SHRILL

SHRILL

BOOK ONE OF REALMS OF SHADOWBLOOD

TROY M. WILLIAMS

First published in 2020 in Melbourne, Australia

Copyright © Troy M. Williams 2020

The moral rights of the author have been asserted.

Typeset by BookPOD

ISBN: 978-0-6489664-0-1 (pbk) eISBN: 978-0-6489664-1-8

A catalogue record for this
book is available from the
National Library of Australia

For Angela, Balian and Declan
With a special thank you to Leeola

PROLOGUE

AS DUSK DESCENDED and the bright orange sky sparkled through the tops of the swaying pines, a four wheeled ranger pulled off the main track onto a small dirt road. It was heading higher into the dark of the Klamath National Forest of northwestern California, its occupants hoping the directions the locals had given them in town would lead directly to a campsite.

"Are you sure this is the way?" Stacey said with a hint of concern in her voice.

"Trust me, have I managed to get us lost yet?" replied Eric. "It shouldn't be far now."

Eric Kirkpatrick, Stacey's father, had been a great navigator in his time. He had climbed mountains, hiked through jungles in Africa, and even spent a fair amount of time in his thirties traveling back and forth to South America, where his work as an anthropologist kept him very busy. Eventually he settled down and created WOSER: "Western Oregon Sasquatch Evidence & Research" team.

Now in his late forties, Eric mainly worked in a lab, scientifically analyzing data, DNA, and bones from different finds and digs across the Pacific Northwest, hoping to finally prove the existence of the elusive Bigfoot, or Sasquatch. Although Eric didn't conduct fieldwork too often now, he decided to help his daughter. Stacey had been studying anthropology as well as cryptozoology and, although only twenty-one years old, was already showing signs of becoming a great asset to the field.

Half an hour later, the two excited explorers were nearing the summit of the lower mountain area.

"There, Stacey, I told you," Eric said.

The ranger rolled off the rarely used but still visible track. It had got dark and although there was a clearing for a tent or two, a cave of dense trees and shrubs seemed to swallow most of the campsite.

Stacey and Eric wearily stepped out of the ranger, shining flashlights on what would be their "home" for the next week and thinking, "Maybe we sleep in the car tonight."

"Well, looks like cold beans in a can and a rough night," Eric said.

Stacey laughed as she pulled the passenger seat down. There were plenty of nights of camping in the past, she thought, and some involved a lot worse than sleeping in a car.

They ate dinner and sat talking for hours as the night wore on, about Eric's adventures and the excitement of what the future may hold. Eventually they grew quiet. Stacey yawned.

"So, who's keeping first watch?" she said with a smirk, obviously joking. She stifled another yawn.

It wasn't long before both succumbed to the night and fell asleep.

As time slowly crept into the early morning, a branch snapped a few yards away from the car. Then, without warning, a large mass emerged from the darkness of the woods, creeping quietly, trying not to be heard or seen as it headed toward the sleeping humans. Slowly it leaned over the passenger side window to get a closer look at what was encroaching on its territory.

The huge beast had its nose on the glass of the window, breathing heavily. It seemed fixated on Stacey, barely visible through the steamed-up glass, and with each passing second became more agitated.

Suddenly Stacey rolled her head toward the window, still fast asleep but under a torrent of dreams. The beast, startled by Stacey's unexpected movement, pulled its giant neckless head back from the car, and with its dark red eyes looked back in the direction it had come from. The creature then made a mad dash for the shadows of the forest with a heavy stride, and was gone in an instant.

Stacey shot up to a sitting position at the final sounds of the trees rustling from the swift departure of the beast. She thought to herself that the forest was inhabited with many nocturnal creatures and was bound to make noises. Years of camping experience helped her mindset and with that thought she lay back down and fell straight back to sleep.

A howl and then a squawk eventually led to a cacophony of deafening sounds, as a concentrated beam of light hit the passenger window of the ranger. It was so bright, Stacey strained to open her eyes, shielding them with her hand, and then realized that dawn had struck up without warning.

"Make it stop," she groaned.

Eric rolled over, looked at her and mumbled, closing his eyes again.

Stacey was blinking profusely from the strain of the bright streams of early sunlight shooting through the pines. She shook her head in frustration.

"Wake up, Dad. Dad!"

Eric jumped up, hit his head on the roof of the car, then keeled over, rubbing the spot.

"Did you have to do that?" he said.

Stacey laughed, pulled her long blonde hair back, and stepped out onto the damp grass. She looked around, breathing in the fresh air, and stretched her arms high with a mighty yawn that could have swallowed a small bird.

"What an absolutely beautiful morning, Dad, you have to see this view."

As Stacey panned around the landscape on the other side of the track, admiring the mountain scenery that seemed to sprawl forever, Eric slowly poured out of the car and stretched his back with a hint of pain on his face.

"I'm getting too old for sleeping in cars," he moaned.

Stacey turned toward her father and smiled. "Come on, Dad, let's get the camp set up and I will make you a cup of tea."

"That sounds wonderful," Eric replied.

After breakfast Stacey thought she might make the most of her time by studying some of the animal life and making notes for her upcoming thesis on wildlife and human interaction.

The morning was slowly disappearing. Even though the air was still quite cool, the sun's rays on her face felt intoxicating, but this would be short-lived as she slowly made her way from the clearing at the riverbank up to the haunting entrance to the dense woods. The half-light of the late morning sun slicing through the thick foliage made it hard to see at times. Stacey, with camera in hand, had to carefully plan each shot she took so as not to get flaring or sun glare in her pictures.

"Hello there." Stacey lowered her camera to a lonely duck that had wandered into the woods. She took several shots and thought it might be interesting to see how close she could get to it and how it would react to her as she approached it.

The duck was not interested in Stacey at all. Its black eyes seemed to be fixated on a bird chirping above, while its shiny green coat glowed in a thin stream of sunlight sneaking through the trees. Stacey could not resist and was able to get close enough to pet the duck once before it woke from its deep trance and made its way back down the hill toward the river.

"Goodbye, little fellow," Stacey whispered.

Excited at the thought of being able to get close to something so beautiful, she was now motivated to get some shots of rare birds, especially the Northern Spotted Owl. Without realizing, she headed deeper into the monstrous blanket of woods and before long found herself standing in front of what seemed like the tallest of the trees in the area.

Crack.

Bang.

Stacey turned suddenly as the noise seemed to be right behind her, but upon inspection she could see nothing.

This time there was a crash in front of her, echoing from at least two different locations. "Those sounds are not natural," Stacey thought, and suddenly realized she was not close to the campsite anymore.

"Hello, is somebody there?" she called out with a quiver in her voice. "Dad? Is that you? Quit trying to scare me."

No response.

Stacey had a huge fascination with Bigfoot and along with her father had researched the elusive creature for many years. Now that she was here all alone, many thoughts flooded into her mind, like the possibility of encountering bears, wolves, and even psychos. "But if Bigfoot is real, what would it do?" Her thoughts were creating all sorts of scenarios and she was now so scared, her heart felt like it was going to explode from her chest.

Crash. The sound was quickly followed by a howl unlike anything Stacey had ever heard before, so loud that all the birds in the area shot out of the trees as if they'd been launched from cannons, and the deer were gone in seconds. Stacey was scared but she had to find the strength to run. The fear had consumed her and her legs were jelly, but she managed to garner the last amount of strength she had and took off like a bullet.

Eric was still adding data to his website and was so lost in thought that he hadn't noticed Stacey leave the camping area. Sipping his hot tea, he thought how happy he was to be spending time with his daughter, which he so loved doing. Eric was enjoying himself.

He was wearing his favorite flannelette shirt, jeans, and black boots, as he always did on camping trips. A few small battle scars on his right eyebrow added to his rugged good looks. The slight gray stubble, along with the silver-tinged short brown hair, gave away his increasing age, but he didn't seem to mind getting older.

Eric turned and faced the woods after hearing the first scream, but told himself it was nothing more than wild animals. Turning back to his tea, he reminisced about his first time out in the field all those years ago and the excitement that came with it, until another scream suddenly shattered his calm demeanor. He heard the howling and saw the birds fluttering in all directions. Jumping to his feet, he ran up the incline from the river to where the noise seemed to be emanating from.

"Stacey, where are you?" he shouted with fear in his voice.

Stacey and Eric had been through a lot together over the years and although they'd always been close, the tragic events in their past made their bond even stronger.

"Stacey, please, this is not funny!"

Eric was now in a panic as another, more intense howl came from the entrance to the woods. He rushed back and grabbed his rifle from the back of the ranger, and then was inside the darkness of the trees with a couple of leaps. The sun had disappeared behind some clouds, so visibility was poor, even though it was the middle of the day.

A high-pitched scream again pierced the air through the trees. Eric knew it was Stacey that time and changed course, heading in the direction of the noise. Another howl, this time closer and more aggressive. Eric knew something was in the woods and was gaining on or maybe even attacking his daughter.

Stacey, camera still in hand, stopped running, turned, and snapped random shots with it, hoping the bright flash may scare away whatever was hunting her. Looking in all directions, she took picture after picture, the flash going off each time, but there was nothing visible to aim for. Then came a crack of branches and a bloodcurdling howl, and before she could compose herself to continue running, she felt a painful blow to the back of her head.

Her camera clicked and flashed from her reflex, and as Stacey fell, she registered an ominous shadow standing over her. The pain was blindingly sharp. Stacey hit the ground, the camera smashing over a log. She grabbed at the back of her head, then looked at her blood-soaked hand. Shaking violently, she raised her head toward the beast and screamed.

Two blood red eyes looking back down at her were the last thing she saw before she passed out from shock.

Eric now saw a beast, standing over nine feet tall and weighing five hundred pounds at least, lowering its head to take a closer look at

Stacey, who was lying limp and looked lifeless. He aimed his rifle at the beast, but before he could fire a shot, it turned, snarled, and within five or six steps was on him.

The beast stood over Eric, who lifted his head slowly and made eye contact. He thought, "I have to do something," so he punched it in what he believed was its stomach. The creature didn't flinch, only howled and backhanded him so hard he fell several feet away.

In pain, Eric closed his eyes and played dead. The beast watched him for a few moments, then turned, and started moving back toward Stacey. Ignoring his injuries, Eric carefully reached for the rifle lying nearby. Somehow, while still in great pain, he managed to line up the beast, and fired.

The giant creature took a shot to its shoulder and let out a monstrous cry that would wake the dead. It fell back and lay there, but only for a moment. Slowly it began to stand, clutching at its wound, blood soaking the leaves on the ground and creating a crimson pool around it.

Eric had to finish it off. He lifted his rifle to fire again, but before he could even take aim, the beast grabbed his gun and snapped it in half. Then it picked Eric up like a rag doll and threw him against a tree, knocking him out.

Eric came to moments later, unable to move his legs. He instantly looked around for the beast. It had Stacey by the hair and was dragging her along the coarse dense brush away to an unknown destination. Stacey was screaming for her father while coughing up blood.

"Dad!" she spluttered, as blood began choking her airways.

"Stacey!"

He saw the butt of his rifle more than ten feet away, but as he dragged himself over to it, he realized the rifle was in pieces and remembered it had been ruined.

Father and daughter shouted back and forth to each other until the beast bent down and gave Stacey another crack to her head with its enormous hands.

"Stacey!" Eric's voice waned, hopelessly, until he couldn't scream anymore. "Stacey ..." he croaked in despair.

The beast was too far from him now, and in the final moments before it disappeared into the darkness of the woods, it let out a horrendous cry like nothing Eric had ever heard before. He watched as the creature, with his daughter, disappeared into a swirl of blue light. Then there was nothing. The beast and Stacey, along with the noise, were gone, leaving only silence. Not even the birds were chirping.

Eric crumpled to the ground and lay in a pool of blood, crying and shaking, until it was too much for him and he passed out.

≈

About thirty minutes later two hikers who had heard noises while they were lower down the mountain decided to come up and investigate.

"Daniel, look!" Veronica said, as she grabbed Daniel's arm. She pointed at Eric lying on the ground next to a piece of his rifle. "There's a body over there."

"Let's make sure he's OK," Daniel said calmly. "Do you have any signal? We'll need to call 911."

Veronica pulled out her phone. The service was poor, and she went to three different spots before finally succeeding.

"I have a signal!" she yelled out. As she was calling the authorities, Daniel ran over to Eric, who was now mumbling incoherently.

"Are you OK, sir?" Daniel asked, not making sense of anything Eric was trying to say.

Eric looked up at Daniel and managed to shout at the top of his lungs, "Stacey!"

Then, his eyes slowly closed and his anguished face relaxed as he descended into darkness.

STRANGERS IN FEDORAS

ERIC WOKE UP, mist all around him. He was still in the woods, although now it was very dark, and he could not see two feet in front of him.

He gathered his thoughts, looked down at the ground, felt around his body, and knew he was OK to get up. He tried to stand but fell over, more from his heavy heart as he remembered what had happened. He tried again, this time managing to get up onto his feet and stand firmly.

He thought to himself how quiet it was in the middle of the woods. No animal or wildlife noises at all. Something was off. He pulled out a flashlight from his belt and started walking. It wasn't long before he heard whispers. He stopped in his tracks and looked around, concentrating on where they were coming from.

"Dad."

There it was again, although this time it was coming from all around, repeating itself.

"Dad, I'm over here."

"Dad?"

He registered concern in the voice as he heard, "Over here."

Eric shook his head. This wasn't right, it didn't sound like Stacey, but he couldn't take the chance. He turned to where the voice was coming from and he saw two glowing red eyes pierce through the blanket of mist and fog. Eyes the size of golf balls.

He took several steps back in panic before falling to the ground. Swirling around the beast were tiny lights floating and whizzing very fast, some splitting off and hovering over Eric's head.

Eric lay there for several minutes, waiting for an attack. He swore the tiny lights were laughing, one even stung him. He swiped at them and with a high-pitched scream that came from all around, they disappeared.

He now started sobbing like a scared child, whispering, "Stacey, Stacey, I'm so, so sorry."

After what he thought was more than enough time to pass without being attacked, Eric looked up. Nothing. The beast had disappeared too.

His thoughts were now out of control. "What is happening to me?" he kept saying to himself. Then, from out of nowhere, as if by an out-of-control rocket, Eric was struck down by an almighty force.

As he regained his composure, he looked up and there was the beast, staring down like a hunter ready to pounce. Eric was now in total shock and could not move as the beast slowly bent down. Eric started praying in his mind as he had nothing left to give and was preparing to die. The beast snarled, grabbed Eric by his legs and started dragging him away; to where, it didn't really matter anymore.

Eric dropped his flashlight on purpose to leave a trail, then his wallet and other objects he could reach, before he heard an awful high-pitched scream coming from the beast.

Eric knew he was in trouble. The scream stopped and he was now in a room. Looking around he saw bodies everywhere and heard moaning from all around him. As the beast gave out a loud cry again, it vanished into nothing and Eric was left with some of the most frightful things any man would ever set eyes on.

He screamed like a child watching a horror movie. "Get away! Get away!" The screaming was so intense, Eric's vitals went into meltdown.

He sat up, sweat all over his body, still screaming. There were doctors trying to hold him down. He was squirming and fighting, and he managed to knock one nurse to the ground before he was administered a shot, instantly calming him down. Still he tried to scream, but was only capable of saying, "God help me, oh please, God help me," until finally passing out.

The doctors strapped him to the bed where he then lay for several hours.

Eric had been in a coma for a few weeks with many injuries. The fact he wasn't dead had amazed the doctors and emergency services who attended the scene. There seemed to be a will or determination inside him to fight hard and keep himself alive.

≈

"Eric ... Eric."

He was slowly coming around from the heavy sedative the doctors had administered for his outburst earlier in the day. A nurse and Doctor Emmen were there, along with a couple of security guards posted outside in case Eric was violent again.

"Hey, why can't I move?" he said, with a hint of desperation in his voice. Eric was very groggy but had enough in him to rock back and forth trying to free his arms from the bindings.

"It's OK, Eric, you have just woken up from a coma and there was an incident when you came out, but we are here to help you," Nurse Serena explained in a calm voice, hoping there would not be a repeat of what had happened earlier on in the day, when he inadvertently assaulted a male nurse.

"Coma? Incident?" Eric looked confused.

Serena did her best to keep him at ease and explain the recent events. "Eric, you have been in a coma for a few weeks due to major trauma, both physical and mental. You woke up earlier today and went into a violent rage, so we had to sedate you again. You have only just woken up which we have all said is a real miracle."

"I ... I ... can't remember being violent, I can only remember visions of evil and ... oh no, Stacey." His voice broke as he whispered her name, a tear slowly moving down the contours of his left cheek.

"We will take it from here, nurse, thank you."

The nurse turned around to see who was talking to her, as she had not witnessed many visitors coming in or out over the last few weeks.

"Who are you?" Eric looked up at two men dressed in black suits, sunglasses still on, with black fedoras and trench coats. He clenched his fists, and his pulse rate registered high levels.

"Relax, Mr. Kirkpatrick. My name is Agent Anders, and this is my partner, Agent Wilkes. We are from the government and would like to ask you a few questions about the incident that occurred in the Klamath National Forest near Marble Mountain. Sir, do you remember anything that happened there?"

Eric looked at them with disdain.

"I will never forget!"

"Agents, I don't think this is the best time. Eric has only just woken up from a coma and major ordeal. He obviously has mental issues in relation to this, and I would recommend you come back after he has come to terms with his current situation." Doctor Emmen was polite and sincere in his comments and very concerned about Eric. But, the agents were not in a compromising mood.

"I'm sorry, doctor, but we have a missing person on our hands and the only witness to her disappearance is this gentleman, so please move aside and let us do our job."

Doctor Emmen was suspicious of Agent Anders, thinking he was very insistent, as if he wanted information that wasn't necessarily relevant to the whereabouts of Stacey Kirkpatrick but something more.

"Remember, gentlemen, I am his doctor and I can override any law enforcement decision if—"

"If you like your job, doctor," Wilkes said in a calm voice looking straight at Doctor Emmen while he took off his glasses, "I would take a step back and let us do ours, or you might find things won't be so good for you."

Doctor Emmen stared into Wilkes' now visible eyes. He took in his pale skinny face, long slender build, and stood back as if he was hypnotized. The doctor agreed with the agents before Wilkes replaced his sunglasses in their original position. Eric was furious.

"Do I get a say in any of this? And what do you mean, *this gentleman?* She is my daughter and I resent any kind of insinuation that I had anything to do with ..." Eric was getting more and more agitated and he pulled his arms up to try and get loose. "Why am I tied here? Let me out of this!" His frustration was again turning into aggression.

"Calm down, Mr. Kirkpatrick, this won't take long. Nurse, take off his restraints, please."

Agent Anders pulled up a chair and moved in closer to Eric, while Nurse Serena released his straps. She thought to herself that something wasn't quite right. "Have these guys been waiting somewhere until Eric woke up?" It just didn't add up to her. Local police had been in and out over the first week and were told they would get a call when Eric awoke from the coma.

The air was filled with tension. Everyone wanted to know the truth about his injuries, and the details of the disappearance had made their way to mainstream media; however, there was a process for this kind of thing and these agents weren't playing the game.

"OK," Eric whispered, and he started crying. This was a hard-core man who had seen the world and held a black belt in karate. He had dedicated his whole life to studies of anthropology and cryptozoology, and could put Bear Grylls to shame with his knowledge of survival. But he loved his daughter so much, he was now feeling broken. His memories were flooding back, mixed with his dreams and confusion as to what was real, imagined, or just plain ridiculous. He couldn't work out the logic, couldn't put it together.

"I'm going to ask you a number of questions, Eric, and I just need you to answer me as best you can. This will be one of many interviews that we will be conducting over the course of a few weeks, are you OK with this?" Agent Anders said.

"If it helps find my Stacey, sir, I will do anything."

Even though Eric had previously been restrained, his injuries were significant: two broken ribs, a broken collarbone, bruising of the kidneys, and major concussion, along with multiple contusions.

Anders opened the questioning without any consideration for the staff, or for Eric. He was an arrogant man who seemed to only follow his own rules. Wilkes sat back blank-faced without movement, like a grown-up doll that was put down and left until someone picked it up again. It wasn't a normal scene. Again, Nurse Serena thought to herself that this was wrong. A sense of familiarity hit her as well, and as the doctor left the room, she quietly switched on an intercom.

"Are you feeling OK, Eric?" she said with legitimate care in her voice.

"Yes, nurse, I'm fine, just a bit thirsty is all," he said, his voice shaking.

"Call me Serena. I will bring you in a drink."

"Thank—" Before Eric could finish, Wilkes stood up and ushered Serena out the door.

"We won't be long, nurse. He can have his drink in a moment. We will let you know when we are finished, thank you." And in saying that, Wilkes closed and locked the door, before sitting back down in his original zombie-like position.

Anders took a water bottle out of an inside pocket of his trench coat, opened it, and passed it to Eric.

"Have a big drink, Mr. Kirkpatrick, you need it."

Eric wasn't going to argue as he was so thirsty, and he sucked it back like it was his last.

In the meantime, Nurse Serena sat at the nurses' desk with the intercom to Eric's room open. She knew it was unethical and would most likely lose her job if anyone found out; however, there was just something about those agents that did not sit right with her and if she could help her patient, she would. Her next move was a sackable offense as she set her mobile phone up next to the intercom and pressed "record".

≈

Eric's tension level was still very high, although his pain levels were coming down due to the last shot of morphine that was administered to him; at least that's what he thought it was.

After a lengthy interrogation by the agents, they finally left, and Eric went to sleep.

Nurse Serena's phone had just beeped as the battery was close to running out of charge. She knew they were on their way back to the desk, so she quickly turned the intercom off and sat back down with a magazine in her hands, shaking nervously.

"All done, nurse, thank you for your assistance, we will be—"

Before Anders could finish his sentence, Wilkes chimed in, "Is everything alright, nurse? You seem to be very upset about something."

Serena had to compose herself very swiftly, because she knew she would be in more trouble than she wanted if they found out the truth that she had heard the conversation.

"I'm fine, gentlemen, I've just had an emergency in another ward to deal with and I knew the person, so I'm a little shaken up. Just part of the job, I guess. You never get used to it."

Wilkes looked back at her. There was something wrong with his face, she thought, and she could not shake the feeling of déjà vu with him, so she did not stare for too long.

"I'm sorry to hear that. We will be back in the morning to see the patient again. If he is up to it, we would like to take him outside for a chat."

Serena stood there silent for a few seconds. She knew she had to go along with it, though.

"Sure, gentlemen, but my shift will have ended by then, so I won't be here. The doctor will have to approve it before you can take him, so see him when you get here tomorrow."

Serena thought it was time to stop talking. The two agents looked at each other, then back at Serena, and before departing Wilkes said, "OK, nurse, thank you for your help. Can I ask your name, please?"

She was now worried, but she knew she had no choice but to give them her details.

"My name is Serena O'Halloran."

"Thank you, Serena, I do like your accent, are you from County Clare?" Wilkes said with a smirk, like he had known people from that area before.

Serena, feeling quite disturbed, whispered, "Yes, sir, I am."

The two agents glared at her for a long moment before Anders turned to Wilkes with a look of confusion. Then they slowly marched out of the ward and into the lift like they had no plans or anywhere else to be, leaving Serena in a mess of emotions.

She pulled out a small bottle of whiskey from underneath the desk, left there for nurses having a particularly hard night. She took two big sips and for the remainder of her shift, in between rounds, tried to work out how she could help both Eric and herself.

—

Eric woke up in a violent state again. This time he was on his own. He looked around and realized what he had seen was just a bad dream. He reached over to grab the leftover drink on his bedside table.

Eric had been breathing heavily when he woke up, and the change in his vitals had alerted the nurse. Just before Eric took a sip of the water, Serena slapped it out of his hands as if she was fighting off an offender. Water went everywhere, and as it hit the floor, it started turning a blue color. Eric sat there looking shocked and confused yet again.

"What the frig?" he exclaimed in frustration.

"It's early in the morning. The agents you saw last night are evil and we need to get you out of here."

Serena was very adamant about what she was saying. She started picking up Eric's clothes and packing them into a bag.

"Can you tell me what you are doing, please, as I'm in pain and am not in the mood for any kind of bullshit."

Serena whispered into Eric's ear very softly but confidently, "You will die if you don't come with me now. This is very serious and those agents that came last night are not who they say they are."

"Wait, what agents?" Eric couldn't even remember the previous night, making Serena even more anxious to help him. "Hang on, what are you doing and why do I need to go? I'm in bandages and I'm not in any fit way to travel." He was starting to panic.

"Eric, look at me, you need to come with me now or you will *die*." Serena said it with more conviction this time. "Now listen to every word I say."

Eric's inability to remember anything had left him feeling vulnerable. He was still trapped in dream, memory, and real-life states of mind so at this stage he had no other choice but to follow Serena and get the truth later.

"OK, OK, let's go."

He was still in a huge amount of pain and in need of help, but Serena seemed to have it all worked out.

"Here, get onto this."

She had a massive gurney ready to go. Eric climbed on while Serena put his medications and other items underneath. There were some things that caught Eric's eye as she packed them.

"What are they?"

Eric was asking too many questions.

"Just be quiet and trust me," Serena said. She was getting agitated.

Trust. Eric was unsure who he trusted now, though there was something in Serena's voice and her eyes that led him to accept it. He had to trust someone!

Walking along the corridor on the fourth floor, Serena pushed Eric to the double lifts. Staff had started to arrive for the morning shifts so there was nothing out of the ordinary, she thought to herself. She needed to make her exit quick, as those "agents" would be back soon enough to interrogate Eric some more and maybe even take him to another facility, which was discussed the night before.

Serena pressed the down button, so she could get to the basement car park. Her finger shook as she did it.

A doctor walked up, and also waited to descend to a lower floor. "Busy night, nurse? Where are you taking this gentleman? None of the technicians in the scanning area are in yet."

Serena's voice shook a little upon answering. But she had only one attempt at this, and she was not about to crumble, especially with Eric's life, and now maybe hers too, on the line.

"Yeah ... I mean ... he's ..."

The doctor looked at her as they entered the lift. Serena composed herself well.

"Sorry, doctor, it's been a very long night. I'm just taking him to level one as he has a friend he wanted to see, but both can't walk just yet so, you know, the extra bit we do for our patients."

The doctor stared at her blank-faced, scanning for any kind of oddity as it wasn't something that was common practice. Still, at this time it wasn't busy yet at the hospital, and he thought it couldn't hurt this once.

"Alright. It's a bit early, but it's probably better than when the rush starts. You are very good for doing that. Make sure he is back before nine."

The doors opened on level two and the doctor walked out of the lift, looked at his chart, and started down the corridor to the children's wing. Serena pressed the basement button relentlessly. She was holding her breath as the lift was now going to open on the first floor.

Eric had his eyes closed all that time so as not to say something wrong to the doctor. He did not have all the facts yet and knew he had to get out of that hospital.

Ding!

As the doors opened to the first floor, Serena stood staring like she was about to explode. It felt to her like time was in slow motion. The door took forever. When it opened, standing before her was Dennis, the nightshift cleaner. Serena nearly fainted, although she composed herself again knowing this was easier than dealing with another doctor or even worse, a nurse from the same ward that she worked in.

"Hey, Dennis, are you going down?"

Dennis looked at the gurney, then looked at her and said, "No, Serena, I'm going up, although you seem to be going to the basement."

Dennis had his hand in the doorway holding the lift open. Serena knew she had to think quickly.

"It's all good, Dennis, I hit the wrong button, and anyway I need to get something from my car so he can stay in the outpatient ... oh shit. Sorry, Dennis." Serena kicked Dennis's hand away from the door and as it closed, she smashed the basement button again. Seconds, only seconds, she thought she had before security would be notified. Although Dennis was slow, he still knew protocols.

Dennis had fallen back as the doors closed on the lift. He was in shock, not sure what to do or think at that moment. He was more upset that someone he had known for many years had done that to him. He slowly got to his feet and made his way to the first floor nurses' station to make a complaint.

≈

Serena had the gurney at her car. She took all Eric's personals out and slipped something in her pocket. Eric was in no mood now to even comment on any of the recent events. He wondered if she was alright, mad, or if it was again all in his head.

"Sorry, Eric, I'm so sorry for all of this. I promise I will explain everything when we get to a safe place. You need to help me now so we can get out of here safely."

Serena was in panic mode, and it wasn't helping that she had to lift Eric into the car. She was very tall, just on six foot, and very lean. Going to the gym and doing martial arts certainly helped her in this case.

She finally got Eric into the back seat of the four wheeled ranger, pushed the gurney away and moments before she could turn the ignition on, an alarm rang out from all speakers. The noise was deafening, and Serena's anxiety was now peaking.

She started the car and reversed it at high speed, smashing into another car, before she punched it into gear and floored it. She crashed through the boom gates and headed south, away from the hospital, breaking all speed limits. Serena knew she had to slow down, as any attention to both of them would follow with an arrest. She slowly took her foot off the pedal to maintain a normal speed and continued onto Interstate 5 headed south into Albany.

"You OK back there? Eric, I'm sorry about this."

Eric tried to get comfortable, all the while grasping his leg. "Sure, yeah, I'm totally fine, for someone in extreme pain."

Serena was dreading telling him what she had heard. The whole conversation was going through her head and although she had heard it with her own ears, she could not believe it herself.

"I'm so sorry, Eric."

Eric raised his head, catching her eyes in the rear vision mirror, and said calmly, "Yeah, you say that a lot. *Sorry. Sorry. I will explain this. I will do that.*"

Serena looked back through the mirror and in a tone that would make even the most hard-core person whimper, she said, "Are you ready to die, Eric? I'm sorry, but are you?"

Eric shut down, closed his eyes. He wasn't going to entertain any more of this. He started thinking about his wife and daughter, trips they had when they were all happy and together. Before long he was asleep, away from the reality haunting him now and into a place he belonged, his memories. But Eric's happy family dream was about to get crazy.

Serena knew she couldn't go home anymore. She didn't have many other places to go either, so thinking of what had happened, she went to the only person she could trust, Father Michael Larsen.

TWISTED
DREAMS

FATHER LARSEN WAS A PRIEST, with a twist. He had a passion for the strange and Serena had heard him talking about different subjects on the paranormal, UFOs, and even at times conspiracies. Serena attended church as often as she could and felt that the priest may be the only person who could help Eric at this stage and hide him until all the truth was revealed.

Serena pulled up to Michael's house at the back of the church. Serena had visited him a few times over the years with her mother and friend Louise for lunches and conversations. Michael had majored in physics, philosophy, and theology, and had a military background. The lawn was always kept very tidy, Serena thought, as she rolled up to the end of the driveway. It had been a few months since she had seen Michael as her workload had been so busy; nevertheless, Michael was the first person on Serena's mind. It was a no-brainer to go there.

Serena parked and left Eric sleeping in the back. It was a long trip and major ordeal, so she thought it better for him to just rest. She made her way to the front door. Father Michael was already there, waiting for her.

"Hi, Serena."

Michael was an impressive figure, always wearing his traditional cassock. He was polite but strong, hard but fair. He had a way with people which Serena thought made him a great priest and probably soldier too, though she didn't know too much about his background, not that she wanted to.

"Hey, Father, it's been so long. I'm glad to see you."

Michael had changed somewhat from the last impressions that she remembered. It wasn't so much appearance, or clothes, but a look in his eyes that she had never seen before.

"Please, Serena, call me Michael, you know that. It's so good to see you and hear that wonderful accent of yours." Michael was sincere with his statement and a little concerned with the "out of the blue" arrival. "So, what brings you here?"

Michael was now looking over Serena's shoulder. He saw a ranger that had obviously been in an accident. Its rear left brake light was hanging as if from a piece of dental floss and the scrapes across the side of the car were quite severe. His concern escalated when he saw movement in the back of the car.

"Father, I ... need your help." Serena lowered her head slowly, like she was asking the last person left in the world. She was desperate.

Michael put his right index finger underneath Serena's chin, lifted it until she made eye contact, and said, "Hey, you've come to the right place. No matter what, I will help. Well, I hope I can, and anyways, it can't be that bad, right?" There was an awkward silence between them. "Right?" Michael was now getting really concerned.

Serena did not say a word.

"Oh, my Lord in Heaven, give me strength," Michael whispered to himself.

"I'm sorry, Father, it's not good." The crackle in her voice made Michael even more determined to help.

"Come, let's figure this out together."

Michael and Serena spent the next twenty minutes getting Eric from the ranger and into a comfortable bed. He was tossing and moaning, although never woke. Once he was settled in the spare room, Michael suggested Serena take a seat on the sofa at the end of the lounge, close to Eric's room, just in case.

"Would you like a drink, Serena?" Michael said as he poured one for himself.

"Sure, vodka with a twist of lime, thanks, and I would love a pizza too."

Michael glanced over his shoulder and smiled.

"How about a cheap wine and some fish fingers? Sorry, a priest's wage isn't that great."

Serena laughed and so did Michael. It broke the ice and relieved some tension, although the elephant was still in the room and needed to be addressed.

Michael sat down on the chair directly across from Serena, leaned all the way back with his wine in hand, and said, "So, tell me the story."

Serena looked at him and said softly, "You will never believe what I am going to tell you."

"Try me."

"OK." She was silent for a moment. "Mind you, once you start down the rabbit hole, you are stuck there, so I am warning you that your life may not be, no, sorry, *will* not be the same afterwards."

Michael didn't utter a word. The kindness in his eyes said it all. And so she started.

≈

Eric woke up in yet another violent state from what seemed to be an ongoing rendezvous with terror every time he closed his eyes. The funny thing was, he thought to himself after he calmed down, that before the incident at Klamath National Forest, he could not remember a single nightmare ever.

Serena came into Eric's room after hearing him screaming. He had slept for the whole day and was still affected by his trauma and injuries. He should still be in hospital, she thought to herself, as the guy had only recently learned of his daughter and woken up from a coma. But if he had stayed, he would most likely be in the custody of those "agents" now.

Serena was, without words, just calmly stroking his head. Eric was sobbing now, still trying to come to terms with it all. Serena administered Eric with his painkillers, and he sat up and looked her in the eye. With a breaking voice, like a child, he said, "Why are you doing this for me? I know something is wrong and I've come to terms with the fact you have saved me from something, but my memory is struggling. I'm not sure what's real and what's nightmare."

Serena frowned. Her world as she knew it was over because of what she'd done, but it had been the human thing to do.

"I'm just a sucker for a broken man with a bandage on."

Eric looked at her, confused for a moment, although once he noticed a slight smile on her face, he then began to chuckle quietly. Serena smiled, then laughed, and for a moment the previous drama had been put behind them.

"There it is, I wondered what your smile looked like," Serena quietly said to Eric just before grabbing his arm to give him his shot.

"Ouch, you could have warned me," he moaned as the needle went in. Eric was known for his strength and high pain threshold. He just was not himself at the moment.

"In my job, sweetheart, surprise is best sometimes. Now get some more sleep and tomorrow I will be checking your bandages." Serena really put on her accent to try and relieve the stress and Eric couldn't help but smile.

"Sleep, really? I think I've slept enough and was hoping for some answers."

Serena knew he was going to say that, so a little extra sedative was administered to give him more time to recover. She was not looking forward to revealing the recording to him. If he was rested enough, he may be able to take it. Eric looked at Serena's uniform; she was still in her nurse's garb.

"Why was I in Salem Hospital?" asked Eric, now slowing down and getting sleepy.

She could at least answer that question, Serena thought to herself. "After your accident, you were flown to Medford, but then due to your injuries they flew you to Salem. There you have been for the last few weeks, where you had me taking care of you." Serena winked back at him with another smile. "Sleep now and I promise tomorrow we will have a very big conversation where I will explain everything."

As she was telling Eric this, he could not fight sleep anymore and within seconds was completely out. Serena thought now was the best time, if any, to show Father Michael the recording and get his ideas on the events.

$$\approx$$

THE PREVIOUS EVENING

As the door closed behind Serena, Anders offered Eric a drink. He guzzled it down, unaware that it had turned a light bluish color inside the clear bottle. Eric thought he was in his right mind, but whatever substance was in that liquid, it would influence his memory during and after the interrogation.

After Eric had had enough "water," he handed the bottle back to Anders, who placed it on the bedside table, and he sat waiting for the questions to start.

"Do you know why we are here, Mr. Kirkpatrick?" Anders fired with a contemptuous tone. As he asked the question, both Anders and Wilkes stood up and the skin on their bodies gradually started to melt away, revealing two gray-skinned creatures with huge black eyes and long slender arms ending with two long fingers and an opposing thumb.

The liquid had helped Eric see the real beings that were underneath the black suit costumes they were wearing not more than a moment ago.

"What are you? Why is your skin melting? Am I dreaming again?" Eric stammered.

"All you need to know is what we tell you now. Has your daughter Stacey been sick before with any blood illness or any diseases?" asked Anders. "She is a very important key to the success of our mission, and if

you help us figure these things out over our meetings, then we will make sure your daughter will survive this ordeal."

Although Eric was still drugged when Anders began threatening his daughter, his instincts kicked in and the anger started to override the drugs in his system.

"Stay away from her, you monsters. I want her back. That big hairy beast took her and if you have any part in her disappearance then I will kill you both." Eric was very agitated, but he knew that he would never get her back if he continued to make threats.

"She will survive if you answer these questions. Has she had any type of blood illnesses?" Anders stood and stared at Eric, waiting for his reply.

"Do you promise she will be OK, and you will let her live?"

"Yes," Anders replied.

"OK. No, in fact she has never really ever been ill. I can't remember her ever really being sick at all, maybe just a head cold here or there, but she has always been very healthy and looked after herself. Why?"

"Has Stacey ever been married or had many partners?" Anders asked, his bulging black eyes staring into Eric's. His tiny mouth did not open at all and although he wasn't talking directly into Eric's mind, the sound was emanating from the slender figure somehow, as if Anders' mind had a volume switch and it was flowing directly from that source into the room.

"What! Why do you need to know those things? I am dreaming, aren't I? Yes, that's what it is. I will go along with this because it cannot, you cannot, exist and these questions are absurd and offensive."

Eric, frazzled by the creatures in front of him, frantic with worry about his daughter, just couldn't quite get a grip on what was happening.

"Please, Mr. Kirkpatrick, answer the questions," Anders said like a statue, with Wilkes in the corner just listening and ready to back Anders up if needed.

"No, she has had some boyfriends over the years, but nothing like a long-term relationship. She has been too busy for anything serious like that with her schooling and her work, although it's something she would like eventually. Why?"

"We think Stacey may have two types of genomes that are extremely important to our existence. We are trying to get into your world, but we cannot survive here for too long as the bodies we make eventually succumb to diseases and illnesses. Stacey has a genome that is so rare, we have only been able to find a very small portion of the population with it. Our beasts have a sense for searching for this particular DNA strand that fights off all diseases once accelerated and manipulated. The other genome that she has sits dormant. If activated, it can wipe out our whole population due to its destructive enzymes. Therefore, we need her pure, as any flaw may turn the genomes into any disease. Even a cold would kill us all."

Anders had finished. Eric looked at him without even blinking. The liquid had now subdued him completely and like being under the influence of some sort of truth serum, he was completely in Anders' control. Eric would answer any question and would not remember a thing after it.

The two agents interrogated Eric with a barrage of questions about his daughter's medical history and their family tree.

"These will be the last questions for the night. We will return in the morning with some more. What did you see in the woods that day, what creatures?"

Eric had been calm and a willing participant in these queries and continued to answer.

"I saw a Sasquatch, which nearly killed me and took my daughter into a blue light. I saw tiny golden lights flickering and at a closer glance they had faces and wings like tiny people only inches tall. I can now remember people looking over me and helping but in my mind, they did not look completely human. Lastly, I saw a very large wolf, so large I could not miss it. Very black like night, with dark glowing red eyes, far away deep in the woods, before it took off into the dark."

Eric started to shake and convulse. The serum was starting to wear off as the interrogation had been going for a long time. Wilkes walked over to Eric and put his two fingers on his forehead, seeming to calm Eric before plunging him into a deep sleep.

The gray beings headed for the door and as they were gliding along *without touching the floor, their bodies slowly reverted back to the human-looking men in black they were beforehand, fedoras and sunglasses included. By the time they made it to the door, they were both making sounds on the ground from their footsteps and were now fully "normal" again.*

Anders opened the door and as they walked out Wilkes turned around, looked at Eric, and a dream sequence began in his mind, directed straight to Stacey. Wilkes closed the door and entered the corridor where no one would see their true form as they both made their way to the nurses' station where Serena was sitting very uncomfortably.

≈

Father Larsen and Serena were both deep in thought. Michael had only just heard the recording and it was the first time Serena had heard it other than originally, so she picked up even more information. Michael showed little emotion, as if he had expected to hear something of that nature. He was a mysterious man, strong and compassionate.

He held his index finger and thumb to his chin, rubbing it for a while before saying, "You cannot let him hear this recording, Serena, you know that, right? It will destroy him."

Michael's comment just flew off Serena like a leaf in the autumn wind.

"Yes, I will, and you know why? Have you heard him screaming in his dreams? I have, and I've picked up bits and pieces from hearing some of his comments when he's experiencing them. There seems to be a consistency with what he's dreaming of and what's happening with his daughter. Father, we may be able to save her!"

Michael was very worried about the poor innocent woman caught up in the creatures' evil plans and about how Eric was going to handle it all. He was also concerned for the rest of his congregation, but his focus was on what they were both going to do now.

"What is the plan then?" Michael said in anticipation of her idea.

Serena sat there for a moment and without blinking leaned back on her chair, twirling her long dark hair.

"I will set up a drip, we put him back on the gurney, and strap him in like he was in hospital. This way I can keep him under observation and at any sign of extreme or dangerous behavior I will administer more sedatives. I've seen Eric lash out, and he is a strong man. Who knows what his reaction will be when he hears the recording."

Michael sat there with a finger on his chin, and muttered, "We cannot let him hear that recording at least until he is a little better and can make more rational decisions. I believe we should leave this place as well. I have commitments tomorrow with the church so after that we should move up to my cabin. At least until he is out of danger. Then he can hear it."

"Let's get to work then," Serena said and smiled while they started planning the next few moves.

Michael hid the car and took the plates off it while Serena checked on Eric.

It had been a long and emotional afternoon and Serena was getting ready for bed. Standing in front of the wooden framed Victorian mirror before her, she looked at her reflection and thought something had changed. Changed only in her mind, she thought, although, as she stared at her brown eyes, pale complexion, long hair, and running mascara, the realization had finally hit her hard. She did not want to leave her previous life. She loved every minute of it, was very happy with her successes and had many plans for the future. She looked at herself, and then wiping the makeup from her face she started crying heavily.

Serena was a very attractive woman. She never had trouble gaining attention from the opposite sex, although her busy lifestyle was always in the way. With her height, and her dark hair, which was quite uncommon for someone from her town to have, she could have almost been mistaken for a model in her younger years. She could thank her Italian background for her looks. Most of her friends growing up had red, mousy brown or blonde hair, with green or blue eyes. Her sisters both had blonde hair which caused teasing when she was younger. They would often say she was dropped off by the faeries.

She sat back down on her bed, sobbing quietly, before composing herself and trying to shake off the events that had just transpired, along with the awful feelings they brought on. She then changed for bed and turned the lights off, still upset.

She wondered if she would ever see anyone she knew or loved again as the realization that she was a fugitive now hit her so very clearly. She opened her bottle of sedatives and took a triple dose, knowing it wouldn't make much of a difference sleep-wise. Within five minutes she was out. Exhaustion had taken hold, and with the weight of the world at her feet, she couldn't fight any longer.

Serena was born in Ireland, in Shannon, County Clare. Her father, Liam O'Halloran, was a well-respected Irish psychiatrist, while her Italian mother, Grace, raised their three girls, Serena, Maggie, and Siobhan. When Serena was only sixteen, the family migrated to America, where Liam furthered his medical career in psychiatry and established quite a reputable name for himself with a lot of hard work.

Serena never wanted to leave her little town of Shannon. It was where her friends were and the thought of going to a new country and starting over seemed to overwhelm her.

With no choice but to go, she used that energy to focus on schooling, where she studied psychiatry like her father but also did nursing part time at the local hospital.

Serena never had much time for dates or a social life. She was picked on in school due to her strong Irish accent, however in time that became a door for her as it was always an icebreaker with potential employers. She began Taekwondo when she was in her last years of high school to help with her social skills. With all the study, sport and different jobs over her forty-two years of life, she hadn't had much time for a family, which was something she had wanted for herself ever since she was a girl playing in the green fields next to the cold Shannon River with her friends.

She had felt lonely for a long time and it wasn't until Eric was admitted into the hospital those few weeks earlier that she started feeling something, a compassion for him of sorts and at what he had gone through. Losing his daughter, and the many injuries he had to deal with. What would his reaction be to the news?

There were rumors going around in the media that Eric may have been the one responsible for Stacey's disappearance, however Serena knew better, and she thought with the injuries that Eric had sustained that there was no way he could have been responsible for any of it. There was something far more sinister in all of it and she waited patiently, looking after him until he woke up so the full story could be told.

She felt that a trauma in her younger years had similarities to Eric's story. Something that wasn't quite right. It niggled at her and she just wanted to find out the whole truth of what had happened and who those people really were that were following Eric. She struggled with parts of her memory from that time many years ago, but she knew that either a doctor or something else had helped to suppress some of the horrifying images and experiences that she had gone through. At least, that's what she imagined happening as it was all a blur, just dreams.

Later in the night she started tossing and turning, sometimes sobbing in her sleep, dreaming of the previous events and what was going to happen. Would she ever see her family again, would they be safe? Her years of psychiatry and medicine would help her through a lot of this. She was more prepared than someone without that kind of background training, although it was still a very big toll to bear, and with much more to come out in the future.

She tossed and turned some more, before finally gaining the upper hand and falling asleep, properly this time, until morning.

～

Light crept through the curtains of Serena's room, creating a tiny bit of warmth as a gentle stream of sun hit her face. She moved little until the smell of bacon and eggs was too much for her to withstand any longer. She slowly dragged herself into an upright position, fighting every fiber in her being calling for her to lie back down again. Giving in to the hunger pangs and aroma, Serena finally made the effort to stand, although she felt as if she hadn't used her feet in months and she swayed from side to side, getting her balance back.

Her arms stretched high like she was reaching for something. At the same time she yawned and a fly landed on the edge of her cracked lips. She brushed it off and made her way to the mirror. With a look of horror she quickly turned away and mumbled under her breath, "I'm getting too old and wrinkly." She washed her face, still trying to avoid the mirror, put her robe on. After a quick check on Eric, who was still sleeping, she followed the aroma to the kitchen where Michael was busy hunched over the cooktop, making what looked like a feast for an army.

"Wow, Father, what is all this food? It smells amazing." Serena walked over to the massive plate of eggs, crumpets, and scones.

"Hey, get out of it," Michael snapped with a hint of a smile. "This food is for the ladies' church group luncheon after the service today. I will have to leave you for a few hours."

Serena thought she needed some time with the Lord to help her through these tough times as well, but she couldn't leave the house.

"Now get this into you, we have a big day."

Michael handed her a plate of bacon and eggs that he had kept for her, along with a side of toast and orange juice. Serena smiled, quietly took the plate, then sat down to enjoy it before getting ready for the day.

She noticed Michael was in a much better mood. He must have prayed on it last night. He always had a way of bouncing back quickly from anything, and that's what made him such a likable and helpful person, she thought.

He presented Serena with some women's clothing he had found from donations he had received for the church.

"It's not much, but they are new, clean, and much better than being in your nurse's uniform."

Serena took the clothes and smiled, and then concentrated on finishing off her breakfast.

GHASTLY
VISIONS

D ARK SHADOWS of withered trees swayed in the half-light in
the park as Valinda Mannix walked home from work. The long
shadowy fingertips reached and vanished without any noise. Each
step Valinda took became more uneasy. The trees shifting in the wind
reminded her of the harshness of life, and the ghosts and the creeping
shadows seemed to whisper to her, "Stop, Val, stop now!"

Valinda fell, and though no one was around, she could swear
someone had tripped her. Once on her feet, she started running,
looking behind her thinking that something elusive was out there. This
wasn't the first time she had felt this.

Once out of the park, her thoughts became more rational and the
fear subsided as she made her way to her two-bedroom apartment on
the edge of the park. Her neighbor was an elderly lady called Emilia,
who kept to herself most of the time. She did, however, love Valinda's
cat and had a spare key so she could look after it whenever needed.

Valinda finally reached her front door. Upon opening it, she was
greeted with a surprise.

"Hello, Tiny, do you want some dins?"

Valinda loved her cat and her company. Because she was so busy
with her job, her cat was basically her only friend. Tiny looked up at
Valinda with hunger and approval while she emptied the last of the cat
food into the bowl.

Tiny gulped her dinner down, each piece of chicken seeming to disappear as if she had not been fed in weeks. After she'd finished her last swallow, she made her way over to the sofa where her master and best friend was sitting with her head in her hands, sobbing.

The cat brushed along her leg to show she was there for her, and Valinda bent down and picked her up. Rubbing her smooth cheek on the furry one, she whispered, "What is wrong with me, Tiny, am I going insane?"

Valinda put the cat down and went to pour a wine. She lifted the bottle and tipped it upside down.

"Great, I'm out of wine too, anything else?"

She knew as soon as she said that comment that she shouldn't have, and in that moment her mobile phone rang. Valinda nearly jumped through the roof. She was already on edge and this was another fright she did not need.

"Hello," she said in a quiet voice.

"Are you OK, Val, it's only me, love, it's Mom."

Valinda had been on edge lately with work, but more so due to the unholy apparitions she thought she was seeing and feeling.

"Hey, Mom, yeah, I'm fine, another long day, another lonely night." There was a massive pause, so Valinda decided to speak again. "No, Ma, I am not going home to live with you and I'm not in a relationship yet or in the near future. Why are you calling me?"

Marjory Mannix was a widow and she was into the church dating scene. Dating likewise parishioners was something the baby boomers in the town seemed to be going for. Valinda just wasn't there yet, so her reaction was, in her mind, justified.

"Honey, I was only calling you to see if you are alright, that is all. Do you want to have lunch this weekend?"

She felt bad, it had been a long day, but her mother was relentless at times, probably due to her love for her but also obsessive control factors, she thought. Valinda wanted to make it up to her, so decided to say yes to lunch.

"OK, I'm in. So where will it be this time, Ma?"

Marjory tended to make dinner or lunch dates with others and Valinda always felt left out, although she was willing to go anywhere, at least just to get rid of some of the stupid visions she was having.

"Oh, sweetie, it's at the church function hall. Bring a friend if you like."

Val, as her colleagues called her, knew that her mother thought her only friend was her cat Tiny.

"OK, Ma, see you on Sunday, but no church stuff."

Marjory was concerned that her daughter's visions and hallucinations were the work of evil. She had made her feelings clear to Valinda in the past.

"Oh no, sweetheart, you don't need to attend the service; however it is before the luncheon and it would mean a lot if you could attend with me," Marjory said in an overconfident tone that she hoped would make her daughter feel guilty. So Valinda agreed and suggested her mother come to her house before leaving for the service.

"Love you, see you on Sunday." Valinda hung up the phone, took the cat with her, and crashed on her bed, so exhausted she didn't even get undressed.

≈

Sunday came swiftly. Valinda had no idea what to wear, or what to say when they arrived at the church. Her only solace was seeing some familiar faces like Mary Jennings, the church counselor, and Garcia French, the guy she grew up with and played cards with at times. Then there was Father Michael himself. A great person to confide in and the best advice giver in the world about any subject asked, although, it wasn't as easy to share her concerns anymore. Her issues were getting bigger, and even though Mary Jennings was the qualified one, Michael was the "hearing one," the one who took people's problems and listened to them. Besides, Mary wouldn't understand her problems.

Valinda had been seeing Michael about her visions and dreams for some time. She was looking forward to seeing him today and hopefully getting to chat about the latest encounters.

Bang, bang ... The loud knocks could be heard from a county away. Valinda jumped from her lounge chair and bolted to her door. She thought to give the early "intruder" a big spray of courtesy, but as she opened the door, ready to launch, she saw her little mother standing in front, looking angry that it took so long to answer.

Valinda had been going through enough, so her mother's bullshit didn't warrant any attention; well, she had to at least pretend it didn't. Val greeted her mother with a hug. Marjory entered, along with three of her friends who had given her a lift here and couldn't resist the chance to take a sneak peek at Valinda's place.

"Come on, ladies, let's hit the road, we don't have time to dilly dally." Stephanie brushed passed Valinda while giving her a nasty side-eye glare.

Stephanie was a troublemaker and the regular gossip queen in the church. Valinda did her best to avoid her at every occasion she could, although today she thought to herself that she was not going to let this woman get under her skin.

Valinda was an investigative journalist and had been overseas in war zones. She investigated some of the most strange and unbelievable cases which others would never touch. "Some people are too protected from the dangers and harshness of the real world. What if one day their protection was gone and the truth actually came out?" That was an idea that Valinda had thrown up in her mind from time to time, but she just needed that big break and enough evidence to open it all up and tear it all down. All the little stories and information that she had collected over time were still not enough to make a dent in the disclosure of the truth. So she thought, once again, that the Stephanies of the world could walk around and say what they liked while remaining in the safe false reality that kept the sheep living their ignorant lives.

Valinda shook it off. Her mother and friends had had a good look around her lounge room and now seemed eager to get moving. Valinda opened the front door and let the others go out before her. "Let's hope I get to speak with Father Michael for at least a moment," she thought.

She got to the car and let her mother in, just as Stephanie's car slowly drove past them. But then she realized she'd forgotten to bring her small satchel with her tablet and notebook. Valinda never left the house without it, a typical journalist's mentality, she was told. Even though this was a family and friends event, she thought there might be some time to finalize another web report she was working on.

She ran back to the front door, unlocked it, and while nearly tripping over the cat, managed to make it to her room where the satchel was sitting at the end of the bed. But as she leaned in to pick it up, she heard a growl coming from her bathroom.

She jumped in fright, hoping it was her imagination as those things had never shown up in daylight before. She took a deep breath, and gathering her wits was about to turn and head back to the front door.

Whoosh, an icy breeze came through the bedroom doorway, sending an almighty chill down Valinda's body, then there was a *crack* and a bloodcurdling growl came from the bathroom again, that time too much for her to ignore.

She gradually opened the bathroom door, each step calculated and slow. One foot, then the other, as if not wanting to wake someone or draw unwanted attention. Once inside the room, she scanned for any threat, reminding herself that those entities were random.

After examining the shower curtain, she slowly moved it to the side but then a hand grabbed her from behind and yanked her to the floor. She had occasionally been physically attacked by the ghosts, but this was by far the most violent time.

Valinda jumped back to her feet as she looked feverishly around the room. But she could not find anyone or anything. It was then that a grotesque creature appeared through the bathroom mirror. It didn't look human, even though it had human features, large dark eyes, a long face, and a skeletal chin as if the skin didn't quite stretch far enough to cover it, showing the extent of its vicious-looking teeth.

Valinda nearly fainted. Her attention was now on what it was saying, like something out of a horror movie, with its deep-growl tone yelling out to her in a language Valinda had not heard before.

The ghostly creature's dark hood fell back, revealing more of its ghastly features as it growled again, this time in English, "Stay away ... no more reporting of us ... no more exposing us ... the end is coming. You will perish if you continue ..."

The creature repeated it over and over, switching between the two languages, howling and hissing in the breaks. Blood and yellow plasma fluid leaked from its chin as it gradually dissipated into nothing.

That felt like a lifetime for Valinda, although it was only moments. But before she could compose herself, the bathroom door slammed behind her and with a final deafening growl the face appeared again in the mirror yelling, "Stop!" before finally vanishing for good.

Valinda, now shaking all over, scampered out of the bathroom and collapsed onto the bed. But she had to get out of there. She picked up her satchel off the floor and ran out of the apartment, slamming the front door closed behind her.

"What's taking you so long? We'll never catch up to Stephanie and now we are running late," Marjory snapped, as her daughter opened the door.

Valinda, still with tears in her eyes and shaking, got into the car without saying a word. Marjory knew she'd had one of her turns or visions, and could see she was trying to hide it, despite obviously being very upset. So she decided not to say anything. Besides, she knew Father Michael would be there to help.

After a few moments of sitting still and staring ahead, Valinda got out of the car, went to the passenger side, and handed the keys to Marjory, who knew at this stage not to argue. She glanced at Valinda with concern, then made her way over to the driver's side and climbed in. They drove all the way to the church in complete silence.

SHANNON, COUNTY CLARE, IRELAND, 1990

RUNNING AWAY FROM HER fast cousins while searching for somewhere to hide and cheat the sting of being tagged, Serena ducked underneath an old table outside a post office. She hoped that by hiding and remaining still she could avoid the humiliation of getting caught. The boys ran by, glancing both ways to try to find their target. Serena smiled and jumped out of the safe haven she had held for such a short time.

Stepping out with her head held high, thinking she had beaten the boys, was a rookie mistake.

"There she is, over there just near the post office!" Jason shouted, and the boys made a beeline to her position.

Serena looked back and screamed as she tried to maneuver a way out of the current situation. It wasn't just getting tagged, she thought, it was the name and reputation you get for failing or losing the game, so she had to win.

Serena found an old hole near the entrance to one of the bakeries and sat there, happy with her new hiding place. Suddenly the rotten wooden floor gave way. She fell, hitting bags of flour piled up high and hurting her wrist on impact. Serena grabbed her arm and started crying without making any noise.

Where was she? It wasn't just a bakery cellar. It looked more like a dump leading into the rear of some offices, definitely an area she should not be in.

She looked around and felt a familiarity, although did not know where to go or what to do. "Should I climb back up? Should I just run out? Or should I look further?" she thought. Serena was a very inquisitive person. She loved her father and listening to all the great stories, but she felt that she was too protected by him, so in her mind investigating was her only option to "escape" that.

Walking through the long basement, Serena had to open door after door, trying to find her way out. She wasn't like many other twelve-year-olds. She was bullied for her different features, especially by the girls. However, she didn't let that bother her. She hung out with the boys instead and helped them when they got hurt.

As she gazed ahead into the half-light of a hall, she heard voices coming from above. She found an old staircase that used to lead to the top; the only problem was that the opening was sealed over, and the only exit seemed to be back where she had fallen in. Serena did not like the idea of going back, especially knowing that the boys would be hovering around there somewhere. She'd had enough of the game, but still, she did not want to be caught. So she pushed hard repeatedly on the old cellar door, bump after bump, on and on, until exhaustion took hold and she fell off the crate she was standing on and onto the ground.

Serena sat up and composed herself, thinking, "Why am I doing this?" when the cellar door she was trying to open creaked, then rattled. Serena sat back in shock and looked up at the door, expecting it to open. Nothing. Somebody must have heard her and had gone to check it. She decided it was a good time to find another way out, but then the voices above, though muffled, started getting louder, and she even heard some yelling, providing her with motivation to stay and investigate.

She made her way to where the voices were coming from and realized she was probably under the medical doctor's residence. Everything seemed different when you were underground.

Serena grabbed several large crates and climbed up on top. From there she could see into a doctor's office through the cracks of a door which led down into the basement and which could only be unlocked from the inside. She saw her father sitting in a chair and she knew where she was now. Her father had an office next door to the medical center where she had been many times.

Serena adjusted her position to get a better view and there on another chair she saw Graham, an old bricklayer in his later stages of life who had some obvious issues. Serena moved her feet on the crate so she was a bit more stable, her new focus being not getting into trouble for listening in. She even managed to get a little comfortable, although what she heard next would change her mindset and her life forever.

Graham Fallon had recently been involved in an incident with his granddaughter. She had disappeared on the day they were both out for a picnic. The media had been ruthless about it and the police were at a loss to explain what had happened two weeks earlier. Graham was passed on to Doctor Liam O'Halloran to try and find something new in his story or to find anything that could incriminate him. His family had turned on him, blaming him for neglect, and he was going on trial soon if he couldn't get any proof of the sudden disappearance of the girl. He was telling wild stories of creatures and monsters coming out of the woods and taking his granddaughter, so he was willing to participate in regression, hoping it would help his case.

· *"Are you ready, Graham?"* Liam asked in a calm voice. His earlier yelling had obviously echoed into the other offices, so Liam now wanted this to go as smoothly as possible.

"Yes."

"Recording. Can you slowly count back from 10 to 0 for me?"

"10, 9, 8..."

"Now, I want you to go back to the earliest time of the day on the morning you took Mackenzie to see the faery forts and have a picnic"

"Yes..."

≈

Graham woke up after a big night looking after his granddaughter, playing games, and running around the fields he owned.

"Granddad, when are we going to the faery forts?" Mackenzie was so excited about their trip, she could hardly wait.

Graham was getting a coffee and trying to get the picnic packed up; however, he knew how much the little one was looking forward to their big adventures. He quickly finished his breakfast, sat up, put his flat cap to his head, and whispered, "Are you ready to catch a sprite, or do you want to pick an—"

"Don't say it, Granddad, the faeries will get us!"

Graham laughed in a low, soft, comforting voice. He knew she loved faeries and believed in them but was worried about how much knowledge she had about the folkloric creatures.

"Let's go. If anything, we will see some great landscapes and the faery forts are historic places full of wonder."

Graham had been looking forward to caring for his granddaughter for a long time. They didn't get to see each other often and since his wife had passed away, he was feeling the loneliness. His daughter and son-in-law had planned a long overdue holiday together and needed a break, so when they asked Graham to have Mackenzie for the fortnight, he was ecstatic. His daughter had dropped Mackenzie off two days early so she could get some last-minute packing and errands done before their big trip began.

They couldn't take Mackenzie as the trip was also for business. They owned their own computer programing company together. Trying to establish themselves, they had to travel to promote it, so they made it a working holiday, and that was hopefully going to boost the company.

"OK, Granddad, let's go. I want to see the forts." Mackenzie grabbed his hand and they walked to the jeep.

Mackenzie, now strapped in and ready for the day's adventures, asked her grandfather to tell her some stories, so he turned the radio down and thought of his best childhood tale about the sprites that tricked a town. After an hour traveling, Graham pulled up to a nice little spot where they could have some lunch first, before heading out to the forts. Mackenzie had other ideas. The seven-year-old poured out of the car and started making her way over to the trees.

"Hey!" Graham shouted to Mackenzie, worried she was heading too far away.

"Hey!" Mackenzie ran back to Graham, tripped on a log and fell flat on her face. Graham ran to her like an overprotective parent.

"Are you OK, sweetheart?"

Mackenzie picked herself up, smiled, and said, "Of course I am, now let's go." Mackenzie just wanted to find the forts, but it was taking too long, she thought, for her grandfather to get ready.

"Hold your horses, little one, we have to unpack the picnic hamper and all the gear. We need to have lunch first because I have heard that you cannot go faery hunting on an empty stomach, and besides, granddad needs some coffee really bad."

Mackenzie looked up at him and said, "OK, sounds good to me."

They found a very nice spot looking over the lush green valley. Not a soul was around. There they set up the picnic and Graham started telling another story over his sandwich and long overdue coffee.

After the story Graham sat back on his chair and closed his eyes for what he thought was only a moment, reminiscing about the times he would take his wife Sian-Anne to some of those locations when they were younger.

Mackenzie had been so patient. She had a little walk while Graham was asleep. She knew he would be mad if he found out, so she only went to the first structure, a small one. Mackenzie had knocked a couple of carefully placed stones over when she stood on top of the ancient structure. She tried to put them back where they had been, but they kept falling off, so she ran back to the picnic site hoping no one saw it, after which she managed to fall asleep for a few hours along with Graham.

"Wake up, wake up." Graham woke from his dream with a start. His granddaughter was standing over him, shaking him, and hitting his chest.

"What ... what's all this?" he said with a stutter and hint of concern in his voice.

"You've been asleep for ages, Granddad. It's going to get dark soon and we still have a big walk to the forts."

Graham sat up, took his glasses off, and rubbed his eyes. He then grabbed his white beard and gave it a tug. "Yes, it's time to go, what are we waiting for?"

He picked up his backpack, grabbed Mackenzie's hand and they walked toward the forts.

After fifteen minutes of hiking Graham set his backpack down and said, "Look, Mack, over there, the hills of the faeries."

Mackenzie was so thrilled, even more so than her grandfather had anticipated. She ran off to look at the mounds and forts, not worrying about waiting for him. After a few minutes, when he had set up his chair, he headed over to the mounds to find her. He ran to the first fort, then the next, and at the last one he felt an almighty pulse which knocked him to the ground onto his back. By the time he got himself together, he could hear Mackenzie screaming.

"I'm sorry, I can't do it."

"You can. You are strong, and you are doing so well, please, it will help us."

"There were ... I'm sorry ... I'm sorry, but it's not easy to tell."

Mackenzie was standing on top of the ring mounds, jumping up and down, shouting to her grandfather, "Hey, look at me! Look at me!" There was no one there, only lights flickering all around her, dancing from her head to her feet. Mack bent down to pick up the little purse she dropped. As she looked up, hundreds of little lights exploded through the forest even though it was late afternoon. Graham was concerned. Never had he witnessed anything like this in all his years of living. Something wasn't right.

"Look, Granddad, real faeries, they are talking to me and whispering lovely words." Mackenzie was so excited she was screaming for joy, all while Graham was moving forward to try and get her off the top of the mounds so they could start making their way back to the car.

The next few moments would change both of their lives forever. Graham was now close enough to try to get hold of Mackenzie. While he reached both arms out to grab her, several of the lights hovered over his eyes, and while they had been quick as they darted around to start with, they now seemed to slow down and hover. The light dimmed and he could make out tiny humanoid faces and long pointy ears, along with the buzzing of fast wings. Their clothing revealed intricate details, green leafy patches and gold stitching, along with gold wrist and leg bands. One of them even had a gold headpiece. All had friendly faces and quivers on their backs.

He looked at the one to the right of him who was lining him up with a bow and arrow. Time seemed to have slowed down. He was trying to lift his hand up to swat them away, but he couldn't do it quickly enough, and as soon as he attempted that movement, all their faces turned violently angry. Their bodies went dark and gray as they let out piercing screams that seemed to affect the lighting in the forest. There was a boom and Graham and Mackenzie were knocked back and fell to the ground.

Time seemed to go back to normal then, and as Graham picked himself up for the second time, Mackenzie started screaming again. This time it was more bloodcurdling, indicating she was in a great deal of pain. Graham, angry now, threw his hands around, trying to swat all the "little people" away. He managed to clip a couple of them and sent them flying into a rock. This just made them all angrier and he could hear the words uttered in unison, "Kill, kill, kill."

Graham kept sweeping his arms around until he glanced at the ground which had started shaking as if a giant was stomping his feet. He turned toward the forest, and there in front of him was an enormous hairy beast. The stench emanating from it was horrendous. Its red eyes glaring, it had its arm raised back as if ready to strike.

Mackenzie was under attack. Twenty or so of the two-inch little people were scratching her and picking her up by the hair. Not knowing what to do, Graham could only think of saving his granddaughter. As he tried to rescue Mackenzie, the beast lowered its fist and struck him on his right shoulder, knocking him down. It stood right over him and put its foot on Graham's back to stop him from moving.

Graham was shouting for Mackenzie, whom he could see hovering five feet in the air calling out for her grandfather to come save her. He kept struggling helplessly while Mackenzie was lifted higher and higher. Little people tugged at her feet, arms, and hair. She was being pulled to breaking point.

The beast lifted its foot off Graham's back and rushed over to the faeries. It took Mackenzie from the sprites and carried her off into the woods. The lights surrounded the beast, and with an almighty shriek, they all vanished into a blue glowing maelstrom. Then ... silence.

Graham, in immense pain, passed out for several hours. When he awoke, he managed to stagger to his jeep and drove to the nearest phone booth. He called the police, along with his daughter. He knew there was no chance of finding Mackenzie after what he had witnessed, even though all his instincts told him to go into the woods to try.

"Well done, Graham. I know this is hard for you, you have done an amazing job. All that is left for us to do is the lie detector test with the police. Upon passing that, along with the photographic evidence of your injuries, and the geographical data they found, I think you will have a good case."

"I just want it over. I just want my granddaughter back and my daughter to talk to me again. I want the truth to come out and I don't care if I spend the rest of my life in an institution."

Suddenly the crates shifted and fell and Serena dropped to the ground. In shock, she ran to the pile of bags where she'd fallen in and scrambled out of the basement, into the street. She sprinted all the way home, not looking back, and not worrying about any of the boys that had previously been chasing her. She could only think of getting home to the comfort of her mother and siblings. She knew they wouldn't believe her, and because her father was the one conducting the interview, she would get into a heap of trouble for eavesdropping if she said anything.

Her mother was in the middle of preparing dinner. Serena hugged her with everything she had before her mother reacted.

"You are trembling, sweetie, what is the matter? Are those boys teasing you again?" Her mother Grace was always kind and she felt safe with her.

"No, Mama, I'm fine, I just wanted a hug." Serena was never going to tell anyone what she had heard.

"OK then, love, go into the living room with your sisters and I will call you later for dinner."

Serena bypassed her sisters, went straight to her bedroom, and passed out on her bed.

THE FIRE AND
THE CREATURE

SERENA HAD TERRIBLE DREAMS all night after hearing Graham's story. She couldn't get the images of a huge beast stealing little girls in the fields out of her head. When she woke in the early hours of the morning, she was still very shaken by her dreams, although knew that no one would ever believe a story like that if she were to share it with anybody. The recording would never make it to trial as it would do more damage to Graham's case than it would help him. There wouldn't be a lawyer in the country that would touch it, so she needed proof.

As she dragged herself out of bed, an idea came to her. She knew her father always kept a copy of the recordings from each of his patients so he could listen to them over time and come to a diagnosis of what each particular patient may be suffering from. Serena knew that she couldn't approach her father about the subject as she would be caught out for listening to the whole private conversation. The punishment for that would be severe because the confidentiality of his patients was paramount, not only to their progressive recovery, but also to keeping his job as a psychiatrist. If anything were to get out, it would be detrimental to the health of his patients, but also his livelihood would be gone. Serena knew this, but she had to be sure what she heard was right, if anything just to alleviate any doubt in her mind.

Serena was always an inquisitive person and wouldn't let anything go if she thought it would be important. So she quickly put on some clothes, rushed downstairs, took a banana from the fruit bowl, and made her way out the front door, being as quiet as she possibly could.

It was a Saturday morning, and everyone was still asleep. In order to get a copy of the recording, she needed to be quick, as sometimes her father would work on the weekends. Serena threw her banana peel into the shrubs, grabbed her push-bike, strapped on her helmet, and took off like she was racing her cousins for a prize.

The dirt path from her family's driveway was very long and bumpy, so when she turned onto the main road it suddenly felt like she was riding on clouds. It was also a still a dirt road, but it was much smoother, and she could cover more distance in less time.

The only people out and about were the milkman and the paperboys, whom she knew by name. She gave a wave to Riley, who was throwing the last of his papers to the O'Donnells' house, and she didn't notice a rock sticking up on the road. Serena lost her balance and tumbled off her bike, scraping her knees on the gravel. She screamed in pain and Riley came rushing over to see if she was alright. He dumped his bike next to hers, but before he even got to her, she shouted out at him, "I'm fine!"

He stood back, and with a hint of anger said, "Well, I'm sorry, Serena, I was only trying to help you. No need to be so snappy."

Riley was clearly worried about her, but Serena wasn't as bad as he thought she was. She just wanted to get back on her bike and finish her journey to get the recording. She was more stressed that she would get caught by someone who knew her father, or even worse, by her father himself.

"Sorry, Riley, I know you were trying to help me. I'm sorry for snapping at you. I'm just a bit embarrassed about falling off my bike in front of people, that's all. It was just a bit of a shock as well." She hopped back on her bike, and as she peddled off, waved to Riley, yelling, "Thank you, I will see you at school next week."

Riley waved back and watched as she rode away.

Serena finally made it to her father's office. She knew where he hid the spare key for those days when he forgot his. No one was supposed to know, but she saw him hide it one day when she went to visit him at work. She lifted the brick next to the pot plant, and to her surprise it wasn't there. She thought, "But he always leaves it there." Serena put the brick back in exactly the same spot and then lifted the pot plant next to it. Nope, it wasn't there either. She was starting to panic as her father would most likely be getting ready for work by now.

"Maybe he moves it every now and then," she thought, and she lifted the doormat. There she saw a small tile that was loose. Sure enough, underneath the tile was the key. Serena was relieved. She knew she had limited time, so she opened the door, locked it behind her, and made her way to her father's office where she could finally get the job done.

Serena looked around the room but couldn't find any recordings. She remembered hearing her father say one day that he had them locked up, just in case someone tried to rob him.

"This is going to be an obstacle," she thought. If they were locked up, how would she be able to copy it. So Serena searched through cupboards and in the desk, even in places where it definitely would not be, until she came to the main interview room where he conducted the hypnotic regression of his patients. There in front of her was the big reel to reel with the recording of the previous day's session still in its place. "He must have run out of time last night and just left it there for this morning," Serena thought.

With no time to waste she picked up a smaller recording device, slipped a spare cassette into it and began to rewind the reel to reel to the start of the session where Graham first started talking. Serena had to stop and start the machine to check for the precise part of the recording that she was trying to find.

Suddenly Serena heard a bang coming from the main office. She stopped the machine and ducked underneath the table. Another bang, then another. They seemed to be getting louder and closer.

Serena didn't know what to do. If it was someone bad, what would they do? If it was her father, that was probably even worse. All those thoughts kept swimming in her mind until the door flew open and there standing in front of her was Riley, the paperboy.

"What are you doing here, Riley?" Serena called as softly as she could, so as not to alarm any of the other people who would be starting work nearby.

"Sorry, Serena, I finished the last house of my round and I wanted to make sure that you got to where you were going safely after you fell off your bike. I saw you go into your father's office and found the key where you put it. I'm only making sure you're OK. What are you doing here without Doctor Liam?"

Serena knew she couldn't lie to Riley as he wasn't silly. She had no choice but to let him in on the plan, reluctantly though.

"OK, firstly, did you hide your bike at the back of the bushes like I did, so my father doesn't see?" Serena did not want this to go pear-shaped.

"Yes, Serena, right next to yours, out of sight." Riley smiled because he knew she would ask.

"Secondly, what I'm about to show you, you must swear to me that you will not tell anyone, not your best friends in the whole world, your parents, my father, or anyone involved. This could be a matter of life and death if it were to get out. Now swear to me."

Serena, still affected by the horror of her dreams, seemed to Riley to be acting incredibly dramatic. He had a shocked look on his face. What was it that was so bad? he wondered. He thought she was just there to steal some paper and pens as she loved to draw. This was getting very interesting.

"Sure, Serena, whatever you say. You know me—if I say it, I mean it."

Serena knew this, but she couldn't take any chances.

"OK then, you need to be quiet as I am going to record something and no matter what you hear, you cannot make a sound."

Riley thought to himself, "How bad could it be?" then nodded to Serena and sat on the floor, waiting for the recording to start.

Serena pressed "play" on the reel to reel and "record" on her device.

It started at the time Graham was talking about getting into the car with his granddaughter.

After some time, Serena looked over at Riley. His mouth was wide open, like he was attempting to catch as many flies as he could. Serena felt bad that he was now involved in her little conspiracy, but she had no choice but to put him through it, despite the outcome.

The recording finally finished, and Serena stopped the playback and recording. She put the original back in its spot so her father could not tell someone had touched it. She then picked up her device and reached down to help Riley up off the floor. Before he could say anything, she said, "Don't say a word. Don't ask a question. Just let it go for now."

At that moment both their heads turned sharply at a sound. "What was that?" Serena whispered. There was definitely someone at the door.

She grabbed Riley's hand and they ran to the door to the basement behind which she had stood the previous day listening. The good thing about being on this side was that the lock could be opened from here.

Crash ... The front door was flung open and two men entered.

Serena and Riley had just managed to get out of the office and were in the basement, on top of crates and peering through the gap in the door. The noise from the front door being smashed open had scared them and now the constant rummaging through drawers and shifting furniture could only mean one thing ... it was not Serena's father; it must be thieves. "But why would robbers do something like this in broad daylight? And what's going to happen when Dad comes into work and finds them? What will they do to him?"

It was all getting too much for Serena. She had to come up with a plan, she thought to herself. The door to the end office was suddenly flung open all the way. She couldn't see very much, but it appeared two businessmen dressed in black suits and ties, with dark sunglasses and hats, were the ones causing all this chaos. She glanced over at Riley who again had his mouth wide open, looking like he was ready to scream or cry. Serena grabbed his mouth with her hand and like stones they sat there very still.

"Check the latest tape on the reel to reel," one of the tall men in black said to the other as he went back into the first room.

The man turned it on, but ... nothing. Obviously it was at the end of the tape. He rewound it for around thirty seconds, stopped it and pressed play, right in the middle of the abduction.

"Found it. Now what?" Wilkes called through to the other room. Anders raced in like he had won the lottery.

"Play it for me so I know."

Wilkes started up the machine again and in no time at all Anders was convinced that this was what they were looking for. Graham had been spreading all over town the circumstances of the disappearance of his granddaughter, which had led to his referral to see Doctor Liam.

"What do we do, now we have the tape?" Wilkes said with some hesitation in his voice.

"We'll burn it. Make it look like an accident, so no one knows we have even been here."

Anders took the tape from the reel to reel and placed it in a suitcase sitting on the floor. He closed it and pulled a device from his pocket. Glancing up, he saw a bottle of whiskey sitting next to several glasses on a shelf. There was no more than a swallow in the bottle, but it was enough to do the job required.

He grabbed the bottle and spilled the contents over some documents. He turned on the device, and with a whirring sound, a bolt of blue light emanated from the end, which started a fire the instant it met with the whiskey. Then he turned the device off and placed it back in his pocket.

"Let's move, Wilkes, before there are too many witnesses."

Wilkes headed for the door and Anders followed. There was furniture everywhere, with papers and equipment strewn all over the place. It didn't take long at all before the whole office was on fire. The two men left the office, walked to an isolated area, and vanished behind some trees.

Serena and Riley were waiting for the right time to leave, but not before smoke started billowing through the cracks in the door did they move. Knowing they didn't have much time, they quickly made their way to the front of the basement. Riley coughed as smoke started to affect him.

"Come on, we have to get out of here now. I need to find my father so I can warn him not to come here today."

Riley couldn't stop coughing. Serena hoped that no one heard it, especially those men in black.

"Hurry up, we're nearly there."

Serena found the hole where she had fallen through the previous day. The heavy bags of flour piled on top of each other formed a step up to the outside, and luckily they were still there so they could get out. That was the only way out. The main entrance doors were closed as it was after hours, and besides, they couldn't have gone through the fire.

They heard sirens and people coming from everywhere, but they managed to climb out before anyone saw them. Otherwise, they would have been blamed for the fire for sure. They ducked out of sight behind a fence near the medical center and then, having realized they wouldn't be able to get to their bikes just now, they ran off down the road to try to find Doctor Liam.

≈

They finally reached Serena's home. She knew she had to think it through carefully, for two reasons. She did not want to be blamed for the fire, and secondly, she did not want it known that she was in the office listening to the recording. She may have seemed dramatic before when she was warning Riley, but this was the new reality for her now. It was life and death.

"OK, Riley, you need to listen to me very carefully. This is what we are going to say to my parents, and to everyone else, for that matter, and we need to keep it consistent or else we will get caught out, do you understand?" Serena's tone was assertive.

"What do you want us to say?" Riley knew he couldn't tell anyone, but the level of shock in his eyes told Serena that maybe he wouldn't be the best at keeping a secret.

"We will tell my dad that I went to get some milk and the paper, then I saw you, so we just got talking. Then we saw two men dressed in black suits, hats, and sunglasses go into his office, so we came straight here to tell them, OK?"

Riley looked blankly at her and nodded.

"Swear to me again that this is our secret." Serena was on the verge of getting angry.

"I, I, swear it." He just wanted to go home, but was willing to go through with it for Serena.

They headed inside to the kitchen where Grace was making breakfast for Maggie and Siobhan.

"And where have you been at this early hour, young lady?" Grace seemed annoyed, yet she had a soft heart when it came to her children.

"Mama, something awful has happened, where is Dad?"

Grace walked around the kitchen table to Serena and sat her down.

"What are you talking about, child?"

Riley came out from around the corner as he was very shy and still in a bit of shock.

"Young Riley, are you part of this horrific news that Serena is about to tell us?" She smiled slightly, thinking it was just kids being kids.

"Yes, ma'am," he said quietly.

"Then you better sit down as well." Grace pulled out a chair and as Riley sat down the dog started barking at the door. "Maggie, can you get that dog, please, and see who is at the door."

Scansy always barked when there were strangers out the front. Her instincts, or senses, were very good, because when it came to family or friends, she wouldn't make a sound.

"Mama, there's no one at the door," Maggie yelled.

Grace thought it was very odd as Scansy only ever barked when it was a stranger.

"OK, I will get your father, although he is very ill today. That's why he didn't go into work this morning."

Serena felt relieved that illness most likely saved his life.

A few minutes went by and Grace marched back down the stairs to inform Riley and Serena that they could go and see her father. Serena knew she should have told her mother and her sisters, to avoid delaying it any further, considering it was an emergency, but she wanted to tell the story to him first.

Serena sat by her father's bedside and told her version of events. Grace and the girls were there too, and all were crying. Liam tried to make his way out of bed, but staggered and fell back down. His wife placed the blankets back over him and assured him that the authorities would deal with it. That wasn't good enough for Liam, though, as he knew he had many files and recordings in the office. His whole livelihood was completely gone.

Scansy started barking again and Maggie rushed down the stairs. This time there was a loud knock at the door. Wiping away her tears, she opened it to find the local police chief standing there.

Chief Duggan was a good friend of Liam's. They had worked on many cases together over the years, so he wanted to update his friend as soon as possible. Maggie called out to her mother while she let the chief inside. Grace raced down the stairs and was in the kitchen in no time, eager for news.

"Hi, chief, how bad is it?" She was a little out of breath and held his hand as she asked.

"It's not good, I'm afraid, Grace. Is Liam around?"

"He's very ill and in bed, I can pass it on if you like."

"I am sorry to hear that." The chief pulled out his notebook and began to explain the current situation. "Let him know all I can say is that the medical center is engulfed. Firefighters are working very hard as we speak to contain it. Two strange men in dark suits, hats, and sunglasses were witnessed in the area and we are looking into that as well. I'm sorry, but that is all I can tell you at this stage, it's more than some people know."

Grace lowered her head. "Thank you, chief, for thinking of us, I will let him know when he is feeling better."

The chief put his hand on her shoulder to comfort her, placed his cap on, and disappeared out the door to inform other unfortunate owners about the fire and the destruction.

Serena felt like she was off the hook, but she was still worried about what Riley would say or do. She took him aside and told him that it was OK and that she would come and see him later that day to make sure he was still alright. Riley left the house quietly while the O'Halloran family were consoling one another. He didn't want to go back to the office where his bike was, he just wanted to get home.

About halfway home he began feeling like he was being watched, but upon turning around couldn't see anybody. He kept moving, but before too long the trees started rustling loudly, though there was no wind.

Riley picked up his pace. He was freaked out and was stressed about his mind playing such tricks on him. His paranoia was getting too much, he thought. But the noises got louder and he could now hear a wolf howling, even though there were none in this area.

He started to run, but the howling was getting closer, to the point he thought it was right behind him. He glanced over his shoulder, thinking that whatever it was must be about to attack him. There was nothing.

He stopped in the middle of the road and looked all around, puffing and panting, trying to catch his breath. This was the edge of an overgrown parkland area and there were no cars or anybody around. A path through the shrubs would lead him home. By this stage all he could think about was getting back to his family, so he broke into a run again and turned into the bushy path. As soon as he did, the howls started again. This time there was more than one, he thought. He was crying now and tried running even faster. The howls seemed like they were right on him again. "Why?" he thought. "What have I done?"

Riley tripped over, as his tears made it hard for him to see and the track was uneven and rocky. As soon as he fell, the howls stopped.

He lay there for a moment sobbing, too scared to look up. His house was only five hundred yards away, but he didn't have the nerve to get up and go. He lifted his head slowly and opened his eyes. Nothing ...

He glanced behind. Nothing ... He closed his eyes again and lowered his head, thinking to himself that this must be some kind of nightmare.

He had to get home, though, so Riley mustered up every bit of courage he had, raised his head, and opened his eyes, ready to stand up. Before him stood a creature so horrifying that Riley's heart began pounding in his chest so hard that he thought it would explode.

The monster in front of him had sharp claws, a long snout that was always either snarling or smiling, and a long braid on one side of its black fur covered body. Its terrifying eyes were fiery red. It lowered its long wolf-like face closer to the boy.

Riley looked into the dark red eyes and screamed hysterically. Shouting for his mother, he quickly jumped up and turned around, about to run, but blocking his path was a man, like those he and Serena had seen at the office. In fact, it was the same man dressed in black.

Riley called out, "What do you want from me?"

As he yelled the wolf-man slowly leaned over and grabbed Riley around his throat, lifting him up by his neck, not caring about the long claws lodged deep into his skin. The creature stood at full height, with legs bent at the knees, waiting for the man to come over and give it permission to end the boy's life.

Riley was trying to talk but couldn't, as Anders moved up closer to his face and whispered in his ear, "You have two options here, son The first one is you agree to never speak of anything you saw here today, including the recording, and you can go on to live your life normally as if nothing ever happened. The second, which is my favorite, is I get my very angry friend here to dig those claws all the way in and snap your tiny neck. Now, I personally hope you go for the second option as Savage, which is what I like to call him, is very hungry and I've told him there is a snack for him today. However, if we can come to an agreement, I will look after you and your family for the rest of your lives. Maybe even make you an important part of our future plans, which will give you wealth and power. Now, what do you say?"

Riley was in terrible pain. Tears streamed down his face. He was aware of what had just been spoken and in a gurgled whisper he replied, "One, number ... one, I ... won't say anything, I promise."

Still held up by the seven-foot bipedal wolf-man, he began to pass out. When he was right on the cusp, Anders smiled and said, "Great, excellent, that wasn't so hard now, was it. Savage, let our new friend down gently."

Savage was Anders' pet, a wolf-man creature he had created. The monster slowly let the boy down onto the ground, and then crept back into the bushes. It howled loudly, and then ... it was gone.

Anders bent down to Riley's level, took out another device, turned it on, and healed the wounds on his neck. The boy pulled away at first, but when he found the pain was going away, he let the man in black continue. When he was finished, Anders offered his hand to Riley and helped him upright, saying, "My name is Agent Anders, now let's go home and have a chat."

They walked along the path together until they arrived at Riley's doorstep. They entered the house together, and the door slowly closed behind them.

No one in the town ever saw Riley or his family again.

BROKEN FAERY

THERE WERE MANY STRANGE events happening in the area around the town where Serena's family lived. One even made the local papers. Another incident was quite creepy. Some locals found the remains of what looked like a very little person. It had a grotesque face and wasn't considered human. High up official scientists came to collect it and it was never seen again. Witnesses said that it looked like a gnome or a goblin of some sort.

Other weird events were the many lights in the sky and through the trees. There were different kinds of howls and high-pitched animal screams at night in the forest areas. The Shannon River even dredged up an aquatic humanoid being. Humanoid, as it had the features of a human, but with the scales and appearance of something aquatic. The creature washed up on the shore one day and was found by two kids fishing in the area, who reported it to local authorities. Again, the scientists came and took it away for tests, and it was never heard about again.

The area was a hub for paranormal activity and unexplainable events, until one day it all just stopped. The media were told not to write about any of it. Only one story made it to the papers and that was the first encounter, the one Graham had been witness to.

Serena was broken after hearing about what happened to Graham. The public had turned on him and he was blamed for the disappearance of his granddaughter. A week after the fire at Doctor Liam O'Halloran's office, Graham was found in the same area that Mackenzie had vanished, at the edge of the woods, swinging from a tree. It was all too much for him and he couldn't bear the pain anymore. He did have some support, but the resentment in his daughter's face was too much for him to live with, so one night he went out and did not return.

The unfortunate part about it, Serena thought to herself, was that he would have had some more supporters if he had just held on over the next few weeks, because of some of the unexplainable sightings happening across the area.

Not long before all the activity stopped, Serena asked her mother if she could go up to the spot where Mackenzie had disappeared. She said that she wanted to pay her respects, although deep down she just wanted to see the place for herself. She hoped it would answer some questions she had about the whole ordeal. No one knew what she knew. She kept it that way, especially after Riley's family basically vanished, moving away without anybody knowing. It was like they had just dropped off the face of the Earth.

After some persuading, Grace decided to take the three girls up to the area. She was hesitant about it due to all the hype over Graham and Mackenzie, but Serena sold it to her on the grounds that they were paying their respects and that they would all say a prayer for both of them.

Later that day they arrived at the exact area. They had packed some lunch and made their way to a nice location where the forts weren't too far away. Upon finishing lunch, Serena picked herself up and turned to start walking toward the forts. Many others were there on this day as it was a tourist attraction, even though it was far out of the way for most tourists. There was also a family of three kicking a soccer ball to each other.

"Wait, Serena, you are not to go without the rest of us. After all that's happened, I want us to stick together. We will walk over to the forts, say a prayer, and then we will leave all together, understand?" Grace was quite assertive in her tone. She knew too many weird things were happening in the area lately.

Serena nodded. Her inquisitive side was taking over, and she scoured the area, gazing past the hill where the first of the forts was and thinking to herself how beautiful it was. Although she had not been to this exact location before in her life, it all felt very familiar, as if she had seen it in a dream.

"Come on, Maggie, stop dawdling," Serena insisted. Maggie was the second eldest and could think of a thousand things she would rather be doing right at this time. Her mother was quite insistent that she come today as it meant a lot to Serena. Serena was acting quite strange lately and Grace thought this may settle things down for her, like some sort of closure.

"Coming ... and I'm not dawdling, I'm enjoying the scenery." Maggie looked at Serena and poked her tongue out quickly before her mother saw it.

They made their way up the hill to the fort and sat down. They held each other's hands and Grace said the Lord's Prayer along with a couple of comforting words of hope. They all sat in silence for a good ten minutes afterward, reflecting on their own thoughts.

Serena had her own poem she wanted to recite, as she thought it may appease the faeries and help anyone else who may have trouble. Faery lore at the time was considered just that, folklore. There were those who believed wholeheartedly that they do exist and that they had an impact on farming, rain, harvest, and so on. Serena was also witness to Graham's testimony that the public didn't know about, which was enough for her to believe while her sisters sniggered to themselves.

"Mother, can you make them stop, this is important to me and it may help Mackenzie," Serena pleaded.

Maggie and Siobhan sat back as their mother glared at them.

"OK, dear, say your poem and we can go home." Grace made herself comfortable as Serena stood and faced the forts. She spoke the words with a loud voice.

To all the ones of tiny wings
Mischief, warriors, and magical things
Appearing only to those they choose
Granting wishes and dreams in twos

But some are dark, mean, and scary
There are many forms of a Faery
They can take your children in the night
Or leave you with a nasty fright

A horseshoe fastened to your door
The changeling will bother you no more
But be aware and don't speak ill
Or change your life they certainly will

This poem is to all a Sprite
We acknowledge you and shine a light
To keep us safe, we say to you
I'll protect this fort and keep it true

As Serena finished her poem, she glanced over to her family sitting quietly. There were no remarks or sniggers, just the three of them looking up at her with caring eyes.

Serena sat back down. "What did you think? I stayed awake all night writing it."

Grace and the girls nodded with approval.

"Very nice, dear," her mother said as they all stood up and started to make their way back to the car.

Not far from the forts, as they were descending the hill, Serena thought she could hear a scream or cry coming from nearby. It was so faint, she dismissed it as just the breeze and kept walking behind her family.

There it was again. This time she stopped and listened carefully, trying not to miss any kind of noise at all. As she was standing there with her eyes wide open waiting for it, she noticed an impression in the ground that wasn't visible unless you really concentrated. She bent down to have a closer look and upon investigating noticed it seemed to be a large footprint. Serena jumped back and wondered if it could be the creature that had attacked Graham.

She slowly moved forward and placed her foot into the slight indentation in the ground. Her tiny shoes didn't even make it halfway up the imprint. Now that she was comparing, she could see toe marks at the end, five toes and a long foot shape. She stepped out and heard the cries again. She turned around and upon examining the ground a reflective glint caught her eyes. Serena bent down to get a better look and found the smallest arrow she had ever seen. Next to this was a tiny sword. If she hadn't been looking in that direction at the same time the items reflected the sun's rays, she would have missed the whole lot. It was only because of the cries and screams that she was in that area of the mounds in the first place.

Serena tucked the two items into her pocket, then scoured the green terrain for any more trinkets, before finally setting her eyes on another reflective glare. As she went to pick it up, she realized it was attached to some very tiny arms and legs, moving fast so they caught her eye. She found where the cries were coming from.

"Help me, please help!" The distressed little thing was calling out so intensely.

Serena lowered her head all the way down to the tiny creature. She knew what it was now. It was a faery, she thought. A slight smile hit her face and she felt a tingle of excitement. Her mother was calling out to her, so she had to be move fast. Whatever happened, she had to be quick.

"Are you OK, are you hurt?" Serena said in a very soft and caring tone.

"No, I'm broken. Help me, they will come soon." The faery screamed in despair.

Serena pulled out her unused handkerchief and very carefully picked up the creature. She placed her gently on it and put it in her pocket, making sure she was OK to do so. Then she made her way down the hill where her family were waiting, their impatience visible in their scowls.

"Right, time to go," Grace insisted, as they packed up into the car and made their way home for the evening.

Serena looked over her shoulder at the mounds and forts to see a bright light shining through the trees. She knew what it was and turned her head back around to face forward again. It was after that day that all activity in County Clare went silent and the town went back to normal life.

≈

Serena arrived home. Not quick enough, she thought, as her little find could be very hurt or even worse. She bolted from the car, opened the front door, and sped up the stairs to her bedroom. She closed the door behind her and locked it just in case her inquisitive sisters wanted to know what she was up to. Once she knew she was secure, Serena carefully took the tiny creature out of her pocket and placed it on the desk next to her bed light.

The creature was either sleeping or severely hurt. Serena found a small handkerchief and folded it like a pillow. Then she lifted its head and gently put it down onto it. As she was doing this, there was a flutter of a wing. Serena looked closely at its face where she saw some movement, so she gently blew some air over it. Its eyes opened and it looked up in horror. Its movements weren't like a human's, Serena thought, they were fast then so slow, very jerky like a pigeon's head moving, but much more pronounced and awkward.

She took a step back as she didn't know what the tiny thing was going to do. After all, little Mackenzie had gone missing, and as far as she was concerned, this creature could be responsible for the whole thing. It was best to just be cautious.

The creature seemed to be slowing down. One of its wings didn't seem to be working at all.

Serena whispered to it, "Are you OK?" Her voice was calming and soft.

The creature looked up at her, waving its arm for her to come closer. Serena leaned forward, then remembered she had a magnifying glass in her top drawer. She quickly grabbed it and put it up to the miniscule being.

She could now see the creature more clearly. It had little yellow and green wings, and dark green clothing that looked like it was put together from tiny leaves. At a closer glance, it was all natural, like the forest faeries she was told about growing up. The creature looked female and had on what seemed to be a golden tiara, wrapped with green vines encompassing a jewel. She had gold bindings on her tiny arms, along with green pointed boots. Her long blonde hair, with waves of purple and silver through it, was fuzzy and needed combing, and her ears were human-like although much longer and pointed. Serena was mesmerized by her and after what felt like an eternity of gazing at the creature, she was startled when it spoke.

"Please, help me." Her voice was high-pitched and quivering.

Serena could barely hear her but the looking glass made it easier to see her, which helped with understanding.

"You aren't going to hurt me, are you? Like what happened to Mackenzie up at the forts not long ago?" Serena was a little anxious. She was thinking, what if they all come into the room and try to take her. She had heard all those stories when she was little.

"No, my dear, I will explain. I just need you to help me first. I have injured my wing and my arm. I have some special healing powder in my sack that fell out into your pocket."

Serena, now in care mode, quickly reached into her pocket where she remembered she had also put the other items she had found on the ground back at the forts. She pulled out the contents and placed them all on the desk. There was a sword and a quiver attached to a bow.

"There, that's it." The faery pointed to the quiver with arrows, which had a tiny satchel tied to the bottom of it.

Serena picked up the quiver, but it was much too small for her to untie the bag, so she placed it next to the faery while she sat and watched.

"Thank you, my dear," she heard as she watched the creature struggle to open the satchel.

Her injuries must have been worse than she thought, so Serena rummaged through her drawer and found a sharp paper knife that she used to work on school projects. She gave the tiny bag a little nick and bright glowing powder dropped out of the bottom. The small being picked up some of the powder and rubbed it on her injured arm, then onto the gash on her wing, while talking in some sort of old language. Within moments she was standing upright and flapping both wings. She then flew all around the room for a few moments and disappeared.

Serena was panicking. She wanted some answers but knew that there was no way she could find the faery if it didn't want to be found. So she sat on her bed and just stared at the ceiling. "So much has happened. I'm still not sure if it's all been a dream," she thought.

Then, at the end of the bed, from out of nowhere came a bright flash of purple, blue, and yellow mist, and there in front of her, in full human size, stood the faery, smiling.

"Now, my dear, thank you for helping me. I would surely have perished if you had not said that poem and found me at the fort."

Serena sat with her mouth wide open, just staring at the wondrous sight in front of her. The tiny thing was now a beautiful being dressed in purple, green, and brown, with her hair straight, although now only slightly silver and blonde, falling from the sides of her dark green hood. Her tiara was now plain gold without any forest attachments, but it seemed to have Celtic patterns and lines all through it.

The faery pulled her hood down, revealing her ears, still pointed at the top instead of rounded like a human's, and her beautiful face, which was long and slender, with an immaculate jawline and thin pointed eyebrows.

Serena could not stop staring. The faery was mesmerizing and elegant, like a princess in the tales she had read as a child. She was dressed like a warrior, with dark brown leather pants, and dark green boots adorned with leafy swirling patterns, which came up to below her knees.

A fitted dark green vest flowed down to just above her knees. Flaps were cut up to her waist, producing four sections of the garb, one each over the front and rear, then two underneath on either side of her hips, creating a small cape or flowing tail coat with the same Celtic patterns all the way through.

Her arms had brown Celtic vambraces with velvet underlining that protruded through to the first digits of her hand, and on her shoulders sat silvery blue metal armor carved with more Celtic patterns, creating layers that went across her shoulders and molding into a chest plate with more leafy swirls.

Her green undervest protruded through the chest guard and came up to her neck, under her chin line, opening to reveal the front of her throat. At the back it led all the way up, creating her hood that was now resting on her shoulders.

What caught Serena's attention the most, after looking past her bow, quiver with arrows on the left, and sword on her right shoulder, were her amazing wings. Serena had never seen anything more beautiful in her whole life. They were in four sections, purple-green and gold in color, although translucent with amazing patterns running all over them. As the faery moved, the colors would change, fascinating Serena even more. The wings were very long, and while pointed, they were rounded off slightly. The top two rose two feet above her shoulders, protruding through specially designed openings in her clothing, and the bottom two, which met in two sections at the middle of her back, hung down to just above her calves.

Serena snapped back to reality with a barrage of questions.

"Why were you on the ground? What happened to Mackenzie? What do you mean, my poem helped?" Serena let fly, but she was stopped midway into her question-fueled rant.

"OK, OK, child, I will tell you, but this mustn't go anywhere no one must know about me."

Serena was getting used to keeping secrets by now. She felt she was involved deeply in these events, without knowing exactly what it was she was caught up in.

"My name is Shaylee Aethelwyne. I am a princess from Faelyrn, a kingdom of many kinds of magic and faery folk. Our realm was invaded by a sinister force and they have taken our Queen Tianna, my mother. In the process, some of our kind were taken as slaves and our magic was not strong enough to break their mind control over us. When the young girl was taken, I was leading the group but was attacked and knocked to the ground. The monster opened the doorway, but I was too far away and slipped between worlds, stuck nowhere, injured and weak, until you opened the fort portal. It was enough to send me back here, and that's when you found me. In the process, the control over me was broken, and I am now here with you. I owe you my life, young one."

Shaylee knew there would be more questions, so she sat at the end of Serena's bed, waiting for her response. The silence was long as Serena struggled to take it all in.

"What is the creature that took Mackenzie and who are the invaders of your realm?" Serena wasn't quite as eager now to know, as she was starting to feel scared about what the answers may be.

"The monsters are large hairy creatures of many names. Sasquatch, I think, is one term for them you may know. They use us to help with their evil, which is to capture as many girls and boys with a special type of DNA which they use to do medical research. We cannot open the doors to the dark realm where they are from, so we must stay with the beast as it opens the door using a vocal scream. If we do not hold on to it or are not in its vicinity when it opens the realm door, then we are stuck. If we are stuck here while still under their control, we perish within weeks, as faeries cannot stay in the Earth realm without the magic of Faelynn's atmosphere to charge us. Only a group of faery folk together can open the doorway to the dark realm."

The faery sighed, and then continued, "The control is too great. We are doing things we do not want to, the power over us is too strong. The ones we call the 'sinisters', who are responsible for this, have an agenda. I think they are also known as grays or Zeytars, but we are unaware of the whole plan as the monster locks us up when we are no longer needed. I cannot explain any more than this." She lowered her head. A single tear fell from her left eye, rolling down her pale near-human face.

"I'm sorry, Shaylee, I had no idea. We are not safe, are we?" Serena passed her a tissue.

"No, these sinisters have taken over many worlds and have control of many creatures. This is the last world that hasn't been affected and all I know is it's the world they want the most. We are not safe here. I must go back to Faelynn to build an army, as our defenses are down and we have had other enemies that could now be a threat. With my mother held captive, I must help my people. If I am found here, I will be killed, as will anyone I have encountered. My hope is that they think that I have been killed, which will give me time."

"Take me with you, please, I can help," Serena said, looking desperate. She knew she could help. She just didn't know how yet.

"No, I'm sorry, child, it's much too dangerous. Besides, you are just a child."

Serena jumped off the bed with her hands on her hips and a demanding scowl on her face that would make any adult laugh. She shouted, "This child saved you! All I want is to help your world." The scowl had turned into more of a begging look now.

Shaylee did not say a word. With a mighty flash she turned back into a tiny sprite and flew out the window. It was getting late and Serena watched her fly off before she disappeared out of sight. Serena lowered her head and slowly crept over to her bed.

But before long, Shaylee was back and hovering in front of her face, now begging Serena for help. She had advanced to the closest faery portal, a lone oak of very old age. She was too weak to open the portal and needed Serena's help.

"Please, Serena, can you help me yet again?"

After everything was explained to her, Serena did not hesitate to pack a bag and climb out the window to find the nearby tree. She left the house and ran up the path, unaware there was a stranger standing at the side of her house, a stranger she would get to know very well later in life.

They finally came to the old oak that towered over the area. Serena knelt and whispered, "Are you sure this is a faery door?"

She was yet again confused, but was quickly told, "Yes, my dear, these are the oldest trees with the highest magic. Now say your words and believe."

Serena closed her eyes and repeated the poem. A blue swirling light appeared in the middle of the tree. The branches came alive and started spreading, as if opening a door for them, reaching out for yards. Shaylee instructed her to quickly get up and follow her through.

Serena did exactly what she was told and within a blink of an eye they both disappeared into the light while the old oak tree twisted its branches back into their original positions, closing the door immediately after they entered.

Five hours later the same light appeared. Serena crawled out of the oak along with Shaylee, both looking tattered and exhausted. Serena was dressed in strange clothing as if she'd been a part of their culture for some time.

She got to her feet, and looking behind her, she ran through the brush toward the main road, eventually coming up to her house. Without speaking, Serena climbed up the ladder to her room, and entered through the window, with Shaylee flying right behind her. She staggered to her bed and dropped onto her stomach, hitting the mattress and pillow. Her head was tilted toward her desk. The low light of her lamp showed the scratches and bruises on her face, as well as the dried blood along with abrasions on her hands. She noticed the date on the clock was the same as when they had left.

Shaylee transformed into full size and sat next to Serena. She pulled out some golden dust from her satchel and sprinkled it onto Serena's wounds, watching them all heal as the powder did its job. Before long Serena had sprung up out of bed without a mark on her.

"Why is it the same date as when we left, ages ago?" Serena asked Shaylee.

"You know that time is different in all realms and from ours to yours time stands still, so a year can feel like a second, or a second can feel like a year. The magic depends on one's perspective. I always knew this and I wanted you to have a normal life. With everything we have been through together, I must now leave you to prepare for the end battle coming up."

Serena cried out, yelling "no" repeatedly. "You can't go, I need you!"

Shaylee put her hand on Serena's face and said, "I will be back. One day I will be here for you. There will be people you will meet who will help you and you them. When time gets near to the ending, I will be back for you. Now lie down, close your eyes, and think of all the great things you want to achieve in your life."

As Serena lay back sobbing, Shaylee sprinkled some blue powder over her face and sang a song in her native tongue. Serena closed her eyes. She had stopped crying and fell asleep.

Shaylee took her hand off her face and whispered, "Sleep, my dear, I will miss you, but I will be here when you need me."

As she said those final words, Shaylee turned toward the window, tears slowly forming in her blue eyes. She picked up a cassette tape sitting on the desk and with a spark she returned to her tiny size and flew out the window.

In the morning, Serena jumped out of bed and ran down the stairs like she was full of life.

"Morning, Mama," she said brightly, sitting down to have some breakfast. "So, what's been happening?"

TENSIONS RISE

ANDERS AND WILKES HURRIED into the hospital's front entrance like they were late for a very important meeting. They had just heard on police radio about the recent events in the building. Local police were already on the scene, but the men in suits didn't care to stop and wait for approval to gain access to witnesses.

"Wait, gentlemen, who are you and where do you think you are going?" said Detective Barnes in a deep low voice, in a tone that indicated no interest whatsoever in the answer. Before Wilkes could say anything, Barnes snapped again, "Men, I'm not interested. We have an incident here that I need to get to the bottom of. If you would like to go over to my partner—"

Before Barnes could finish, Anders took off his sunglasses and looked Barnes directly in his eyes. Anders' pupils were completely black and Barnes just stood there mesmerized, as if he had been put into a trance or was daydreaming about someplace nice.

Anders spoke softly to Barnes. "My name is Agent Anders. This is my partner, Agent Wilkes. We have overseen this investigation from the start. I suggest you take your men and leave the scene without any hesitation and pass on to us all the information you have already gathered."

Barnes stared back at him like a child, as Anders slowly placed his sunglasses back into position. Then the detective seemed to snap out of his trance with a somewhat calmer expression and agenda.

He turned away from the two agents and walked over to his own men, ordering all witness statements and evidence be handed over to them both. Upon gathering all the information, the two agents made their way up to the ward where Eric was admitted. Doctor Emmen had just arrived, missing the early onslaught of Barnes's questions and interrogations.

Anders grabbed the doctor, sat him on the chair, and whispered in his ear, "Do yourself a favor and tell me where they went, and who is involved."

Doctor Emmen was quite a popular doctor and knew most of his staff well but liked to keep to himself. He was a very busy person and barely got to see his own family at times, so any personal details about others escaped his notice. He knew these guys weren't playing games, so he tried to give what he could.

"Well, Serena is the nurse on duty who is alleged to have kidnapped Mr. Kirkpatrick. The files contain both his address and her personal details, which I assume you already have, and I can't tell you any more than that."

Anders looked at Wilkes, then back at the doctor. "Can you tell me where she might go, any hobbies or private places that she has discussed?"

Emmen lowered his head, trying hard to remember any conversations they may have had over the years that would indicate any places or people she may spend time with outside of work.

"I'm sorry, gentlemen, I just don't know. I'm very busy and try to stay out of everyone's business; however, there is a nurse that works here by the name of Louise Carter. She has spent the most time with Serena over the years."

Anders moved his lips into a very slight grin, which if you didn't look closely enough would easily be missed by most. Doctor Emmen caught a quick glimpse before the agent returned to his stern, cold as a robot expression.

"You understand how important this is. We need information to locate the whereabouts of his daughter."

The doctor nodded his head.

"Yes, I agree, I just don't understand why Serena would do this, there has to be more to it."

Upon hearing the doctor's response, Anders shut down the conversation.

"Thank you for your time, doctor. I hope this hasn't disrupted too much of your day. Oh, before we go, do you mind if we take a look at the CCTV of the last twenty-four hours, please? This will help us immensely with our investigation."

The doctor nodded and gave the two agents directions to the main control room.

Before going to collect the security footage, Anders and Wilkes first headed down to the main reception desk where the dayshift duty nurse had just started work.

"Can I help you, gentlemen?" The duty nurse was a large woman named Carly Manning. She had worked at the hospital for over thirty years and had a nickname around the place, "Butch Manning", for her no tolerance, hard-line stance on the way she ran her shifts. She was also a sucker for a young attractive man.

"Good morning, this is Agent Wilkes and I am Agent Anders. We need your help with locating one of your staff members. We were hoping you could assist with our enquiry."

Anders needed to tone it down a little, Wilkes thought. His robotic methods could sound too manufactured sometimes and nurse Manning was already seeing through him.

"Sorry, guys, I can't help you. That would break all of our privacy rules and even though you are from law enforcement, I don't have the authority to give out that information. I'll get you a form you can complete, and I will hand it to my superiors."

Anders clenched his fist at his side, clearly getting agitated. Wilkes noticed this and took over the negotiations.

"OK, Carly, is it?" he said, looking at her name tag, while trying to build some rapport with her. "We are agents of high classification and this case is part of one of the biggest investigations in the history of the United States. There are people in a great amount of danger and we just don't have time to be filling out forms. That is the most I can say about the whole thing, so any help you can give us would be much appreciated and you may even save some lives." Wilkes gave her a smile, more natural than any expression Anders could maintain.

Carly smiled back and after giving him a wink, started typing. "What would you like to know?" she said, her mood having changed almost instantly.

"Could you please give us the home addresses of two staff members, Serena O'Halloran and Louise Carter."

Information on Serena had been forwarded to them by the detectives, but finding out more about this other nurse, her friend, was what they hoped would lead them to her.

"OK, bear with me."

After some more typing on the computer, she scribbled the information the two agents needed on a notepad. Carly handed the note over to Wilkes, but didn't let go. Wilkes looked at her with some confusion until Carly smiled, and then winked. "It's yours for another smile."

Wilkes glared at her, smiled intently showing teeth, and grabbed the note from her hand.

"Thank you, Carly, please have a nice day." Wilkes' smile quickly went back to his normal expression as they turned around. Carly stared at the men as they made their way back to the elevator, asking herself what had just happened.

The men soon reached level four where they would gain access to the security footage, hopefully finding something they could use for their investigations.

"Who are you guys?" Stanley asked, as the two agents just strolled into the "secured" hospital control room.

Anders showed his badge and after reading the guy's name tag said, "Do you have something for us, Stanley?"

Stanley didn't answer for a moment, taking in their hats and sunglasses, and then responded, "Oh yes, I've been expecting someone to come take a look at the footage of this morning. I have saved the event from all cameras involved, from half an hour before the event started to half an hour after. Here, I will show you."

Stanley pulled up two chairs and played the footage.

"Here we go, this is the best angle. I have recreated the pathway of the nurse and the patient, from where they started to where they finished," Stanley explained as the two agents watched every frame intensely as if they were trying to find something others would not pick up.

Stanley sat back, letting the agents watch the footage, selecting parts and replaying some two or three times each. Anders seemed to be becoming more agitated as they watched and rewatched.

Wilkes leaned over to his fellow agent and whispered, "We have missed something, there has to be a reason this nurse has risked her career and her life for this man."

Anders nodded and then addressed Stanley. "Hey, Stan, is this absolutely everything you have? Did you miss something? It's very important we see it all."

Stanley seemed a little puzzled. "Yes, sir, I have spent every minute of my shift copying files and following the event. There is absolutely nothing I have missed."

Anders was getting angry as he usually did. He stood up and started pacing. Wilkes sat back, in deep thought.

"Maybe something happened through the night that we missed. Stanley, can you bring up all camera footage of the nurse from the time we walked in late last night until the event?"

Stanley rolled his chair forward and nodded.

"What are you thinking, Agent Wilkes?" Anders asked in a calmer tone.

"I'm not sure, but there must be something else."

They all sat down, staring at the cameras while Stanley brought up every scene from the previous night, until Anders jumped out of his chair as if he had just won the lottery.

"There, this camera right here."

The scene was showing Serena at the nurses' desk around the same time they were interrogating Eric.

"What are you looking at, Anders?" Wilkes said.

Stanley rewound the scene again.

"Can you blow the image up and play it slowly," Anders insisted.

Stanley nodded and they both looked intensely, again and again, watching Serena turn on the intercom and place her phone next to it. The camera's resolution was good enough that they could see a recording light flashing on her phone's screen.

Anders whispered in Wilkes' ear, "Look at the time stamp, it's exactly the same time we were mind-stalking subject 112."

Wilkes' face dropped. This changed the whole plan, he thought to himself.

"What did you find?" Stanley asked, even more confused than before.

"Are there any copies of this footage or backups anywhere?" Anders said.

Stanley looked around for a second, thinking about the question. "Ahh, no this is it. Our backups are all here. When the hospital's power goes out, the emergency generator goes on, so all backups are kept here as there is always power, and after twenty-four hours all footage goes to the mainframe system backup for three months, and then it's erased automatically. Why is that?"

Anders pulled out his firearm and faced Stanley before pulling the trigger and watching him fall to the ground. Blood hit the computers in an explosion of crimson, with pieces of gray matter sticking to the keyboard and mouse. Wilkes had reached over to stop Anders, but he was too late.

Stanley Connor lay there in an expanding pool of blood, with open eyes and a hole in the back of his head the size of a grapefruit.

"Are you crazy, Anders? We could have handled this better. He didn't have to die. Now what are we going to do? People are going to know soon enough with or without your silencer being on."

Wilkes was very upset. As hard as they were as investigators, Wilkes never wanted any harm done. He would always try and erase a memory with other techniques. In this case Anders was getting desperate and dangerous. Wilkes knew what was coming up and he had to make a plan for himself and others who would possibly end up the same as Stanley.

Anders didn't even look at Wilkes. He took the disk from the hard drive and shot up all the computers, along with the mainframe. Before walking out the door, he pulled out a tiny bottle of flammable oil and squirted it all over the room, barely missing Wilkes in the process. Once finished, he took a lighter from his left pocket, lit it, and threw it to the ground.

He then opened the door and turned to Wilkes. "Are you coming or staying here to fry?" Anders had a smirk on his face as he walked out.

The flames were starting to spread as Wilkes made his way to the door. He looked back over his shoulder, watching the flames climb higher for a moment, before walking out and shutting the door behind him.

By the time the two agents made it to the old black car, the hospital was well alight. The fire alarms and sprinklers had kicked in as the flames had taken on a life of their own. There were sirens in the background and evacuations were already taking place. Wilkes climbed into the car on the passenger's side, and sat quietly, looking out the window at the unfolding catastrophe with potential for further loss of life. He lowered his head, deep in thought.

Anders was in the driver's seat, smiling.

"Come on, Wilkes. You know what has happened and you know what's next, it had to be this way."

Wilkes looked across at him, not prepared to be all accepting, but cautious of how to react. He knew Anders would kill him given the chance.

"Really, it had to happen like that, though? OK, I know, I get it What is the plan?"

Anders studied him for a moment. "Are you sure your feelings are with us on this, or are you getting soft for this lot? Remember who you are and what our mission is. Don't drift off the path or I will have to finish it myself, are you good?"

Wilkes nodded. "Sorry, I'm good. So, what's the plan?" Wilkes asked again, knowing the answer to the question already.

"It's time. She knows too much, we must get the phone from her and destroy it. We must kill Eric and all the witnesses. In order to do this swiftly, we have to turn on V.I.Z.I.N.D.A.L.E.X."

Wilkes dropped his head, thinking to himself, "It has started, the beginning of the end." Aloud he said, "It's too early. Are we ready for it yet? Don't we have another three months before Zero Time?" Wilkes again knew the answer but thought that maybe he could stop it for now. But then he thought, "No, remember who I'm talking to."

Anders didn't answer.

"What about one of your minions?" Wilkes knew that the lesser of all evils would be one of Anders' creatures. Despite causing mayhem and destruction wherever they went, it was nothing to the destruction of V.I.Z.I.N.D.A.L.E.X.

Anders sat there for a moment, staring at Wilkes for what felt like an eternity, before he snapped. "Wilkes! Sometimes when I think you are ready to desert your mission and give up on me, you turn around and kick me in the balls with a surprise like that. We have worked together for a long time and I still get surprised by your methods and ideas. Knowing you hate my creatures more than anything else is testament to that, but I know you secretly get off on it."

For the first time in a decade Anders moved his unwavering lips to an awkward full smile, then not more than a second later he was back to his robotic self.

"Let's go, we need to find a clearing so that we can get a signal to Agent Xandar to discuss subject 112. I will find out when the X-Clock will awaken."

Anders turned the key in the ignition and slowly moved out of the parking lot. By now several fire trucks could be heard and people were pouring out the doors of the hospital.

***

Anders found a space on top of a building where he pulled out a silver device, nothing that was sold in any phone or electronic store.

The "phone" had unusual markings and with the touch of a button a holographic image appeared. Anders pressed another sequence of buttons and after a few squeaks and whirs the blue and red hologram of a silhouette turned into a face. The face was human, but the language was not English. Anders hit a button and the person on the other end of the hologram was now speaking perfect English.

"What is it? Anders, we don't have time for this. You understand some of the latest sightings, along with some of your handiwork, have sparked panic. Now tell me something I don't know."

Anders hated Agent Xandar. Although they were all masters, Xandar was one of his direct superiors due to being the Leader's direct contact, so Anders needed to show respect.

"Sorry, sir, we have new information that is vital to this mission and the ongoing end game. I understand we are no longer connected so I have established this call as it cannot be traced," Anders nervously answered.

"What is your information?" Xandar asked.

With a low tone in his voice, Anders responded, "There are a few things, sir. The first is we have found evidence of a breach. The nurse looking after subject 112 has recorded our mind-stalk and has escaped with him. We have good information on where they are, so we are pursuing them now."

Anders swallowed hard. The pause was deafening. The only thing he could hear was the whir of the device he was holding, everything else was silent.

Then, Xandar responded, "You are right, this was unforeseen. We are having to silence many rogues now. The closer we get to Zero Time the more podcasts, video blogs, and brazen disappearances are occurring. The veil is becoming weak and some of the slaves are working hard to reach our target. I have agents all over looking for them. You concentrate on these ones. Has Wilkes seen the subject 111 girl yet and injected her Geno-drones?"

Anders smiled as he had been expecting to get a negative response from his superior. But things were getting desperate and they all knew that this day was coming.

"Yes, sir, Wilkes saw the girl, hours after she was taken, and then again a week before subject 112 escaped. He has injected her, and the Geno-drones are awaiting the global switch along with her DNA samples and manipulations of the genomes." Anders paused.

"Is that all, Agent Anders?" Xandar snapped.

"No, sir, I'm worried about Wilkes. He seems to be gaining compassion for the people, and I'm concerned he is going to defect. We have lost others in the past and I don't want to have to kill him because I actually like him." Anders was still holding the device high enough so they could see each other face to face while awaiting Xandar's response.

"I don't believe he is going to be an issue at this late stage. He has proven his loyalty in the past and I have no reason for second-guessing him. Keep an eye on him and at any point if he shows signs he will apostatize, shoot him without hesitation. We are close. Stay the course and annihilate these people. I will see you at the end." Xandar switched off before Anders could respond.

Anders knew things were close if he wasn't going to talk to Xandar again. He turned off the device and placed it back inside his jacket pocket.

He returned to the car where Wilkes was waiting for him.

"By the look on your face, it went better than you thought?" Wilkes commented.

"Are you reading my mind, Agent Wilkes? Yes, much better than expected. We now have a plan of attack. Our next task is to find this nurse. What is her address again?"

Wilkes grabbed his notepad. "Louise Carter is her name. I know where to go, just head onto the freeway," Wilkes explained as they moved toward a new target.

A LIFE IN PIECES

LOOKING UP AT THE BRIGHT MORNING SKY and feeling the cool summer breeze on her face, while listening to the trickling of flowing water from the tap next to her back door, Louise Carter was enjoying her only day off in ages. She filled her bucket with water to tend to her many roses spread throughout her back and front yards.

Roses were her passion and her favorite hobby. She loved to just sit in her backyard with a nice red wine and listen to the birds, while taking in the beauty of the many different colors and smells that her garden provided her with. She had felt in recent times that she had neglected her babies as she was at work a lot over the last several weeks. With a little tender loving care Louise knew she could get her garden back up to scratch in no time.

Louise was single, in her forties and was a registered nurse. Nursing was something else that she had a passion for. Helping people and taking care of those who needed it. The only problem was it took up most of her time and, not unlike her roses, her personal life suffered. This was until she met Serena a few years ago while they were on nights together. Over time their friendship blossomed into a very close one as they were both in the same situation.

Serena would often get the roster clerk to put them on the same shifts so when they had days off, they were always together. Serena would often take Louise to her parents' house for dinners, go to movies, even do some Taekwondo classes, which Louise liked but never had the time to commit to. Louise had attended the family's church services and that's where she met their family friend Father Michael. She thought he was a strong priest with a great knowledge of life and who had a heart of gold. He was also a great person to confide in and call a friend when times were tough.

Louise knew that something had happened the night before. Without knowing the details of the situation, she figured Serena was headed to Michael's house, as that's where she would go if in trouble.

Louise took her bucket filled with water and made her way to the first bunch of roses on the east side of her garden. Her thoughts started running away with her now. Was Serena really in that much trouble, or was it just a misunderstanding over something that could easily be sorted out? She sat down, took a deep breath, and whispered to herself, "This is Serena, she will be fine." Louise then took a cup of water out of the bucket and spread it over the first lot of roses.

After an hour or so Louise finished watering the flowers and, wiping the sweat from her brow, made her way into the house. She grabbed a glass from the cupboard, sat down, and had a cool drink of water. Her eyes were closed as she sat at the kitchen table. The fan had been put on earlier in the morning as she knew it was going to be a very hot day, which is why she was outside in the garden so early.

She enjoyed the breeze for a moment or two as she finished off the last of her drink, placed the glass on the table, and savored the peace. The silence soon became oppressive as the noise of the fan started to diminish and she could no longer hear any bird noises or cars driving past. In fact, it was like she was completely deaf albeit some unusual scratching and movement was coming from the spare bedroom.

Louise got to her feet. She felt a little dizzy and confused, as if she had just been drugged. There was blue light coming from the spare bedroom. She placed her hand on the wall to gain some stability. Louise felt like she was about to fall over, and before too long gravity got the better of her and she eventually passed out.

When she awoke, she was on her bed, confused as to how she got there. Did she just have a dizzy spell? she wondered. Then a noise came from the kitchen. This time it wasn't a scratching sound, more like a squeak of some kind, then moments later she saw what she thought were hairy fingers reaching around the door, accompanied by a deep growl. She passed out again from shock.

Louise woke up. It was the early hours of the night. She had slept all day and through some of the night. She put it down to being hot and having a bad dream. She was a nurse and knew there were rational explanations for most things. Heat could make people sick.

She got out of bed and made her way to the kitchen. As she went to turn on the light, something scratched her hand. She let out a mighty scream and ran in the opposite direction to another room of the house. Louise tried to flick another light on and a scrape sliced down her hand once more. She screamed and dropped to the ground.

It was still eerily quiet and she could hear the drops of her blood hitting the wooden floor. She clasped her hand to try and stop the bleeding. The cuts felt deep, as if a handful of nails had torn at her skin.

Louise yelled out in desperation, "Who's there? Please, don't hurt me, I have money!"

She dropped her head to her hands and let the tears come. The silence told her that whoever was there wasn't about to reveal themselves.

Eventually Louise stopped crying. Still whimpering, she felt for something around her to use as a weapon. She had never known darkness like this before. Even a streetlight would normally be shining in at least one of her rooms. As she was feeling around, she noticed a hard object, a doorstop, she thought. She picked it up, threw it to the other side of the room and in the same motion stood up and flicked the light on.

Nothing!

She was expecting to see a band of thieves or at least someone, but there was no one. She scampered through to the kitchen, pulled out the first aid box and had a look at her hand. Blood was dripping continuously onto the floor. The lacerations looked like an animal scratch, a big animal, she thought. Louise grabbed a bandage and was wrapping up the injury when the lights started to flicker.

"Oh no, no, no, not now ..."

Desperate, she quickly finished up with the bandage, tied it off, and went to find another light switch, but before she could do that the power went out completely.

Louise ran for the back door, tripping over a chair before she could get there. Lying on the floor, she glanced up, and seeing nothing, she couldn't help whimpering again. Her heart rate was so high she nearly went into cardiac arrest.

As she slowly started to lift her head to have another look, Louise felt heavy breathing on the back of her neck. The smell was putrid like rotting flesh. She wanted to be sick.

Louise put her left hand over her mouth and began to breathe shallowly while trying to be quiet. She felt a drip on her head, then another. It was like a leaky tap. Something was standing right over her, drooling. Louise plucked up all her courage and scrambled in a speed crawl toward the back door. Jumping onto her feet she burst out into the backyard and ran for the rear gate.

Before she could reach the halfway mark, she felt a violent pain on her back, and something pushed her to the ground and held her down. It was still very dark, but Louise sensed that whatever was out there was large, as she felt the claws dig into her back.

She screamed out in pain as the creature stepped off her. She looked around but there was nothing. Louise was shaking violently. Her legs were like jelly and the pain in her back was horrendous. She started crawling again on her elbows when she felt a knife-like sting go across her legs. She let out another scream and turned to see her attacker while reaching for her legs. Nothing. Her ankle was missing on her right side and was just barely attached on the other side. Louise threw up and midway through vomiting she felt a claw dig into her back, lifting her up off the ground. She was now convulsing.

"Enough, Savage. Bring her inside," Anders, standing nearby, ordered the beast.

One of the creature's right claws was still attached to Louise's back and upon entering the house he threw her onto an armchair.

Louise fell onto the chair like a rag doll. She was going into shock due to blood loss. Her left foot was hanging off from her ankle by the last few threads of skin and muscle. All she could do was shiver and twitch as life slowly drained out from her body.

"Stand over there out of sight, Savage. We need her alive for the information. If we don't get what we are after, you don't get your reward."

Savage growled at Anders, then put his head down like a naughty puppy. Knowing that even a creature like that could not mess with a master like him, Anders petted the large beast's head for a moment before he disappeared behind the door.

Anders walked over to Louise and in a calm voice said, "Hey, my dear, I have taken care of the awful creature. Now let me take care of you."

He took her by the waist and sat her up in the chair. From his pocket he pulled out a ring with two finger holes and a long metal band that fit onto his palm underneath his fingers, like a glove that fit only part of his hand.

Anders waved the ring device over Louise's ankle. Blue light emanated from it and her ankle began to repair itself. Louise woke out of her semi-conscious state and her screams filled the room.

Anders said, "It's OK, pet, we are nearly done."

Louise looked down at her foot and she could see all the sinew, tissue, muscle, and skin fibers reattaching themselves. Her ankle was fully healed in a few moments and there was no longer any pain. Anders then did the same for her other foot that had been dismembered, holding the body part to its original position while it mended entirely. Her back and fingers received the same attention from the ring until she was completely healed.

"How ... how did ...?" Louise couldn't find any words as she was still in too much shock.

"It's new technology in medicine. Sorry, I'm Agent Anders from the CIA. The reason I am here, as you can imagine, is because of some dark experiments that have gone wrong in one of our government labs and we are trying to clean up the mess. It's completely top secret and I am hoping you can help me with my investigation of the disaster."

Louise took a moment before answering, as this wasn't to her a nightmare that she just wanted to wake up from.

"Is that creature one of the experiments?" Louise whispered.

"Yes, a nasty one, we have it contained now. So, can you help me with some information, Louise?"

"How do you know me?"

"Let's just say it's your friend who we have grave concerns for. This is how we know who you are. Some very sensitive information about the hospital you work at has been leaked and some of the experiments have to do with escaped monsters which your friend is involved with, that is all I can say."

Anders was even starting to believe his own lies. Nothing he had said was true and he was marveling at his own storytelling. He could go down the mind-breaking path like what he thought they had done to Eric, but that took too long, and he needed information right now. Telling lies to get what he wanted was fair in his mind.

Louise seemed even more frightened now. She was thinking that this bizarre story just kept getting worse. Not only was she in danger, but so were her colleagues. "Who is in danger, which friend? Please don't say Serena."

"I'm sorry but it is Serena. Time is of the essence and if we don't find her soon, another thing like the one you encountered will be doing worse to her if we don't stop it. Can you think of any place that she would go when she is in any kind of trouble or danger? We know she is not at her house or with her parents either as we have guards looking over those locations as we speak. It is imperative we find her before sunrise."

"You promise she will be alright and that I will be OK as well?" Louise was trying to get a sense of safety for herself. She thought, "But if he healed me and he is from the CIA, then he can put me into protection."

"Yes, you have my word as a man of the government."

Anders was loving every minute of this. Wilkes was back at headquarters following up on Eric's daughter as he wanted no part of what Anders was doing, but he also needed to get word to Eric and the only way was through Stacey.

"Alright, Serena always visits her parish priest Father Michael who is also a family friend. He is someone that both Serena and I find comfort talking to. He is like a priest, psychologist, and philosopher all in one, so I would definitely say she is with him."

Louise was shaking, she wasn't sure if she was doing the right thing or not, but she wanted to help her friend.

"Fantastic. Thank you very much, Louise. You are doing very well under the circumstances. Tell me the address there and I will be on my way."

Anders was stone-faced and cold again. He had finally obtained what he came for, so the niceties were over. Without Wilkes to pull him up on his approach, he went back to default mode every time. Although other tactics had worked in more recent times, Anders thrived on intimidation, violence, and suffering. His dark glasses were off for once due to the lighting. He had managed to hide his eyes and his veiny skin from the angle of the light, hoping not to deter Louise too much while he was trying to get what he wanted.

Louise turned to her side table where her mobile phone was sitting. She flipped across the screen a few times. Several seconds later she had what she was looking for and after a quick exchange of the address Louise said in an almost childlike voice, "Will you take me with you?"

Anders looked at her for a moment, put his sunglasses back on his face, and murmured, "Thank you, Louise, you have been more than helpful."

As he finished his sentence he leaned across and cut a length of her brown hair before placing the knife on the table. Louise just stared at him in horror, too shocked to react. He went to the room where the beast was hiding, grabbed the braid on the side of its head and attached the section of Louise's hair to Savage's collection. The wolf-man kept them as trophies, and judging by all the different colors and sections on the braid, there had been a lot. Anders then rubbed the beast's facial hair, and made his way to the front door, where his final words for the evening would be, "Savage, your reward awaits."

A moment later Anders was gone.

The wolf-man appeared from behind the doorway of the room, drooling as he crept toward Louise. His smile was ghastly as he knew human flesh was a rarity. In anticipation of the feast, he gave a bloodcurdling howl and leaned over the now screaming woman, tearing at her like a razor machine.

He pulled out her stomach, lifting part of her intestines up to his wet face, and chewed on the first of his reward. Louise was writhing in unimaginable agony as Savage slashed across her face, tearing an eye out in the process. She was convulsing. The creature held her down with his long claws while he tore her left arm completely out of its socket and then chewed on it like on a chicken bone.

Louise was losing too much blood and the creature knew it. He usually liked to eat his victims alive, but not today. So he dropped the arm and sank his enormous head and snout deep into her throat, ripping out most of her neck. Blood filled the room, splattering every surface. After he had swallowed, he went in again, this time straight into her stomach, tearing and pulling at it.

Louise was dead. Her remaining eye was wide open with a blank glare of nothingness, blood dripping from her eyelid, her head moving from side to side from the force of the beast.

Savage had had his entrée and now wanted the delightful main. He pushed his claw up through her stomach under the rib cage and pulled out her warm heart. As he held it up to his face to take a good look at it, Louise fell to the ground, a lifeless doll, empty from within. The wolf-man, standing tall, put the tiny heart in his mouth and gave another howl of pleasure. The sight of blood all over the room only excited him more and he spent the next half an hour finishing off the "good parts" until he had his fill.

When he was finally done, he let out a high-pitched scream and disappeared into a blue vortex. All that remained was a horror scene that no human could possibly stand to witness.

Anders turned up again no more than a minute after his creature had disappeared. He looked around and whispered to himself, "Wilkes would love my work here." He gave himself a robotic little smile, pulled out the same oil bottle he'd used in the hospital and squirted it all over the room, before lighting it. With one last glance at the growing flames, he opened the front door and got into his car, driving slowly up the road to await Wilkes' return.

THE DESERTER

PEOPLE WERE GATHERING OUT the front of the church before the Sunday service. Some had been waiting all week to get to this day, considering this their social event. Others were very devout and had built their lives around the Catholic Church. Then there were those attending out of guilt. One thing was for certain, the sincerity of beliefs of some of those attending was questionable.

Nancy Wright was one of the devout ones. Much like Stephanie, she had an annoying tendency to take charge, tell people where to sit, and give the evil eye to people who coughed or sneezed in the middle of the service. Although, when people were in trouble, she was quite compassionate toward their needs and would help when she could.

Marjory and Valinda had just arrived. The usual crowd gazed at them for what seemed a lot longer than was normal. The rumors about Valinda were rife and Nancy seemed to be the great instigator, with or without facts. The tales of Valinda dabbling in occult activities, along with witchcraft, were all started by her, with no proof, originating only from her own nasty ideas. Nancy didn't care, though, as it kept her profile of gossiping up and her followers distracted from what was real and truthful.

That's where Father Michael made a difference to Valinda. He would always provide an ear and offer sound advice to her, especially now with all the UFO sightings, unexplained disappearances, and odd creatures spotted around the world lately. Valinda's podcasts and video blogs were busier than ever, so she needed Michael's comforting guiding voice to settle her nerves at times. Particularly lately, with the harassing visions she was having, Valinda needed that assurance that there was a good force to counter all that evil.

Michael was standing out the front of the church greeting all the parishioners as they entered. He was happy leaving Serena and Eric for the morning as Eric was sleeping most of the time and Serena seemed to be more settled now after the initial shock of everything that had happened. Michael knew her well and admired how strong and independent she was under times of stress, much like Valinda who he was looking forward to seeing today.

Marjory and Valinda made their way up the stairs to the entrance, where they met with Father Larsen. The look on his face when he saw Valinda was that of happiness. He leaned forward and with no words gave her a hug. He could see in her eyes she was troubled.

Nancy looked up and saw the two embracing. She dropped her plate of cakes in shock and marched into the side entrance of the church, leaving her son to clean up the mess she had made.

Valinda pulled back from Michael and whispered, "Father, I need to talk with you quite urgently. May I have some of your time after the service?"

Valinda knew that he would meet with her even if he was busy with other things. He always made time for those he called "the chosen strugglers," people who were challenged in life with different things, because he believed they were chosen by God, and their paths would eventually be for a higher purpose.

"Of course, Val, you know that I always have time for you. I have some people I want you to meet who I know you will be interested in getting to know."

Valinda nodded. "Let me know when."

She made her way into the church while her mother finished hugging Michael. When they entered, they both took holy water and blessed themselves before going to the middle section of the pews. Marjory waited for her friends before taking her seat, while Valinda looked up at the huge statue of Christ on the cross and quietly prayed.

Father Michael Larsen stood at the altar and waited for the congregation to finalize their positions before he started. The altar boys were still preparing their items for communion and the church seemed to be packed for such a small service.

Once there was complete silence, Michael began with a prayer: "Lord, in these most desperate times protect us from the evils of the beast, give us strength to help others suffering from these dark times of hate, drugs, racial tension, and wars. With the strange events that are upon us now, Lord, guide us to stay strong, endure, and overcome these trials. We give thanks to you, oh Lord, and ask that you bless every one of us. Amen."

"Amen."

Michael then went on to talk about all the strange events that were happening in the country and the world at the current time, warning everybody to be ready for the return of the Lord as the time was nearly upon us. The signs were showing, and the beast was busy.

While he was preaching his sermon, he looked across at Valinda and gave her the slightest of smiles with a wink only a few took notice of. Most in the room were ignorant of the exchange and Valinda felt a sense of calm being there, knowing she had someone on her side and feeling a closer connection to the Lord.

After the sermon, Father Michael took some time with the ladies who were organizing the dinner later that evening and the luncheon which was always on after a service. They were very chatty sometimes, but it was all part of the job. He loved every single one of them, even Nancy who tested him at times. They all brought something special to the congregation and he appreciated all the hard work they put in. He didn't mind their little "social nights" at the hall, as it was a chance for them to let their hair down and have a little fun (in a church sense) once a month.

After Michael finished up with the ladies, he went to look for Valinda. She wasn't where he had asked her to meet him. The ladies took up more time than he had anticipated, so the thought crossed his mind that maybe Valinda got tired of waiting and returned home. But then he saw Marjory talking with Stephanie and a couple of the other church group ladies. They were discussing where to set up the sandwich table inside the hall adjacent to the church for lunch, something they discussed every week.

Michael knew that time was getting on, so he approached Marjory and asked in a concerned tone, "Hey, Marjory, have you seen Val? I was supposed to have a meeting with her before the lunch started."

"Yes, Father, she is sitting under the tree with her laptop. You know that girl, she is always working on that thing. I would love for you to talk with her, Father. I am getting quite concerned with her mental state and I'm just worried that she is overstressed or overwhelmed with work or something."

Marjory didn't have to tell Michael that, as he already knew her feelings about the situation. "From a mother's point of view, she is just doing her part to protect her child," he thought.

"Thank you, Marjory, I will. She will be OK, you will see. I have some very good friends that I want to introduce her to later that will definitely make her feel better and maybe even solve some of the issues you are concerned about."

And with that Michael skipped down the steps and made his way over to the large tree out the front of the church that Val was sitting under. She was wearing a red skirt with a yellow blouse, so she stood out from the crowd, as all the older parishioners were wearing more conservative attire, this being a church service.

"Hey, you, I've been looking for you. Sorry, I was caught up with the ladies' group, but I'm all yours now. Would you like to come into the meeting room, and we can have a chat about the progress of your research and the issues you want to talk to me about?"

Valinda looked up at Michael and smiled, shut her laptop, and jumped to her feet. "I figured as much, let's go."

Valinda seemed to be calmer now after the service. There were things she needed to get off her chest and she hoped Michael would be the one who could reassure her that she was safe.

Meanwhile, back at Michael's house, Serena had finished packing everything in Michael's car for the trip. Eric was sitting up in bed watching television while slipping in and out of sleep. His painkillers were still strong, but he was managing to stay awake longer.

Serena went into the bedroom to check on him, as he was still upset about the last dream he had had. It was very disturbing to him and Serena hoped to get more information. He was going on about a robot that would end the world and that the agents were getting close. Stacey was the one warning him in it, but it was very cryptic.

Eric woke up from his daze as Serena gathered the last of his medicine.

"All ready, Eric? The cabin is a couple of hours away, so you will be able to sleep in the car."

Eric nodded. Serena had found an old wheelchair that was used sometimes for the elderly parishioners, so she put her arm around Eric, and eased him from the bed into the chair. He grimaced in pain but didn't make a noise.

"There we go. I have the car packed and we just have to wait until Father Michael gets back so we can head off."

Eric didn't know Michael at all as he had barely seen him since they arrived. Serena had reassured him that he would be the one to help get Stacey back, and he trusted Serena. She wheeled him to the main television in the lounge room and turned it on.

"What channel would you like it on?"

Eric turned his head and sluggishly answered, "Documentary, please."

He ended up watching a documentary on how the Democrats had won the election three years prior and managed to beat the NRA by bringing about a complete ban on firearms and weapons of all kinds. The amnesty nearly started a civil war. It was done now, and the penalties were huge for anyone found with any kind of weapons that had been deemed unsafe or dangerous. Eric thought about the rifle destroyed in the Sasquatch's attack and the couple of rifles he still had left. They were only for protection and he was very careful who knew, as some of the harshest penalties for keeping them included life in prison or the death penalty. One of the reasons Eric thought the agents were after him at the hospital was for the firearms that he had back in the Klamath woods.

Serena was in the kitchen, making some last-minute sandwiches for the trip, when she heard some whispering coming from the front of the house. She didn't think too much of it, so she went back to finishing what she was doing. There was a bang now at the side of the house near the kitchen window. She could hear the whispering again, and this time she was a little more concerned.

She ducked from view of the window and took a sneaky look, only to gasp in horror at what she saw. Serena crumpled to the ground in shock. She managed to get to her feet and unsteadily ran toward the next room where Eric was, but she slipped and fell before she could reach it. Serena just couldn't get to her feet quick enough. Her legs were like jelly, and before her heart gave way, she finally made it to the lounge room.

She took some deep breaths, grabbed Eric's wheelchair, and cautiously headed to the garage door where the cars were. Eric had fallen asleep watching TV, and she knew if he woke up, there would be all sorts of commotion and questions she just couldn't answer at this stage.

She made it to the side entrance to the garage door, but she did not want to open it, just in case they were there. She needed some sort of confirmation that she was alone. But then, without warning, Eric snapped his eyes wide open and looked at Serena. He was in another of his states, but this time with no noise at all, just whispers, telling Serena to open the door and get inside the car.

Serena didn't know what to do. Should she trust Eric, or should she go with her gut? She debated with herself in her head, until Eric said one word that made her listen: "SAFE."

Serena remembered that part of the recording she had listened to was of Eric being used as a vessel to communicate with. Something in her mind kicked in and she knew it was time to go.

Serena opened the door very slowly. She could hear whispering from the front of the house again, so it was now or never. She tried to get Eric out of his chair and into the car as quietly as possible. Just before he was completely inside the vehicle, as she leaned on the chair to give her strength to lift his legs in, the chair gave way and smashed into the wall.

Serena knew they would hear that so before she could get his seat belt on, she slammed the door, and ran to the driver's side of the SUV. Shaking like crazy and fumbling for the keys, she heard the front door fly open. As she tried to put one of the keys into the ignition, she accidently dropped them. Fear was threatening to overwhelm her as she knew that if she did not get that car started, they would both be dead. She reached down to the floor feeling around for the keys, knowing the intruders would be on them in no time. Through tears she said to herself, "Come on, come on, please, Lord, help us."

She felt the keys with her hand, scooped them up, and put the correct key into the ignition. With a blast of fuel and a high rev, she reversed the SUV at high speed out of the garage, smashing the roller door and crashing her way out into the backyard of the house. As she was putting the car into gear, she could see Wilkes and Anders, both with guns drawn ready to shoot. Serena floored it.

Anders started shooting at the car, but then Wilkes grabbed Anders' arm. "No, not here, there are too many witnesses."

Anders looked back at Wilkes and gave him an elbow across the face, smashing his sunglasses and leaving a huge mark on his eye.

"Never, *ever* do that to me again. Do you know who you are dealing with? This is our mission and we are close to completing it."

Wilkes stood up. He seemed taller now. As calm as ever, he responded, "It will be easier if we used tactics that don't involve going full throttle into crowds where there are mass gatherings. We are wasting time, let's split up."

Anders did not like this one bit and disregarded everything Wilkes had just said, thinking he would sort out his shit later. Now he just wanted them stopped and he took off at a fast run. Wilkes followed. He knew where they were heading so he had a jump on Anders.

Meanwhile, at the church, Michael was just about to enter the building with Valinda to have their meeting. He had been sidetracked again by some parishioners who had some more questions for him. He heard all the commotion coming from his house, then the gunshots. The SUV tearing around the corner was now in Michael's sights. More gunshots were fired at the vehicle creating an atmosphere of fear, panic, and screams.

Serena skidded to a stop in front of the church screaming in desperation for Michael to "Get in now!"

Michael glanced at Anders, who was only thirty yards away. He was not going to let whoever this crazy gunman was hurt anybody he knew, although this notion didn't last long as Anders fired straight at the SUV again, barely missing the passenger side window but hitting Marjory's shoulder, throwing her instantly to the ground. More shots were fired and now it seemed Anders wanted more casualties. He was firing at the fleeing parishioners, slaughtering them. Michael managed to grab Val's arm and get her into the car. As he did, a flurry of shots came, barely missing him. He ducked down and hid behind the open door yelling, "Under the rear seat there is a towel, get it, Val!"

Valinda, who had been screaming for her mother, clumsily started feeling under the seat.

"Hurry, Val, he is nearly on us!"

Valinda found the towel and as she felt the weight of it, she automatically knew what it was. She threw it to Michael who was breathing heavily. He dropped the towel to reveal a fully loaded Smith & Wesson shotgun. He fired at Anders, each shot missing for some reason, until Wilkes grabbed Anders and threw him to the ground. The last of Michael's shots hit Anders in the thigh while the two agents rolled around the ground fighting.

Michael rushed out of the car and ran to Marjory who was in shock. He picked her up and carried her to the rear of the SUV. After opening the back door, he jumped in with her.

While Michael was escaping with Marjory, Wilkes managed to put his hand on Anders' face, which put him in a trance. Wilkes then got up and sprinted to the SUV. It had started driving off, and Eric yelled,

"STOP!". Then he repeated it in an aggressive manner, "STOP, STOP, STOP!", over and over, until Serena finally pulled the car to the edge of the driveway.

"What is it, Eric, why do you want me to stop?" Eric looked blank-faced and then passed out. While they were all staring at Eric and wondering why he was saying that, Wilkes put his hand in the driver's side window with his fingers on the keys and his other hand on Serena's face. Serena was now in a slight trance, but only for a moment, until she snapped out of it and yelled, "He's coming with us."

"Are you crazy?" Michael and Valinda both shouted. "They are trying to kill us."

"No, I'm sorry, Serena, something isn't right here. We must go. Please just leave him and get going." Michael was angry that he didn't have a choice.

"I'm sorry, everyone, but he is coming with us. We have to leave now."

As Serena was talking, Anders started coming around. He slowly looked up. In his groggy state he couldn't see Wilkes, only the SUV. He looked around for his gun.

Meanwhile, Wilkes took the keys and Serena quickly shuffled over to the passenger side. Wilkes jumped in, turned the key, and skidded off out of the car park and onto the main road, headed somewhere out of trouble, they all hoped.

"I hope you know what you're doing, Serena, this is our lives you have here," said Michael as he held Marjory and kept pressure on her wound.

Serena turned to Wilkes and without moving her gaze from him, said, "It's OK, I know him."

Everyone in the car except for Marjory looked at her in amazement. Even Eric, who had been entering in and out of his dream state, seemed suddenly lucid and wanted answers.

As the SUV sped away, Anders got to his feet. He had his gun in his hand and was reloading it. He went over to every single person left, chasing them down and shooting them all in the head one by one, leaving no witness alive. It was a massacre. There was no remorse or even the slightest blink in his uncovered eyes. It was pure evil. His sole purpose was to cause as much carnage as possible.

He grabbed the last woman alive by her throat because he had run out of bullets. As he lifted her high, a loud scream emanated out of nowhere and a beast appeared, taking Nancy with a swipe. It bellowed into the wind, letting out another high-pitched shriek until all three disappeared into a blue mist.

≈

The group had been driving for hours, with no idea where they were going and without any word from Wilkes, who was still in control of the vehicle. Wilkes continually repeated that all would be answered when they arrived at their destination.

Valinda was asleep. She had looked at Michael about fifteen minutes after they had left, and from the slow shake of his head she knew her mother hadn't made it. She had lost too much blood and it had been too risky to stop at a hospital. Val had broken down, crying for much of the journey, with Serena comforting her until she finally fell asleep from the stress of it all.

"How much longer before you can tell us anything?" Michael asked in an assertive tone, hoping that if he kept prodding, he might finally get the truth. It had no effect. Wilkes just stared at the road ahead without so much as a twitch, even though they knew he had heard every word.

It was getting late and the last signpost they had seen was Caldwell. After several hours of driving without filling the car up and with no bathroom breaks, it was time, Michael thought.

"Sit back, Father. We are here."

Michael with a blank face stared at Serena, thinking to himself that he had really fallen down a rabbit hole. As the car pulled onto a dirt track heading into a secluded area of dense forest, they could make out a sign saying, "Lake Lowell Deer Flat National Wildlife Refuge, No Entry, Trespassers Shot On Sight." After a rough drive down the track, they finally pulled up into a clearing. They all piled out, everyone except Valinda who was still asleep, and obviously Eric, who may have had an accident. There was a quick dash to the trees for a much-needed bathroom break.

Wilkes got out and walked over to the rear of the SUV where Marjory was lying. He looked over her lifeless body and quickly dismissed any intervention to help, as she had been gone for hours.

Michael was first to get back. There was an awkward silence as they stared directly into each other's eyes. Michael couldn't quite grasp what Wilkes was about, but Wilkes thought he knew what he needed to know about Michael.

"Come, we need to hide the car and get rid of the body." As he said that, he realized he lacked the empathy of humankind. "Sorry, I meant we need to take her with us."

Wilkes picked up Marjory's body just as Valinda was slowly waking up from her deep sleep. She rubbed her eyes and saw Wilkes with her mother. Before she became hysterical, Serena gave her a sedative that she had been keeping for Eric. Val calmed down and Michael managed to pick her up, comforting her with prayer as they followed Wilkes to the edge of the lake. The wheelchair wasn't taking to the soft edges too well, but Serena and Eric soon joined the others.

Before they could ask any questions, a mighty shriek emanated out of a device. They all looked around in alarm and within a blink of an eye they were all sitting inside another vehicle. This one was like nothing they had seen before. Outside the windows they could see fish, green plankton, and other marine creatures. "Are we at the bottom of the lake? How did we get here?" Serena wondered.

"OK, follow me."

Wilkes walked into another room, larger than the one they were previously in. It seemed to be set up for medical procedures and goodness knows what else.

"First things first, I need everyone to just relax and sit here. After this I will tell you whatever you want to know."

The group was already in so deep that whatever happened, they would get through it together. Serena was first up. She felt strong now and confident she could be the one to keep everyone together and safe throughout the continuing ordeal. She sat up on the operating table. Wilkes had placed a two-finger device on his hand, which went onto his middle and index fingers. This device was like the one Anders had used previously on Louise.

"OK, Serena, can I get you to lie back and just relax. You may feel some slight tingling and a little pain all over, but it will be brief."

Serena thought to herself, "I know what was done to Eric at the hospital, but I feel calm with Wilkes, like I have known him for years."

She kept coming back to this feeling but couldn't grasp why. She was no longer petrified of him. As she relaxed her body, Wilkes waved his hand with the silvery blue device all over her body, some five or six inches above, slowly going back and forth. Serena was moving slightly, feeling just a little uncomfortable, until Wilkes finished.

"OK, now for the hurt."

Serena braced herself while the device made an electric sound over her right hand, where a small silver ball, no bigger than a tiny ball bearing from a kids' toy, was pulled right out of her skin and onto the device. She jumped slightly in pain. Wilkes quickly waved the device back over the hole from which the silver ball had come. Her hand was completely healed, as if there had been no trauma to the area at all.

"What is that?" Serena said as she jumped to her feet.

"As I said, after this you will get your answers."

Michael was next.

Wilkes looked at Michael strangely after finding no sign at all of any tech in his body. It was odd that a human could have no levels whatsoever, he thought to himself, although he didn't mention it to the others.

After Michael was Valinda. She seemed somewhat reluctant, yet was still semi-sedated. Michael and Serena lifted her up onto the procedure table and Wilkes waved his device like he did with the others. He soon stopped, turned to Serena and Michael and whispered, "This is why I haven't said anything. Your friend has an active Gen—"

Before he could finish his sentence, Val's eyes opened wide, and then with a dark deep voice that sounded like it was out of a horror movie, she growled, "I have found you. You cannot hide from us. We are going to kill all of you." Then she shouted it out repeatedly in a language not from Earth, until Wilkes found the spot, and with a final blast of electricity, the chip was sucked out and destroyed, before falling onto the floor with the one removed from Serena.

Valinda, back to normal and aware, wept. "Please don't let that happen again, I can't deal with them any longer."

It seemed that Val had a story of her own to tell when they finally had an open forum to discuss everything. *Everything* being the key word at the moment, as nothing was making sense.

"It's gone for good. You will no longer have this happen to you, I promise."

Valinda didn't believe Wilkes. She slid off the table and made her way over to Father Michael and Serena, who comforted her.

"Is there any way to help her mother?" Michael said with his arm around her shoulder.

"No, I'm sorry, it doesn't work that way. If the heart is still beating, we can fix almost anything. If there is too much damage to major organs after death, then it is impossible to resuscitate with this tech. It works on combining with living tissue in the body as a way of replicating cells and repairing them. Once the body is dead, we need to get them to the main facility where equipment for that is available, and at this stage that is one place we need to avoid at all costs. She was gone before I could do anything. As you know we were, sorry *are*, being hunted."

Michael bowed his head and pulled Valinda a little closer. "Well, can we at least give her a proper burial?"

Wilkes looked up, a little annoyed, not that it showed on his emotionless face.

"We don't have time for it right now, we need to get this done. The best I can do is put her body on ice for the time being. When we get to our safe house, we will then be able to slow down and take care of all our needs, along with all the questions you have."

Michael was happy enough with that answer and made his way over to Eric.

"OK, big guy, it's your turn," Wilkes said to Eric, who was himself the quietest, yet the most agitated. He was over all the drama and just wanted some answers. Like Serena he felt there was something about Wilkes that seemed to be familiar and positive, but he just couldn't pinpoint it. Like her, a day earlier he just wanted to kill both Wilkes and Anders.

Michael and Wilkes lifted Eric out of his wheelchair and laid him on the table. He closed his eyes and was thinking about Stacey when he felt a sharp pain in his leg and then looked up at Wilkes with contempt.

Wilkes focused on Eric's injuries and slowly healed every part of him. As this was happening, all the others were just watching in awe, eyes transfixed. It was something so far removed from reality that they thought they must be dreaming.

As Eric's pain started to subside and the healing continued, Wilkes began to feel faint. He stumbled but remained upright and pushed through until Eric was finally healed completely and the device was removed.

Eric slowly moved his legs from the table and left them hanging over the edge. He swung them back and forth while rubbing his chest, looking for any signs of broken ribs. He slipped off the table and took an apprehensive step as if he was a baby learning to walk. With one foot in front of the other he walked then skipped around the room. In his excitement he gave Wilkes a hug and kissed his white, bald, veiny face, before realizing what he'd done and backing off awkwardly to the rest of the group.

Wilkes had physically proven that he could be trusted. Now he had to verbally prove it. This would take the most out of them so while Wilkes was removing their Geno-drone devices, he had also administered a strong sedative for all of them. They would need rest to face what was coming up next.

Wilkes took them into separate rooms and they walked behind him like zombies following a victim. One by one they lay on their beds and fell victim to the administered drugs as well as the long harrowing day that had just unfolded. When they awoke, they would be far away, in another place.

Wilkes moved into the pilot seat of the craft and after pressing a few key tones, a red and white three-dimensional chart appeared out of nowhere in front of his face. His outer body dissipated and what remained was the form of a gray skinny figure with two slender fingers and an opposing thumb on each hand. His huge black eyes focused on the ethereal touch screen in front of him, and after a swipe and scroll of a few sections of the map, Wilkes put his right hand into a groove on the front console and closed his eyes. Three straps snapped across his two fingers and thumb, and while it looked like he was asleep, he was actually moving the craft up and out of the water. A sharp nudge of his head and now it was flying extremely fast over the water before a huge blue cloud appeared and the craft disappeared into it, leaving no trace at all.

STACEY KIRKPATRICK

A HARD FLOOR, ALONG WITH PAIN and noise, surrounded Stacey. She groaned in agony, and then lifted her right arm to push herself up. But she was weak and kept falling on her face. She tried one more time, this time with success, and finally she could sit back against a wall.

As soon as she looked around, trying to get her bearings, Stacey started screaming, before she slapped her hand across her mouth to dull the sound. Next to her were mutilated half-bodies along with human entrails, and half a skull filled with blood and partial brain matter. She was becoming aware of the number of ghastly images around her, but it was the smell, seemingly emanating from every vent and opening inside the dimly lit cell, that made her eventually pass out.

Stacey was born in Washington but then moved to Eugene, Oregon, when she was little. Her father Eric worked there as an anthropologist. When she was young, she would often listen to her father's stories about all the adventures he had been on when he was younger. At this time, he was still very active, frequently going overseas and researching, although he'd started to concentrate more on the group he had created called the Western Oregon Sasquatch Evidence and Research team.

Stacey thought he was her own private Indiana Jones and looked up to him very much, so much so she wanted to follow in his footsteps and become an anthropologist as well. She would listen to his stories at night—not from a book, though. They were tales only he knew, about Bigfoot, the Loch Ness monster and even Mokele-mbembe a creature like a sauropod that local people still believed existed around Lake Tele near the Congo River in Africa.

The stories were special to her and after the passing of her mother Felicity from a rare form of cancer when she was only eleven, the stories became her outlet. She loved her mother and missed her every day, making her connection to her father very special. Particularly as they had no other family in the area. Her grandparents on her mother's side were in England and her father's parents were in Florida. She didn't really know her cousins either, so she would only see relatives on special occasions or on the rare trip to England.

After the passing of Stacey's mother, Eric had to tone down his bigger trips, although he took her with him whenever he had to. This built her love for the field even more and when she finished high school, she started studying for a degree in biological anthropology, concentrating on primatology and crypto-anthropology. She only had one more year to finish.

Due to her unusual upbringing and first-hand home schooling from her father on such topics, along with the many years of traveling, she was always at the top of her class with distinctions and honors. The trip to Klamath was a dream come true for her and was going to be part of her final thesis and research test for the end of year score. If she could somehow find substantial evidence to expose Bigfoot as a hoax, find evidence of its existence from samples, or establish the connections of sightings to Gigantopithecus, then not only would she have her degree, but she would also already have established a major name for herself in the crypto and scientific world.

But she knew this was never going to happen, so part of her study was to watch the native animals and their reactions in the wild along with photography. It was also going to be a special trip to celebrate her big achievements over the years, but no one could have predicted what had happened.

Stacey woke up. She was still in a lot of pain from the beating she had received. Struggling to come to terms with it all, she tried to get to her feet, but her injuries were worse than she thought. She tried again, this time using the slimy wall to help her gain some balance. She managed to get up and slowly hobbled in the direction of the locked door. Her vision was still bad, which she thought was a good thing. There were some very ugly scenes all around, so she avoided making any sudden turns of her head.

Stacey kept shuffling along, getting closer to the door, when something grabbed at her ankle and she tripped over. Once she opened her eyes, she found herself staring at another creature, one she did not recognize at all. She screamed as she tried to move away.

The eyes looking back at her were all black. The creature's face was covered in green scales and it had a crest on top of its head. As she scanned the rest of it, she noticed it had on clothing like military garb. It definitely wasn't human. It was more like a giant lizard wearing human clothes.

She got closer to its head and noticed burn marks on what would normally be its cheek. It had no ears, just holes. Stacey had just gained the courage to touch its arm to see if it was alive, when the door sprang open like a reverse guillotine snapping up, letting streams of light into the darkened room.

Stacey saw more clearly the mess that surrounded her, bits of bodies from things she couldn't even imagine. The room was so much bigger than what she had thought, so looking at it all took some time. Heads, fingers, arms, squirming torsos trying to scream, green fluid mixed with blood, blue blood, heads of animals, and all types of horror. She had never seen so much gore. This wasn't a nightmare she was in but a "terror-mare."

Stacey threw up. The whole experience was just too overwhelming for her. After finishing her contribution to the muck on the floor, she wiped her mouth and looked up at the door. She was expecting to see the huge beast that took her, but standing in front of her was a tall slender man in a black suit and hat, with veiny pale skin. She wiped her eyes and looked up again to stave off confusion and make sure she was seeing correctly.

The figure took his sunglasses off, walked over to Stacey and slowly bent down. He grabbed her hand and said, "Hi, Stacey, my name is Agent Wilkes. I am here to help you. I need you to trust me."

Stacey felt, exhausted. Wilkes picked her up and walked out of the horrid room, the room where the beast dumped its captives. The ones that survived got moved. The others were left to rot or became food for the many creatures lurking around.

Wilkes closed the door behind him. He was very strong and walked with ease along the bright hallway. Stacey drifted in and out of consciousness as they continued through different rooms and hallways. When they got to the main hall, her eyes were opening and closing, still drifting in and out, but there was something she saw that stuck, something even more horrific than the previous place. Stacey was now out cold.

When she woke up a few hours later, her body was strapped down to a bed. She was in a completely white featureless room with no windows or any entry. She tried to pull her arms up, but they were strapped, as were her legs.

Stacey heard a door open and looked over. From nothing, an entry appeared in the wall and disappeared again after the visitor entered. It was Agent Wilkes again.

"How are we feeling now? All your wounds have been attended to and you have been given sedatives to help with sleep. You should be feeling like new in no time." Wilkes was smiling and although it looked fake, it was somewhat soothing for Stacey, at least for the moment.

"Where am I? Who are you? Was that a Bigfoot? What were all those gross creatures? Where's my dad?" Stacey just let it all out and she wanted answers immediately. She was still in shock and Wilkes knew it.

Wilkes put his hand on Stacey's face, placing his fingers in a sequence. Stacey tried to pull away, but soon settled back as Wilkes was now talking to her in her mind.

"It's OK, Stacey. I will give you all the answers in time. All you need to know is that I am a friend and I'm going to help your father when he wakes up. He is fine, just resting while his body heals. The first thing you should know is that there will be medical practitioners taking bloods and samples of your DNA. The world you know has ended, the Earth is under attack, and you are the only conduit for the chosen who can stop this. I have set up a link directly from you to your father. He won't understand at this stage, though over time it will all be explained to you and to him. I need him, as he is close with one of my chosen who will help stop this invasion. The link I have set you up with also blocks and hides you from the hive so you will be safe here. Your bloods will be taken, and a double will be put in place of you so that no one will be any the wiser."

Stacey looked at Wilkes with a blank stare before responding, "I'm sorry, sir, I just don't understand any of this. It's like a bad dream. All I want to do is see my father and go home."

Wilkes gave her a little smile to reassure her, then kept on with his explanation.

"I know it's a lot to take in, but we are running out of time and there are few we can trust. I have some 'agents' on my side who will be here to hide you and keep you safe, but you cannot leave this room for now. It is not safe unless you are with me. I have disconnected myself from the hive ..." Before Wilkes finished his explanation, he looked at Stacey who was still blank-faced.

"What's a hive? What's a link? What's ...?"

Wilkes spent the next hour with Stacey showing and telling her enough of the plan and the history to satisfy her questions. Stacey, although still very scared, seemed to be a little more content afterward.

"OK, I'm going to leave now, as I am needed back at the hospital to help your father. You can talk with him through dream sequences, but remember he is still very weak so only give him little bits of information at a time. I will be back soon to start it all as I can only reach him through you at the moment."

Stacey was overwhelmed. However, she was strong and felt calm with Wilkes; there was a definite trust with him.

"I have left my very good friend and colleague to guard you. This is Agent Rovan. He is a trusted friend and a great agent."

Stacey smiled and after the medical staff had finished doing all their tests, they undid the straps, and Stacey was then left alone to get some proper rest.

The next day she woke feeling refreshed and pain-free. She glanced over at the corner of the room and after she finished rubbing her eyes and quickly got her bearings, she noticed the agent who was left to look over her while Agent Wilkes was gone. It was all still surreal to Stacey, and as much as it felt like a dream, she knew it wasn't.

"So, I wonder what's out there," she thought to herself before Agent Rovan stood up and made his way over to her bedside.

"Wilkes has asked me to keep an eye on you and to make sure you are OK. He has suggested that you help your father wake by opening his mind up. You need to close your eyes and concentrate on your father's face. Once there, help him remember what happened to him. This will assist him down the track."

Stacey questioned the methods. "Is it safe?"

Rovan nodded and continued to explain. "Close your eyes and concentrate on your father's face. I will open a pathway until you get used to it. Over time you will be able to visit him and communicate with him on your own."

Rovan placed his hand over Stacey's face as she closed her eyes and began. The first few times she didn't have much luck, although over the weeks she started establishing a connection. Right before Eric woke up from his coma, she had a successful attempt, relaying the events from the forest in a more detailed way. It was horrific for Eric at the time, but necessary for him to remember and start to understand. Stacey continued at times to mind-meld with her father, which in turn would build his connection up.

≈

Stacey had been in that room for weeks now and she was getting cabin fever. She had worked out how to open the doors by always watching Rovan's movements. The only problem was that Rovan or some medical staff were always in the room with her, either watching, taking more blood or trying to establish some sort of bond or connection with her to help pass the time away. Wilkes had been in a couple of times, but Stacey could not stop thinking about all those creatures she had seen when she was in that awful room weeks ago.

She decided that she would go back if she could and try to find out some more information to pass on to her father. She also kept having flashbacks and visions of a massive window she saw when she was being carried by Wilkes to the medical room. In these dreams and visions, she saw people inside cylindrical tubes of some kind, just hanging in the air. Stacey only caught a glimpse of this, and she needed to know more, even if her life was in danger. It was the inquisitive side to her personality and the strong woman she was due to her father's upbringing that made her question things, and knowledge is power, she thought to herself.

Knowing the bits and pieces of the story that Agent Wilkes had given her, she realized there were more parts that she needed to know. Even though it was "for her safety," Stacey just couldn't sit by and wait while the world was being overrun by beasts and creatures.

Stacey waited and tried to time how long she was alone for and when she was supposed to be asleep. This was difficult as she was given sedatives at times and even though she didn't always go to sleep, she would be too dosed to move.

Rovan, still in the room when Stacey woke up, was staring at nothing like he was plugged into a machine uploading information from an unknown source. Stacey hadn't seen this before and she thought how odd his behavior was, not that anything now made sense.

Taking a chance, she slowly climbed out of bed and walked over to Rovan. She was in a hospital gown and not very covered, but curiosity set in. "What is he doing?" She didn't care about her lack of dignity and she moved closer to Rovan, saying his name and waving her arms in the air around and around, begging for his attention. Nothing. Rovan continued to be as still as a stone although with head movements like he was acknowledging something.

Stacey was now in front of his face. She poked his veiny white cheek and waved her hand in front of him, all without any reaction. Stacey knew this was her chance to get out. She ran past Rovan to where the door was and waved her hand across the small keyhole opening. The door flung upwards with force and without hesitation she ran out and down a corridor, praying she would not get caught.

As she was running down the barren hall, she recognized the next hallway. Taking another chance, she slowly crept around the corner and made her way to the entry of a huge doorway. The room was massive, and the door was already open, permanently, it seemed. She slowly and strategically moved her head around to see if it was safe, and upon making eye contact with another human lying in a medical bed, she realized that other human was her, staring straight back at her but not moving at all.

Stacey gasped as she held her hand over her mouth. There were small creatures, like Wilkes but much smaller, as well as a taller slender figure. This figure was dressed like Wilkes in human form, but there was something not quite right about him. Still holding her hand over her mouth she noticed there were chunks of bloody meat on the floor under her doppelganger's bed. Further inspection revealed that it, whatever it was, was not alive anymore as the small creatures finished taking bloods and pulling the last of her organs onto the floor. They were brutal and as they pulled, cut, and wrenched at her body, the lifeless corpse kept staring at Stacey, its body movements coming only from the destructive nature of what the barbaric medical creatures were doing to her.

The tall slender man became angry, and was throwing around tools, medical equipment, and even pulled one of the medical beings' arms off in rage, causing a stir throughout the room. Stacey's double's lifeless body hit the floor, exposing her inside cavity and the empty mess left behind.

Stacey turned away from the ghastly images she had just witnessed. Wilkes was right, she thought. "How do I get back to Rovan before they find me?" She turned and without looking behind her started running back the way she came.

In the heat of the moment and not thinking clearly, Stacey took a wrong turn and headed down a dark corridor. When she reached the end, she knew she was in the wrong place, but she was definitely not going back.

Meanwhile, in the operating room Stacey had just left, the tall slender figure all dressed in black, heard a whisper and movement coming from Stacey's swift departure. As he turned around to see if someone was there, he noticed nothing, but he knew someone had been there.

"Who is that? Someone was here watching us."

In the corner of the room was another medic. This one was human-looking, and responded quickly, with a hint of fear in his tone. "Sorry, Agent Anders, I only caught a glimpse of a female running down the hall. I'm not sure who it was."

Anders was now angrier than ever. He looked directly at the medic, who was staring back at him, and less than a moment later the medic had blood running from his ears and nose before dropping to the floor, lifeless.

Anders stormed out of the room and headed in Stacey's direction, before turning the other way and into a room that Stacey hadn't noticed. The room was full of human-looking hybrids in gray uniforms holding guns, standing at attention like they were already preparing for Anders to enter. He called out, "Bring her to me now. I want her alive. If she escapes, you will all answer to me."

The guards marched out of the room. Anders hit a button and set off a short-range alarm to flush out the intruder. It flashed blue and red lights, but just in the local vicinity, so it would not bring any attention to this farther afield. The Leader would not forgive Anders if anything slowed down the end process.

Anders pulled out a small electronic device, blue in color, and upon pressing a button, a high-pitched screech flooded the room. While the sound traveled down the halls, Anders disappeared into thin air.

Stacey, now in real panic mode after the alarm was raised, was running low on options. There was what looked like a small door on her left and a chute of some kind on her right. With only moments before she was caught, she needed to do something.

Stacey waved her hand across the wall and the door opened. She ducked her head, hoping it was a closet or junk room of some sort, however when she entered the room, she dropped to her knees as the door slammed down.

There in front of her was a glass window with a control panel in front of it. The room was tiny and unoccupied. It wasn't the equipment that brought her to her knees. It was the sight beyond the window. Stacey was staring at hundreds of levels in hundreds of layers of human-looking beings inside cylinders of orange liquid. All looked asleep or dead. They were connected by wiring and large scaffolding all lined up next to each other in rows upon rows going as far as she could see and as high and low as she could see.

Her eyes wide and heart rate through the roof, she felt a blackout coming on, yet knew they would find her if that happened. The control room she was in looked like it was used to move cylinders around and upon further investigation Stacey could see there were many of these rooms along the other side. She could see them being pulled out and taken in for maintenance or clean-outs of broken cylinders.

Looking closely at one of the nearer life pods, she noticed a twitch from the pink hairless being inside it. As she stood up and moved in for a better look, its eyes opened, staring straight at her, before writhing around in what looked like pain.

Stacey stepped back slowly, while noticing blood leaking from the humanoid's nose and ears. The being convulsed again before a large metal arm reached out, grabbed the cylinder, and as a red light flashed on the top of it, the bottom opened and the being, along with all the fluid, fell to what seemed like forever. The large arm brought the cylinder into a room on this side of the walls, several sections to Stacey's right.

"What the fuck is this?" Stacey whispered to herself. She normally didn't swear but could not find appropriate words to say at the time.

She had to get out. She turned and clambered around to find the opening. She could still hear the alarm and the steps of the soldiers' feet getting closer. Stacey was getting desperate but then the door managed to open by itself. There standing in the doorway was a short hybrid male in a gray uniform and with a clipboard. Stacey knew she had to get past him, so without even thinking she kicked him in the knee, then followed with an elbow to the face, and finished off with a roundhouse kick to the head, before the worker, who was obviously back to take up his post, fell to the ground in pain.

Stacey ran past him, looked to her right, and saw that the guards were now on her. She had nowhere else to go so without hesitation she dove headfirst into the chute in front of her. Loud blasts came from a plasma rifle, barely missing Stacey. She fell for ages and as she was sliding down the chute, others opened and closed like a conduit of pipes before finally coming to an end, and she landed on her back in a pile of humanoid carcasses, like the ones in the cylinders.

THE DRACONIAN

STACEY WAS OUT OF IT FOR A MOMENT. As she slowly came too, she noticed the bodies all around her and before long the stench hit her hard, making her throw up. She feverishly scrambled off the pile. The pit was dark, but with enough lighting throughout for maintenance workers and clean-up crews to get what they needed done.

Stacey was very cold. The gown she was wearing was saturated with bodily mucus and fluids from the humanoid bodies she fell on. She needed to get out of there.

She started down a corridor to find an exit point. After walking for what felt like an hour but was only minutes, Stacey's exhaustion kicked in. She found a spot against a wall and sat back, trying to catch her breath and gain some composure. She thought, "What would my father do?" and realized she needed to warn him as Wilkes did not explain exactly how horrific it all was, and how many of them there were.

She closed her eyes and tried to gain a link to him. She was getting better at it now and Wilkes had opened a nice clear connection that no one else could interfere with. She only hoped her father was strong enough now to reciprocate. Stacey concentrated and built a link. She didn't have long so she explained as much as she could in that short amount of time, pleading to her father to find Wilkes, before being ripped back to her current state.

She opened her eyes and looked up, gathering her thoughts, and slowing her heart rate to a normal rhythm. Not far from where she was sitting was a cell of some sort. The bars were emitting a crisscross section of lasers and through it she could just make out something inside.

Stacey stood up and quietly moved toward the lone cell. Once near enough for a better view, she could make out a creature sitting back with its eyes open, looking directly at Stacey. It wasn't moving, although it was breathing deeply.

"What You Look At, You Not Belong Here, Girl." The creature had very broken English but managed to communicate enough for Stacey to understand.

Upon hearing its question, Stacey fell back, shocked for a moment, not expecting something so horrid to speak. She was learning fast over the weeks, though. Nothing was what it seemed and the rules of normal were out the window. She managed to get back to her position and sat down in front of the laser grid before answering back.

"Who are you? Why are you locked in this cell?"

Stacey stared without blinking, amazed at the sight of such a creature. The creature had a reptilian but humanoid face, a crest on its head, yellow eyes, and a mouth with lizard-like features. It had a dark greenish yellow tinge to its scaly skin and was dressed in military clothing like the one she had seen in that awful room; in fact, they could have been twins, if not for the burn marks on the other's face.

"Me Vargzin, Come, Help, Hurt Not, You?"

Stacey was establishing a connection with the creature by saying its name. "Hi, Vargzin. I'm Stacey, I saw another like you weeks ago, although he was ..." She paused for a moment, realizing Vargzin may know him. "I'm sorry, did you know the other?"

Stacey could see Vargzin's head lower before he answered, "Yes, Brother, Taken, Killed, Me Locked, Hate Us."

Stacey put the pieces of his words together to establish what happened and repeated back to him.

"I'm so sorry. He was your brother and they killed him, but locked you away because they hate you?"

Vargzin nodded. "Yes, And Daughter."

Stacey looked next to Vargzin through the gaps of the laser and could see a younger reptilian humanoid lying lifeless next to him.

"Oh, my goodness, is she OK?" Stacey exclaimed in desperation upon seeing her lying there.

"No, Gone, Sad, Mad." The creature looked scary and tough, but the single tear meandering through the contours of his scaly face said it all.

"I'm so, so sorry, Vargzin. Why do they hate you? Why did they do this, who did this?" Stacey wanted to know as much as she could. As intimidating as he looked, he seemed to have a good heart and looked sincere and sad about his daughter.

"We Fight Zeytars, Thousands of Moons, We Fight, Evil, Control, Kill All." Vargzin stood up and moved closer to Stacey. "Please, Escape, Me."

Stacey sat back for a moment taking it all in. She had run out of friends and needed help. "Do I trust him? Is it a trick or could he actually be someone who could help?" Stacey didn't take long to decide. She thought there was no other choice as they were still after her, and if this decision ended up being the wrong one, then maybe it wasn't a bad thing, as waiting to see the world end was not on her to do list. Surviving as long as she could was, so taking a chance was all she had left.

Stacey looked around the opening, but could see no obvious controls to open the cell. She went farther along to the side and saw three levers, well away from anyone inside to reach them.

She pulled the first down, but the laser grid now went all the way across without a crisscross, so she quickly returned that lever and pulled down the second. This time there was a change of color and a pulse emanating from the lasers so no one could get too close. She returned that lever and went to the last. As she pulled it down, she heard a crackle and buzzing before the laser grid disappeared completely, making it possible to enter or exit the cell.

Stacey whispered under her breath, "It's always the last one." She then moved around the front and found Vargzin standing there staring at her. He was at least seven foot two and very strong-looking. He slowly stumbled out of the cell before collapsing in front of Stacey.

Before long he came to and turned, looking up at Stacey, who was now supporting his head.

"Thank," he said as Stacey smiled back.

"Welcome," she replied, helping Vargzin get to his knees.

Eventually he managed to stand up on his own and said, "Clothes, Daughter, Have, Cold."

Stacey looked at him before answering in a light tone, "Do you want me to have your daughter's clothes? Are you sure?"

Vargzin nodded and pointed while he went around the corner.

Stacey stood for a moment. "Wow, who are these creatures? They give humans a bad name," she thought.

She went inside the cell, and in a few minutes she had managed to modify the larger clothing and wear it as best she could. Being military gear, most of it was adjustable anyway, even though the creature, for a young girl, was very tall. As she finished placing the jacket on, she could see a reflection of herself in a shiny part of the cell wall. Her blue and gray camouflage pants, black skivvy with camouflage vest and jacket didn't look that bad, she thought. In a pocket in her vest she found a knife and other implements that would most likely be of assistance. As she walked out of the cell, Vargzin was already waiting to go back in.

He had a small silver device that he pulled from his vest. He entered the cell, and kneeling before his daughter, sang a song out loud in his native tongue, before lighting his daughter's body on fire from the implement in his hand.

Even though she didn't understand everything about what was going on, she knew enough to realize that it was their custom and his way of mourning. After the song was finished and the body had turned completely to ash, he used two fingers to scrape some of the ash left over to mark his face across the top and along his two cheeks. Once satisfied, he stood up, walked out, and quietly said to Stacey, "We Go, Finish Them."

Stacey, staying right next to him, was feeling stronger and more confident, now that she was properly clothed and had a strong partner who would help her go toe-to-toe with these things.

They continued down the corridors of that section, which was obviously used as a dumping level for bodies and prisoners. Stacey turned her head and looked down a darker part of the level. She could see more of the same sort of cell that Vargzin had been in. She stopped in her tracks before she started toward the dimly lit prison section.

"Stop, Not Go There, Bad Things," Vargzin announced.

But Stacey didn't seem to hear or listen as she kept moving. Her thinking was that if Vargzin was good, then there may be a lot of others like him who could help her cause. She would soon realize she needed to listen to Vargzin more in the future.

Stacey stopped at the first couple of cells and tried to peek without getting too close. She could see movement inside it, so she advanced a little closer to get a better view. As she stepped up to the laser grid and put her face close enough so she could see what was moving inside the cell, a hand grabbed her shoulder and pulled her back to the floor. She turned around and looked up at her attacker, and saw Vargzin standing over her.

"Listen Me, Bad, Evil Things Here, All Mantids," Vargzin warned, while Stacey, still in shock, started standing up.

As she got to her feet, she felt pulsating pain in her head, and before long she was back on her knees holding her head and screaming out in agony. The Mantid creature inside the cell was sending out hypnotic and intrusive thought waves, trying to break her mind and create a false reality. Soon Stacey stood up, without pain, and headed over to the side of the cell where the levers to open the doors were.

She was being controlled by whatever was in the cell. Vargzin knew this and just before she touched the lever, he pulled her back. He flicked the second lever, which flooded the whole cell with a pulse, cutting off the severity of the mind control the Mantid had over her.

Stacey shook her head, obviously upset about her ordeal, yet thankful for Vargzin being there to stop it.

"Now, Will, Listen, Me?" he announced in a stern voice.

"Yes, Vargzin, thank you for that. What are those things?" Stacey was confused and worried about what else could be lurking around the place.

"Evil, From Other World, Captured by Zeytars, Kill or Capture, Last Ones Kept Here."

Stacey understood even though not much information was relayed. Vargzin was obviously very smart, he just couldn't use the language very well. But he seemed to be able to capture the right words at the time to get his point across.

As they walked away from the insidious creatures hidden in the cells, they could hear a terrifying screeching or screaming, obviously in response to the failed attempt at freedom. Stacey and Vargzin entered a different hallway, while the cries continued to echo down the corridors before finally dissipating into nothing.

Vargzin stopped.

"Now where do we go, and what do we do?" Stacey said, as he looked down at her tiny frame.

"Me, You, Wait." Vargzin seemed a little vaguer this time. Did he know something that she didn't?

"What do you mean, we wait? The end is here, and if we don't do something about it, no one will survive. We can't just stand here and wait."

Stacey was upset. She was frustrated at not being able to help her father. Although she knew he was in good company and doing a lot better, it still didn't help that she was helpless to do more.

"Wait, Attack, In Time, Have Plan."

Vargzin was very confident that he could do something, and Stacey just needed to hold back and trust his judgment. After all, she didn't really know this creature very well apart from the last few hours they had spent together traipsing up hallways and nearly releasing an evil alien creature out into the area.

They found a well-lit area with what seemed like a group of abandoned rooms where procedures had been done a long time ago.

They looked like they hadn't been used for hundreds of years, judging by the amount of debris covering some of the entry points to the rooms.

With a glance at each other and without saying a word, as if connected in thought, Stacey and Vargzin entered the darkest room at the end of the corridor. They avoided all the strange equipment on the floor until Stacey saw a rifle. When she picked it up for a closer inspection she noticed it was very advanced compared to Earth's weapons. Vargzin saw this and snatched it off her straight away.

"No Shoot, Find Me, You."

Stacey looked shocked for a moment. She knew how guns worked even though they were illegal in the country now, and she wasn't going to fire it.

"Hey, what are you doing? I wasn't going to use it. It looks too old and broken to work anyway," Stacey barked back at Vargzin who stood blank-faced before going over the firearm in detail. Even though it looked like advanced equipment, it also looked very old and well used.

"Gun, Stay, Me, Last Ten Thousand Moons."

Stacey wasn't going to argue with him, especially now he had the gun. They continued dodging the mess and found a nice spot at the end of the room where they could sit and rest until Vargzin was ready.

ROSWELL, NEW MEXICO, 1947

ON JULY 8, 1947, above the skyline in the early hours of the morning a giant craft was breaking through the clouds and moving at a steady pace until it stopped miles above a herd of cows. Happily grazing in a field on a private property in the middle of Roswell, New Mexico, the cows didn't even blink an eye as a huge blue light emanated from the center of the disc-shaped craft, hitting the Earth below. Then red beams, not as large, although still quite impressive, streamed from twelve sections of the craft, each hitting the Earth like the main center one.

The lights weren't like anything on Earth. They weren't harsh or bright; however, they were strong enough to be seen by Earth eyes. There was no sound at all.

Florida, the oldest cow in the herd, managed to take her eyes off the lush grass for a moment to see what all the fuss was about, but then went back to focusing on her food.

The farmhouse, half a mile away, was quite small, only occupied by an elderly couple who kept some chickens, cows, and went to market once a month. They had moved there forty years ago after the children had all grown up and moved on. Besides that, there was nothing but fields of grass and dirt as far as the eye could see.

The disc-shaped craft was the size of a small town, reaching for miles across the sky. Even though it was huge, it was difficult to see due to powerful cloaking shields. None of it reflected at all, not even the clouds or the windows of the house gave its location away, despite the lights. Unless in the direct vicinity of it, no one would know its location. That changed when the first of the small craft came out of the red-light entry point from the ship, soon followed by another, then another, until all twelve had been dispersed.

The blue light in the center got brighter and seemed to be vibrating as it sent something down out of it. As it landed slowly and carefully on the grass, the cows started to scatter, Florida's bell ringing as she ran toward the house.

The small triangle craft, now shooting off in all directions, were flying upwards, roaring like a thousand jet engines, which broke the farmhouse windows and knocked over the cows and some of the trees in the area. The smaller craft were then sent to all sections of the enormous mother disc and hovered like scouts.

As the object lay in the middle of the blue beam, safely on the ground, the light faded, revealing three large beings. They were very tall and thin, with only two fingers and an opposing thumb on each hand, grayish in color with bulbous black eyes and long faces. They were not human but grotesquely different, with an intelligence about them.

They all kneeled while staring at an object lying on the ground. Two of them started making sounds in a language not heard on Earth before, while the other, slightly larger one, slowly put his three digits on the silver object, turning it clockwise until it hit three revolutions. The sounds then stopped and they all had both hands on the object, sliding fingers through strange text that was appearing out of nowhere, until they all stood up in the most rushed movement of the whole event. There seemed to be no sense of urgency in their actions until then.

With all three standing, a blue light came from the square object on the ground. This time the light was extremely bright and the cows were badly burned, some even so bad internally that their organs had completely disintegrated.

The object now began to change from the original detailed cube that stood about three feet high to a melting flow of tiny particles, like a trillion microscopic ants moving about the area, slowly building up to make a solid form. They finally settled into the position that was chosen for them at that time.

A humanoid silver figure stood before the three gray beings. The detail of the alien writing had been moved around, but was still there, blue light glowing through symbols before disappearing as the makeup of the humanoid droid was settling into its new form.

There was a huge detailed clock that took over its whole abdomen, with intricacies that even the finest Swiss clockmaker would have trouble replicating. Two other smaller clocks were where its pectoral muscles would be, with tiny hands and mechanics that went deep into the android's system. Its face was covered in very small symbols, although it had the distinct humanoid look even to the finest detail of metal lips, a slender nose, glowing blue eyes and molded ears on the side. It had no hair.

The bluish-silver creation took a step forward on its metal legs. It had arms ending with hands and slender fingers, five on each hand with razor-sharp pointed metal fingernails at the ends. It took another step and as the three larger gray creatures made unusual sounds, the droid nodded as if to agree, before a blast came from the sky ...

Five Roswell Army Air Field planes from the 509th were shooting at the small scout ships. The scouts transformed from their triangular shape into smaller disc versions of the enormous mother ship. This defense mode made it easier to maneuver. Four more rounds of fire came from the RAAF planes, directly hitting one.

The large mother ship had now closed off the main light beam from the center but not before raising up the three gray beings on the ground. The other scout ships ascended into the red lights from whence they came, leaving one to do battle.

One of the planes circled around again. The mother ship had vanished leaving only one scout to take on the whole contingent of planes. Although the maneuvers were very fast, it had no hope against the Air Force, which was now firing hard on it. Within moments the scout disc had taken too much damage and crash-landed not far from the farmhouse. Satisfied for now, the RAAF planes took off and alerted base they had taken down a foo fighter.

Not long after the Air Force planes returned to headquarters the mother ship reappeared. All the while, the humanoid droid was standing there watching it all unfold. As it slowly walked over to the burning disc-shaped scout ship, the mother ship made a jet-sounding scream. At the same time a blue light emanated from the android's abdomen to the ship before a major electromagnetic disturbance created a maelstrom and energy blast. The mother ship entered into a vortex of lights and sounds and then it was gone.

The droid returned to silence after the ship disappeared and continued to the smaller burning craft. After pulling some wreckage off the entrance, the droid, as if sentient now after the three gray beings had turned it on, transformed itself into thousands of strips of metal next to the debris from the craft.

Soon after, a contingent of soldiers arrived on site to look through the damage, extinguishing the final fires burning, revealing three smaller gray beings hanging out of the disc's doorway which was gaping open.

As the military went into cover mode, a journalist managed to get a single shot of the event. Sneaking in with the contingent of soldiers, how he never got caught, he would never know, he thought to himself. Dressed in military uniform, he seemed to get away with it, blending into the drama which was unfolding. All the others were too busy cleaning up debris, numbering it, measuring areas, and most importantly attending to the three creatures lying in the craft.

Milton, the journalist, was as brazen as they got, although he thought he wouldn't push the issue by taking any more shots. He slid back out of sight and waited for their departure.

The last task of the evening, now early hours of the morning, was to question the farmers. They had been standing out the front of the farmhouse for hours watching it all unfold. The Smiths were unfortunately never reunited with their home; in fact, they were never seen again, despite a missing person's report filed by their children a month after the event.

The media were having a field day and Milton was smiling from ear to ear when he developed his photo and knew he had taken the most important photograph of not only his career but also of any journalist's lifetime. No one would ever get better proof of extraterrestrial life than this.

Milton then sent it to his editor along with the story. They had stopped the press and it made front page news, sparking worldwide panic. The only problem was that before Milton could see the final product, he was pulled into a car and was never seen again. The next day a retraction was made by the paper and they ran a cover story about a "weather balloon" from a military "project" called Mogul, which had been fabricated, setting off one of the biggest cover-ups in the twentieth century.

≈

After the military had finished going into public damage control, they turned to all the other things that needed to be sorted out. Witnesses still needed to be silenced. Staff members would have to be moved and set up in other towns with new careers.

All this activity was a result of the grays, or Zeytars as they were also called, having penetrated the military's armor by leaving three of their own inside fortified areas. The grays, unbeknownst to humans, managed to stage different things through mind control and Geno-drones.

Once they had control of the higher echelon of the military, more beings were brought down into the base and before too long the takeover had begun. Edwards Air Force Base, and later Area 51, was predominantly run by hybrids, a few soldier grays, and humans with Geno-drones that were all connected to the hive in the control ship. Gradually these infiltrators would spread throughout the country and indoctrinate a propaganda that would eventually destroy the world as humans knew it. The only thing left to do was wait for the machine.

After the Roswell crash, the droid was in thousands of pieces. Those pieces were then used to make a weather balloon. Eventually, after everything had settled down and the area was in the control of the Inter-Dimensional Extra-Terrestrials, or I.D.E.T.s, all the pieces of the weather balloon turned into tiny Geno-drones again. Each one individually was microscopic to the eye, however all together they combined into a flowing pool of liquid metal, which formed once again into a sentient humanoid droid. This time the droid took an elevator and went to the last floor at the bottom of the base, where only highly classified projects were located and which was looked after by the three main grays: Wilkes, Xandar, who was the designated chief of the base, and Anders, who hated going anywhere near the base because of Xandar.

The X-Clock, as Xandar had named it, although Wilkes usually referred to it as "ALEX," found its way into a small bunker at the end of a massive room, and welded the door shut with its own hands. It then went to the far corner, melted into the cube it was originally, and turned off, waiting ...

1972 UINTA BASIN

Deep within the mountains near the Uinta Basin in Utah, Anders had set up his own home away from home. Still connected to his dimension, he was able to come in and out of Earth's dimension whenever he pleased. The internal cavities and structures hidden within the mountains vibrated at a different level to the human world, making it impossible for anyone to dig and find anything.

The doorway located on the side of the mountain wall, however, could be opened, but only at a certain frequency. Once the opening sequence was triggered, though the mountain remained solid, a craft could fly straight through the side wall of rock into the dimensional hangars waiting inside. It was impossible to gain access any other way and Anders had made sure he kept it all to himself when he created it in the 1950s.

This was the location he decided to take some of their own scientists to so he could create his own army of aberrations and minions to control and do his dirty work. He used data from the deoxyribonucleic acid manipulation program, or DNA MP PRO for short. This was an early study and his bioengineers were more amateur than the high-level scientists on the mother ship, so the outcome was not the best at times. Gene splicing and recombinant DNA was a complex practice and some of the outcomes were far from normal because of the types of creatures he was combining.

Most of the abominations did not survive very long, particularly in the incubation stages. Although some were more complex and the genomes seemed to combine well enough, they were not things that could walk the streets or blend in anywhere. Not that Anders cared. He just wanted his own little backup army if things got too much for him. They were more of a plan B, though in time they would play a much larger role.

In the early days, Anders' scientists had around thirty-five spliced embryos incubating. The average total growth time differed as it depended on what was mixed and what DNA coding was altered for a more foreboding type of creature.

The first to survive the incubation stage and make it through full stasis was a human and gray mix, not like the ones the main bioengineers created, but a more sinister looking thing. It had human skin and four fingers, along with an enlarged head. Its ears were deformed and protruded to the sides like mini horns. The eyes were blue, half the size of a Zeytar's but very much the same shape. It had very sharp teeth and no nose, only a small bump with nostrils.

Anders named it Goblin for its very small size and grotesque features. He was taunted by Anders constantly, as Goblin's intelligence wavered at times. He would show promise and a high functioning IQ one day, then the next day would hardly be able to talk. It was probably due to the large cerebral cortex and the smaller amount of firing neural tissue at times. Some days Goblin couldn't even walk, other days he was helping the scientists.

Over time some of the creatures escaped the facility, roaming the area. Anders had taken the risk of adding harmonics to the DNA genomes as a way of being able to call for his abominations whenever he needed them. They could open a doorway, using their vocalizations, to appear where Anders was, then disappear back to the facility once they were no longer needed. The key to the success of this theory was to connect the creatures to Anders' own Geno-drone so they could always find him. The tones would only be to open the doorway from their dimension to Earth's; after that it was a matter of the connection Anders had with his creatures.

Anders hated the creatures escaping in and out of the facilities, so he modified the harmonic vocalization DNA later, limiting the ones he wanted to have it and which ones he did not. The ironic thing about that was that some of the intelligent creatures who didn't have it learned the vocalization and adapted it to their coding like a quick evolution of sorts. Anders in time lost some of his creatures due to this, and felt it was becoming too much of a risk, as stories started to rise of beasts, UFOs, ghosts, and werewolves roaming around a ranch near the mountain. Over time more and more witnesses were coming forward and Anders had to go into crisis mode. In more recent times he took over the whole area and fenced it off, stating it was owned by the government.

SAVAGE

In 1983 Anders' team of scientists had slowly started improving and making progress. He was happy enough with most of the creations that survived the process, although was getting annoyed that there wasn't one particular minion he could use all the time. One that was bonded so much that if he needed help, he didn't need to think about it, he could call on it whenever required. As much as Goblin was loyal, he wasn't reliable, and as for the others, well, they were so unpredictable that Anders couldn't take the chance on them turning on him.

So he sat down with his scientists one day and they came up with a very interesting mix. They had decided to abduct a strong human male and extract DNA from him, then splice it with a black dire wolf, the largest wolf known to have existed on Earth.

Anders' team of average Frankensteins now only manufactured one creature at a time due to the serious abominations that had failed earlier. Over time Anders brought in more pieces of equipment and scientists who were no longer required on the mother ship due to the failings of their work, and built his own little lab for more detailed creations away from everyone. It was his own little sanctuary, and as much as it wasn't sanctioned by the Leader, nothing was done about it as it was considered that he was doing his own work for the cause. That's what he let the Leader think whenever he was connected to the hive, anyway.

This would be his last design, though, as time was getting on and the work toward the agenda seemed to be ramping up. His time was needed to silence the truth seekers with Wilkes. The scientists put as much into Savage as they could, creating a human mind with a thirst for blood, keeping a link with Anders and only Anders, so the human loyalty would override his animal instincts.

Occasionally more of the human would come through, like the fetish of how he killed his victims, savoring little pieces for a prolonged kill, and the trophies in a braid of snippets of his victims' hair to remind him of what he had done. Sometimes he would even wear clothing to try and bring that human side out more; however, the bipedal wolf was an animal and he knew it, so those times were rare.

Savage was named after his first kill. It was an ex Air Force pilot in 1984 who had started his own group of truth seekers. He had his own experiences with foo fighters when he was in Vietnam and had been told specifically to keep it to himself, or else.

One day Wilkes and Anders turned up at his house dressed in their full suits and fedoras. As the former pilot answered the knock on the door, he felt something wasn't quite right and so he flicked on the large VHS camera that had been sitting on the table next to him. He had just finished reviewing some UFO phenomena in the sky out the back of his place, although in reality it was only cloud and a plane that was difficult to see flying past.

Wilkes and Anders entered the house and started asking him questions. Before too long there was some back and forth which turned into an argument. Usually these things were sorted out quickly with mind persuasion, however this ex pilot seemed to have a strong resolve which led to Anders calling on Savage to finish the situation. Wilkes had not seen the creature before and was shocked that he had the harmonics of DNA built into his genetic coding. Only the Sasquatch had that at the time.

After Savage had finished with the former pilot, he bent down and pulled at the dead man's gray mullet, then turned to Anders and pointed to his own head. Anders worked out quickly enough what he wanted. He would do anything for loyalty, and Savage was loyal to Anders. He cut a length of hair, tied it to a long part of Savage's fur on his head, and then told him thanks, that would be all.

But before the beast disappeared, he walked over to Wilkes. He was twice his size and Wilkes could only stare. He had seen a lot of different creatures in his time, but this was something else. Savage leaned over, blood dripping from his fur. His teeth were showing, and human flesh seemed to be stuck between three of his sharp teeth at the front. Wilkes noticed that he had a sort of menacing smile that was always there, like he had fun with it all.

Savage leaned further down within a whisker of Wilkes' face, opened his long jaw, and let out an enormous howling scream. Wilkes could nearly see the beast's stomach through the open mouth, but he was not going to let it intimidate him. Most creatures' hearts would stop at such a sight, but Wilkes had a strong mind.

Savage had opened a door back to his lair and disappeared into nothing. Wilkes took a moment to gather himself, then turned to Anders who was standing there smiling.

Anders asked Wilkes whether he liked his new pet, to which Wilkes responded, "That thing is savage. I've never seen anything more disgusting in my whole life. Don't bring it near me again, do you hear?"

"Savage, I like that. Thank you, Wilkes, you just named my new pet," said Anders.

They traded glances for a moment, then Wilkes said, "So what's next on the list?"

Anders went back into normal mode and they both returned their sunglasses to their faces, fedoras to their heads, and exited the house to go to the next job, leaving a scene of carnage that would be covered up later as a serial killer's work.

The camera was knocked to the ground and smashed at the start of the scuffle, so nothing of Savage was recorded, but eventually part of the tape was leaked and became one of the first "men in black" videos to circulate.

AGENT ANDERS NOW

After the attack at the church, Anders went to his bunker and healed his thigh. He was now a different entity. More angry, bitter, and vengeful than ever, after being betrayed by the one he was supposed to see this thing through with. Even though he had had his doubts about Wilkes, he didn't think he was that invested in those stupid humans to abandon his own race and help them. In truth, he was the one that pushed Wilkes to the edge with centuries of his abominable acts, although he would never admit it. He was so furious that he wanted to know the extent of the damage and how deep the rebel went with his plans.

Anders finished brooding and went to his number one scientist.

"Gaald, can you check if there is a chip inside me other than my own Geno-drone. I have a feeling that I have been blocked somehow. I know Wilkes' power of mind is strong, but not that strong."

Gaald was one of the twelve warden grays. Wilkes had Rovan, and Anders had Gaald, although he only required him at times due to Gaald always being in the lab. This was one of those times.

Anders lay down and Gaald scanned him for any other Geno-drones. Zeytars at times needed them to enhance a higher functioning ability and to attach to the hive when in other dimensions.

Gaald stopped midway through the scan, staring at Anders. He was too frightened to go further.

"What is it, Gaald? What is it?' Anders said slowly, assuming Gaald had just had a brain fade.

"You have two, sir. The second one is a highly functioning one. I'm sorry, sir."

Anders let out a horrendous scream.

"Get it out!" he ordered Gaald.

Gaald was shaking as he waved the retraction device over Anders, sucked the device out, and healed his exit wound.

"I'm going to kill him. After I find out what is going on in the mother ship, I'm going to find Wilkes. Then I will kill him and all his dirty human rebels." Anders was at a new level of anger, even worse than before.

"Savage, stand by, my friend. You are about to receive your biggest reward yet. Zeytars taste nicer than humans." Anders didn't know that; he was just trying to work Savage up.

Savage licked his huge yellow teeth but was thinking to himself how much he doubted that scrawny Zeytars would be tastier than his favorite dish, human.

Anders took off and appeared moments later inside the mother ship. He made his way to the extraction point so he could find Stacey and see what Wilkes was hiding. Her father had escaped, and she was the only survivor left that had the proper DNA genome.

Anders finally found her room to see Stacey had been put to sleep awaiting another extraction of bloods and biopsies of some of her internal organs. The beasts that found these people were usually spot on. There were times when they only had a part of the genome they were after, however that was good enough to the scientists as the genome was so rare.

Anders stormed in and demanded to know what was going on. There were several medics, some human, some Zeytar, with hybrid soldiers keeping guard as per orders from Wilkes himself.

"So, this is her, this is Stacey Kirkpatrick?"

Anders hadn't seen her yet as Wilkes oversaw the subjects who were brought in and the extractions of DNA. Anders' role was purely to silence the humans who had stumbled on the truth, and plant deceptive humans with control Geno-drones inside governments and the military where Xandar was primarily in charge, Area 51 and the V.I.Z.I.N.D.A.L.E.X.

So as the Leader trusted all of them to complete their jobs, now there was a problem and Wilkes was public enemy number one. Anders wanted so badly to tell the Leader but thought it better if he didn't know, due to the higher chance Wilkes would show himself somewhere. Anders didn't want anyone else taking away his revenge.

"This is Stacey Kirkpatrick, sir. Wilkes oversaw the first extraction and now we are going to complete the next phase due to his absence. Would you like to stay?" the head medic asked Anders like he was being invited.

"Please," Anders replied in a condescending tone.

The medic proceeded to extract bloods and began with biopsies of her liver and kidneys. The technology was so advanced that they could read the whole DNA codex on a computer in the room instead of waiting for analysis that took days or weeks on Earth. A half hour went by and Anders was pacing up and down the hall just outside waiting, until finally he was called back in.

"I have bad news, sir. She is a clone," the head medic explained to Anders.

"What do you mean, clone? She is here, she has the DNA. Wilkes ..." and before he finished his sentence, he realized exactly what had happened. "Well, if she is cloned there should be the same DNA coding. Look through her whole system, open her up, and find the hidden genome."

Anders had just learned what Wilkes had been up to on the ship when he was gone those recent times. It was just lucky that the current run of Zeytar hybrids was already created with the coding. But Stacey's was so rare that it could be transformed and used as a weapon if it fell into the wrong hands.

Twenty minutes went by and nearly all the clone's organs were on the floor and her head had now dropped to the door side of the room. Her eyes were open, staring at nothing. Anders started smashing things and the anger in him was disturbing. He heard a noise and turned. There was now a new concern.

≈

Anders was back in his bunker. He had left the search for Stacey to the soldiers on the ship. He had no time to be playing cat and mouse with a human, so he ordered the hybrid soldiers to guard all levels of the ship, including the science and biological divisions.

Anders stewed for hours thinking of the ways he was going to kill Wilkes and his precious little human helpers. He didn't want to go anywhere near Xandar as he hated him so much. "So how could I get him, or even find him?" he thought to himself.

Then he remembered that Wilkes' ship had a connection to the main fleet, just like his did. If he could locate it at the right time, then he would at least be able to find him and surprise him at a moment when he was unguarded and least expecting it. The only problem was he had to get one of his "thinkers" as he called them to crack the code.

Wilkes was a smart cookie, the smartest Zeytar he had ever known and the only one besides the Leader to have the ability to control minds at the highest levels. Anders was supposed to be able to have some degree of mind control as a master, however he was lazy and used more medieval methods like truth serums and hypnosis. Therefore, he was an easy target for Wilkes to control him without him knowing. He hated himself for that and this was another reason he wanted to torture Wilkes. Savage would be very satisfied indeed, because after Wilkes there would also be his little collection of humans.

Anders couldn't take any more, he felt like torturing some humans, maybe even running amok in the air and frightening some pilots. He didn't care about the agenda now. That was his sole focus for so long, but now he was purely in hate mode and this was going to drive him until he came face to face with Wilkes.

Anders' ship hadn't been moved for many years and although he was in a parallel dimension of his choosing, he went to power the engines. With a mighty blast, the power cells fired first time as he burst through the mountain and over Earth's Uinta Basin. The power cells lasted for thousands of years so he had no concerns.

Anders was going to have some fun and the first thing he would do was to set down and create some crop circles. In the past people had seen crop circles as a sign of extraterrestrial activity, like a message or landings of some sort. However, they weren't made by Zeytars but another race known as the Pleiadians. They had high-tech machines that left marks when they landed. They would also use them as messages and warnings to others at times, although in recent years it was more human interference and hoaxes that were the talk of the town, as the Pleiadians had been defeated by the Zeytars. The Pleiadians weren't responsible for the cattle mutilations. That was the work of Zeytars, scraping out bits and pieces of vital organs for their experimentations with bioengineering. Anders always liked that part. He was a messed-up creature and was in that mood now.

Savage was with him and after clearing his head with a crop circle or two he was going to let Savage have some fun before the "big meal" later.

Over 90,000 people in the United States of America went missing every year, never to be seen again. Anders knew Zeytars were responsible for a large percentage of that, so one more wouldn't matter.

It was nighttime and Anders hovered above a house in Oregon. He was livid that Serena had started the whole thing by taking Eric and recording some of the most important information about their whole agenda. Anders had a plan for revenge against Serena. He was going to kill her parents, or at least let Savage do it. Louise Carter wasn't enough. Now that Anders was angry, they all had to suffer.

Hovering above the O'Halloran house, Anders and Savage disappeared into the beam and wound up inside the family home's master bedroom. Liam and Grace were both asleep. This was going to be too easy, Anders thought. He leaned over to Savage and whispered in his large furry ear, "Wake them before you start."

Savage was watering at the mouth. He crept over to Liam, who was snoring heavily. Drool was dropping randomly onto his face and with a few more solid drips Liam awoke. He turned over, looked at the beast, and then rolled back and went straight to sleep again.

Anders was confused. Why wasn't he screaming in fear and trying to escape? Was he still asleep and dreaming?

Savage grabbed Liam and shook him violently like a rag doll to make sure he was fully awake. Both Liam and Grace just sat up in bed and stared at Anders and the beast.

"Can I help you, gentlemen?" Liam asked in a strong Irish accent.

Anders was now starting to become aware of a paradigm shift that he hoped was not real. After watching the two in bed for a minute or so, he tasked Savage to finish them.

"All yours, Savage. Don't leave much, take it all in," he said, looking forward to the screams and the manifestations of fear. But the more Savage dug into them both, the more Anders realized that wasn't going to happen.

Savage stopped midway through devouring Liam's lower intestines. He turned to Anders and, shocking his master, spoke for the first time.

"Not real flesh, fake human, no fear!"

He then threw all of it up onto the floor, which turned even Anders' hardened stomach. Anders knew exactly what was going on now and shouted out in rage, "Wilkes, I'm going to eat you myself!"

Wilkes had prepared so much more than Anders had anticipated. He cloned not only Stacey, but also Serena's parents, and who knows who else in the process. It was another blow to Anders' ego and just made his resolve even stronger.

He called for Savage, who felt defeated and sick because Wilkes had added some nasties into the DNA of the fake parents. They beamed back to Anders' ship and flew back to his parallel dimension in the mountains of Uinta.

Where were the originals of them all? How did Wilkes have time to do all of this? How could he, Anders, not know any of it? The whole thing was tearing Anders up and he was determined to find Wilkes and finish him.

Savage went to his lair to recover while Anders got his "thinkers" to find the location of Wilkes' ship. Surely Goblin should be able to find them. It would be a messy action, no matter the outcome, and Anders was more than ready. He was patient and would sit and wait for the first alarms.

DARKNESS OF
THE MIND'S EYE

THE GROUP SLOWLY STARTED WAKING from their deep slumber, many hours after they were first administered the drug and had been freed from the Geno-drone devices hidden inside their bodies. So many questions haunted them and they feared they would get no answers, especially Eric and Serena. They had been a part of this journey now for a good few weeks, ever since meeting each other at the hospital and escaping from the agents who wanted them dead. Now they were held by one of those same agents at a location they knew nothing about. The craziness of the situation didn't escape them, but this was where they found themselves right now and they were dealing with it.

Valinda was the first to wake up. Still upset about her mother's murder and becoming angrier about the situation as time went on, she did notice one thing, though, and that was the silence in her head and the lack of the disturbing visions that had been getting more frequent over the years, especially in the last few months. "Whatever that creepy guy took out of me, it has definitely helped," she thought to herself.

She looked over at the bed next to her where Serena was now coming around. She then took in the room around her, noticing that there were no windows, furnishings, or wall art. It looked like a hospital room, but without any other furniture at all. Even side tables or cupboards which would normally house linen seemed to be lacking. There were only two beds and the plain sheets on them. Other than the door, the only other features were metallic looking walls and a tiny light on the ceiling.

Valinda whispered to Serena, "Hey there, are you OK?"

She was concerned. She remembered her from some church services over the years but that was about it. Serena lifted her head.

"Yes, dear, just a slight headache, although I feel like I've had the sleep I've been needing for ages. I should be asking you that question, though, as all this has been a lot for you in such a small amount of time."

A sad smile appeared on Valinda's face for a moment and she lowered her head in silence.

"I know we don't know each other that well, but I just wanted to say thank you for being there for me after my ..." Valinda's eyes welled up with tears and her voice began to break but she knew she needed to finish what she was saying. "I just wanted to thank you, anyway. I feel very comfortable with you and you have helped me feel a little better after my mother was murdered by that creep."

Serena stood up and made her way over to Valinda's bedside. She put her arm around her.

"You will never need to thank me, ever. I will be here for you and all the others when I can. Whatever is happening seems to be big and getting bigger, and I have a very strong feeling that it's only going to get more serious before it stops. I don't know a lot of what is going on, although I know enough. I have seen and heard things that should not be real, but there seems to be this familiarity with it all, I just can't quite pinpoint what. I know that there will be answers soon and some sort of relief. I just feel it."

Valinda wiped her eyes and sniffed before turning her head to face the other woman.

"Thank you, Serena, I feel better when I'm around you. Even though I'm struggling with all of this, I'm not without my own stories of the strange and macabre."

Serena sat upright in anticipation. She was like a sponge wanting any information she could get to start putting some more of the puzzle together.

"Do tell, my dear."

Valinda sat back on the bed and laid her head down, eyes at the ceiling. After a moment's pause, she said, "How long do you have?" and then she laughed.

Serena assumed the same position on her own bed, also gazing at the ceiling.

"As long as you need."

Valinda turned her face toward Serena and began to explain all the weird things that had happened to her since she was a child.

Valinda was born to parents Marjory and her husband Phillip Mannix. She was named after her great-grandmother who had been a spiritualist back in her early years.

When she was only eleven years old, Valinda's father and brother passed away from a car accident. She was devastated, as she was very close with her father and they had a special bond. It wasn't long after they were gone that the strange shadow encounters started, keeping her on edge ever since, without knowing what it all meant.

One Friday morning, when she was getting ready for school, she noticed an owl at the window. Not thinking anything of it at the time she wandered off and caught the bus. Not two days had passed when at the same hour of the morning she saw the same gray owl. Its eyes looked huge, not like in the pictures she had seen of them in books at school. She also remembered that owls were nocturnal, so why was she seeing this one in the daylight hours? Was it hurt?

Valinda moved to the window on this day, and as she reached out to close it, she was flung back to the other side of the room. The owl flew in and circled around her head for a moment, then without warning disappeared out the window again. This would be the last time she saw that creepy owl or the shadows until she was sixteen.

She and her mom had moved by then, and Valinda was hanging out with her friends and studying, as she wanted to be a journalist later on when she finished school. The strange occurrences escalated, and she would see the owl again when she was walking to school. At nights it would be at her window staring at her. The eyes were glowing at times and in the middle of the night she would wake up in a cold sweat from some of the horrific and strangely realistic dreams about floating in strange rooms, pain in many places, and creepy humanoid creatures looking at her while she was lying down.

These dreams continued to affect Valinda to the point she started missing school and had times where she would have missing days and could not remember where she had gone or why. Over time, the dreams became so real that she started to take medication for depression and to block the constant intrusive thoughts she was having.

By the time Valinda was eighteen the sightings of the owls started to wane, but the dreams seemed to be converting to reality. At least that's what she thought, because she would start to hallucinate or see and feel things that weren't actually there. She finally went to speak to a group of people who had been through similar events. They prompted her to document everything that she had been through, and she went further and researched other cases as well. Her journalism career took off. Valinda spent all her time doing podcasts and video blogs on cases of the paranormal, focusing on people's stories, and obtaining video evidence that would help solidify the information.

One such case was the release of a leaked report about a cluster of UFOs over a period of time across Ireland. Another was the Tic Tac craft seen off the coast of San Diego. A Navy officer leaked the full footage to Valinda, which showed numerous UFOs hovering around an underwater disturbance that was filmed by a Navy Super Hornet. The Pentagon officially released a snippet which became a well-known sighting but Valinda had been given the full high definition version from start to finish, making the officials in the Pentagon very nervous.

There were many other cases on her site over time. Incidents that were so strange that nobody would believe them unless they were there when it happened. The cases were getting more bizarre as time went on so she needed somebody to help validate the content and select what would be most important for the public to hear. This is when she started getting Father Michael to help.

The site received backlash from countless people. There were also threats from government agencies that wanted to know where she was getting the information and threatened her with lawsuits for slander, for spreading panic and fear, propaganda, and threatening national security. This went on until quite recently, when the government threats stopped. The visions and shadowy images, and threats from ghostly specters were becoming more prevalent. She had some new information about an abduction that was filmed by a security camera that she wanted Father Michael to have a look at, before the incident at the church happened.

Valinda had been haunted by some vile ghostly apparitions of little girls standing in the hallway, all repeating the same things about ceasing informing the public about any paranormal events. The haunting images she witnessed in her bathroom were the final straw for her. She wanted answers and had hoped that Michael would be the one who could finally help her.

Now she felt like she was in the company of people and events that would give her all the answers. Well, at least about some of the key pieces to her childhood, visions, dreams, and missing time.

Serena stared at her in amazement after hearing some of the dark times of Valinda's life. She was glad that she had confided in her about it.

"Wow, Val. Can I call you that?"

Valinda nodded. "Yes, everyone calls me that anyway, it's like an old person's name, though." She laughed.

"Well, you have the wisdom of an aged person with all you have been through. Can I ask you one question, though, and please forgive me if it is out of line or too personal?"

"Sure, Serena, go ahead. After all, you have been there for me in the short amount of time I've known you."

Serena sat up and with a smile lightly grabbed Valinda's hands.

"Have you been to any doctors or had anyone explain to you what you have been through, like the missing time and what the owls meant?"

Valinda pulled her hands away and snapped back at Serena, "What do you mean, doctors? I'm not crazy. I told you all of this in confidence as I thought you may understand."

Serena put her hands up in front of her in a stopping motion. "No, no, that's not what I meant. I'm actually a psychiatrist and I deal with regression. It's something that may help give you some of the answers you're seeking and maybe unlock some of these mysteries."

Valinda seemed to calm down somewhat. "I thought you were a nurse. I heard you talking in the car and you're the one administering Eric's medications."

Serena said hastily, "Yes, I am. Part time. I have a psychiatry practice, but I still enjoy the nursing side of things. I actually never left after I got my Doctorate in Psychiatry, and although I work long hours, nursing breaks it up for me. I love helping people in all kinds of ways, medically and mentally."

Valinda opened her eyes wide. "Oh my, how do you have time for a family or anything else?"

"Well that's the real problem, isn't it?" She smiled. "I don't have time for anything else at all. But that's OK, it's not forever. I'm saving to buy a bigger place, as I am sick of renting, and I can then afford to hire more staff and take more clients at a full-time capacity. Now, what I can do for you is help answer some questions, and I think now is the time for your truth." Serena took Valinda's hands back.

"OK. I have put this off for most of my life out of fear. I trust you will look after me and I'm ready to get answers." Valinda stood up and shook herself all over. "OK, where do you want me and what do I need to do?"

"Stay there," Serena said, getting up. "I will go and find a chair from somewhere. I won't be long."

She made her way to the door using the half-light from the ceiling glow. As she went to open it, she realized there were no handles or any buttons to push to open it. Upon closer examination Serena noticed a tiny hole at the center of the wall next to where the handle would be. She investigated it by pressing it and getting in close to check it out. She could not work it out.

Valinda seemed a little confused. "Hey, what's going on? Are you looking for ants or something?" she said and then chuckled. "Try waving your hand over it." She made her way over to the door to see if she could help.

As Serena waved her hand across the small hole, a door snapped up into the cavity above. The women looked at each other in shock.

"How did I know that?"

Serena stepped back before the door snapped down and closed again.

"Maybe now would be a good time to get some of these questions answered." Serena opened the door again by waving her hand above the "switch," and as the door opened for the second time, she disappeared into the well-lit corridor.

Serena was in strange territory. Not knowing where to go, she looked up and down both corridors, which seemed to go on for ages. She went over to a wall in front of her and waved her hand across it, hoping to find an entrance of some sort. To her it seemed like feeling her way around a house without glasses on. She stopped, thinking to herself, "What am I doing?" This time using her intelligence, she examined the walls instead, hoping to find contours or lines that would indicate the same kind of pattern as in the room she had just left. Before too long she found a tiny hole. She swiped it, and there were Eric and Michael, standing at the entrance, looking as confused as she was not more than a few minutes before.

"Now there's a sight for sore eyes," Michael said quietly and Eric nodded in agreement.

Serena smiled at them and whispered, "Likewise," while sneaking a glance over Eric's way.

Eric got the look and smiled back before awkwardly whispering, "Why are we whispering?"

They all laughed for a moment as Serena entered the room before the door shut.

"Ah, that's what I'm after," she said, picking up a solid steel chair from the back of the room. The only difference in rooms was the presence of that chair, all the rest was the same as theirs. "Come on," Serena announced as she swiped her hand to open the door, "I have work to do before that agent comes to get us and takes us to that secret location."

They escaped the room before the executioner door snapped shut behind them. Serena led them back to roughly where her room was. All of them noticed the bland metallic walls and roof that had absolutely no pictures, furniture, or anything else that would give it a homely feel. Perhaps it was all meant to seem the same and without character, maybe even confusing people as to where they were so they wouldn't escape or find something they shouldn't. They would worry about that later, Serena thought, as she found the entrance to her room and they all went in before the door closed shut again.

Valinda ran over to Michael and hugged him, but then snapped at Serena, "Where have you been? I thought you abandoned me."

Serena, confused and worried that Val may have had another episode, said, "I've been gone no more than five minutes, Val, I swear. I accidently found the guys along with the chair, and then we came straight back here. Five at tops, I swear."

Valinda sat back down on the bed wondering if perhaps she'd fallen asleep.

"Now, do you mind if we begin? I would like to get this done before we are moved again, or things get serious. I also think it would be good if Eric and Father Michael were witness to this, so we are all on the same page."

Valinda nodded and repeated to Michael and Eric the events that had happened to her when she was younger, leading up to this moment. Even though Michael knew it all, Eric needed to hear it before Serena started with the regression.

"Could things get any weirder?" Eric announced as he and Michael sat back on the other bed in anticipation of the events about to unfold.

"Now, gentlemen, I need absolute silence from you, or this won't work. Any noises or sudden outbursts may affect the regression and may even hurt Valinda's state of mind."

Both men nodded. Serena placed the metal chair down for Valinda to sit in. She herself sat on the bed, leaning forward to start the process.

"Alright, Valinda, now I want you to count backward from 10 to 0 slowly with your eyes closed," she said in a soft tender voice.

"OK," Valinda whispered.

The men were still as stones waiting in anticipation of what might be released from her subconscious. Michael especially had been concerned about Valinda's troubles for a while now.

"Count from 10 to 0 slowly ..."

Valinda counted down and by the time she got to three she was completely under.

"Now tell me in your own words what happened on the morning when you were young, getting ready for school."

The curtains were blowing softly in Valinda's bedroom as she was getting ready for school. The window was slightly ajar to let the breeze in for relief from the harsh summer heat that had been scorching their area in California for the past few weeks. Eleven-year-old Valinda was almost done dressing in her school uniform and in the distance could hear Marjory calling for her to come down the stairs and have some breakfast.

Valinda finished putting on her shoes. As she looked up, she could hear scratching at the window. Thinking it was a bird, Valinda walked over to have a better look. She went to open it further, but was grabbed by something and flung across the room. She started sobbing while still lying on the soft carpet on her bedroom floor. When she looked up, there was a small gray being with huge eyes, only slits for a nose, no ears only tiny holes, and a long thin slit for a mouth. Its head was quite large, disproportionate to the rest of the creature's body with its long slender arms and long fingers. It was hovering over Valinda, not touching the ground, floating around three inches above it. It was moving around her head, before it whispered into her mind, "You have been chosen. You will give us more, you will be ours and you will be summoned."

The being, not of human origins, reached out and placed its long slender hand with two fingers and long thumb onto Valinda's head. She passed out for a moment and on awakening she could only remember seeing an owl and ran downstairs to tell her mother.

"This is too hard. It wasn't an owl, it was one of them."

Serena whispered to her, *"It's OK, Val, you are doing an amazing job, and we are all still here for you, keep going with it."*

Valinda was reacting to the visions in her head, but although upset, she continued.

Serena went on, *"OK, Val, now I want you to move forward to when you were sixteen. Can you tell me, on the night you had those awful dreams where you were floating and there were others around you ...?"*

"OK."

It was Friday evening and Valinda had been out with her friends all day. She was exhausted as she hadn't been sleeping well lately. The uneasy feelings of being watched and the stresses of her exams were continuing to be a problem after her eyes closed.

At around ten thirty that night she had fallen asleep on the couch watching one of her favorite movies. Marjory gently shook her and eased her up the stairs, before putting her in bed. Valinda went right back to sleep.

Around an hour later things started happening inside the sixteen-year-old's room. Curtains were blowing on the inside of the room, the bed was shaking, and she woke up in a fright from all the light surrounding her. She was completely frozen and hovering three feet above her bed. Her eyes were fixed on the ceiling as she tried to move her head to see what was happening but couldn't. The only movement she felt was the intense beating of her frightened heart, pounding away like a racehorse at a carnival.

The next moment would change Valinda forever as she began to descend back to the bed. There surrounding her were the same little beings as the one she had first witnessed all those years ago. Valinda went to scream but could not get anything out, not even a whisper. She could only breathe and stare, as the beings grabbed hold of her arms and legs. They slowly guided her to the window where a craft was hovering, waiting for them. They all vanished, and the craft took off into the clouds, disappearing into a vortex.

Valinda awoke minutes later. She was now surrounded by human-looking beings, although there was something not quite right about them. They seemed to be very tall and thin, dressed in medical attire. She could move, but she was three feet in the air so moving at this stage was not an option, yet she could still not scream. There were several different-looking creatures in the room. The tall human-like medics helped bring her to a table where she would eventually end up. There were smaller ones, with ears around a foot long that pointed to the roof, long arms, and short legs. They had three eyes—two eyes were either side of a long nose and one was a lot larger, sitting in the middle above the nose. They had green skin and sharp teeth. All were standing over her, holding medical tools with their four fingers. The middle eye seemed to be hypnotizing Valinda. This would be the reason she was unable to remember the events as they put a block on her mind. But the pain would be hard to forget.

The being in the corner showed itself. It was like the equivalent to a doctor but a grotesque-looking thing. She screamed in her mind.

Snapping back out of it again, she began to cry. *"Sorry, Serena, this is way too much for anyone. I cannot look at these images in my mind anymore. Can we please stop?"*

Serena grabbed her arm. *"Just breathe, Val. Breathe with me."*

They sat for the next few minutes breathing deeply, Valinda slowly calming down until she was back to light breaths. The two men kept glancing at each other in disbelief, and Michael was nearly ready to jump off the bed to comfort her, but he trusted Serena and her methods, and knew it would upset the process.

Serena sat back and in a light tone said, *"We are almost there, Val. You are doing an amazing job. Without you finishing we won't know*

what we are dealing with when it comes time to put the pieces together.
Your description of these things will help us all eventually."

"OK, I know, I'm ready now. I know you are all with me."

Valinda sat back and continued to the next, most disturbing part of her experience.

Valinda was back on the table, looking up at the doctor who would eventually be the one to conduct the painful experiments on her. The creature had a white egg-shaped head with tiny round yellow eyes, no nose or hair, and seemed to have all types of colored veins protruding all around its head. There were four arms reaching out with long creepy white fingers. It had no clothing on and did not have what would be genitalia in any area she could see. Brown scales covered its body right up to its neck and the legs on it were long and inverted, making it look like it walked backward.

As it approached, the smaller large-eared beings passed the implements over to the "doctor," the first one being a long large needle which the being shoved without any thought straight into Valinda's neck. Valinda was shaking in pain and that's when the tall medics came to assist by holding her down.

After the first procedure of attaching an implant, the doctor then reached for another, smaller, needle. It was shoved into Valinda's chest and pulled up at least half a liter of blood, which was dispensed into five different canisters held by the tall human-looking medics.

The doctor then made a noise with its tiny mouth hole that in fact looked like an anus, before the three-eyed beings all in sequence used telekinesis to raise Valinda from the table. As she was being raised, her legs were pulled apart by an invisible force before the doctor inserted three metal rods, like hoses, into all her cavities including her belly.

Valinda was convulsing in the air. She was now immobile and could only breathe, like before when she was back in the bedroom. The pain was so bad she started to black out until one of the three-eyed creatures zapped her mind and sparked her back up, as if they enjoyed seeing her feel so much pain.

As the doctor moved the prods around her, something latched onto her insides, and then the rods all released out of her body with tiny bits of tissue on them. The doctor, satisfied that its work was complete, handed the three tissue samples over to the human-like medics, who then placed them into three separate canisters before disappearing into the darkness again. Valinda was in so much pain, her eyes were watering and bulging red like she was ready to explode.

They slowly brought her back down, and as she lay still, unable to move, one of the human-like medics stood over her, scanning across her body with a device similar to the one Wilkes had used earlier to heal Eric. As it continued along, healing all the damage, the three-eyed being put out a last burst of mental energy and the next thing Valinda remembered was waking up the next morning, fresh to start a new day, although bothered by some terrible dreams of hovering owls and floating creatures.

"OK, Val, you are done, sweetie. When I count to 10 you will be completely awake and safe with us," Serena calmly whispered. Valinda had been shaking as she mentioned the final part of her experiences. *"1, 2, 3, 4, 5, 6, 7, 8, 9, and 10."*

Valinda snapped back, opened her eyes with tears flowing down her soft face, and looked over at Michael. The priest came over to her and held her in his arms.

"See, Father, I knew something evil happened to me."

Michael held her tighter and said, "I know, my dear, I know. It's going to be all better now, you will see."

Valinda glanced at Serena and gave her a little smile to indicate that she was happy that she had gone through it for closure. Serena winked and smiled back, just as Eric fell to the floor screaming in pain, covering his head with his arms.

STACEY'S
MESSAGE

A S ERIC WAS BEING LIFTED ONTO THE BED he just fell
from, he shouted out Stacey's name and continued doing so
repeatedly for the next half a minute. Then, silence. He just sat there
blank-faced, as if he was in a trance.

"Give him some space, guys," Serena said as they waited for him
to come out of it. Serena had seen this look a few times, although it
never lasted this long and he was never this quiet. There were always
movements and screaming along with it. Her nursing skills would not
be able to help him at that moment as she knew it was meant to be
happening.

"Stacey, his daughter, must be trying to communicate with him
again. We need to just wait until he's done."

Meanwhile, inside Eric's mind he was seeing nothing at the start
until light began streaming through and he was inside a small dimly lit
room with nothing else around him. Out of nowhere Stacey appeared
from the darkness. Eric ran over to her and held her in his arms so
tightly that it took a moment for Stacey to speak.

"I'm OK, Dad. How are you? You look better than you did on my
last visit," Stacey said, chuckling quietly.

Eric took a moment to respond.

"Where are you, I want to come and get you." He wasn't wasting any time. He needed to know. It had been his mission since the woods in Klamath and he wasn't going to stop.

"In time. You must listen to me very carefully. I'm glad you are now able to communicate with me, but time is short. You need to trust Wilkes. He is the only one you can trust. Do not go near his partner, I am hiding from him at the moment, but there is something else. There is a takeover of massive proportions, millions upon millions of human-looking things are in cylinders where I am and there are otherworldly creatures too. I can't explain much more than that at this moment, but these things, these grays, are sinister and not from another world but inter-dimensional, in-between worlds, waiting. You need to get the word out to everyone to prepare, but watch out, as you are being hunted as we speak. You need to get a message to Wilkes."

Eric stood there dumbfounded for a moment. He loved his daughter and trusted her with every fiber in his being, so he said, "Yes, of course. What is the message?"

Stacey grabbed his hand. She could feel the connection fading.

"Tell Wilkes I'm out of the room and lost, deep in the ship. He won't be able to find me unless you tell him that he needs to get back here as soon as possible to get me, as I don't know how much longer I have before I am caug—" As Stacey was finishing her plea to her father, she faded away.

Eric, still in the mind-grip, shouting out her name and looking around, was soon pulled out from it and sat up with a start saying her name one final time.

The group was just standing there looking at him, a little confused as to what he had seen, until Serena came over and wrapped her arm around his shoulder.

"Did you see her, Eric, is she OK?"

Eric jumped up and started making his way to the door, but then turned around, deciding to include the others in his new plan.

"We need to find Wilkes. Now. Stacey is in danger and everything we know here on Earth is in danger of being lost forever. I cannot explain any more than that until we get some answers from him now."

Eric waved his hand across the door switch and they all piled out into the corridor, heading to the right and running as fast as they could to a destination they had no idea how to get to.

After a minute or two of endless corridors, Eric said, "This is ridiculous, this place is like a maze. We need to stay together but in order to cover more ground faster, we are going to have to split up."

He looked over Valinda's shoulder and noticed the corridor close in and then open two new corridors. It seemed to be changing as they left one part and then entered another, before it changed again. Eric screamed in frustration.

"We need to find Wilkes now, and we have been here for who knows how long. We have to trust that there is a reason for all of this, so we have to go separately to look, not in twos."

Serena approached Eric to calm him down a little, glancing back at the other two and nodding. She took charge as she was good at it, and quietly said to Eric, "Leave it with me, sweetie. Just breathe, let me take it from here. I don't think it's a good idea to split up completely. We just don't know what is happening yet and until we do, we should at least stay in pairs, OK?" Serena had a way of soothing people. It was one of many skills she had.

Eric lifted his head, searched her eyes and smiled.

"OK. I don't know what I would do without you right now. You have been my saving grace."

"You can buy me a beer when it's over." She winked at him, then turned to the others and kept on with the plan. "OK, we will stay in pairs. Valinda and Michael, you two can go down the right hall, Eric and I will go down the left. Watch out for each other and stay close as we don't know what this place is doing right now, and we don't want to lose anybody in the process. Until we find Wilkes, we stick to our partners. Got it? Cool, let's go."

They all headed down their corridors. Looking back, Valinda and Michael saw theirs starting to vanish behind them as they walked. They picked up their pace so as not to get hit by the changing sections. Michael grabbed Valinda's hand.

"Come on, Val, keep moving, it doesn't seem far to the end of the corridor."

Suddenly Michael tripped on a loose shoelace and fell to the floor, breaking the link he had with Valinda's hand. Valinda was about to help Michael up, when a thin wall came out from the side and blocked the hall with a wall. She screamed.

"Father? Father, are you there?"

Nothing, not a whisper. They were separated, which they weren't going to do. It was like something was trying to separate them, she thought. "Why would a wall just come out there for no reason?" Nothing since she met these people had made any sense and Michael was the only person here she knew enough to really trust.

Resigned, she turned and continued walking toward her original destination and when she got to the end of the hallway, she looked both ways. There, again, were more empty hallways. Scared and frustrated, she chose the left corridor and walked that way. The same color theme continued all the way through, with lights that brought to mind a hospital, and that was all. Halfway down the corridor, she had a thought, "Why are we always trying to find new hallways when we should be checking along the walls for doors?"

Valinda slowly scanned along the sides of the corridor when a wall started coming across behind her. She saw what seemed like a small switch, and before the wall could fully block her off, she waved her hand over it. A door flew up. Valinda didn't hesitate. She ran into the room and the door snapped down behind her, leaving her in total darkness not knowing where she was, but at least safe from being sliced in two.

Valinda had her hands out on the wall, trying to find a light source. She heard a deep growl coming from the other side of the room. She stood there, frozen, hoping she imagined it, before hearing another deep growl, this time slower and longer. She was shaking. Before she could do anything else, she heard movement along with heavy footsteps slowly getting nearer.

She scampered around frantically trying to find the door access, but succeeded in finding the light control instead. As brightness filled the room and she turned to see what was there. When she gazed upon it, it let out a huge growling howl. Valinda screamed, fell backward from fright, and then hit the floor, passing out from shock.

REUNION
OF HOPE

AFTER WALKING THROUGH THE MAZE OF HALLWAYS and the never-ending sections of walls and lights, Serena and Eric finally made it to an opening where they could see people working on computers and rushing around like it was some kind of office or business section. They were both just glad that they were finally free of the maze.

As they entered the massive room, the last wall closed off behind them, leaving them exposed to the workers. In a bit of a panic, Eric scanned the figures hoping to find Wilkes, but instead was shocked to see some members of his WOSER team working frantically as if they had to meet a deadline of some kind.

"Hey, Simon," Eric called out, hoping he may have some answers to this whole nightmare.

"Eric, you finally made it. We have been waiting for you and the others for some time now. We've all been briefed, but I'm not able to explain anything yet. There are strict instructions to take you to Wilkes first. All I can tell you, though, is that all our work and theories have been put right to bed with the Sasquatch. All except yours, the one no one believed about being dimensional and not organic to the environment."

Simon would've kept going but another voice echoed out from the far side of the room where a narrow doorway showed a shadow outline of someone standing there giving orders.

"Thank you, Simon, that will be all for now. I think you have more important work to complete before day's end, am I right?"

Simon dropped his paperwork, startled that he had been caught giving out information that he was not supposed to just yet, but maybe more so due to the uneasy feeling of realizing he was being watched all the time.

Wilkes stepped out of the shadows of the doorway, still in his dark glasses, fedora, and black suit, although he didn't look as veiny now and seemed to be a little more relaxed.

"Eric and Serena, I am glad you are getting along and helping each other out, and more importantly, that you didn't succumb to the maze of walls," Wilkes said with a smirk before turning to walk back out of the room.

"Hey, where are you going? What was all that crazy stuff and why were we left in those rooms? You said you would give us answers. And I really need to tell—"

Before Eric could finish his rant, Wilkes cut him off.

"Come, it's time, please follow me."

As they walked to the doorway, Wilkes explained about the walls. This would be a first, Eric thought afterwards.

"I left you all to bond more, to help each other, which is what you are doing, because what is coming up will require all of your skills and compassion for each other to even attempt to succeed. Secondly there are some very, very dangerous rooms here, and things you aren't quite ready to see, if ever. So as a security measure, I initiated the herding walls to guide you back here without witnessing anything before I disclose everything."

Wilkes seemed to know the questions before they were asked, but there were some things that he didn't know, like Stacey's whereabouts. They entered the room and the door closed behind the three of them. It was not as large as the previous one, but it seemed to have a lot of technical equipment, sofas, whiteboards, and an array of racks with gray looking uniforms lined up from one end to the other.

"OK, take a seat and we will begin in a moment. Firstly, Stacey," Wilkes said looking at Eric, who was starting to get a little anxious not being able to relay the message about his daughter to him.

"I was unable to mind-blend with you at the time, though Agent Rovan filled me in about her escape from the safe room. Did she give you any information on where she is?"

Eric felt better now. He could finally start the process to find her.

"She said she is lost deep within the ship and that there are millions of cylinders with human-looking things in them. She needs you to get back there so you can find her and protect her." Eric repeated Stacey's message with a quiver in his voice.

Wilkes paused for a moment before snapping back to the conversation. "I'm sorry, Eric, I cannot go back there. Anders is after me and if I risk myself getting caught by him, his minions, or the Leader, I will be erased, and everything would have been for nothing. Stacey's fate would still be the same. I do have a plan for her, but I need you to find her again and relay a message back."

Wilkes was now back to his old mood, seemingly a little more annoyed and anxious than he was just moments before, giving the impression that getting this new information to Stacey was imperative.

Eric nodded. "Yes, of course, if it means saving her."

Wilkes looked at him deeply, sunglasses now off, as he opened a connection for both him and Stacey.

"What is the message?"

Wilkes knew Eric wouldn't like it, so he would keep that to himself until the last moment. "OK, Eric, I have opened a strong connection. I will relay the message as you are talking with her. First you must lie back on the sofa, get comfortable, and concentrate hard. Serena, can you please hold his hand."

Serena nodded and sat next to Eric.

"Whatever you do, Eric, don't break the link," Wilkes whispered as he positioned himself at the end of the sofa next to Eric's head.

Eric nodded, closed his eyes, and began to concentrate.

After a few minutes, Eric was getting a little frustrated. He was wondering why it wasn't working. He just had to trust Wilkes, though, as Stacey had said to him. After a few more moments, Eric started getting fragments of noise and screams. He could hear a female calling out, but similar to being on a phone that was out of range, he couldn't make out who it was or what they were saying.

Suddenly Eric grabbed his head, screamed in pain, and arched his back as the connection hit him like a wave of electricity. He was now standing in a corridor with dark walls, drips of liquid keeping cadence to the silence that surrounded him. He glanced around and could only see long corridors, not like the ones he had been in recently, but dark and foreboding. It was like something out of a horror movie.

Eric moved down the main hall where he could see what looked like cells. He kept going. The screams were back and getting louder. He knew straight away it was Stacey. He reached the room where the noise originated from. Peering around the entrance, he could see Stacey on the ground, screaming, as a small gray being with long arms and a bulbous head tried to drag her away by the ankles. He looked to his right and saw a massive lizard-like creature aiming a gun directly at another gray standing in front of him.

Wilkes had his hand on Eric's face and could see everything happening in his mind. Subconsciously he told Eric to walk over to the gray holding Stacey. The giant lizard-man stood completely still while the small creature was staring back at him, slowly shaking its head from side to side, like it had mesmerized the tall being.

Eric got to the first gray and as he put his hand on the back of its head like Wilkes had directed him to, a massive surge came through his fingers and the being fell to the ground, lifeless. Eric continued over to the other one, but before he could do anything, it released the lizard-man and turned to Eric, like he could see him. Its dark almond-shaped eyes started making blue, red, and green colors, waving back and forth through them both. It had started to control Eric, but before anything else could happen, Eric's hand came up, open palm facing the gray, and its head popped like a balloon, releasing an array of blue and green goop that redecorated the lizard creature's face.

Everything faded, leaving only Stacey and Eric in a darkened room together like the last time they talked.

"Are you OK, honey? What were those things? In fact, never mind, there's no time."

Eric was relieved that she was away from them but concerned about the lizard-man.

"I'm OK, Dad, thank you. And thank Wilkes for me as well, can you?" Stacey was still shaken, although unharmed.

"Are you safe with that lizard thing?" Eric snapped.

"Yes, Dad, he saved my life. He is a Draconian and his name is Vargzin."

Eric smiled. At least she had someone looking out for her, he thought.

"OK, well that's great, honey. Now I need to relay a message to you from Wilkes. He cannot come and get you as it's too dangerous."

Wilkes now took over the conversation, talking through Eric and using his voice.

"Stacey, I need you to listen very carefully. I need you to conduct a very dangerous mission, although one that will help us bring them all down."

Eric, without expression, was having to send his daughter into the worst part of the ship, without his prior knowledge and unable to stop it.

"OK. I'm scared though, Dad, but if this is how I can save you, then tell me, and I will try."

Stacey thought it was her father asking. Wilkes was very cunning in this mind-blend as getting Stacey to think it came from her father would make it easier.

"OK, you need to get to these coordinates on the ship, L17R72. There is a lift at the rear of the previous corridor that should lead you close to the spot. After you have gained access to the floor, you will need to kill the guards, then find your way to the room. In that room there are thousands of vials, which are all categorized by numbers and colors. I have put a special batch aside, colored red and numbered as the last lot 5000375621. You need to grab all seven of the vials and head back out. Leave the room and turn right. Rovan will meet you at the end of the corridor where he will escort you to one of the main control bays to the life pod cylinders. This is a restricted area and will be guarded. Once there, you need to administer all seven vials into the life pod conduits. That way the formula will run into the main storage vat and drip feed into each of the life pod cylinders. The Geno-drones that were added will replicate it as it runs its course so as to eventually reach the billion in stasis. This formula has your genomes in it, Stacey, and has been turned on. You do not want any of this on you or you may have the same reaction. Once it's in their system, it cannot be passed on. It will activate the very opposite sequence that they have been searching for all this time to save them. The rare genetic coding that can allow them to walk the Earth will eventually be their undoing."

Stacey looked at her father as she had worked out that it was Wilkes talking and not Eric. He was only just beginning to learn what was going on, and he wouldn't have had any details like that. But she went along with it.

"Lastly, Stacey, this is very important, no one must know this is happening. If you are found out they will flush the hybrids' cylinders and administer the last of the original booster. If this happens, there will be no more anti-vials left and they will begin the awakening, bringing all our mind-ripped souls awaiting bodies to enter the stasis life pods and start the process of releasing the new army of human hybrids. When you have completed the task, we will meet you at the rendezvous point at section 2, corridor 5 in the old abandoned medic lab where our team will be waiting for you. Keep quiet and stealthy and we will see you very soon. Oh, and there is a wall near the lift with storage built into it, which has a cache of weapons. Good luck, Stacey."

Wilkes left so Eric was able to communicate with her once again. He had witnessed the whole conversation and could barely contain his fury.

"You can't do this, Stacey, it's suicide!"

She took a deep breath. The numbers and codes were embedded inside her brain and before she could let the anxiety of the whole plan take over, she said to her father, "It's alright, Dad, it's the only way. We all have a part to play and I trust in Wilkes. I know you will be waiting for me, please just let me do it."

Eric didn't speak for a moment. He knew he had no choice, but he still had to try.

"OK, Stacey, as soon as I know what I'm doing I will come find you. Stay safe and I love you."

Eric disappeared before he could say anything else or hear Stacey's reply. As soon as the connection was broken, he passed out from the strain of Wilkes' interception. Blood seeped from his ears and nose and he convulsed until Wilkes, who was also somewhat exhausted from the ordeal, waved his "magic wand" over Eric's head and healed the pressure in his brain.

Eric stayed asleep for around half an hour. When he came to, he jumped off the sofa as if he'd been jolted from a dream into reality. He looked around. He had been placed in another room, on a similar sofa, but this room was huge and had hundreds of people in it. Some he knew from his team, but most he didn't.

He looked around again and there at the front of the crowd were Serena and Wilkes talking to Michael. Eric managed to get to his feet. Surprisingly, he felt good considering he nearly hemorrhaged earlier. As he got to the group, he noticed Valinda was missing.

"Where is Val? I can't remember seeing her when we arrived before," Eric said, the worry evident in his voice.

"Valinda is safe, she will be with us shortly. Now that everyone is in the room, it is time to begin."

Wilkes shuffled to the front near some high-tech computer gear, seeming to indicate he was just about to do a presentation of sorts.

Relieved, Eric looked at Serena and whispered, "Can this shit get any crazier or what?"

Serena smiled and with a wink replied, "I have a feeling this is only the tip of the iceberg."

Eric nodded. He turned and saw that the entrance to the room led out into a dark hallway.

"Can you see something there in the doorway?" Eric asked Serena with a hint of concern.

"Yes, I can, although it's too dark to make out."

Just as Serena finished speaking, Valinda walked through the door glancing behind her, with her right arm reaching back like she had just let go of someone's hand. As it was too dark to see, Eric and Serena didn't think anything of it, they were just glad she was safe and back with them.

"Hey, Val," Michael said, reaching over as he approached and gave her a hug. But he let go instantly. "Oh, dear Valinda, I'm not going to ask where you've been, but you do smell quite terrible." He held his index finger and thumb over his nose to close it.

"I hadn't noticed. It's a long story, though, which will be explained in Wilkes' lecture," Valinda informed them.

Serena smiled at her and Eric gave her a wink to show he was glad she was back safe and had got away from the crazy walls.

Wilkes started talking, however it wasn't just the people in the front row who heard him, as the sound spread across the room as if he had a microphone on.

"Please, ladies and gentlemen, take a seat and make yourselves comfortable. We will be here for a while, and though many of you have already been briefed on the upcoming information, I ask you to bear with me as it is a lot to process and you may have missed some things last time due to shock or the abundance of details presented. I have also put bags next to every chair for any sudden nausea that may come on. To those who have not been briefed, this is going to be extremely hard to hear at times, but I assure you it is all true. I also ask that all questions be raised at the end of the lecture so as not to distract me from my speech. Every layer is just as important as the other to gain an understanding. I have a 3D holographic floating screen that will help visualize some of the harder to understand sections. Lastly, I will show you all my true form. This may take some of you by surprise, so please brace for it," and as he said this Wilkes' human form melted away, leaving a tall, slender, hairless, gray-skinned being, exactly like the ones Valinda described, only much taller.

Serena and Michael both turned to Valinda straight away, concerned this image would cause flashbacks that would be devastating to her psyche.

Valinda just stared straight ahead and whispered to them both, "It's OK, I'm OK," not even turning her head or blinking. Something had changed within her, giving her a confidence or strength. Wilkes stood in front of the crowd surrounded by whispers and gasps. He grabbed a small device from the table in front of him, held it up, and as he let go, it stayed there, floating like it was made of only air. After a few seconds the room was illuminated with lights emanating from the device and a picture came up of a set of star systems, floating around the immediate area where Wilkes was standing. Everyone immediately grew quiet.

"Now, shall I begin?"

DARK
DISCLOSURE

THE HEAVY SILENCE WAS BROKEN as Wilkes began his long awaited explanation.

"We were a race of beings from a section of the universe known as Zeta Reticuli, a binary star system thirty-nine light years from Earth. Our planet was the fourth in line, called Aladoor. We are not 'grays' as we have been colloquially named, but are known as Zeytars throughout the universe, a peaceful race of beings dedicated to advancing technologies and exploring new and exciting worlds, including Earth. This was one of our favorite places and was a great source of scientific exploration for us, until our Leader at the time thought it would be a great exercise to see what would happen if we could start manipulating giant lizard DNA. After we started, the risks became too high and he thought it would be better for study if the big ones were gone. So he blasted the Earth. Although it worked and there were no more giant lizards, an overall extinction was also brought about as the blast was too powerful and killed nearly everything. This was the first abomination that would devastate your world.

"Our race has existed from its primitive form for two billion years, hence our evolution of advancement is overwhelming to try to understand, but I will do it as best I can with Earth terminology.

"The Leader who wiped out your ancient creatures was destroyed for his abominations and in our historical data, which we all carry inside us, we continued to be peaceful and helpful. It was especially noted that we did not visit your world again, to let it settle from what had happened. Over many millennia our scientists and Leaders became interested again and over time a clause was voted into our laws that we would help your world, not destroy it.

"Several thousands of years ago in Earth time, we started again, keeping low profiles and helping when we could with advancements in technologies and building monuments on different continents. We visited occasionally for a thousand years, burying tech so when you became more advanced, we would share it. This was until we were looked upon as gods and not sentient physical beings, which created some division at times, stemming from Leaders who wanted to take over your world.

"It was after this absence that the wars started. We had encroached on another world to gain knowledge and take some natives for our research, but when we were discovered doing this, it started the 'war of the zones.' We had made enemies with some of the most advanced civilizations in warfare, which were the Draconians. Then there were the more primitive, although intelligent, Mantids who hated everyone, and eventually many more who sided with the Dracs. Although our tech was too much and some of their worlds were destroyed, the Dracs fled and continue the search for us to finally get vengeance.

"We then started developing and testing out new devices to open portals to sneak into worlds without detection, as traveling was time-consuming and dangerous. The problem, though, was we were foolish enough to test this on our world and in doing so our planet was ripped in time and space, spiraling us into another dimension. A world between worlds or an inter-dimension if you like. But two things happened when this devastation occurred, and the second was the worst. Three quarters of our people were ripped apart. It was lucky that our mind essence was very strong, and they weren't lost forever. Those who survived could not communicate with them, as they were trapped in a higher vibrating zone which took us centuries to find and break through to allow the physical to commune with the ethereal energy. In that time, they had clawed their way back by opening rips and tears in the multiverse, gaining knowledge of other worlds, and eventually the bodiless ones learned to enter the physical realms and take over hosts. But it was Earth's physical plane they hungered for, as it was the closest to Aladoor and harbored the closest DNA constructs for a future body.

"Over time, our physical race dwindled. We would sleep in cycles for thousands of years at a time, leaving a Leader in charge overall, three masters, and twelve wardens to keep things on track, with a thousand drone workers rotating through. Our world turned desolate and we had to start opening small portals as food and water was running out. It was imperative that we do something, or our species would all be lost. Some decided to stay on other worlds, and we have distanced ourselves from those traitors.

"DNA manipulation, cloning, and experimentation was always a part of us but in time became one of two obsessions. We could clone ourselves, but our bodies could not survive in your environment over a long period of time. The other obsession was technologies, building craft, and finding ways to create devices to repair damaged tissue cells. Simple diseases could only be cured for short periods. We needed the perfect DNA.

"We became angry, violent, bitter, and twisted over time, enslaving creatures from other worlds to help with our plans. Eventually the bodiless ones became desperate and they tried to take human bodies to possess for takeover. This was to no avail as the human spirit is strong. Even though our essence was much stronger, they couldn't sustain it for long periods of time without damaging the human hosts, breaking their minds. We made allies with some and enemies with most, always working in secret with scientists on your world to develop our tech and build our ships and drones, until we finally finished a creation that would revolutionize our takeover.

"Hybrids.

"Our first human hybrids kept dying. Due to the mix of DNA, we still had no way of beating your simplest yet to us most complex diseases. We lost millions of our own bodiless minds, as once they entered the body, if it died so did they. That was until a geneticist found a genome that could solve everything by, once it was turned on, curing every single disease known to man. The only problem was that it was very rare, and we could not find many humans to extract it from as it needed to be manufactured for a billion hybrids.

"Our soldier drones were out abducting random people to see if they had the gene, but it was time-consuming and risky. Eventually the world was starting to take notice so we genetically modified a construct of the genome into some of our beasts which created a scent for it along with a key to the door, so to speak. The harmonics of DNA were programed at a certain frequency that when the beast let out a high-pitched scream, the frequency was set to open a doorway back to our dimension, keeping everything low key, virtually undetectable.

"We created these beasts from a creature you once called Gigantopithecus who roamed the Earth over one hundred thousand years ago. We have a complex and quite detailed amount of DNA from our long history of visitations, so we experimented on many of these until we perfected it at the beginning of our first hybridization programs. We adapted it in more modern times after we started searching for this particular genome. Once we realized we had a body that would sustain all our waiting people, we got to work creating hybrids that looked human but also had all the neurological upgrades to sustain our intelligence.

"Thrusting us into the twentieth century, where our agenda had been well and truly on its way, we were still abducting subjects, however more discreetly and only for crossbreeding and implanting Geno-drone chips to start getting government officials and more scientists on board. The crossbreeding was deliberate to create aberrations that would help to spy and send back information for our agents when they started getting close to truths and disclosure. You labeled them black-eyed children, although we like to call them our skin pets. They never lived past sixteen due to diseases. We were also responsible for MKUltra and all the subsidiaries of this to make people conform to our will. Although great in theory, it had negative effects on some brains with the drugs given at the time. We had not realized the human brain was so frail. Eventually, we started having some power in governments and as we encroached into the CIA even further, we found it easy to manipulate and control who or what we wanted, trying to cover up all the reports and witnesses behind our agenda. There were several of us agents, although it was only Anders, Xandar, and me who knew everything and eventually it would be Anders and myself to initiate any consequences for those leaking truth. We had our spies everywhere.

"We knew this would be hard, so as we infiltrated governments with our control chips and began releasing propaganda, from Roswell being a hoax, up to the discrediting of sightings and experiences with Project Blue Book, the Montauk Project, and the falsifying of Majestic 12 or Majic-12 as it is also known. We let some things slide. We kept everyone busy with wars and civil unrest among the population along with disease, hunger, and false alien agendas. We also polluted the air and your bodies with chemtrails as you call them. All your vaccines and water systems, as well as the abductions, led to our Geno-drone technologies lying dormant inside all your bodies, awaiting the global switch."

Eric had grown angry. He wanted so bad to hurt Wilkes but knew it was a bad idea. He needed clarification on the global switch.

"The global what and Geno-whats? You destroyed your world and now you want to do the same to ours? I feel sick."

Wilkes turned to Eric, not happy he was interrupted.

"Yes, I'm getting to all of your answers. When I'm finished and you need a question answered, I will do it then. Now, can I go on?"

Eric sat back with his arms crossed, fuming but hoping for some better news.

"The Geno-drones are the microscopic single cell metal organisms created by us to work together to control all of you. When you receive enough over time in your system, they lie dormant in your body, camouflaged until the global switch is turned on. The global switch is when our Leader is ready, and once turned on, every single Geno-drone cell will come together inside the body creating a tiny multicomplex cellular chip, just like the one Valinda had. Then we activate it. Once they are on, the Leader can control every single human being on Earth for his own doing."

Eric lowered his head in disgust, saying under his breath, "Son of a bitch!"

Wilkes didn't blink in his emotionless grayish body. Not even the two tiny nostril holes quivered. The creature seemed to have a resting angry facial expression, though, with his hairless brow naturally angled over his huge black almond-shaped eyes, so whether he was indeed angry, no one would ever know. He continued with his disclosure.

"It gets worse, I'm afraid. Your military will be under our control and we have managed finally after all these years to infiltrate enough of your government to arrange the weapons bans, making it now impossible to fight back."

Silence in the room.

Wilkes continued.

"Now, about the Leader. He is in the control facility on the mother ship and has been there for twenty years. No one has seen him, although we are all connected to the hive, so we hear from him at times. He is overseeing all the hybrids in life pod stasis, communicating everything through a system of conduits directly to their brains in the billion cylinders. He is like a central computer uploading data and getting them ready for Zero Time, which is the time they wake.

"The Leader has been far too busy to worry about anything here on Earth, as he has instructed the three of us to handle it. I have blocked myself from the hive, a technique I acquired from MKUltra that the others could not and do not know about. This has enabled me to do things without their knowledge. I have also put blocks on Anders and Xandar, which has been instrumental in getting this rebel group organized. I will elaborate more on that later. First, I need to explain the most horrific part of our agenda, the one that will be the biggest struggle to defeat if that's at all possible. This is V.I.Z.I.N.D.A.L.E.X.!"

Still no one made a sound. Wilkes had his holographic hand device ready again for the next part of his disclosure, about the unstoppable android. He showed the hologram in color as he spoke.

"The problem was, in order to get all our massive ships and bases into your world without destroying ourselves, we had to create a rip from our dimension to yours. Only the smaller ships could come through as the rips needed a lot of power due to the vibrational sequence changes and magnetic fields making them unstable. This, at least, allowed us to come into your world and slip back whenever we wanted. We could open them to come through and they would close back again, like a portal although less stable. Problems have arisen lately as more and more of us are tearing into your world. Some of the tears are staying open longer and our bodiless Zeytars have been coming through to cause fear in some people who are disclosing truths, like you, Valinda. They could follow you through the Geno-drone you had inside you by lowering their vibrational states which they had learned to do over time.

"So, two hundred years ago we started on a project that would allow us to keep the door open on your world while we opened it on ours. Big enough and long enough for our entire fleet to come through at once, which lowered the risk for reprisal. Eventually, after putting everything into it, we created V.I.Z.I.N.D.A.L.E.X. just in time.

"All who worked on it were killed after its completion. The remaining few who knew it existed were myself, Anders, Xandar, and the Leader, Xandar being primarily responsible for it. In 1947, what you know to be the Roswell Incident was true, however with a twist. We set the android down on Earth and it was spread out to be camouflaged with the actual debris of the saucer that we sacrificed. Unaware of this, your military took it and there it waited in Area 51 in a secret vault for over seventy years. When the Leader is ready, he will turn it on and begin the countdown.

"The V.I.Z.I.N.D.A.L.E.X. is a:

Virtual
Intelligence
Zero-Time

Inter-dimensional
Nanotech
Droid
Activating (high)
Levels (of the)
Electromagnetic (field)
X-Clock.

"I will break this down as it's very important. It is a 'virtual intelligence,' however, it is also an 'artificial intelligence.' The virtual side keeps it on its mission without distraction from the AI, but it is a learning machine, adapting and researching human behaviors to stay hidden and act out its mission.

"Next is 'Zero-Time.' This is when it reaches its destination and opens the door from this side. The next part may be somewhat confusing. It is an 'inter-dimensional' machine so it can vibrate on all levels and enter another world as a physical entity, adapting to most conditions. This will sustain it from breaking apart when the doorway opens.

"It's made up of three different types of nanotechnologies, as you would say on Earth: Geno-drones, Medi-drones, and the state of the art Inteli-drones. We tend to use only Geno-drones to explain all of them, for example: The Geno-drones as I have discussed are the microscopic metal Nanos that sit dormant in millions of pieces inside a host. Once turned on, they come together in the body to form one very tiny chip that can communicate with the hive and control or manipulate one's thinking. It is a highly functioning piece of tech that if used in multiples can create a symbiosis like the X-Clock.

"Then there are the Inteli-drones. They are the smartest piece of tech out there as they communicate with the Geno-drones and Medi-drones to make sure the workings of the X-Clock stay functioning and that it is on its path at all times. If there is damage to the machine, the Inteli-drones inform the Medi-drones. It's like centillions of tiny brains that work in symbiosis with the others, learning as they go, giving the X-Clock its neurological self-awareness and learning abilities.

"Lastly the Medi-drones, which are the medical Nanos that can manipulate DNA and copy tissue to heal nearly any kind of trauma. Although they cannot grow bone, they can heal it. On the other hand, if someone is dead, they cannot bring them back if the drones are in small numbers, like in the hand held devices we use or if the person's brain has been inactive for more than twenty minutes. In the X-Clock's case, they are the Nanos that copy DNA and fix flayed skin onto the android's external casings. When the skin starts to fall off, they can fix the damage. All three types of 'drones' work together making the X-Clock a very powerful machine.

"Geno-drone is the terminology used for all different types of Zeytar nanotech. They can break apart into centillions of pieces and build their way back to form the full android, changing shape on its body to form solid weaponry for self-defense.

"The next part of the name is self-explanatory. It is a 'droid', or 'android' to be specific, looking as human, or in human form, as possible, which was key for it to remain incognito.

"The next three terms are how it activates high levels of the electromagnetic field in our environment to gain power, and when it comes time to open the doorway, most of the power in ripping into worlds is electromagnetic.

"The last part of the name explains what its mission is. It is called an X-Clock, X being the final destination it needs to be in before Zero Time, or the opening of the doorway. The android has three clocks on its body—two where the pecs or breasts would be on its chest, and one larger one in the center of its abdomen, as you can see here. Once the droid is woken, the clocks start, whirring and ticking along with a precision that is flawless. They are incredibly intricate and as they whir and count down, the closer to Zero Time they get, the stronger the android becomes. One clock will stop when it reaches a power milestone, then it internally alarms the droid and it sends a signal to the Leader. Then the next one will do the same until it's down to the final clock, which is so detailed it was designed by the best Zeytar chronometers.

"We have an idea where it will be heading as we started work early on a Superconducting Super Collider in Waxahachie, Texas. It was shut down during development to distract the attention of protests. However, it is very much in operation and bigger than the Large Hadron Collider near Geneva. It's ready for the android to arrive. As soon as the last hybrid is completed and given the serum, all our awaiting souls will begin transference into their new bodies. Then an alarm will ring, activated by the Leader in response to a silent signal from V.I.Z.I.N.D.A.L.E.X., or ALEX as I call it, and everything will start counting down from the ship."

Wilkes had shown the whole makeup of the droid on his hologram. Now he searched the faces in the room. There was complete silence. Even members of WOSER who had already been briefed were still flabbergasted by hearing such a far-out story, one that would even have science fiction readers scratching their heads.

"Are we all OK?"

Serena turned and threw up in the supplied nausea bag. Eric rubbed her back and tried to make her feel better although he felt the same. Valinda wasn't as shocked, with all she had been through. With all the stories and information she had received over the years, she was probably the best prepared out of the whole lot of them, though Michael didn't bat an eyelid.

"Now, questions?" Wilkes reluctantly asked.

"So why *you*? Why are you the 'good guy' and trying to help us? By the sound of the story, you could just be creating another diversion to prevent us from stopping all of you," Eric snapped.

"You are right, it could all well be a good diversion. So, I ask you this, why did I save you, why did I save all of you, why did I save Serena when she was a child, and connect you to your daughter for warnings, healing, and so on? I know you are angry, but I am on your side and I will tell you why."

Wilkes, in his humanoid form now, pulled out a chair and sat down to explain his role in it all.

"I have seen the most horrific things done to this world, to good people going about their business not interested in hurting anyone else, just raising their family and working hard. I have had to be a part of killing, maiming, mind destroying and other unspeakable acts over my time. Being partnered with Anders took its toll. Around one hundred and twenty years ago I was working with a female scientist on the android. She was controlled by the Geno-drone, but I told her more than she was supposed to know, especially after I took the chip out. I tested her by turning it off and explaining everything to her. She was so open about it that we built a connection and the hive tapped in and found out. After she had finished her part on the project, Anders took great pleasure in slowly killing and dismembering her."

Wilkes lowered his head before returning to his story.

"I swore after that happened that I would dedicate myself to destroying the agenda, so I learned techniques and created my own chip to block myself when required, from the others and from the hive. I am far more superior in the mind control field than any other Zeytar out there. Even the Leader struggles to be at my level at times. I was ready to give myself to this cause, and in the process, I have been waiting for the right people to come along and help me. It's been so hard still having to watch and act out some of Anders' destructively violent acts to silence people. He has grown ever more twisted, spending too much time in other dimensions and creating abominations and beasts to do his dirty work, while he watches on like it gives him pleasure. Before my last act, I wish, if anything, to see him gone for good."

Wilkes paused again, seemingly exhausted from all the years of waiting and working toward this moment.

"I have been around humans and seen more good in people than in any other species I have come across, and I feel we have no right to do this, even if it means the destruction and extinction of our species. I wish to eventually build back our race of peaceful Zeytars. I hope that this is enough now to gain your complete trust. We do not have much time and we have to plan our defensive attack before they find out."

They were all intently staring at Wilkes, affirming their support. Even Eric now was a convert after hearing that, although he was still wary.

"This concludes the first part of my lecture. I will answer anyone's questions if they feel they need to talk to me privately. Now onto the next and most important part."

As the hologram shut down, Wilkes turned to the doorway and called out, "LVI738319, come out now, it is time."

Wilkes stood there staring into the darkened doorway where there was some obvious movement, although nothing was coming through. Wilkes shouted out again, this time with a little more assertion, "Come, LVI, these people want to meet you, we are all looking forward to it."

Again nothing, a tiny hiss and groan, then no movement. Wilkes was obviously getting annoyed. Even though he could communicate without words directly with it, he wanted to be more human in his approach.

"Let me, Wilkes."

Everyone in the room now looked directly at Valinda. Michael was more shocked than anyone.

Wilkes responded swiftly, "Yes, perfect, thank you, Valinda. It seems our friend is a little shy today."

Valinda stood up and made her way to the darkened doorway where she stretched out her right hand and whispered, "It's OK, Levi, come with me. These are our friends and I want you to meet them. Wilkes, can you please lower the lights just a little more, he may be a little overwhelmed."

Wilkes hadn't even thought of that. He lowered the lights enough that it wasn't pitch dark but took the edge off the brightness of the room, still allowing everyone to see clearly.

"Come on, it's OK," Valinda said in a kind, soft voice once again, and then her hand was met with another and they both entered at the same time.

Eric jumped up upon seeing who it was and flew into a rage, before he was stunned by Wilkes knocking him out. The visitor screamed and took off down the corridor with Valinda right on its heels, leaving everyone sitting there in stunned silence.

MALEVOLENT
METAL

SEVENTY THREE YEARS AFTER IT settled in a sealed bunker at Roswell, without a twitch, buzz or whir, "ALEX" turned on. It was different now. Something had changed. As all the Geno-drones turned on, it slowly transformed into the humanoid android shape it had been all those years earlier. Without a blink or grunt, like a freshly well-oiled machine it stood in the dark waiting until the last of its symbiotic friends took their posts, then its eyes turned blue like it had just woken up from a deep sleep, lighting the whole bunker around it.

As it made its way over to the door where it had sealed itself in, it lifted its hand and five long knife-like nails extended out, cutting through the solid bunker like it was made of soft butter. Dropping the last of the shredded door to the ground, the android looked around, taking in all the changes that had occurred over the years and updating its neuron processor by scanning the whole area. This took no more than a few seconds.

ALEX was always sentient, but now it was on a mission and all the cogs, hands, and fine clock pieces were moving, like someone had wound it up and turned the clock on. They were whirring in sequence, although the hands were not pointing to any Earth time. It was set to other symbols not used on this planet, counting down to something, with each clock set for different times. The middle, largest clock had parts going one way with a deeper level going another way, and so on, with its hands moving at a slower pace. The other clocks were timers for the main central clock.

ALEX moved forward from the bunker. It was now ready to leave that level and start on its mission. As it made its way to the lift, a guard who had just started his shift noticed the robot walking toward him. As he stared into its eyes, the guard froze in fear. V.I.Z.I.N.D.A.L.E.X. had only one mission and was programed for that. Anything else was a distraction and deemed expendable. No guard, employee, human, hybrid, or AI knew about the X-Clock android. Only the three master grays and the Leader were privy, making it the biggest secret of the whole agenda as it was the most important part. That's why the agents worked so hard to cover it up all those years ago, and still to this day, because if V.I.Z.I.N.D.A.L.E.X. failed, so did the end plan.

The guard raised his firearm when he saw ALEX. But the droid moved so swiftly toward the soldier that before he could fire a shot, ALEX had its right hand inside the soldier's abdomen, thrusting it deep within his body and moving up into his chest until it finally found his heart. Gripping it tight, it pulled hard and fast, ripping it out. The droid held the still pulsating and quivering organ up close for inspection as the soldier's last wail ended and his lifeless body slid down the wall.

ALEX threw the heart on the floor and examined the corpse. It knelt down next to the body and scanned the name tag which read Private Evan Hicks, then ripped it off. The tag melted into its hand. Then the droid's index finger molded into a long needle device as it pointed at Hicks' face. A thin red laser emanated from the needle and sliced around the outer edges of the face until it had completed a full cut. With the precision of a surgeon, it peeled away Hicks' face until ALEX had it in its hand, like a thick piece of tissue paper flopping to the movements of the android. The device turned from a precision laser cutting tool back to a finger and ALEX placed the facial skin onto its own robotic face. It waited while all the Medi-drones programed as part of the makeup of the machine molded the flayed skin to become a physical DNA-blended match over the android's face, looking like

Hicks' head on a robot's body, even using micro tech to genetically modify eyes using DNA from Hicks' own blood.

Anyone who knew the soldier, wouldn't have even been able to tell the difference, except for the fact that the rest of ALEX was still an exposed X-Clock machine without hair. But after resizing itself to fit, it put on Hicks' uniform and hat, so the robot looked completely like the soldier.

The last thing to finish it off was to place the name tag back in its place. ALEX didn't place it on itself. Rather, it appeared from its body, pushing out of the uniform, and settled into position, as the last of the machine's tiny workers fixed the fabric and blended the blood stain so no one would be the wiser. ALEX then lifted its head, satisfied with its new disguise for now, and continued up into the lift to the surface.

The doors opened on the ground floor. Taking in its new surroundings, ALEX noticed several guards dressed like Hicks, although heavily armed. It scanned the area, picking out each soldier one by one, even reading the details of the faces, skin, clothing, and more importantly, weapons, like it was trying to build itself a database for future reference. As an Artificial Intelligence it was designed to learn, adapt, and create self-awareness, so as to protect itself for the completion of its primary programing. Its Virtual Intelligence kept it on track without letting it divert off the mission for any reason at all.

ALEX moved toward the first soldier. Before it could do anything, though, another soldier came running over to the android shouting, "Why aren't you at your post, soldier? You have only been there for a half an hour and it is the primary post. I have had orders from high government departments that you haven't even heard of stating the importance of watching for any movement coming in or out of that area, so get your ass back down the hole now!"

After the soldier finished screaming at ALEX, the android looked directly at the officer and nodded its head, before lifting the officer by his neck and snapping it like a twig. The sound could be heard down the end of the hall.

Staring in disbelief, the first soldier, Corporal Damien Ventrice, yelled, "Are you crazy, Hicks? That was the Lieutenant! you've just killed the frikin Lieutenant!"

ALEX turned to Ventrice and as it lifted its right arm, the skin glove on its hand disappeared revealing the silver blue metal of its own body. The hand turned into a long five-way prong with all its fingers now knives. They pierced Ventrice's head as if it was a watermelon, which then exploded.

As the soldier dropped to the ground, convulsing until his final nerves lost all signals, ALEX moved toward the next two, who were now spraying the android with multiple rounds from machine guns until they emptied both. They were reloading when ALEX pounced on them like a panther on a deer, ripping the first one's throat out before turning onto the second soldier, Private Lesley Dawson, and driving both arms into his chest cavity. The soldier had nearly finished reloading his gun right before the sting and pain of the android reaching deep into his body and pulling out a lung, together with some other internal pieces vital for life. Dawson looked at who he thought was his friend Hicks with eyes wide open. The confusion would follow him into darkness.

The last man standing just stared. After witnessing what his colleague had just done to all his friends, he didn't know what to do himself. "Do I shoot, or do I run?" were the thoughts traveling through his mind. Time was running out, though, and a decision had to be made for he would surely end up the same as the others. The soldier, shaking but confident, slowly placed the gun on the ground. He then placed his hands in the air as he knelt.

Corporal Scott Mulver had been at this location for less than two years and was always told that if anything unusual happened they were soldiers first and answers would be last, if they came at all, so he knew he was now on his own.

ALEX moved ever closer, with the vague look of Hicks as his mantle.

Mulver said calmly, "Hicks, hey, remember last week when we were chatting up those girls from the Desert Inn, remember, pal?"

The soldier lowered himself even more. He knew what this place was, even though they were all told it wasn't what they thought. They all had to sign disclosures and were all told never to ask questions or to go anywhere classified, which was a good portion of the fortress. The stories that had been told over the years through whispers of ex-soldiers and workers featured horrors ranging from creatures running loose to ghostly alien beings and other abominations. They were clear in Mulver's mind and he knew this was one of those stories playing out now. To survive, he thought he needed to talk, keep speaking calmly, without violence or aggression.

"What about that time we played football and you slipped on the ice, do you still have that scar?"

Mulver noticed a change in the pace of the rogue soldier. It was slowing, as if his friend Hicks was remembering, and as his friend was now right upon him, Mulver started to smile. But as he did this, ALEX grabbed the soldier's hair, lifted him up into the air, and opened its own mouth wide releasing a silver cord that pushed through Mulver's lips, breaking some teeth in the process, and ventured down into his body.

Mulver tried to scream and breathe at the same time, swaying violently to try and break free—to no avail. His so-called friend was very strong and as the cord made its way back up from his lower intestines, it switched direction and pierced Mulver's brain. Spreading tiny microscopic nerve-sized cords all the way around his cerebral cortex, it sucked all the information out of his skull, harvesting his memories and all other data it needed.

Before Mulver died, he saw a blue light glowing deep inside Hicks' eyes. ALEX retracted the cord back into its own mouth, ripping half of Mulver's jaw off from the force so the soldier was left looking like a zombie.

ALEX took no more time than needed to finish what he was doing and left Mulver in a lifeless mess on the ground, bleeding and drooling over the floor, eyes open wide. The android stepped over his handiwork and continued to the front entry point of the fortress where it would face the biggest challenge since it awoke.

Minutes later ALEX was at the entrance. The Geno-drones were working hard to repair the damage to the uniform and to make the droid look like the normal soldier it was supposed to be. The disguises were new to ALEX, just like everything was at this early stage of its mission. There would be errors and learning, but the end result was the most important thing. It wasn't bothered about lives, or whether it would be on the six o'clock news that night. The mission's success was the only thing it cared for. But learning more about human behavior and avoidance techniques would make the path much smoother for the android at the end of the day. Therefore, the priority, as part of its programing, was to at least try to maintain some sort of invisibility to the best of its own ability, and it would become better at this as "time" ticked on.

The door opened and there were at least a hundred soldiers standing there with machine guns all pointing at ALEX.

"Get down, son, now!" a voice echoed from the front of the containers giving the soldiers cover. Before ALEX could react, the soldier yelled out again, "You better move, kid, because there's something coming this way and you are right in its firing line."

ALEX had no human emotions. Even though it was an Artificial Intelligence, it hadn't built up enough to engage, so the robotics were still making it expressionless. After sucking all the information from Mulver's cerebral cortex, it was now processing that knowledge fast and using it as data, like a program being uploaded to a computer. The only flaw with this was that while it learned, its behavior would be jerky and over the top, like a glitch.

It processed all the files into categories to pull from when required, dropping the emotional side out and deleting irrelevant files as it did this. Even though it was a highly sophisticated piece of equipment, it was taking more time than anticipated, because humans were complex systems of knowledge, emotions, and memory.

ALEX started running, then it stopped, fell to the ground, opened its mouth, and tried to scream. By now all the soldiers were looking at who they thought was Hicks. Some snickered and some were just shocked, thinking this was not how a soldier should act.

The General had received information from security that no vision from cameras was available, only noise, probably due to interference of some sort. He was constantly getting updates. The alarm was sounding all over the base and more soldiers were coming out of every door.

Seconds after ALEX's outburst, the files were sorted and the android stood up, turned to the General who had shouted out the orders, and said, "Sorry, sir, I tripped. Please help, it is coming after me."

All the soldiers who knew Hicks were stunned. The voice was Mulver's not Hicks'. Hicks had a slight accent and his voice was deeper. Mulver was from the south and had a very distinct way of speaking. The flaw would be a costly one for the android.

The officer yelled, "Fire with everything you've got! Get those electrons on it! Get the flamethrowers on it! Get that thing down now!"

What General George Branton would soon learn was that sometimes top secret meant TOP SECRET and the next course of fire would do very little. But very little damage to ALEX physically could still cause great damage. Not to its systems, but to the timing of its mission. Every single second counted, and there was hardly any room for delays. By Earth time standards there would only be a leeway of a day in reaching its Zero Time, which was calculated and factored into the probability of success of its mission.

ALEX was swimming in endless streams of bullets, fire, and electrons. As Hicks' flesh burned off its face and the uniform turned to ash revealing its raw shiny humanoid physique, ALEX just stood there. Of course, it was taking in all the rounds and the electrons. But what the General and all his minions didn't realize was that the more electricity it took in, the more power it would get. As an electromagnetic energy source, ALEX sucked it all in like it was breakfast and once full, the circular clock at its front started spinning like a dryer at top speed. A blue light swirled from it, as ALEX lifted its arms out like it would be a conduit for its surroundings. A hurricane of electricity and blue fire emanated from its middle and the ends of its hands. Its center core started spinning at the top twisting its body so fast it was now just a whir of blue light. All anyone could see were its legs standing as still as a stone.

The soldiers were burning and falling. Their bodies were disintegrating and being blown to pieces, along with the weapons. The buildings that made up the complex exploded and as the power from the android became increasingly stronger, the whole fortress crumbled beneath it, leaving ALEX in mid-air from the force of the power it was exuding, like a small nuclear weapon had been set off. Once satisfied it had obliterated everything it intended to, it began changing back into its android form, using the last of its power to hover upward out of the deep pit it had created.

ALEX hit the dirt hard when landing right next to the rim of the destructive hole. It was so close to the edge that it had to send out a range of spears from its fingers to pierce the dirt, holding it back from the pit. Nothing would escape a hole such as that, and with no power left in the tank, this preventative maneuver had been necessary. ALEX surveyed its handiwork. The pit went for miles, with dust and smoke billowing out of the canyon and across the skies. Its program kicked in as it turned and headed into the desert and on to its mission, without a second thought or any remorse about what had happened.

≈

ALEX had been walking for hours. Its navigational systems were all in check and it was on its way to receive final instructions from its minder, Agent Xandar. There it would find out where exactly it needed to be for its final act to play out. In order to get there on time, it would need to stay focused on its destination. As each time milestone edged closer to the final countdown, the clocks over its body would signal the Leader. Once each clock reached its time, it would stop until the next time milestone, and then that one would signal and stop, until the last clock in its center would be the final countdown to Zero Time. Once this happened, the droid's power capacity would be at full unlimited charge and its mission to bring about the end would begin.

The clocks were so sophisticated that even when ALEX was in destructive mode at Area 51, its clocks had not vanished, but were hidden internally up in its core matrix system until it reverted to its original state. They were still counting down and without missing a beat the clocks would still work at power-downs and even in major blasts.

The extensive workings and precision, along with the defensive systems, power consumption, and pure intelligence of the android's neurons with the Geno-drones, made ALEX the Zeytars' most complex and pure piece of machinery that had ever been designed and created. They had always been known for their tech, but this was beyond anything else, and had been researched, designed, and built by the best minds over a long, long time.

≈

ALEX was now well clear of the devastating aftereffects of the previous events. Without any new information coming from the hive or from Xandar, its mission was in jeopardy of failure and that was something that it would not let happen. Every single event had been planned and it was programed to trust in its creators to pass on the last of its uploads.

As the desert wind whispered and swirled around the android, a bright light appeared over the night sky. ALEX knew immediately what it represented and as it lifted its metallic face up to the sky, a green light hit the ground like it had escaped the vessel that hovered above. The light switched to a light blue color and then disappeared completely, leaving a tall, slender Zeytar standing in front of the droid.

Without a sound, the large diamond-shaped craft turned on its multicolored side lights to scan for danger, not realizing a scan had already been completed by ALEX. The lights stopped, and now only one was visible, just enough to illuminate the two figures that were standing facing each other.

Xandar walked over to ALEX and without any expression from his bulging eyes and massive forehead said, "V.I.Z.I.N.D.A.L.E.X., you are ready. I knew a day earlier. The Leader only mentioned it to me as there has been some major conflict with Wilkes, who is now a deserter, this is why you have awoken earlier than expected. Anders is dealing with the betrayal as we speak. We informed our brethren from Area 51 and they were taken out of the facility just before you awoke. The hybrids and humans left were expendable. I have come to inform you of your destination for Zero Time."

Although ALEX didn't or couldn't smile, there was a change in energy, whether it was his way of smiling or due to acceptance of this new information it had been waiting for.

Xandar moved even closer to ALEX and using his long slender index fingers started sliding and pressing symbols over its body, coding into its systems the final programing it needed. This was the destination. Xandar poked, pressed, and slid the unusual array of weird shapes, swirls, cosmic numbers, and binary coding for minutes, before ALEX said in a deep robotic voice, "Waxahachie, Texas, Superconducting Super Collider."

Its default voice sounded eerie to even Xandar. It would only be used to communicate with any of the masters and the Leader. Well, most of the masters, as Wilkes was now on its list as number one to destroy if in the vicinity.

"Yes, now calibrate and synchronize. I need to tell the Leader how long it will take you."

ALEX's eyes turned bright blue. It was internally calculating with its GPS and the length of time before the clocks ran out to determine a pace to set to reach his destination in time for the Leader to turn on the machine from his end. Then, after a pause of a few seconds, the android's eyes went back to a silver color.

"Why can I not reach the hive or the Leader?"

Xandar responded swiftly, as he knew he had forgotten to explain something to it. "Sorry, the Leader disconnected you from the hive completely in response to the deserter and his rogue helpers. The less information they have, the more likely our mission will be successful. It has become known that they are disclosing to the world all our plans with real evidence and are gaining quite a big following, with people preparing themselves for an attack. So even though we have the upper hand with the global switch and all the humans being under our control, in the meantime, until both the doors are open, the switch can't happen and they can retaliate. It is why we destroyed Area 51 so no military will be close enough to tell anyone of your destination. Let us handle the deserters and you concentrate on the end game."

ALEX didn't seem to care. It had its mission set now and it was time to fulfill it.

"Seven hours at maximum pace with an error margin of two hours and thirty-five minutes, making final calculation before Zero Time to be nine hours and thirty-five minutes from now," ALEX explained.

This was the most important information in the universe to the Zeytars right now and only Xandar knew it. The Leader had already started preparing the billion hybrid Zeytars. The only thing he was awaiting was the Zero-Time signal from ALEX. Knowing the precise moment was imperative, so that he could connect the door without delay.

Xandar seemed happy with this last meeting. He had spent over seventy years protecting this machine and helping with the cover-ups and disinformation to pave the way for these events. There was only one more thing to do, he thought.

"Here, V.I.Z.I.N.D.A.L.E.X., you are too exposed for now. Until you can find another source of disguise, this will cover you."

Xandar handed over a plain white mask with only two eye holes and a mouth slit to cover its face, along with a long black cloak and hood to cover its body, and a pair of gloves. ALEX took the items. The mask went on first and the Geno-drones did their part in syncing it to its face. It then put on the gloves and the hooded cloak, while the Geno-drones did the rest by darkening its legs and any exposed parts, mimicking the cloak color. This would allow it to hide in dark places and stay out of sight until it was in a more built-up area.

The deserter's spies were out there now trying to find it and any exposure was too risky. Xandar wanted so much to just take ALEX with him on the ship and drop it at the site; however, the Leader's plans all along were quite specific. ALEX had been designed and programed for this task and any deviation from the mission could put everything in danger. If Xandar was to take it to the location and someone blew the collider up searching for it, then to find another power source close enough and in the same time frame would result in the doors not syncing in time, stranding them all in their dimensions.

The other reason was that it was a learning machine and after the doors were open it would play another major part in the Leader's plans, so it was required to learn. Lastly, its mission was to count down, and while counting down it would build its power continuously, moving forward and gaining momentum. There was no collider there seventy years ago, and it was built in that spot to make ALEX's mission accessible and without too many witnesses.

Xandar took another long look at ALEX, turned around, and walked back to where the original beam had sent him. A green light once again lit the ground and Xandar entered the beam and disappeared up into the craft where he would notify the Leader of the progress. The ship changed shape to a large saucer before taking off at high speed into the night and vanishing inside a bright flash of red and blue electricity.

ALEX started on his new path, each moment getting closer to reaching the Superconducting Super Collider, where the beginning of the end for humans would be waiting.

IMPOSSIBLE MISSION

STACEY AND VARGZIN HAD BEEN in the room for ages. Even though it was only hours, it felt like days. Stacey was getting anxious and restless as she wanted to do something. Vargzin said he had a plan, but he had been meditating for most of that time.

Stacey was constantly hungry, barely surviving on disgusting rations that Vargzin had in his satchel. "I could kill everyone in the ship just for a hamburger," she thought. "Hey, maybe that kind of thinking is actually going to help me," she quipped. Her energy levels were now very depleted and with the number of soldiers out looking for her, she really needed something to eat soon.

Vargzin was still deep in meditation when Stacey thought it would be a great idea to go and look for some food. She quietly snuck out of the end room and started on down the hall to see if there were other rooms that may hold what she was after.

As she was nearing the first room on the left, she lifted her gaze to see two small gray beings rummaging around in some debris. Stacey froze like a statue. She slowly stepped back with one foot, hoping like crazy they wouldn't glance in her direction. But when her foot hit the floor, it made a loud crack as she stepped on broken glass.

The Zeytars both looked up together and made a beeline for her as she broke into a run. Stacey shouted out at Vargzin to wake up, and when she got back to the room she saw the startled Drac was already on his feet with the gun aimed at the door. Stacey ran in but suddenly tripped over a fallen surgical tray, and struggled on the ground, trying to get back up. The Zeytars were now in full view at the door, moving swiftly as they glided into the room like hovering drones.

The first one went straight for Stacey, grabbing at her ankles and dragging her toward the door. The second was on Vargzin in no time. The Drac had the gun lifted ready to fire, but the Zeytar put its hand out and stopped Vargzin in his tracks. Just then, the first gray who was holding Stacey dropped to the ground, lifeless. The remaining Zeytar turned, confused, and could faintly make out Eric. It focused and tried to hypnotize him, but Eric lifted his hand up and in the blink of an eye the remaining Zeytar was splattered all over Vargzin, pushing him back onto the floor. Stacey stood up. The faint image of Eric was now gone and she was standing in the middle of the room in a trance.

Vargzin growled and huffed as he wiped all the blue goo from his face and upper body, although he wasn't upset about it too much because the intrusive images that were being blasted into his head by the tiny Zeytar would almost certainly have driven him insane. Vargzin figured Stacey was communicating with the helpers, so he left her to it. He picked up his gear, ready for a swift departure, as the hive would surely have been alerted that they were both down here.

Stacey finally came to. "Change of plans, Vargzin, I know what to do." Stacey seemed scared but pumped, like she finally had a purpose and a focus to move toward.

"Varg," Vargzin insisted.

"Sorry, what did you say? Varg?" Stacey replied, a little confused by the comment.

"Call Me Varg," he said.

Stacey understood. She went on to explain the plan that her father and Wilkes had just given them. Varg had had his own, but after hearing this news he was happy to switch and go along with it.

With soldiers now definitely in hot pursuit of the two, they had to be quick about it. They ran down the corridor, then headed left toward the end of the hall where the lift was supposed to be. Stacey remembered there was also a wall next to the lift with guns and weapons. As they headed further down the hall Stacey had a plan to add to the existing one.

"What do you think about releasing all of the prisoners down here as a diversion?" Stacey was happy with this idea, although convincing Varg would be the challenge.

"No, No, No, Too Many Bad," Varg snapped as they finally made it to the end of the corridor.

Stacey heard his answer although was more concerned now at the lack of lift in front of them.

"Where is it, Varg? Wilkes said it would be here."

She turned to the walls either side of the dead end. There was no indication of any storage facility. Had Wilkes lied, or was he wrong, or, she hated even thinking this, had he set them up to be caught?

"No Lift, No Guns, Let's Turn."

Varg was insistent and with time running out before they were surely captured and killed, they needed to do something. Stacey felt all along the walls of both sides hoping for a hidden button or switch, but there was nothing. After a few moments she gave up and fell to her knees in disappointment.

As she slumped there just staring at the joinery of the wall and the floor, she noticed a tiny hole. Thinking nothing of it, she at least knew that anything they came across had to be investigated. She crawled on all fours over to the hole and put her face on the ground. There was nothing in it, so she then placed her index finger inside it and could feel something right at the end, but she was just short of putting pressure on it.

"Varg, there is something here. Do you have anything I can use, a piece of metal or something to try to reach it?"

Varg looked at Stacey for a few seconds. He broke off the side metal handle of the rifle he was carrying, handed it to Stacey and said, "Waste Time Must Go." He was becoming agitated. He wanted to pursue his plan now.

Stacey grabbed the piece of metal, nodded to Varg, and dropped back to the ground again. As she placed the piece of metal at the entrance of the hole, she heard noises coming from deep within the other corridors. She thrust the metal in, and a switch activated, opening a door and revealing hundreds of different kinds of weaponry, enough for a small contingent of soldiers.

The masters and wardens were the only ones who knew about these caches and created them just in case there were ever rebellions on the ship, as a safety measure.

Stacey lifted her face to the ceiling and whispered, "Thank you, Wilkes." She then ran over to the end of the corridor wall, and there in front of her, sure enough, was another hole.

Varg was like a kid in a candy store, picking all the best weapons he thought would do the most damage, modern flash grenades, pulse rifles, de-materializers, and the straight-out lightweight handheld rocket launchers. A whole artillery that would require an army to carry on Earth, but this advanced tech was so light and small he was able to fit most inside his satchel. He had been at war with the Zeytars for many years so knew their tech and how to use most of it.

Stacey had just opened the lift's outer door and as the inner doors retracted to the side, she glanced at Varg who was finishing updating all his gear. She needed some weapons herself, so when she was satisfied that the doors wouldn't close on her, she made her way over to the cache of weapons where many were still sitting there awaiting use.

"What do you recommend for me, Varg, and don't say nothing. I can sure as shit handle myself."

Varg smirked. He knew she could and was happy that he wasn't being burdened with a helpless human.

"Here, Pulse And Plasma, Bad, Damage, Zeytars."

Stacey smiled. The guns were lightweight and she could put one in the back of her trousers and carry the other. She grabbed some clips and some flash grenades. There was a small carry bag, so she grabbed that as well and stashed them all inside it.

"No Need All That, Varg Has Plenty."

Stacey didn't even listen. She wasn't going to be told what to do now. Time was catching up with them.

Stacey looked at the pistol she was carrying and wondered how the Zeytars could use such weapons with only three fingers, before realizing that most of the soldiers were hybrids and other abominations. The masters would have access to the cache and in turn issue the weapons to their minions.

"OK, Varg, it's time. While I close the door to the weapons cache, you head over to the lift. I won't be long."

Varg nodded and headed toward the lift. Stacey closed the door until it looked like a wall again so the others wouldn't find the secret cache, and then started running back toward the entrance of the corridor where they had come from. She turned and yelled, "Wait for me, Varg, I won't be long."

She disappeared around the corner, making her way to the prison cells. Varg knew what she was doing and thought to himself, "I'm starting to like this human, but she's going to get me killed."

Stacey knew the only cells not to open were the ones with the Mantids, although there were plenty of other unsavory looking beasts that she wasn't sure of. But she didn't have time for a full report on who was naughty and who was nice. Mind you, this would give her a full pass for her final college report that she still needed to finish.

She went to the furthest spot, as she could hear a full contingent of hybrid soldiers on their way, and they were close. Stacey started opening the side switches and kept on doing so, making her way back to the lift. One by one doors opened and creatures' heads poked out of the entrances of the cells.

She continued, until the hybrid soldiers arrived at the far entrance to the corridor. Instantly they began blasting the beasts and prisoners as fast as they could, trying to fight their way closer to Stacey. Some of the larger prisoners, too frightening to even look at, retaliated, crushing the soldiers' heads in, picking them up, and throwing them against walls. Stacey watched the action, as the door to the final cell was opening, not realizing what she had just done, too distracted by the commotion coming from further down.

Stacey turned to run back to Varg, but in front of her was a giant Mantid. Its eyes were piercing and lifeless. Its long claw-like front legs reached out and grabbed her. Stacey let out a scream as the grip tightened and she was being crushed. The creature was putting thoughts into her head and Stacey was going into convulsive shock. Suddenly, the top of the Mantid's head just disappeared, leaving enough room to see Varg standing there with his pulse rifle still aimed. The huge bug let go of her and as she dropped to the ground, Varg was already by her side to help pick her up.

Stacey needed a moment to correct herself. If the Mantid had held her much longer, her brain might have been lost. She shook it off and Varg assisted her getting up.

Just as they were about to move on, a blast came from behind them and hit Varg in the back of the left shoulder. Stacey let out a scream and returned fire, taking out hybrids one at a time until there were five or six lying dead on the ground. After the first wave, more started coming through. There were only a couple of the larger prisoners left now so Stacey threw some flash grenades at the lot and now it was she who was assisting Varg to stand up.

"Come on, Varg, we have to go!"

They were both in a bad way, although Stacey seemed to be getting back to normal. She held Varg around the waist and they scampered down a corridor and then into the main one with the lift.

Stacey could hear the hybrids firing and shouting as they neared the lift corridor. It seemed longer now that she was assisting Varg, however she persisted and kept going. When they were three quarters of the way there and could just about touch the doors, the hybrid soldiers found them, firing as they entered the corridor.

Varg fell. He yelled, "Go, Go, Leave, Now."

Stacey didn't even blink. He had saved her life a few times now and there was no way he was getting left behind, no matter how important her mission was. She managed to get him to his feet once again.

The hybrid soldiers were only yards away, lining them both up and ready to fire. Stacey dipped into her satchel and grabbed another flash grenade. As she picked it out and went to throw it, the grenade slipped from her hand and rolled onto the floor. She was so close, she thought, bracing for the end. She closed her eyes and waited.

Stacey heard an almighty blast and fell to the floor. Then there was silence. She was out cold.

When she came to, moments later, she opened her eyes. There in front of her was Rovan along with some of his rogue soldiers.

"I got to you when I could, Stacey. I'm sorry, but without a connection to the hive and with your Geno-drone inactive, I just couldn't find you. I don't have the ability Wilkes has. I had to follow the whispers and the flurry of soldiers, hoping they would lead me to you. Now come on, we don't have long before more will arrive."

Stacey did not say a word. She was too relieved. She had been sure she was dead, but Rovan's timing was impeccable, to the finest millisecond.

They all loaded into the lift while two rogue soldiers remained outside, just in case. It was suicide, but it was worth it to them. Stacey looked at Varg as the lift closed. He was standing upright and smirking at her.

"You're OK, Varg, how?" and as soon as she finished asking, she realized Rovan had healed him.

"Varg, Fine, Stacey, Fine," Varg said, also happy that she was alright.

Rovan pulled a small electronic patch from his vest and reached out to place it on Varg's neck. "Here, this is a translator, it will help you with communication."

But Varg slapped it out of Rovan's hand and with an assertive growl replied, "No, No Chip, No Longer Yours, Free."

Stacey grabbed Varg's hand. "Yes, you are, Varg, you are free like the rest of us, and we are one now."

Stacey smiled as Rovan went on to explain, "Sorry, it was meant to help."

"Help You, Not Me, No More Control from Zeytars."

Stacey squeezed his large hand before saying, "No more, now it's time to destroy the Zeytars." She paused, then looked over at Rovan and said, "No offense."

Rovan looked blank-faced. Humor was not one of the Zeytars' strong points.

With the six of them squeezed together in the lift, Stacey asked Varg to punch L17R72 into the control panel. In no time they were sucked up and spun around to the exact level and corridor they needed.

The lift opened and the soldiers poured out first, only to be met with direct gunfire, hitting them with multiple electropulses and putting them on the ground. Varg jumped out of the lift, not knowing what was waiting for them, and used his remaining flash grenades, before aiming his launcher and decimating the whole corridor.

As the smoke finally dissipated, they all carefully exited the lift. Stacey was behind Varg, with Rovan at the front. As they moved closer, they could see several hybrid soldiers on the ground, dead.

"The Leader must have awakened some more of the lower form hybrids to assist in protection and has placed them on all floors of the ship. We have to be very careful now," Rovan informed the two as they inched closer to the destined room.

"There, 72," Varg said as they stepped over chunks of flesh and blood, trying not to slip on the mess. Varg accidently stepped on an arm and as he adjusted his position, he placed his foot where the head would have been.

Rovan opened the door. This was a restricted area, and the lift was only used by the masters, so they had bypassed all security points. Once inside they all looked around in awe.

This was the place where they kept every single life-form's DNA and modified genomes, along with all diseases and cures. When they finally snapped back to reality, Stacey yelled out the details, "It's at the end of all the other vials, blue section, beginning with five."

Rovan knew where that was. He was the one who assisted Wilkes in cloning Stacey for the deception model so they wouldn't get her DNA coding in full which, after the first sample was taken and manipulated, set off the chain of events that gave chase to Eric.

When Stacey first arrived, the Sasquatch was responsible for letting the master or head scientists know that another life-form with the rare gene was on the ship. Wilkes was the one notified of the very rare genomes and took Stacey to an isolated room where she was tested. She was then cloned, cutting the genome off and making Anders and the rest think she was the original, all while Wilkes manipulated her coding into the seven vials to corrupt all the hybrid Zeytars with diseases once on Earth.

Stacey's body would eventually have been cut up and used as backup for future hybrids, and to be tested and kept, as she was the first one with the rare gene since the 1980s. All the others who were brought in had only the first genome required.

Rovan made his way to exactly where the vials were. He didn't even need the numbers. To make out he wasn't aware, he asked for them anyway, as he did not want to be the one who had to tell her that Wilkes and his team cloned her for Anders to hack at.

"What are the numbers?" Rovan yelled.

"5000375621," Stacey answered, while Varg stood watch.

"Got them, let's go."

Rovan had the seven last manipulated vials that would give them an advantage over the Zeytars if they did make it through Zero Time. They raced out the door and turned right down the corridor. Rovan punched in a special code on the control unit and a few seconds later a door opened, they all entered the lift, and the door closed behind them.

"Listen very carefully, I will take you to the control bay that I know is left unattended more often. Set your guns to stun, it's quieter, we can kill them after they are out. We cannot afford to get caught. If the Leader finds out, we are in trouble. He will dump the first lot of tainted ones and wake the rest. He won't know, though, that this mixture is dangerous as it is coded to look the same as the antidote. The only way he can know is if we are seen here. Vargzin, you need to stay with me after it's safe. Stacey has to be the one on her own to do it. She is nimbler, with smaller hands for the vial taps."

Stacey nodded and took a deep breath. Their stun guns were set and pointed, ready. As the doors opened, they pounced, moving the stun guns around, looking for a target, but found nothing.

"Just as I thought, although we will stay in the lift in case they return. The only other entrance is a side door."

Before Rovan could finish, Stacey explained, "I know, I have been in a similar one of these, I will check it. You two head out, I will be fine."

Rovan nodded and they started moving back into the lift, but then he turned and added, "Oh, I almost forgot, do not get any on your body and do not let any of the others see you. Even the hybrids awaken at times and if you are seen, it will be relayed, as they are all connected to the hive. Even without the mindless Zeytars' essence in them yet, they still have a sense of consciousness."

Stacey nodded and watched as the doors closed behind them both, leaving her in the scariest situation since it all began. The fact that the human race depended on this working was unbelievable to Stacey. She didn't want to fail anyone, let alone everyone. She felt sick with fear, took a couple of deep breaths, and whispered to herself, "You can do this, Stacey, you can do this."

She kneeled and crawled closer to the control panel. It was even more intimidating than the first time she was in one of these places. There were so many bodies just hanging in their cylinders awaiting the start of their lives. Stacey nearly felt bad for them. They never had a choice in being created like this and used as tools for a Leader who didn't care personally about them as individuals. However, as a collective, they were a powerful force and therefore important to him.

THE FACE BEHIND THE GLASS

STACEY CONCENTRATED as she fumbled around in the dimly lit control booth. Like at a box seat at the football, she could see everything, and if she could see, so could others. She kept low and examined the controls. She was looking for a specific nozzle that fit the large vials.

After some time and lots of stress, she found what seemed to be the correct hole. She remembered, though, that the lever was to be pushed all the way forward. This would allow the contents of the vials to be sucked through to the main nutrition-medical vat where all the nutrition and medication was drip-fed from.

Stacey took the first vial and attached it to the nozzle. As she twisted it and locked it into place, she heard something behind her. Looking back over her shoulder, Stacey couldn't see anything. "I'm spooking myself out," she said to herself, turning back to the controls. She pushed the lever forward and all the reddish fluid was sucked out.

Stacey grabbed the second vial. She was losing her grip on the others, so she placed the satchel on the ground. Her position was very uncomfortable, but she had no choice. She screwed the second one in and released the lever, and she continued this sequence, like a nicely flowing machine.

After the third one was done, she lined up the fourth vial, and just before she could turn it a scout drone flickered past. Stacey dove onto the floor in a commando roll so as not to be seen. The scout drone flew up to the window scanning for any abnormalities. It was a security device for the Leader along with other measures to ensure everything ran smoothly.

Stacey looked up at the canister. It hadn't been fastened and as the scout drone finished and moved on to the next window, the vial started rocking from side to side. Stacey couldn't stand up or even attempt to grab it as she would be heard and most likely seen if she did. Meanwhile, the vial rocked more and more, back and forth, until finally it jumped out of the nozzle and hit the control panel hard, bouncing along, hitting one side then the other before launching into the air.

Stacey knew she was in trouble, but she wasn't going to allow herself to be beaten yet. She moved into position and caught the vial before it hit the ground and ended her mission. She was just happy that all those years of catch in the backyard with her father had paid off.

Stacey waited there until she couldn't hear the whirring of the security drone any longer. When she thought it was safe again, she climbed back up to the control panel and loaded the fourth vial in. She was getting tired. She hadn't eaten properly since she was in the room with Rovan. She was thinking of upgrading from a burger to a full pizza with everything on it, even pineapple, as she drooled.

After the fifth vial was loaded, Stacey heard movement coming from the room behind her.

"Not now," she whispered.

She slid down from the control panel like a snake to the floor and she waited behind the door. Soon enough the door opened and a Zeytar walked through like it had just come back from lunch. Stacey pounced and kicked its legs from underneath it. She knew it couldn't get too close or it would tell the hive, or even worse, get into her mind. Once it was on the floor, she stunned it and dragged it to the side before closing the door. She remembered that it could still activate the information to the hive, so she had no choice but to kill it. As she leaned over to break its neck, she heard the buzzing of the security drone again. It must have picked up the vibrational disturbances when she kicked the Zeytar's legs out. With an almighty twist, she broke the stunned being's tiny neck.

Stacey quickly lifted the Zeytar and placed it in the chair, positioning the arms and hands on the controls. The only problem was that its head just flopped around, so Stacey was forced to hide behind the chair and discreetly put her arm up to hold it in place.

The drone eventually arrived at her window and scanned the area. Stacey was as still as a stone, although her arm was tiring quickly. She had no energy to start with, let alone enough to give her shoulders and arms extra work. The drone continued scanning across.

Stacey couldn't hold on any longer and the lifeless Zeytar's head went limp, tipping forward. The drone turned quickly toward the movement, but at the same time a deafening alarm activated all around the ship. The drone tucked its scanners inside and stopped what it was doing as if it was recalled with the others for some reason.

Stacey wasn't sure what was going on and as she hadn't finished yet, she needed to get to work.

At that same time Rovan burst in and through the noise of the alarm said, "Have you finished yet? Wilkes told me this would happen, it's the start of the countdown. It is very close now and the Leader is getting ready to open the doors to Earth. We must hurry."

Rovan was a little agitated but still focused. Varg had poked his head around the corner and looked at Stacey's handiwork on the ground before giving her a wink and retreating back into the lift.

"I have three to go. This has been a nightmare. I will finish off and meet you at the lift in a moment."

Stacey didn't need to be told to hurry up. She was already under the pump enough and she didn't see Rovan trying to help. The Zeytars were a selfish race, she thought.

She continued her work with the fifth vial, still in stealth mode as there were others in the windows across from her who could possibly catch a glimpse at the right time.

She just could not get past the haunting vision of the thousands and thousands of bodies lying naked in the cylinder life pods. Women, men, children, they all looked like humans, but she knew very well they were different. Some would twitch, some would open their eyes and close them again and some were as still as a rock.

She placed the sixth vial into position and pushed the lever forward, then lined up the seventh. She was nearly there, a home run with a couple of strikes at the start. Stacey lined the seventh one up and screwed it into position.

As she was about to push the lever, her eyes caught another pair of eyes straight ahead in a life pod cylinder. There, looking back at her, was a boy no more than ten. His hands were held up to the glass of the cylinder and he was staring directly at Stacey. It was the creepiest thing she had seen in her life, more so than any previous events that had occurred along the way.

Stacey couldn't move. It was like it had some kind of hold over her. The tubes that were meant to be attached to his body were now removed, along with the brain and the stomach conduits. He was completely detached. Stacey saw a single bubble coming from his mouth and as she regained her composure and pushed the lever, she felt that he was in trouble and was just about to get the flush. He couldn't be awake as the Zeytars hadn't mind-blended with the bodies yet, so how could this one be conscious and lucid?

Blood came from his nose and he started convulsing. It would only be a matter of time before the other controllers would see it. She had to do something, she thought. Looking over the panels she could see coding like in the lift and the same coding on the cylinders. Eventually she figured she was looking at row and individual numbers. Stacey pressed the row 783 and then the cylinder number 17. The symbols were similar to Earth's, and she figured math was a universal language, so she went with that.

After locking the details into the computer, she couldn't find the right switches to bring him in, nor did she want to press the flush button, or he would fall straight to the ground with the piles of flawed meat that they deemed unworthy. Stacey was panicking. She had finished her part of the mission, however she now had a new one. She had to save him.

"OK, think, girl, think," she said softly to herself and just as she was going to give up hope she saw a release button. It wasn't a flush but a cylinder release, for lowering it down for repairs or to enter the embryo for a new hybrid. Fortunately, there were pictures on some buttons. The flush button had a picture of the cylinder's bottom opening and this one had the same but lines at the top indicating down. So much for their high-tech equipment. They concentrated too much on other things and not new age control panels, she thought, laughing to herself.

Stacey hit the button and a jolt came from the line. All the other cylinders moved along and the one with the boy in it came forward, lowering slowly down all the floors to the maintenance area.

Stacey opened the lift and yelled, "We have to go, now!" Her voice was assertive and both Rovan and Varg thought it wise not to argue

"Did you finish the job, were you seen?" Rovan demanded.

"Finished, yes. They were all too distracted with the alarms going off, and before you ask, we are going to the basement where the cylinders come down for repair. Can you please punch in the coordinates, Rovan?"

Rovan yelled straight back, "Are you insane?"

He wasn't scared of her, that was for sure. The look on his gray face was like on most of the other Zeytars, angry. Rovan had changed back to blend in with the rest, knowing that he was probably being hunted by most of the other wardens, so he didn't want to look like an agent.

"Yes, and this is non-negotiable. Now, Rovan, move it or I will make our location known."

Varg didn't care what Stacey was about to do. But he did not like Zeytars, and if Stacey wanted to go somewhere, then he was going with her. He looked over at Rovan and gave him a little growl. He was a Drac of few words, but he had an intelligence and inspired a sense of awe.

Rovan punched in the coordinates and they whizzed around and headed down to the maintenance floor, getting ready with weapons now at full power and not stun, as this would be a dangerous exercise.

"Wait, I have an idea." Rovan stopped the lift and redirected it to the floor just above.

"What are you doing? We need to get there now. I can save him," Stacey pleaded.

"Save who, Stacey?"

She didn't answer as she knew he wouldn't believe her.

"We need to blend in more. Varg, I'm sorry, but you will have to try as best as you can."

As much as Varg was a Draconian and they were the Zeytars' enemies, there were some beings used as slaves for the Zeytars so the plan Rovan had could include him. That's what he hoped, anyway.

"OK, we are here, this is the storeroom. When the Zeytar hybrids awaken they will all receive uniforms with this patch on it so they are all identified and together, as the first few years will be a battle to clean up all the humans and find the rebels. This is the military uniform they will be wearing. Some of the new batches are already wearing them," Rovan explained as the doors opened revealing a massive warehouse floor with all the uniforms. There were gray pants, gray shirts, and vests, along with tunics and caps. The patches had a Zeytar face, with a saucer shape above the head, and two plasma rifles on either side, with gray, red, and blue coloring.

They quickly got dressed, after which they ran back to the elevator and down to where the life pod repair section was. Stacey was hoping that they were not too late.

The lift opened and Varg was the first one out, creeping around the corner and maintaining a level of security so Stacey would be safe when she exited. He turned, then nodded. Without making a sound, the other two quietly caught up with Varg. There was no real plan at this stage as it was a rush job, although there was always time for safety and self-preservation. This mindset was across the board with all three of them, no matter what, at this stage. Things were ramping up on the ship and it wouldn't be long before all the life pod cylinders would be dropping to awaken the newly blended Zeytars.

Varg dashed across to the other side of the entry point to the room. He had a better visual now and only noticed three workers. He indicated to the other two to follow him, so Stacey and Rovan ran to his location, ducking behind so as not to be seen.

"OK, this is good, follow my lead now," Rovan said. "They will do what I say as there are no other wardens here yet, but it won't be long before all these areas will be flooded with soldiers and low-level workers to assist with the transition from stasis to getting uniforms and taking their posts for the upcoming entry to the Earth realm."

Rovan seemed to be confident in his plan working, although he purposely neglected to mention that if he was caught out, the hive would know straight away, and he would be number one on the new Zeytars' hit list.

Rovan confidently walked into the room with Stacey behind him. Varg stayed back at this stage and was a backup if it went south.

As Rovan inched closer to the main section of the life pod release area, a repairer bowed his head and then looked up, saying to Rovan, "Hi, sir, it's not quite time yet. The first alarm is for the awakening of the X-Clock, the second is for the Zeytars' mind transference, and the third alarm is for the doorway portal. We were not expecting a warden just yet. How can we help you?"

The small hybrid worker seemed confused and a little frightened, as the wardens tended to have big egos and were very controlling. The wardens wanted the authority of the masters but didn't get the respect from them as they only had the ability for hypnotic trances like the lower drone workers, not mind altering or control like the masters or the Leader. So they took out their frustrations on the lower level workers.

"Relax, hybrid, I am here to oversee everything and to make sure all your work is ready for the releases. I don't want any problems when it all happens. The Leader will not tolerate any failings from this part of the agenda, and he will destroy you from where he sits. Now go, and take the other two. Forget any life pods that are awaiting repair as it is too late to add new ones. We need all hybrids and worker drones on deck now in preparation. This will be your only chance for a rest, so take thirty Earth minutes and then call upon your team."

The hybrid still looked confused. He was specifically told not to leave here until all the Zeytars had been released, but he was not going to argue with a warden. So he took the other two and they left through another door.

The whole area smelled bad, Stacey thought. She knew why but didn't want to think about it as it reminded her of the other dumping site of the failed bodies she was in earlier on. This wasn't as bad, though, as it was more "remove and repair" than "dump and leave."

Rovan looked around at Stacey, and said, "I don't like this. The hybrids are easily led, however they are black and white. If they have previous orders they will go and question the original source if that order was supposed to be changed, so we don't have much time at all."

Rovan nodded to Varg to meet up with them. The Drac was a little disappointed that he didn't get the chance to blow anything up, although he knew he would get the chance soon enough. War was pretty much all his race knew because of the Zeytars, so they had to expect retaliation sometime, Varg thought to himself.

"Come, this way." Rovan led the two around the corner where five life pods awaited repair.

The hybrids had been attending to one before Rovan and Stacey turned up. The other three had lifeless corpses inside, and the last one had the young boy in it that Stacey had seen. He appeared lifeless, sitting on the bottom of the life pod cylinder. Stacey ran to it, and peering in, she gave the glass a few soft taps.

"We have to hurry. Rovan, how do we get him out? We need to flush the embryonic fluid and get him to breathe."

Stacey was agitated and desperate. The Zeytar hybrids were the most sophisticated life-forms ever created by their science teams, far more superior than all the others they had experimented with. However, they had human DNA, which meant they weren't fish. They had lungs

230

designed for Earth and they needed to breathe. Even if they had near on immortal genes, they weren't one hundred percent invulnerable.

Rovan started pressing buttons and punching in codes. He was not a scientist or a qualified repairer, so he had no idea exactly how to unlock the fluid and release the body without assistance.

"I'm sorry, Stacey, I just can't understand the sequencing. It's like it's got a special code and order to unlock, probably a security provision."

Stacey stared at Rovan, not content with his answer and getting angry that there was no solution. She looked around the room for something heavy or metal, only to find most things were of a synthetic nature. The only item she could see that might work was a piece of metal from a broken life pod cylinder sitting on a bench awaiting repair. It was far too heavy for any of them, and she wanted something smaller.

"Varg, are you able to pull one of the metal conduits from the stasis cylinder's hatch over there? I will break the glass."

Varg made his way over to the bench, while Rovan exclaimed, "This glass is the strongest synthetic glass known in the universe. It was crafted to withstand anyth—"

Before Rovan could finish, Varg had smashed the cylinder into a thousand pieces with the whole hatch, not just the conduit, releasing all the fluid and gaining access to the boy's body for extraction.

Rovan just stared at the reptilian. All the rumors were true about them, intelligence and strength, along with a great fighting mind and compassion. The history books stated different, which was designed to teach soldiers not to fear the reptilian race. But they should be feared and Rovan was having an awakening of his own right now. His own race not only deceived other worlds, including Earth, but also their own people. Who were these Leaders that had been in control all this time? Rumors about Draconians had been spread by soldiers over time, but the Zeytars were always coerced not to believe them.

Stacey called out to Varg, "Help me with him. I can't seem to get his legs out."

Varg pushed away the large shard of glass that had the boy's legs trapped, lifted him up, and placed him on the repair table.

"He's not breathing, Rovan, can you bring him back with your tool?" Stacey asked desperately, while Rovan tried to fix the problem in the boy's body.

"I can't seem to locate the issue. I need to bring him up to the medical lab and there I can bring him back. At this moment it looks like the boy is dead and there's nothing this device can do to repair dead cells and organs. I need a medical lab."

Rovan looked desperate. He knew his device worked most of the time; however, this boy had no Zeytar mind and was not connected to the life pod. Who knew what kind of damage had been done to the poor kid? Stacey was not going to give up, though. She jumped onto the table and gave him chest compressions, over and over, then some breaths and more compressions. This went on for some time, and as she was just about to give up, she felt a jolt and a choking movement, but then nothing.

"Did you all see that? I have to keep going."

Stacey was crying now, knowing well she had done her best but it was not enough. The poor boy's face was lifeless. He looked human. A larger than normal head, five fingers, five toes, a bald scalp, and hair follicles that would eventually grow. She didn't see a menacing hybrid Zeytar, but a defenseless, lifeless boy who had not been given a choice or a chance.

Feeling helpless, she hit the boy's chest one last time in anger. At that, his eyes opened, and a stream of embryonic fluid spewed out of his mouth. Coughing and splattering, he was trying to gain a breath as this was the very first time the boy had ever used his lungs.

Stacey's tears became those of happy relief. She wiped him down with a large cleaning towel the workers would use to polish off the cylinders when they finished repairing them. It wasn't the cleanest thing, but it was all they had. She wrapped him up and Varg carried the boy, giving Stacey the weapons.

"We have to go now, I'm sorry, this took far too long." Rovan was very distressed. This boy had put them in so much danger and he hadn't planned for it. Wilkes would not be happy about it if the mission failed because of it, so the stress levels were high.

They ran to the exit and could hear movement coming from the white-walled doorway where the hybrid and his workers had previously departed. By now they were in the lift, and as the doors closed, they heard the second alarm.

Time was running out, so Rovan hit the lift buttons and they made for the rendezvous point that Eric/Wilkes had told them to go to. The boy was shivering, so Stacey gently rubbed his bald head and sang quietly until he succumbed to the soothing tones and fell asleep.

SCREAMING THROUGH TIME AND SPACE

ERIC AWOKE AFTER A FEW MINUTES, dazed and confused. He looked up from the floor and saw Serena's face smiling at him. He wondered if he'd been dreaming as he smiled back, before turning his head to search for Michael and Valinda. He was greeted with an enormous hairy long face staring back at him. He recognized it instantly and remembered now why he was knocked out. He gave out a yell and started scampering backward with his hands, trying to grip the slippery floor to pull himself back up. The creature grabbed his head and stroked it softly before standing up and letting out a growl.

"OK, Levi, thank you, you have helped Eric, just give him a moment," Valinda whispered.

Eric slowly stood up, not taking his eyes off the beast standing at least nine feet tall in front of him. He took in every detail, from its thick mousy brown hair to its large hands and feet. Its head seemed to have two parts to it, the large dome-shaped skull and forehead down to the chin which then extended, making its face seem very long. It had fur that covered all of its body except its actual face, which had a darker brown tone to it compared to its hair. Eric continued scanning the creature, looking at the pointed ears slightly poking through its hair and its dark brown eyes that seemed strangely friendly and kind. Its long hairy arms seemed to extend further down than what a human's did, although its legs seemed to fit the proportions nicely. Eric couldn't help staring at its huge shoulders that complemented its whole physique with a strength that nobody would want to take on.

"Are you OK, Eric? Wilkes had briefed me about what his own appearance would be like due to my abductions, but no one thought about how seeing Levi would affect you after what happened at Klamath with Stacey. I assure you, he is not like the others," Valinda explained to Eric calmly.

Wilkes moved in closer and had his turn.

"Yes, I only realized when you started reacting. I'm sorry I had to do that to you. If you had been closer, LV might have given you a bit of a swipe to protect himself and I've already healed you once for that so you know what kind of damage they can do."

Eric nodded slowly, still staring at the beast.

"It's really him. I mean this is a Sasquatch or Bigfoot? Not an altered thing you made to look like one?" Eric asked like he was a schoolboy again.

"Yes, Eric, we created them thousands of years ago, what your native people told stories about. They are the same ones. It wasn't until recent history that we programed them for abductions. The early ones we classed as aberrations and let them loose on the world, but over time we realized their stealth abilities and only modified the genes enough for the harmonic vocalizations and in-built genome tracker so they could return to us after they found a subject." Wilkes had twisted the truth a little to appease Eric, although he would never find out anyway.

"May I?" Eric asked, as he slowly put his right hand out palm up to touch him. Simon had ventured over to Eric. He was the second-in-charge of WOSER and was excited for Eric to meet it finally.

"Yes, of course. I know all the work you have put into this field over the years and was devastated that your 'close encounter' with one was negative. They are all programed with a control Geno-drone. They aren't like that generally, they are shy, quiet, and keep to themselves mostly, just like LV here," Wilkes explained.

Simon chimed in and quietly whispered to Eric, "I told you, buddy. didn't I?"

Eric smiled at Simon, and as he did this Levi gently placed his enormous palm over Eric's. There seemed to be a change in him. He realized that the anger he had for what had happened to him and Stacey had been pointing in the wrong direction. This creature in front of him was not what it had seemed from his previous encounter. The realization that they were all victims of this malevolent agenda redirected Eric's focus to finding Stacey and then destroying the Zeytars.

"Why do you call him LV and a bunch of numbers and why does Valinda call him Levi? And how did you come to be in his good company, Val?" Eric asked, still holding Levi's hand and staring into his eyes.

"I'll go first!" Wilkes exclaimed. "Agent Anders was creating some abhorrent creatures in a secret facility. The Leader knew of it and as long as it was kept under wraps, he didn't seem to care. Over time there have been some horrific abominations that should not have been created. Anders found one that he connected with, called Savage, a ghastly beast that is part human, part dire wolf, a massive bipedal creature that is as destructive as it is loyal. I've seen its dirty work and I can tell you, it's not pretty, so I needed something that would protect me if Anders ever found out about my betrayal. I went into the creature side of the hybrid program and found one in its junior form, part way through creative stasis. I took him, damaging the cylinder so the caretakers thought it was just dumped, like they do with all the beings that have flaws or defects.

"His life pod cylinder was numbered LVI738319, LVI meaning Life-form Validated Interspecies, 73 being the row it was in and 8319 being the number of the life pod cylinder.

"He was the equivalent to a full-term newborn and in stasis. Usually they are kept in life pods to be grown to full adult; however, they took up too much room and the Leader wanted that for the Zeytar hybrid scheme. They grow quite quickly to full term, only a couple of years, so I took him and raised him to protect me, blocking him from anything that Anders or the others would ever know about." Wilkes turned to Valinda and asked, "Yes, Valinda, why do you call him Levi?"

Valinda smiled and responded, "It sounds better than all those numbers, it's easier to say, while keeping some of the letters, and more importantly, he likes it, don't you, Levi?"

Levi gave a positive grunt, before Wilkes nodded and responded with, "I gathered that, I was messing with you."

Everyone was in shock. Did this "Gray inter-dimensional ex Aladoorian Zeytar" just make a joke? The surprise turned to smirks and before long Valinda was explaining how she came to be in Levi's company.

Time was getting on and Wilkes wanted to explain the last part of the information to everyone as this was something that no one had been briefed on just yet. So, it was very important that all of them listened carefully.

"If I can have everyone back in their seats, please, I will begin. Then we can rest up." There was a desperate tone in his voice, and it seemed like even he was becoming exhausted. "Come here, Levi, and stand over there."

Levi left his new friends and walked over to the spot where Wilkes was pointing, a clearing in the middle of the room that nobody was close to.

"Now, what LV, I mean Levi, is going to demonstrate is the opening and closing of doorways from this plane of existence to your own. We are currently in another dimension to Earth's, hidden inside one of the older medium ships, floating in our inter-dimensional plane of Aladoor. We have been able to calibrate and modify it so physical things, living or dead, can vibrate at the right speed inside the dimension. However, step outside and you will cease to exist."

The crowd just stared with their mouths open, awaiting the next part.

"Like I said previously, the Leader needs an exceptional amount of power from both dimensions, Earth and here, to open a door. If one side tries to open it, they may get one ship through and then it will close after some time. If both are opening at once with a significant amount of power, the door can be held long term. In order to start the rip, ALEX must use a particle accelerator to start the process, then after the rip is made the droid can tear it fully open."

Wilkes was starting to struggle a little, but he was nearly there.

"Now, why can't they just open a door and send one or two through at a time, you ask. Why all the power? Well, this is because there are a billion hybrids in either cryo or life pod stasis. Each of the ships that has been built here using materials from other worlds is connected to the mother ship. There are hundreds of medium and large life pod ships, specifically designed to only host the life pods. They are all connected to each other by conduits and cables, creating the hive, where the Leader has control and is connected to all at the same time. So, when they come through it must be all at once and that is a significant amount of power to sustain. If they get cut off halfway through, all the hybrids stuck will perish, as they will be cut from the mother ship, and the bodiless minds will be lost."

Wilkes looked around at everyone. There was still no reaction until Eric chimed in, "Could you repeat all of that, Wilkes, I missed the start."

The room erupted with laughter. Wilkes stood there glaring at Eric like he was not impressed, although he knew it was only to break the tension.

"Sorry, Eric, I was hoping you were writing it down for everybody," Wilkes casually sniped back, while the group let out another burst of nervous laughter. It seemed Wilkes was becoming more human after all.

"I want to demonstrate for you just how the vocalization of a Sasquatch works. There are tones that can manipulate dimensional doors by opening them up and closing them. Each of the tones can open the doors and over time the creatures have learned to adapt where they open. Like changing the frequency of a radio station, they can choose where to go. Levi is mind-blended with me so if I'm in trouble, he can concentrate, and he will find me using just one vocalization tone. These were embedded in the construct of their DNA. This is why all you WOSER scientists haven't been able to find one yet. If they die outside in the woods, we can track them and take them away, leaving no trace, just footprints."

Wilkes was nearly finished. He was looking forward to showing Levi off.

"Levi, are you ready?"

Levi gave a grunt and nodded, awaiting instruction.

"Levi, I want you to pick me a rare jade vine from the forests of the Philippines. Here is what it looks like."

Wilkes showed a hologram of it, along with the coordinates of the area, to Levi. A shriek and prolonged howl billowed across the ship, leaving some to cover their ears. Then blue swirling light appeared in front of Levi, creating a whirling vortex blowing air around the room until it reached a size large enough for the beast to fit through. The crowd could see through the mix of blue swirls, making out trees on the other side. When Levi had finished with his howl, he walked straight through the vortex and disappeared completely, as the maelstrom of wind and light dissipated into nothing, leaving an empty area of the room where the behemoth had been standing no more than a moment before.

"As you can see, this is quite an effective tool of stealth and invisibility." Wilkes heard all the little whispers coming from the different groups he had chosen over time to help with the mission.

Eric stood up. "That's exactly what I saw when it took Stacey, but there's something missing. There were fireflies or small bright creatures flying with the other one. I remember seeing them while I was under in hospital, or was that just a dream?"

Eric kept standing, waiting for his answer. Wilkes stared back at him, not sure if he should tell him just yet, as it wasn't going to be part of his direct mission, but he was becoming closer with Serena and he would most likely end up helping her anyway.

"Yes, Eric, you are right. They are creatures from another place called sprites, deep within a dimensional world that was taken by our kind to assist the Sasquatch with capturing victims. They are also a peaceful, friendly race and are among those being controlled. They are at the beasts' beck and call and are locked away when not in use. The symbiosis between the two has worked well over the years and that is why when you see a Sasquatch in the wild, the sprites are usually somewhere close, if you know where to look."

As Wilkes finished his answer the doorway started opening again. The noise was crazy, Eric thought to himself, but effective, because the vortex became larger and larger until it was the same size as before.

Valinda smiled, as she got a small glimpse of Levi through it. The blue light swirled around and the wind of the maelstrom blocked the view for a moment. A massive hairy leg then stomped through, followed by an arm and a head, until Levi was completely through it. He stopped howling and the vortex dissipated again into nothing.

Levi turned to Valinda and walked slowly, like an awkward doofus with his long stride and heavy feet. He bent down, and reaching out to her, handed Valinda the beautiful jade vine that was asked of him. Valinda smiled and gave him a rub on the side of the chin, before he stood up and returned to the exact spot he was in before venturing into the jungle just minutes earlier.

"There, that's my demonstration. This is how we will be getting in and out of our locations. Get some rest tonight as tomorrow morning I will brief everyone on the mission, who is doing what and where, along with the equipment we will be using for it."

The audience didn't budge. They were still in shock over the last demonstration. Valinda turned to Serena and Eric and whispered, "Have you seen Father Michael? I haven't seen him since we sat down at the start of the lecture."

They all looked around the room. People were finally starting to leave to go to their quarters, this time on the other end of the ship away from the maze walls and surprises.

"No, I haven't seen him. Have you, Serena?" Eric asked, as they took note of the concern in Valinda's face.

"He can't be far. We are only in another dimension in a ship who knows where." Eric smirked. "Wilkes, has Father Michael gone to his quarters? Can you find him for us, please? Valinda is just a little worried, is all," Eric asked, thinking Michael had most likely gone to bed, but he wanted peace of mind for Valinda. She was vulnerable and had been through so much in her life, especially having just lost her mother.

"Michael is gone," Wilkes said as if he himself had only just realized.

"Gone? What do you mean, gone? We are in the middle of nowhere," Eric snapped.

"I'm sorry, I cannot pick him up. I can see everyone and where they are, but he is not here."

"It's OK, Val, we will find him, and Wilkes is just tired, I'm sure of it," Eric whispered to Valinda.

Wilkes said, "You may be right, Eric, it's all taken a mental toll, and I too need rest. Nothing can leave this place without me or Levi, so he has most likely gone to bed as you all should too."

Wilkes seemed far too drained, and they trusted him, so they started making their way to where the others were going, hoping not to get lost in any other mazes or surprises along the way. As they followed the last of the groups into the sleeping quarters, Wilkes called out, "Serena, I almost forgot, can I have a moment with you? It's very important and it won't take too long."

Serena turned and slowly walked toward Wilkes.

Eric said, "I'll come with you, Serena."

But Serena was content with her situation. She was far removed from the frightened woman shaking because of Wilkes and Anders back at the hospital.

"No, Eric, I'll be fine, go to bed. I will see you in the morning, or afternoon, or something," she said. There were no windows or clocks, so who knew what time it was, if in fact there even was time here, she thought.

"OK, but be careful?"

Eric was developing feelings for Serena and his concern was genuine. Serena walked off into the section of the ship where they were all caught up in the maze walls, although she was now with Wilkes, so he wasn't too worried.

Eric would wait for her. He made his way to a chair and sat back, staring at the ceiling, taking in everything that had just happened and thinking of his little girl who was lost on a big ship with monsters. Before long he succumbed to fatigue and was snoring away.

WINGS, STEEL, AND HOPE

WILKES AND SERENA ENTERED A DARKER part of the ship, not in terms of evil but because of the lighting. It was a part where humans were off limits. The only reason the humans were near this area earlier was that Wilkes hadn't expected them to find their way out of their rooms. He had planned to get them later that day, but got caught up. He wanted them separate from the others when they awoke as he had to be the one to inform them about things. Their impetuous curiosity was something that he liked, though, and he knew he had made the right decision bringing them all together for this mission. There was one huge piece missing, though. He needed to explain things to Serena about her childhood and the reasons for watching and choosing her.

They entered another corridor and at the end of that one a door was open. The inside was dimly lit so it was hard to see what was there, but it was light enough not to fear entering. Serena was a little hesitant but not scared.

"Serena, this will answer a lot of questions for you and explain your part of the mission. I will be waiting, and we can talk afterward. Don't be scared, it's all OK."

Serena looked at Wilkes, then at the room at the end of the hall, and started making her way to the ominous entrance. She walked up to the door and glanced behind her, but saw Wilkes had vanished from the area. As she entered the room, she could see two chairs and a table in the middle. The chairs were on either side, facing each other like in an interrogation room. The walls were blank like in the rest of the ship and the lighting was now flickering on and off. She walked over to the chair on the left and slowly sat down. As she made herself comfortable, waiting for the next guest to wander through the door, her thoughts were racing, trying to work out who this would be and why her.

While she was sitting there for a few minutes, the lights flickered relentlessly, bright, dim, off, and on, until the light snapped on and lit the room completely. Serena could see everything now and scanned the space for any details, but was let down. Nothing but walls.

A bright flicker of yellow light appeared in front of her. She got a shock and threw her head back. The tiny light flew around her like a firefly, although a little bigger. Jerking and moving like it was not quite right, it was so fast that Serena could not get a good look until it slowed down and hovered in front of her nose. Now Serena could clearly see its little body, golden hair, and tiny wings. On its back was a bow, arrows, and a sword in a scabbard. It was no more than two inches tall.

Serena fell backward hitting her head on the floor as the tiny creature buzzed to the other side of the room and then changed instantly into a full-grown woman with large wings and a green Celtic dress and tiara. She raced over to Serena who rubbed her head vigorously. Serena could see the beautiful woman leaning over her.

"I'm so sorry, my sweetheart. Are you OK? Here, let me help you."

The woman helped Serena up off the floor and then assisted her into the chair before making her way to the other side of the table and sitting down to face her.

"What was that little thing and where did it go?" Serena was confused and looking around the room for it. "Thank you, I'm sorry, who are you?"

The woman was smiling at her like she had been waiting for this moment.

"You don't remember me, my child?"

Serena shook her head and stared at the mesmerizing wings, green medieval Celtic dress, amazing face, and ears that she could just make out, pointing through golden hair.

"Well, firstly, that tiny little thing you saw was me, and secondly, I have waited a long time for this."

As she said that, the room started falling away, and the walls seemed to melt into the ground as grass and trees grew up through the floor, pushing away the ceiling to show a perfect blue sky. The table turned from hard metal to an old oak one with knots and flaws as if it was very old. The same happened to the chairs they were sitting on. The dull boring room disappeared completely, leaving them both surrounded by the richest array of green and different-looking fauna. Birds were singing and one landed right in front of Serena who felt like a little girl again, smiling and giggling as the sun shone through with gentle rays through the thickness of the woods.

"Do you remember now, my dear?" the woman whispered.

Serena shook her head again as she took in all the wonders she was witnessing.

"No ... no, I don't," she said as the woman reached over and sprinkled a tiny purple and gold substance onto Serena. When she finished, she placed her hand on Serena's head, whispering some words that seemed ancient until she began to understand some of them. She opened her eyes, rubbed them, and then she sat up straight.

"Shaylee, is ... It's you, isn't it?"

Serena's memories come flooding back to her with a wave of emotion and excitement. She was putting back together the pieces of a long-lost memory and time when she was a child.

"It *is* you," she screamed, flying off the chair and running over to her long-lost friend, hugging her tightly like a little girl while tears flooded her eyes.

"Yes, dear, it's me. Oh, I have missed you so much, child, and my how you have grown into such a beautiful woman. I am so proud. I have watched you at times grow and succeed, and have longed for this day."

Serena was overwhelmed. Some of her memories were now restored, of the adventures they had when she was young. She had so many questions, but she couldn't let go of Shaylee.

"I know, my dear, come, sit. We have much to catch up on."

Serena loosened her grip and slowly returned to her seat, looking at the forest around them where there were all sorts of creatures near large toadstools and oak trees, and high up in the branches. She knew where she was. She was home in Faelynn.

Serena, now back in her chair facing Shaylee, was rubbing her eyes to adjust to the vibrant colors, when a little creature poked its head from behind Shaylee's dress. It was a rabbit, with long ears, one pointing up around a foot into the air, while the other flopped back behind its head pointing to the ground. It was standing upright and had a thin grass band around its head, like a headband or headpiece of some sorts. A satchel made from large leaves and twigs was hanging from its shoulder angling toward the other side of its hip. Its eyes were a perfect blue and its whiskers were long and silver, matching its light grayish fur. On the other shoulder was a scabbard attached to a baldric that went across the chest with a wooden implement of some kind.

As Serena took in the shy little creature, it jumped up onto the table and said in a young boy's voice, "Did you miss me, ugly?"

Serena looked sternly at the bipedal rabbit, but her expression slowly turned into a smile before exploding into laughter. Picking up the two-and-a-half-foot creature, and hugging him lightly, she said, "Are you kidding me, snotty face? Seeing your head makes me want to puke."

"OK, OK, put me down, stinky breath, I missed you too."

Serena lowered the rabbit down onto the table, still amazed at seeing him again, with his little brown leather overalls covered in leaves and grass.

"Come along, Van Coinan, you can catch up soon enough," Shaylee said.

Van Coinan leaned over to Serena and kissed her on the cheek. "I missed you, kid," he whispered, before bouncing off the table and disappearing into the thick green grass.

Serena stared as he vanished, before turning to Shaylee and asking,

"How come you left me? Why couldn't I stay with you? I loved you so much, and knowing that, you still left me. We'd spent ages together." Serena quivered as tears started rolling down her face.

"I had to, child. You would have eventually forgotten your family and while you never aged, time would eventually have caught them. They would get older, and you wouldn't. I managed to keep it at bay for several hours, but no one has enough magic to hold time forever. It would have been damaging to spend any more time with us, staying the same age and missing years of your family's life.

"Secondly, you know of the war with the 'sinisters' and the dark ones of Faelynn. My mother is still a captive and that vile thing with his pet dog would have taken you too. I wasn't even going to take you to Faelynn; however, when I first flew out the window to leave, Wilkes stopped me and explained what had happened to your friend Riley, and that Anders was on his way to find you. Wilkes waited at your house and as Anders approached, he used everything he had to block you and make him think you perished in the fire, even though your friend spilled the beans before that vicious pet of his tortured and killed them all.

"Wilkes knew that even if you were gone just for a few hours it would be enough for him to clean up the mess and to save you and your family's lives. He saw something in you at the time, when he realized you had the tape of your father's, of the events surrounding the beast and my people. He knew you were strong and well worth being on his list to end all this."

Shaylee passed the cassette that she had taken all those years ago to Serena, who was looking a little disappointed. As she took the tape, she asked, "So, you weren't going to come back, you were told to come and get me from—"

Before Serena could finish, Shaylee grabbed her hand and whispered, "I don't regret a thing, I would have come back anyway, I was only frightened about my mother and our people. That's a promise. Besides, my dear, you are one of us."

Serena had her head low, and through her disappointment said, "I know I am one of you."

Serena knew in her heart that all that time in Faelynn meant she was part of the family.

"Serena, you are one of us," Shaylee emphasized, holding Serena's hand tighter. "This is why I had to block your mind. If Anders and his puppy dog had discovered you with the tape, they would have found out about your past. Having that tape was dangerous, and if you knew about it all, even with the promise of a secret, eventually he would have found you and conducted horrendous experiments and tests on you for your special blood. So, the decision, as hard as it was, had to go that way."

Serena was now looking wide-eyed at Shaylee, thinking she was missing an important point.

"What do you mean, my blood, and being family?"

Shaylee took a deep breath. The creatures all around quietened, the mushroom folk, the Pixies, the under folk, the tree sprites, gnomes, and all the nature folk around the area, trying to listen in.

"Go about your business, my people, she will know soon enough." After Shaylee said that, all the creatures went about their usual activities, creating a natural sound in the mystical forest, as it had been before.

"Serena, this information was told to you when you were with us. I thought it better not to block it, but to remove most of it completely on the off chance that when you returned, it would come out.

"When your mother was young, she was at a local bar. This was right before she met your father. Being Italian, she didn't know too many people and she didn't know a lot about the local folklore. On this night she was tricked by an elf who was a known trickster and drunk. He had turned himself into a handsome young man and swept your mother Grace off her feet with romance and sweet talk. They spent the night together, and in the morning, he had gone, returned to Faelynn. Two weeks later your mother was crying outside your father's office and he went over to help her out. Grace did not want to be hurt again so she was a little standoffish at first, but Liam, being a gentleman, just spent time with her and helped her transition into her new country. He learned some Italian and taught her some Gaelic in return.

"Eventually they got married and you were born. Liam knew you were not his, but he loved you just the same, if not more at times. When you were born the wind blew in a swirl, like a small hurricane. This said to our world that a faery was born outside of Faelynn. When the council found out the elf was crossbreeding with a human, which is forbidden, he was going to be put to trial. But just before this was to happen, Faelynn was attacked by the 'sinisters', as they found a way into our world, taking our queen and many of our people. So, we forgot about you, as you should have been raised here with us. It wasn't until we met that I knew straight off it was you. Why do you think you could see me on the ground? It wasn't the poem you recited, as lovely as it was. No, you found me because you are one of us, now and forever."

Shaylee finished with relief in her eyes, as she had thought keeping this from Serena all this time was not fair on her.

"Are you saying I'm half elf?" Serena asked, desperate for closure. She felt like she was in a dream state, but she knew this was very real.

"Ha, ha, ha, no, my love, you are half Fae, part of the faery folk, elves included."

Serena smiled and thought to herself how it all made sense, her being different from her sisters, the teasing about being taken by faeries, even the fascination as a kid and the relationships she built in Faelynn all those years ago, as some of the missing pieces started coming together.

"So, if I'm part faery, then does this forbid me to be with a human?" Serena thought she'd better get some rules straight because she didn't want to be punished.

"Ha, ha, no, no, my dear, you are half human, so this exempts you. In fact, I encourage you to be with whomever you want in the world."

Shaylee giggled, but then became serious.

"You have limited time here. If I don't send you back soon you may not get back at all, so we must be swift. I have a request, no, a favor, more like. I hate those sinister things called Zeytars. I only tolerate Wilkes because he has done right by many of my kind, including you.

I must get onto that ship with you to save my mother and our people. Wilkes has approved that I help you and I am asking, can you please help me save them? You are a strong woman and only with you can I succeed. You will be required to be part of the mission, though we will deviate for a small time to release them and then we will all help your friends. Wilkes doesn't know that part, he only knows that I will be coming to help you all."

Shaylee didn't like keeping things from Wilkes due to the number of things he had done for her. She was worried that there wouldn't be time to prioritize her people if it all hit the fan.

"Of course, Shaylee, you know that I will. In fact, it reminds me of that adventure we had in Toozookus, remember?" Serena was so excited, all her worries were gone. She felt like she had such a strong network around her now with all her friends old and new.

"Wonderful, my dear. Now here is a small crystal from the palace. Whisper into it and I will appear wherever you are, but make sure it's just before we enter. I will hide in small sprite form until needed, to blend in."

Shaylee handed over the blue and red crystal. There was still so much about faery magic that Serena didn't understand. Although, thinking about it, was it really magic or just their own sciences working in with their culture and world that gave that illusion. Serena liked the magic idea more, she thought.

"Oh, Eric's daughter is lost on the ship. After we find your people can you help us find her? She is very important to Eric." Serena remembered why they were there in the first place.

"Of course, my dear. He is special to you, isn't he? He is a good man, you will be a great match for each other after all this. Oh, I nearly forgot, I have something for you, an old friend so to speak."

Shaylee bent down next to her and picked up a scabbard with Celtic symbols all over it. Inside was a sword. The scabbard was slightly bent, with a detailed handle made from ancient bone wrapped in maroon and green binding to hide it.

Serena jumped up.

"Long Leaf! You have her."

With much excitement, Serena took the sword from Shaylee and pulled it halfway out of the scabbard to look at it. She was an elegant sword, with a slight bend in the middle, a green and maroon handle, and detailed pommel. It had beautiful patterns all through the steel, much like Shaylee's own sword. Serena loved it very much, and when she was first given the sword by Shaylee all those years ago, Serena remembered it was shaped like a thin bent iris leaf, so she named it Long Leaf.

"I knew you would be happy with her. She was the love of your life when you were young. But now it's time to go, my dear. I will see you in the blink of an eye," and as she said that, Serena found herself sitting all alone inside the dull room just as it was before.

She took a little time to adjust and gather her thoughts. So many questions were still unanswered. Then she grabbed her sword, the cape, and crystal, and made her way out into the corridor, where Wilkes had reappeared again.

"Are you happy, Serena? Now that you know, please understand it was the right thing to do." Before Wilkes could continue with what he'd been waiting to say to Serena, she put her arms around him and kissed the side of his bald, pale, veiny face.

"Thank you, Wilkes, thank you. I will pay it forward and help you with all I've got."

Wilkes was expecting to have to explain a little bit more as Shaylee held back on a lot of information, but he liked the fact he didn't have to and that she was on his side.

"OK, good, well, I'm going to finally recharge. We have one more day of information and plans, so I am going to rest my beautiful face." Wilkes said and he smirked this time.

Serena thought she liked this side to Wilkes and could understand why he was so reserved and tense. If you were organizing the absolute destruction of your own people, you would probably feel the same way, she thought.

"No worries, Wilkes, I will see you then."

Serena made her way back to the main information room where she saw Eric sitting asleep in a chair, waiting for her. Serena thought how sweet it was and stared at him for a moment, before snapping out of it and wandering over to wake him up.

"Hey, Eric, time for bed."

Eric's eyes opened and he took in his surroundings before acknowledging Serena there.

"Hey there, are you OK, how did you go?"

Serena smiled and whispered, "I will tell you all about it tomorrow, it's time for sleep."

Eric yawned as they both stood up, and they made their way into the sleeping quarters. Two doors were still up.

"I'll take this one if you like," Serena said.

Eric nodded and awkwardly leaned over to give her a kiss on the cheek. "Thank you again, Serena, for everything you have done for me. And I can't apologize enough for how I acted when you were trying to save me. I—"

Before Eric could finish his sentence, Serena moved in close and gave him a passionate kiss on the lips that lasted for a very long time.

"You will never need to thank me," she said. "You are always looking out for me too."

Serena then let go of Eric and made her way to her sleeping quarters. She looked back, winked at Eric, and then watched him until the door snapped down, leaving Eric standing on his own in the hallway.

As he turned toward his room with a large smile on his face, Serena's door flew back up. She ran out and they embraced, kissing passionately for minutes until Serena grabbed Eric's hand and led him into her room. The door snapped shut again and there was silence once more in the corridor.

PLANNING
THE ATTACK

A N ALARM SCREECHED THROUGH the entire ship. Eric launched out of bed, nearly pushing Serena out too.

"I'm so sorry, sweetheart, are you alright?" Eric asked.

Serena was smiling, as she pulled the covers back up to her chin.

"Yes, Eric, I'm fine. You need to be less jumpy, I'm sure it's just someone burning the toast or something."

She knew very well, with everything going on, that any kind of alarm meant something. But Eric was so tightly wound since his daughter was taken, that she just used some calming psychology on him to ease him into whatever crisis was about to unfold.

"Didn't Wilkes mention that there would be alarms that would connect to all the ships, the first being the VIZZY LEX, or something, the robot that opens a tear for the Zeytar hybrids to come through?"

Eric was still tired and even though he was rambling a little, Serena understood.

"Yes, the V.I.Z.I.N.D.A.L.E.X. We need to get up. If that thing is awake, we don't have much time at all to prepare."

Serena looked over at her sword Long Leaf and the crystal sitting next to it, and smiled. Memories tumbled through her mind and a sense of wonder and adventure filled her heart like she was a child again. She gazed at Eric who was getting dressed, and gave out a little wolf whistle. Eric turned around revealing his muscular physique. He was a little older than Serena, but he took care of his body by going to the gym whenever he could. After Eric finished putting his shirt on, he walked over to her, leaned in, and gave her a passionate kiss, before grabbing the sheets and saying, "Come on, sexy, it's time we find out exactly what is going on."

Serena let out a yell and quickly grabbed her clothes, giving Eric an angry smirk before getting dressed and heading to the door where he was waiting. But she realized she had forgotten something and asked Eric to wait outside for her. Eric nodded and went out.

Serena rushed back to the bedside and grabbed the crystal. Then she fastened her scabbard over her shoulder with Long Leaf safe inside. She wasn't going to let any of those things out of her sight now. She ran for the door, and as she opened it, Eric was standing there with his lips pursed and eyes closed, waiting for a kiss. Serena laughed and gave him a peck on the cheek, before pushing past him and moving toward the large meeting room.

Eric turned, disappointed with the outcome, and whispered to himself, "I've been cheated."

Serena heard it, turned, and smiled. Eric caught up with her, grabbed her hand, and they entered the room together. Everyone else was already seated and waiting for Wilkes.

"What, no breakfast in bed?" Eric said as they took their seats up the front. Valinda, who was next to Serena, was staring straight ahead, not saying anything, lost in her own thoughts.

Serena knew something wasn't right with her, so she whispered, "Hey, kiddo, are you alright?"

Valinda snapped out of her trance.

"Oh, hey, guys, I didn't see you there. What did you say, Serena, I'm sorry?"

Serena had a newfound respect for Valinda, with the things she'd had to continually overcome and deal with, all while showing resilience and the drive to keep going. It was admirable, she thought.

"It's OK, sweetie, I just asked if you are alright," Serena said in a soft tone.

Valinda flashed an awkward smile. "No, Father Larsen is still missing. I'm not sure where he is, and no one has seen him at all. Wilkes said again this morning that he is not on this ship and if that is the case, then a man who doesn't know where he is in another dimension just vanished into thin air. He wouldn't survive outside the ship, so if he went outside somehow, he would have been killed. I'm so worried about him, Serena." Valinda couldn't hold it together any longer and cried.

Serena leaned in and gave her a hug, Eric reached over and rubbed Valinda's shoulder, comforting her as well. They had not known each other for long, but they were all becoming very close, very quickly.

"He will show up, Val, he has the Lord on his side, and I have never met a tougher priest in my life. He was always strong for me when I needed him too over the years. I know he will be alright." Serena had tears in her eyes. She too was very worried about Michael, although she had to give the illusion that she wasn't too concerned, for Valinda's sake.

Wilkes appeared through the other doorway in his Zeytar form. He looked like he was in a hurry to get this all sorted, as he arrived at the desk where he had stood the day before.

"Everyone heard the alarm, I gather. There will be two more. The android V.I.Z.I.N.D.A.L.E.X. is awake and on its mission. It will reach its destination fast, so we have very little time. We need to be on the ship no later than the second alarm. This is when the bodiless Zeytar minds will blend with their new hybrid bodies and be released from stasis. The third alarm is Zero Time, which means the X-Clock has reached its destination and the doors will open, starting the dimensional transition from here to Earth. This is what we are here to stop, so before I go any further, can I have everyone into their teams so I can run through what your role will be and where you need to go."

Wilkes had no charm about him this day. It was game on and everything had to be done to perfection. There was no room for error, so everyone was strategically selected for their own special skill sets, knowledge, or background to be used specifically for this mission.

There weren't any tourists on this ride and Wilkes had worked very hard for decades planning how it would all go down. The problem with that was you could plan for every scenario, but at the end of the day you had to put your trust in the people selected to come through. Humans were not robots programed for a task, so free will and decision-making could affect the whole dynamic. This he knew and tried to account for. It was also the reason he was in rather a stressed-out mood, for if one zigged when he or she was supposed to zag, the whole thing might well be over before it started.

Everyone was pretty much all together in their groups, except Eric, who was meant to be with his team WOSER to be briefed on the first part of the plan. This was for him to learn as much as he could about the Sasquatch and its strengths along with its weaknesses, so if they were confronted with the gatherers on the ship, they could deal with them and teach others how to avoid getting hurt.

The hardest part of this was they had to find them, release them from the mind control Geno-drone chips, and send them out into the wild. Wilkes wanted that specifically as he did not want to see them harmed or for them to perish with the Leader's ships, as they normally were very peaceful and compassionate creatures.

Wilkes knew that Eric would not be a full part of that side of the mission, not until he at least had his daughter with him. His knowledge of the beast was very good, and all his research pointed out many similarities in theory to the actual creature, without even having set eyes upon one until he was attacked.

Wilkes first asked the pilots to stand up. He would nominate each one their role as required right up to the last detail and then move on to the next group and so on.

Alan, Terrence, and Alexandra were the pilots. Each had access to a stealth bomber, courtesy of Wilkes. Their mission was to wait until the android entered the particle accelerator and fire as much as they could, hoping to blow enough up above ground to cause chaos underground. The accelerator had to be as still as possible, so any distraction was encouraged. One pilot would do this while the others waited until the ships started coming through, then they would release a barrage of firepower as they entered, hoping to cause a chain reaction and destroy them all.

Wilkes moved on to the next group. These were the soldiers, fifty in total, half of which would be allocated positions inside the grounds of the Super Collider, while the others would assist in the protection and tactics for the groups on the ship. The two contingents were led by Lieutenant Stone, who oversaw the ship's men, and the other was Staff Sergeant Felon, who had been selected personally by Wilkes two years earlier, so he had quite an understanding of the mission ahead and the logistics of the whole place.

Wilkes moved forward looking at the third team. That was the weapons control team. Each group had to have at least one of these men and women as they were briefed on all the locations of the weapons caches on the ship along with the ones here that Wilkes had yet to explain and show to all who were going to use them as part of the plan.

Lastly, there were the freelancers who had individual missions to complete in order to achieve success. Stacey had already been one of those, completing one of the hardest parts of the plan and setting up a hope for all humans if the Zeytar hybrids managed to succeed in getting through to Earth. Not even Wilkes knew of her success yet. It was all blind hope that she had managed to complete her mission. However, if she had not, the other plan was to wipe out as many of them as they could.

The freelancers were Serena, Eric for the most part, Wilkes, Rovan, Stacey, and three others whom they hadn't met, Eleanor, Dakota, and Spencer, who would be part of freeing as many slaves as possible. The group would be split and those freeing the enslaved ones would be given a map of the area.

The others were expendable. They were to help Wilkes find the Leader and kill him.

The only one left was Valinda. She had to gain as much public confidence as she could before the imminent attack, by exposing as many things as she could to people. She already had a large following, but she would use some hard-core evidence to prove the threat was real by means of tapes and recordings. Two from Serena: Eric's brush with Anders in the hospital, revealing their agenda, and the second being a hypnosis regression recording of beasts stealing a child in Ireland.

There were many others that Wilkes had accumulated over the years to help with disclosure. His hope was that if they could warn as many people as they could, then there would be a formidable amount of power to deal with the threat. Wilkes' own mission, besides the Leader, was to guide Valinda through her mission at a secret radio station, then to destroy the command center on the ship where the control Geno-drone chips would be turned on from. This should be enough to stop the global switch and at worst they would only have to deal with the Zeytar hybrids which would fall ill quickly if Stacey had succeeded.

There were so many things that could go wrong, Wilkes thought, but he felt he chose well and had faith in them all to succeed. They were all worth saving in his eyes.

≈

Wilkes had sent the pilots and the twenty-five soldiers as the ground crew for Waxahachie off to their posts after which he began working with Valinda to gather all the evidence and put it all together for a livestream. Wilkes had access to a satellite and had some tech experts awaiting them when they arrived, which would be very soon.

Eric was now with his team WOSER, looking at all the DNA, their previous research, and how it compared to the actual Sasquatch, along with how they could use this knowledge to better understand the way the beasts acted and reacted to events, especially in their controlled state, as this would be the most dangerous part. Wilkes had videos uploaded of some abductions and how they maneuvered in the wild, although it wasn't so much the beast itself that was the most dangerous, as strong as it was. If always monitored, and not lurking or sneaking, it was slow in comparison, apart from its stride which was what they had to look out for most. It was the tiny flying folk accompanying the beasts that were the dangerous side, as they were super-fast and, when working together, super-strong. Only a few of them could lift a small child off the ground. They seemed to have weapons as well, and in one video, a young boy's eyes were lost as he struggled too much. He had been too fast for the Sasquatch to catch, and the little humanoid creatures, or faeries as Serena had mentioned before, used tiny arrows to blind the boy so the Sasquatch could take him. It was barbaric and inhuman, and they seemed to work very well in unison.

Serena was with the group when they were analyzing the data and had explained some, not all, of how they are a peaceful race under the control of the Leader just like the Sasquatch. Eric knew there was some major link between her and those tiny sprites as he saw the sword and the crystal. He knew she would tell him everything in time and this was not the time.

Levi was a very good model for the WOSER team as they analyzed, poked, and prodded him, even making him laugh with a snort from a ticklish spot near his underarm. Eric spent the day with his team, passing on as much information as he could and working with Levi, even scanning his whole body for any internal clues which might help.

Eric found something that could change things, he thought. If Levi had the ability to naturally harmonize a frequency from his larynx and open a doorway, then could that same theory work in an inorganic copied version? Eric took some scans of Levi's larynx physiology and then asked him to open a door to Earth, only for a few seconds, then stop, as no one wanted to go just yet. Levi lay calmly on the scanning table and then let out a horrible cry. As the vortex started to open, Eric took some more scans. When he was satisfied, he tapped Levi on the arm and the beast stopped immediately. Eric could not believe how human-like and understanding these creatures actually were, and would love to study them more when this was all over.

"OK, Levi, thank you very much for your help. You can go and find Valinda now and get ready for your journey with her."

Levi climbed off the scanning table, looked at Eric, and gave him a hard pat on the head, before stomping out of the room. Eric rubbed the back of his neck, and as sore as it was, he could only smile and admire the strength Levi had.

Eric took the scans and uploaded the data into the computer. He hoped his idea worked as it would be a fantastic backup if something happened to Levi or Wilkes. After he had set up, he commenced the 3D printing, which was much more sophisticated than Earth's and able to use Geno-drones to replicate each fibrous muscle, tendon, bone, and tissue for an exact copy, like it was pulled from the beast itself.

Once completed, he took the original of Levi's first scan where he was calm, and gave it a blow inside it. It was modified so air could not escape quickly, and the muscles and tendons worked on air flow like a flute. There were even tiny blood vessels that filled when Eric blew air inside the tiny opening.

Eric had no luck. It just made a loud unpleasant array of animal noises. He then tried the second where Levi had opened a doorway. Eric blew wind inside the tiny hole once more and a high-pitched scream came bellowing out. He continued, and as he did, a vortex started opening. Eric had to breathe, although he held on until the portal was fully opened before stopping. As he stopped the vortex slowly closed and they were left in silence again.

Eric looked around the room and all his team were staring in disbelief. All his years in science and anthropology had worked for something spectacular. He then broke the silence with a scream of joy and jumped up, kissing Simon on the forehead, before bolting out of the room to find Wilkes.

Wilkes was finishing up with Valinda. They had prepared all the evidence and placed it into a folder, and Valinda had finished a voice-over for the compilation of the evidence. This meant she didn't have to stay at the station, but she could turn it on and play it on repeat until the authorities shut it down. It would be played over all stations and networks with a code that would be hard to crack if anyone wanted to silence it. If the power was turned off, it would be uploading through the satellite as it played. So the only way to stop it would be to find the satellite and destroy it. This would keep the authorities busy for a long time and that would hopefully be enough.

Eric rushed into the recording room and explained to Wilkes what he had just uncovered. Wilkes looked surprised and a little concerned.

"That is great, Eric, I never even thought of that one. However, be careful of two things, the first, if you use it, only one or two can go through at a time as your lung capacity is not as strong as a Sasquatch's, so cutting out halfway through could trap someone in a parallel dimension. Secondly, it's not like Levi where he has been trained to use his harmonics to open doors by linking with his mind and with latitude and longitude to the finest point. Where did Levi open the door to when you copied his harmonic vibrations on your scan?"

Eric looked confused, and then he remembered. "I told him just to open a doorway to Earth." Eric was now understanding that it wasn't as simple as just opening a doorway. He needed to know the default setting that Levi had opened just before. If it was in the middle of the Atlantic Ocean, then they would all be stuffed.

It was handy that Levi was there with Valinda and Wilkes to ask.

"Levi, can you open the same door as before when you were on the table, the one back to Earth?" Eric asked calmly, hoping he would remember.

Levi nodded and opened his mouth wide, the sound too much for Valinda who covered her ears. The next moment shocked Eric and Wilkes as they could see through the whirling blue maelstrom a forest, but where that forest was no one knew, so Eric decided to jump through it. Glancing back, he could see Wilkes in panic mode gesturing to Levi to follow him and bring him back.

Eric now looked around the place and was wandering off as the vortex closed and he was left stranded. He was trying to find something familiar that would lead him to some kind of conclusion. Eric had worked in some form or another at most of the major national parks in America, and as he looked at the trees, the sizing of the trunks, along with the vegetation and some of the birds, he narrowed it down to somewhere in the Pacific Northwest. Where exactly, he didn't know, but it was better than being in the middle of the ocean.

Then it hit him hard. In pursuit of his curiosity, he was now stranded in the middle of nowhere. He couldn't even use his model of Levi's larynx, as it was still on the table in the computer room where he was showing it to Wilkes.

"Shit!" Eric yelled, as some birds flew off from their resting perch, startled by his outburst. As he walked around to try and find the area where he had come from, another flurry of birds left the sanctuary of their homes, startled by something else. Eric hadn't made a noise this time and as he turned around to see what was scaring them, a huge shadow fell over him and he was standing in the presence of a massive beast.

Eric dropped back, startled at first, before picking himself up off the ground and dusting himself off.

"Don't do that again, Levi. You scared the crap out of me! I think I've had enough of that to last me a while."

Levi gave Eric a smirk and a huff, as if amused by the situation, before turning around and opening a door back to where Wilkes was patiently waiting for them both.

As they poured into the room, Wilkes walked over to Eric, put his long index finger in front of Eric's face, and whispered, "Please don't do anything as foolish as that again. That kind of action will get you and maybe others killed, do we understand each other?"

That was the first time Wilkes had ever talked to anyone like that. It was clear the stress was getting to him. When he finished with his small lecture, he turned away from Eric, but asked him, "Where did you go?"

Eric looked like a small child who had just lost his pocket money. "Somewhere in the Pacific Northwest."

Wilkes, still with his back turned, said, "You were three miles from where you first got attacked. It is a default for some Sasquatch for some reason to start from there and for others to start elsewhere in the Pacific Northwest. This must be Levi's. So Klamath National Forest will be our starting and ending point when we are ready to enter the ship.

Knowing this, you may now use your device only if Levi or myself can't open it for you."

Wilkes walked out, headed for the last of the teams, to educate them on all the weapons systems.

COSMIC TOYS

WILKES HAD THE LIEUTENANT AND HIS TEAM ready and waiting. It had been a long and drawn out few days for them all, briefing everyone, preparing, and answering questions. It was a good thing the soldiers had been with Wilkes for a while and had been briefed previously on most things. Wilkes wanted to save the weapons until last so as everyone who was going to enter the ship would understand how some of the weaponry and devices worked. Eric, Serena, Dakota, Eleanor, Spencer, and Valinda, even though she would not be entering the ship, were also present for the demonstration.

Wilkes had an array of weapons laid out across a long table, each one for a purpose and for particular individuals. As he walked over to the first lot, he made it quite clear that everyone needed to switch on for this exercise.

"Firstly, I just want to announce that after the first alarm sounded, I sent off several drones to monitor and follow the X-Clock, or ALEX, as it were. The high-tech drones will transmit any kind of imagery or video that they deem out of character for a normal human being. This will give us an understanding of roughly where the android is. The signals and messages will be received by Staff Sergeant Felon's crew, and if deemed important, I have a relay to any information forwarded by the soldiers. The second alarm will sound soon and that means the Zeytars will find their host bodies. I would ask everyone to please take note. These devices and weapons are very easy to use, sophisticated, and advanced, but you need to know how to use them properly."

Wilkes walked over to the first one. It was a long rifle, around the length of someone's arm. It was rounded like a large barrel, although very light in weight.

"This is your bread and butter, especially for those on the ship chosen to release prisoners. It's called the Zaxis 104. It is purely and simply only to deactivate control chips in anyone. The zap is an electroshock through the body, designed to stop the function of the chip. The second blast, which is imperative, is a controlled blast that holds the creature or human in the one spot and pulls the chip from their body. It also releases pain relief to the exit wound at the same time, all while the host is stunned. It takes several seconds for it to work, however the second shot must be administered, as the chips will be reactivated if the global switch happens. Here, I will demonstrate."

Wilkes picked up the Zaxis 104. It looked large under his skinny gangly arm, although he seemed to handle it like it was a part of him. He lined it up to a dummy that was set up for the demonstration, then with one pull of the trigger, a single blast of blue and white light emanated from the gun and the dummy fell over. A volunteer stood the dummy back up and once he was out of the way, Wilkes lined the dummy up and pulled the trigger again, this time holding it down for several seconds until a small object tore out of the dummy's arm and into the large barrel of the device.

"See how that time I held my finger down until the light on the top of the gun went from red to blue? This is how you know it was successful. When we have the chip, all we have to do is dump it. The only other button on the gun is on the side. Just press it and the chip is launched out onto the floor. Without a host it's useless. Then we move on to the next stage. This may seem like it takes a while, but trust me, it's only twenty seconds maximum per person if used at its optimum capacity. You will have one each, so if there are multiple controlled beasts trying to attack, you will have enough."

Wilkes had planted the chip inside the dummy to make it look more realistic. He had found while working with humans that most of the time using a visual aid was the best way to teach.

"Next up we have the Marxis Exo 779. This will be your best friend, people, as it's purely a stun gun. If you are overwhelmed by many controlled ones at once, then you can safely zap them and pull the Geno-drone chip out while they are out. It's as simple as point and shoot. Take note, though, that they will be under for at least a minute, so you may need to get them off the ship while they are out of it. If this is the case, then you can use your cloned portal device to open the doors. Please be aware and make note of what beasts and people have been de-chipped as the rest are controlled by the hive and could fake it. Always do a scan beforehand by just pointing the Zaxis 104 at the subject. It will pick it up and light up red for a positive reading. Never trust that the chip is out purely based on behavior, as it's all over if your skull is caved in by a Sasquatch or worse. Are we clear on those two devices?"

Wilkes looked around the room. Everyone was nodding, so it was time for the harder artillery. This was mainly for the soldiers.

Lieutenant Stone moved in a little closer. He had already been briefed on the weapons at hand, however his troops hadn't, so he quickly addressed his soldiers.

"Listen up! This could save your life. We will debrief after this demonstration, so I don't want any confusion about what these things do and when to use them, got it?"

In unison, like a perfectly timed choir, the response was a loud "Yes, sir!"

Wilkes didn't care too much for the formalities of human military. He was more interested in science and development, although he did spend many, many years developing devices for war and intimidation of innocent victims going about their daily routines. He knew this was a human thing and was what they were trained to do. That discipline they had could someday save their lives or the lives of others.

Wilkes continued, "I have already explained that there are caches all over the control mother ship and in those storage areas you will find all different kinds of weapons. The first is a flash grenade. Pretty straightforward, press the button and throw. Very convenient for large contingents of soldiers to stun for a while. Please don't look after you throw it, though. Second is the Repeater X2. This is a pulse rifle that will basically shatter anything in front of you. It's fully automatic and has enough power for several dozen blasts. It's the top of our range in destructive warfare and we only use these on the Draconians."

Wilkes looked around the room and realized he just mentioned a race no one would know about yet.

"Long story, if we survive this, I will tell you more about your other visitors and the wars that have been playing out under your noses. Now, the Repeater X2 is lightweight and easy to carry, with a strap for over the shoulder carriage. Only the masters and the wardens use these guns, as in the hands of the wrong soldier it can be quite messy. This will satisfy nearly all your needs, but these other three left on the table may also come in handy."

Wilkes grabbed the first one. It was a goggle device that could fit over a soldier's head.

"This is very useful in times of flashes from grenades, to dim the lighting. It adjusts the vision as the lighting changes and can scan beyond the visible light spectrum from ultraviolet to infrared, switching throughout. With this on, it gives the wearer constant updates and information on the screen and a map of their location. Also it provides updates on the kind of species that is in front of them, and whether they are alive or not, with pinpoint accuracy, which will save time. Next is the tiny handgun. It will stop anything in its tracks without killing them, just in case you are unsure if they are on our side or not. It will get dark and confusing at times, so this may help some of you. Lastly, you have the task of setting four of these at specific locations around the control ship. They are flash zeeps, highly powerful electro-explosives that if placed near the power cores of the ship will ultimately bring the whole thing down. They have timers, although I would rather you use the detonators just in case they are found and deprogramed. There will be three detonators that all connect to the flash zeeps, so if two unfortunately are killed, there is still a remainder. If that person is also killed, then I have a backup one. However, I will need to be on the ship to use it, as once turned on, the signal can only be switched within the vicinity of the flash zeeps. Now, Lieutenant, who would you like to be in charge of the detonators?"

Wilkes was well in control now. He had been dreading the whole disclosure and training part, and now that it was drawing closer to an end, he was able to concentrate on his mission, which was to face the Leader and inevitably Anders. Thankfully Xandar would be with ALEX so he only had to face one master and the Leader, as long as his pet wasn't there.

"I think it would be most logical for me to have one myself, my second mate Sergeant Merring, and one of your rebels, maybe Eric, to hold one, in case we run into trouble." Stone was convinced he was right and wouldn't take no for an answer. Eric saw it in his eyes even though the last thing he wanted was to be responsible for that.

"Yes, great idea." Wilkes looked over at Eric and winked. Well, it looked like a wink, Eric thought. The eyelid closed in sideways and met in the middle, not up and down like a human's.

Just as they were finishing up, the second alarm went off, meaning the Zeytars were mind-blending with their new hybrid bodies in stasis. Wilkes went back to "panic stations".

"OK, everyone, to give us a heads-up and work more invisibly we will be wearing their new uniforms. I have a size each for you, gray cargos, gray long sleeve shirts, a cap, vest, black boots, and satchels. Disregard the patches on the sides. Also, everyone gets an earpiece on the same channel with a voice activator on the collar so everyone can always check in and know what's happening. Get dressed and meet me back here in twenty minutes. Yes, that means you too, Eric."

Eric thought he was exempt from their uniform because his role was different and Wilkes liked to mess with him at times. It was the human in him which he had acquired over the years, but it seemed to shine through more with Eric, though.

Wilkes went to the main control section to fly the ship to the Klamath National Forest near Marble Mountain, not before getting Valinda ready, though. She would be the first stop. Wilkes powered up the craft and with a loud echo it burst through a small portal rip and into Earth's dimension. He flew as high as he could to stay undetected, before descending at full speed toward the abandoned radio station in Minneapolis. The ship hovered over the outskirts of the city. Wilkes didn't care about it being seen by the public now. A huge saucer-shaped craft with multiple lights flickering all around the underneath, using zero-point energy to power and maneuver was going to be the least of the weird things the public was about to experience.

He took Valinda and they disappeared into a light on the ship to reappear inside the radio station. The saucer then vanished into thin air by Wilkes' mind command, as he thought perhaps he should hide it for the time being.

Wilkes had a team of tech specialists inside the station who were awaiting the video documents to upload to the satellite. Martin Friedman had been one of Wilkes' own personal file encryption specialists over the years and had been looking forward to finally seeing some of his handiwork being shared with millions, if not billions of people around the world. It wasn't just America that would be affected by this apocalyptic event; the entire human race would be devastated if the Leader and V.I.Z.I.N.D.A.L.E.X. succeeded.

Martin welcomed Wilkes and Valinda, who was already working her way around the system to start playing the recording. She was already experienced with this kind of tech, having been involved with journalism and her own video uploads for many years, so it was not foreign to her.

"We need to hurry, Valinda. Martin and Jeffery will take over, I just need you to do a live feed introduction so it doesn't look robotic or like a secret organization is sending out propaganda."

Valinda knew this was her time to shine and what she was predominantly chosen for, so she sat down, plugged in the hard copy, and looked straight into the screen, awaiting the signal from Martin to go ahead.

Valinda was nervous. This was a major part of the mission and she had to be as real and convincing as she could. The tape was in, her opening was ready, and Martin flicked the switch to live. Valinda was on.

"Ladies and gentlemen, boys and girls, my name is Valinda Mannix and I am an ordinary person just like all of you. The interruption to your screens at this stage is unfortunate, although imperative. The way of life we have right now is under direct threat of annihilation. I and many others over time have created this video together. Some very important people and some who were nobody in the scheme of things have died because of this deception that is upon us. Some scenes will be very hard to watch, but I assure you, it is all very much real and true. Hollywood could not even compare with the violent and destructive scenes that will soon fill your screens. I just ask you all to prepare and find solace. Today is the last day you will have as you know it. Don't trust anyone telling you this is fake news. Pool together all your hidden weapons and pray. I will show you right now what the deception looks like. Wilkes, come here."

Wilkes had not planned for this and wasn't happy at first, but on reflection thought it should have been the first thing they did for global disclosure. He moved to the other side of the disc jockey's control table where Valinda sat staring straight down the camera. Wilkes walked around and showed his original Zeytar form. He picked up a sharp implement and used his mind to set it in mid-air, floating. The sharp object then turned, and as Wilkes lined it up with his own eyes, he let it loose, hurtling toward his face, ready to blind himself. The sharp object abruptly stopped a fraction of an inch from his eye. With a blink from Wilkes, the object fell to the floor and the Zeytar vanished into thin air.

Valinda continued, "The deception is real, and the following videos will explain the whole agenda. Trust, believe, pray, and prepare. The end is here, and we are trying to stop it, but we need you to believe us."

Valinda stood up, still in front of the camera, looked at Martin and nodded. Martin then went to press play on the video which had Valinda's original loop recording on it and the last thing the audience saw before the video started to play was Valinda vanish like Wilkes, back up onto the ship.

SAVAGE DESTRUCTION

WILKES MADE IT TO THE DEEP OF THE Klamath National Forest from Minneapolis in only minutes. All the teams were ready and waiting while he was going through the last of the plans in his mind, making sure he had not left any stone unturned. The footage from the drones showed they had picked up something strange in Waxahachie, Texas, but he had faith that Felon and his team would hold it off long enough for them to bring the ships down from the inside.

Wilkes landed the massive saucer in a clearing just outside the dense woods. There he cloaked the ship and opened several hatches around the circular structure of the craft. The teams piled out with large packs, each containing parts to tents, first aid kits, and weaponry.

Wilkes had chosen this location from his radar maps on the ship and believed it to be secluded, with a perfect clearing if they needed to escape quickly. The soldiers erected a large marquee tent and a couple of smaller ones for the three people that would be left behind to attend to anyone who needed medical assistance. One was a medic soldier, and the other two were Valinda, who had remote access to the live feed she had recently uploaded, and a science officer that Wilkes had chosen specifically for his understanding and advanced knowledge of Zeytar tech, including the craft if they needed a quick escape. He was also going to be helping Valinda with the Sasquatch as they were freed and let loose. Valinda had some kind of unknown connection to the beasts and Wilkes thought it might help having her there to calm the bipedal hominids.

Wilkes was extremely anxious. None of the others had ever seen this side to him and although he was trying his best not to express any feelings at all about the mission, they were very obvious to some of the group.

Wilkes moved the team that was going onto the ship into the dense darkened forest, out of the way of the camp. Levi had said goodbye to Valinda and was now standing next to Wilkes. She wanted to watch them all go through. Wilkes would wait until the rest had entered before going inside himself. Levi knew where the door would open. It was an old part of the ship where the beasts brought the subjects in, although it was no longer being used, as that part of their agenda had finished for now.

Eric looked around for Serena. He was standing with his team and the soldiers, but he wanted to go through with her. As he tried to locate her, he called out softly, "Serena, Serena, it's time."

Meanwhile, Serena had ducked out of view and pulled her crystal out. It was time for Shaylee to find her. She pulled the sparkling rock closer to her face and whispered, "It's time, Shaylee. I am waiting here for you."

The crystal glowed a luminous blue and red and within a blink and a breath Shaylee flew out of the crystal and hovered above Serena's head.

"Thank you, my dear," the faery said in a high-pitched tone into Serena's ear. "Lead me to your beast so I may hide within him."

Serena held the tiny glowing sprite inside her palm and followed Eric's calls, which were starting to sound concerned. She appeared from around a very large tree that pointed to the moon, and met Eric's gaze. Smiling, she walked over to him, kissing him on the cheek, before walking over to Levi who was getting ready with some slow breathing for his bigger than ever portal opening. She unclasped her hand near his back and Shaylee snuck deep within his fur to hide until she was through the door. Shaylee was very thankful that Levi, although smelly, was not half as bad as others she had known while under control.

No one was any wiser to what had just taken place as Serena returned to Eric's side and held his hand awaiting the unknown events that were about to play out.

"It's time, Levi. Once the door is open two teams will go through. Once the first is safely through without danger, come back to this place and let the second wave through. I will wait until last, and this will break it up for you, so you aren't too exhausted."

Levi nodded with a grunt and then opened his mouth to begin the process. The next sound they heard was the beast letting out an almighty cry as the process began. Swirls of light, wind, and noise were created as the doorway opened. The soldiers were ready and waiting to go through first and clear the area. After they had quickly piled through, Levi vanished and the last of the wind and blue light dissipated into silence. The birds were no longer singing, and even the trees seemed to slow down. An eerie silence remained.

Within twenty seconds or so the vortex opened and Levi was back with the others in Klamath. Eric still could not believe that this was how they stayed elusive for all those years. Serena clasped his hand tighter and he turned to her, knowing she was a little scared.

"It's OK, gorgeous, I won't let anything happen to you, I promise."

Serena smiled and pulled his arm in closer before responding, "I know, but who's going to protect you? That will most likely be me."

They both giggled like little children for a moment, and then Levi opened the portal again. This time the WOSER crew along with Eric, Serena, Eleanor, Dakota, and Spencer went through, leaving Wilkes with Valinda alone in the darkening forest.

Wilkes turned suddenly. The silence had descended again, but he was picking up a presence and heard rustling in the thick woods and foliage. Dismissing it as animals, he concentrated hard on awaiting Levi's final arrival.

"Will you be OK, Valinda?" Wilkes asked with genuine concern.

"I will be fine, Wilkes, just bring my Levi home safe."

As Valinda smiled back at Wilkes, a deafening howl came from the deep woods. Valinda turned to face the sound and within seconds a large beast was on top of her. She screamed as Savage, standing on her stomach, brought his gaze up at the tall pines and howled at the moon. Then he looked down, his mouth dripping in anticipation of his upcoming feast, wetting Valinda's cheeks and forehead.

While the slimy gunk flowed onto her face, Savage leaned over even more, and then, with a huge powerful swipe, he let loose across Valinda's right cheek, ripping a huge clawful of flesh out of her face and tearing part of her eye out. Valinda let out a bloodcurdling scream.

Wilkes was trying his best to locate Anders. He knew the beast would not be far from his master. He couldn't pick up his signature, though, which could mean only one thing, that Anders had discovered his Geno-drone chip and had Wilkes blocked.

Wilkes turned, and there standing behind him was Anders. He had been there for a good while, enjoying the control he now had and what was about to unfold.

"Hello, Wilkes, did you miss me?" Anders said as he swiped Wilkes across the face with a sharp blade. They were both in their Zeytar bodies, so the blue blood flowing out of Wilkes' face would look odd if any human were to witness it. Wilkes fell to the ground and called in his mind for help, although help was nowhere to be found. "What has happened to Levi," he thought.

Anders leaned over Wilkes. "Your little insurrection ends here. When I am done feeding you both to my pet, I will give Savage his just desserts from the last of your weak rogue humans."

Wilkes had nothing; he was too hurt to get up, and he needed all his energy to try and mind-wreck Anders. Anders slashed across Wilkes again and again, cutting him apart and leaving him in a pool of Zeytar blood and entrails before he looked over at Savage.

"Enjoy, my pet. This will make up for the previous poison Wilkes gave you."

As Savage bent down to taste Valinda's bloody face, the bipedal wolf was struck to the ground by a heavy force, accompanied by a huge angry growl. Levi knew something was wrong so he had returned a little farther away so he could find out what was happening, thereby demonstrating a high functioning intelligence and problem-solving capabilities that weren't really known in Sasquatch research.

Valinda was out cold. Anders carefully retreated and crawled behind a tree, out of the large hominid's gaze. Savage was on his back howling as he bit down hard on Levi's arm. The Sasquatch let out a huge cry and reciprocated with several flying fists into Savage's jaw. This gave Levi time to get off the ground and back onto a fair playing field. He didn't have the sharp claws or the jagged teeth the upright wolf had, however his strength would match pound for pound any of the strongest animals in the world.

Savage stood up, growled, and with his constant smiling snarl made a dash for Levi who was waiting with his right fist clenched. The huge hairy fist met the wolf's face with an almighty blow. Savage fell to the ground and Levi stood over him and kicked him repeatedly in the chest. Savage struggled to breathe and as Levi lay the boot in, the wolf's howls became softer as yelps developed in their place. Levi did not stop until Savage was out cold.

Levi turned and grabbed his arm, scanning for Anders who had no idea Wilkes had such a bodyguard. Not that it did him any good as Anders' timing was everything and it had worked for the most part. But he would need his own bodyguard now.

Levi could not see Anders anywhere, so he stomped over to Valinda and leaned over to check on her. This would be costly, as Savage had been putting on an act and was waiting for Levi to turn so he could retaliate. As Levi went to rub her face and check if she was alive, Savage swiped the beast over and over with his razor-sharp claws, cutting deep into Levi's back.

Levi's thick fur seemed to keep the slashes from cutting vital organs until Levi was able to turn to face his attacker. Savage swiped across his neck, this time piercing deep enough inside Levi's skin to cause damage. Levi was gargling blood. The attack barely missed a vital artery although the bleeding was still heavy enough. He tried to cry out in pain but couldn't. He had to stop Savage from furthering the damage so he waited until he slashed again, and as the wolf-man thought he was going to finish Levi off, with his last ounce of strength the beast with the big feet grabbed Savage's attacking arm, breaking it, and then the other. They almost matched in size and height although Levi was much broader and stronger.

He pulled the wolf in closer still, gargling and struggling to breathe properly, though fixated now on the task at hand. As he pulled him in, he quickly let go of a limp arm, then the other, to grip the sides of Savage's long jaws. In one swift motion Levi ripped the braid off the side of his black furry head, gave out a gurgling cry, and pulled Savage's jaws slowly apart. The wolf-man was in the air, just a little off the ground, slashing around with his feet and what he could with broken arms, trying to get free.

Levi had the dog where he wanted, and as his grip inched the jaw to its final point, he gave an almighty wrench and pulled his entire face the other way, opening and cracking his mouth so wide it went all the way back. A tiny whimper escaped from Savage as Levi dropped him like a rag doll to the ground. As Savage's final breaths left his body, he gave one last convulsive twitch, and then the beast was still.

Levi waited for a moment. He wasn't going to be tricked again. After a final satisfied look at the lifeless hybrid wolf on the ground, he turned to Valinda and picked her up. He placed her next to Wilkes, who was now struggling to breathe the Earth air. He needed his suit. Zeytars when healthy could survive in Earth's atmosphere, but not for long periods of time without getting sick.

"Go get a medic, Levi. Valinda is alive but she needs help. Tell Carlos to bring my mask."

Levi picked Valinda up and slowly, with great effort, walked across the dark woods and out into the open spaces of the campsite where Jaydin, the medic soldier, and Carlos, the scientist, were sitting peacefully by the campfire, sharing stories and oblivious to the events that had just unfolded.

Levi put Valinda on the camp table, looked up at Carlos, and using sign language gestured for a mask to assist Wilkes. Carlos understood immediately. As he ran off, Levi dropped to his knees, with his arms limp by his side. Then he slowly tipped over and fell onto his torso and face with a thud.

Meanwhile, in the woods, Anders had just witnessed Levi's devastating destruction of his pet. He moved out of the area to escape the wrath of Wilkes' bodyguard. With his device in hand he vanished into thin air, with one less aberration by his side.

≈

The first team made it through without incident. Lieutenant Stone had already briefed his men and women on their roles and which contingent they were on. He had four groups of five along with himself and three others as roamers. They would be able to execute smaller, more individual tasks that would allow the four groups to stick together and stay stronger as a team of force.

Team Alpha went first out of the smelly old holding room which they had arrived in. Team Beta was directly behind them exiting the door and going left and right down the hallways until they reached the ends. Teams Charlie and Delta followed through and cleared the next stage of hallways. Like a perfectly oiled machine, they were tactically prepared and able to execute a safe pathway without any communication. When the rear two teams had cleared enough of the stained, dirty halls, Charlie and Delta kept post, with two looking forward and three covering the rear. Alpha and Beta scurried back to help with the escorting of the civilians.

Stone was awaiting the next lot through and was ready to give them orders. He was a hard soldier but a fair one, and those convictions made him a credible and successful officer with more victories per battle than any other at his level of command.

The room started lighting up and through the vortex Stone could see Wilkes with Valinda. He didn't like the fact that Wilkes was coming through last, as he was the brains of the mission, although he knew he would have had a valid reason and was content enough to trust whatever that was.

As Levi went to turn and pick his master up for the final escort through dimensions, they all heard a shriek coming from down the hall. Levi pushed through all the soldiers to see for himself what was making such a racket, and he was followed by curious others. He was greeted by a Lumping Bug, a common parasite on the ship that had six legs, a frog-like body, and sixteen eyes. It fed off mites, bugs, and blood from victims brought into the rooms. Corporal Bellingham wasn't a huge bug lover at the best of times and with a single outburst had shown her true feelings to everyone.

There was a moment of sniggering and quiet laughter as Levi bent down, picked the Lumping Bug up, and casually squashed it against the wall. He then started making his way back to the room to collect his master.

As Levi was halfway up the corridor, he began rubbing his head. Dakota came over to him and caressed his arm.

"Are you alright, big guy?"

Levi didn't respond. Something was wrong and he had to go quickly. He ran down the hall to the entry where the remaining soldiers were and let out a different toned sound than the last. Another vortex opened.

Eric tried to see through the blue lights of the wind but could see mostly darkness, although it looked a little different than before. He was not too concerned and listened to the last of Stone's berating of Bellingham.

"If you even whistle from your nose, I will shoot you myself, do you understand?"

Eric snickered to Serena as the chastised soldier replied, "Yes, sir."

Stone returned to the original room and they were all back to how they had been beforehand.

"OK, now that you are all here, I just want to give you this one piece of advice, and one rule. You all have missions, I get that, we are here for you all and to help fulfill those missions. However, if you deviate from them due to personal vendettas or any other reason than safety, I will leave you here. If you get any of my soldiers killed due to this, I will shoot you myself. Do we have an understanding?"

The eleven civilians just stood there, shocked, although all nodded in unison.

"Good, now we wait for Wilkes and then we set off."

Stone was smiling like he enjoyed giving that speech, which was obviously not his first time.

INTER-DIMENSIONAL DARKNESS

WILKES WAS TAKING FAR TOO LONG. Levi should have returned minutes ago and now another alarm had sounded for a few minutes. Without Wilkes, there was no knowing if it was the last or not, or if indeed this was related, as the final one meant the doorway opening and it was all over.

Stone was on edge. The soldiers were getting restless and there was lots of noise coming from deep inside the ship, not close enough just yet to cause panic, although knowing they all had to go that way, the nerves were kicking up a gear. Stone made the call and figured Wilkes would find them when he made it on the ship. There was a plan B which was going to be implemented now until Wilkes showed.

The teams were meant to split, but Stone thought it better to go one mission at a time at this stage. If that was the final alarm, they would have felt the power of the dimensional doors, so they still had some time.

The maps they'd been given helped a lot and the first cache of weapons was right where Wilkes had explained. The soldiers opened the weapon vaults quickly. Having the right knowledge and tools made a difference and Stacey would have liked the same information at her time of need. On they went picking out the best and leaving the rest.

The civilians took a Zaxis 104 each and the soldiers mixed between the Repeater X2 and the Marxis Exo 779 stun ray in case of an unknown slave that needed chip checking for extraction. They also grabbed plenty of flash grenades and zeeps each, which would be quite effective with large groups of enemies.

Once they were all tooled up, they moved forward to the slave section. Serena was up the front with Eric, just behind the Alpha and Beta teams. As they approached the lift to descend into the lower level where the slaves were kept, the rear teams called for a halt. Something was happening at the back and as the silence grew from all parties standing together like rocks, a blast sounded out as well as some screams of terror. Stone radioed to the Charlie and Delta teams, to which a response came.

"Sir, the hybrid armies have found us, there are around seventeen on first scan." The goggles were doing their job just like Wilkes had promised, picking out every single enemy despite all kinds of flashes or darkness.

"Stay with them. I will send two more to back you. We need to go silent now, give me a sit rep once you are clear, received?"

Stone was in full military control. It didn't matter if they were little green men or if they were walking giants, war was war and he knew tactics in depth. "Once you know your enemy, the rest is easy" was his favorite saying, although he was about to encounter very soon the one enemy that not even Wilkes could teach him about.

The Alpha and Beta teams continued forward, now split from the main group as originally planned, although under much harsher and more difficult circumstances. Stone entered the lift and cleared it first. It was much larger than others that had been used in the previous mission as this was a holding lift for creatures that were a lot larger, like Sasquatch beasts and Draconian prisoners. All of them were able to fit, the eleven civilians and remaining soldiers. The directions were quite simple, and Dakota punched in the coordinates to the correct section without any issues.

The lift door opened and the two teams cautiously moved out, preparing to clear whatever they needed to, before freeing the enslaved ones. Serena felt a bite on her neck, like a sharp sting from a mosquito.

As she went to swipe the area, she noticed a dull glow coming from her right. The glow moved out into the large room which had multiple corridors branching off it. She knew straight away who it was, and while all the soldiers were gathering everyone from the lift and leading them around the corner to a safe open space, Serena was gone. No one, not even Eric, had seen her disappear around a different corner and down five sets of similar looking halls and doorways, running fast in her gray uniform, cap, and with the scabbard on her back.

The soldiers split the civilian team into three groups. This would allow a swifter outcome of the freeing process. As they cleared each corridor and doorway, a soldier opened the main holding cell at the same time two others did, each time awaiting a beast or malevolent creature to fly out in a fit of rage. But each time a door opened, nothing.

Eric hadn't noticed Serena missing yet as he was with Simon and a couple of others from his team. He was getting quite frustrated, as this was definitely the area that Wilkes had sent them to for the controlled slaves. Eric was fixated on finding his daughter. This was his agenda and source of frustration from the very start. He was confident she would be at the rendezvous point, though, so was content for now to help, but if the last alarm sounded, he was out of there.

Meanwhile, Serena was still following Shaylee, whispering as the tiny sprite led the way through a maze of corridors and dirty floors.

Serena stopped, bending forward and catching her breath. She begged her friend to stop, "Shay, wait, please."

In a flash and without any noise at all, Shaylee was in front of Serena, rubbing her back and trying to assist her in breathing.

"I'm sorry, Serena, I still can't bring myself to show my full form to humans. Besides, I have picked up where they are. My mother is here. I can feel her close, come."

And in another blink of an eye she was back in her tiny sprite mode.

Serena was now upright. She was very fit normally, but the stresses were taking a toll. Shaylee had a way of making her feel better, though, and that would be enough to sustain her for the next part of the journey.

"Shay, you have to start trusting people. This situation we are in right now has affected not only your race of people, but it is also happening to my home with people I love. There are even creatures fighting back who were manufactured by them, along with Wilkes defying his own people to help all of us. You need to let go of the past and trust in all of us now. I promise I will help you get Faelynn back to normal when we are free here, you have my word."

Shaylee fluttered about for a few seconds and flashed out of sight. Serena thought she had really upset her this time, but Shaylee was back within seconds. She hovered in front of Serena's face for a moment and with another flash she appeared in full form again. This time her blonde hair was straightened and in a Celtic knot braid, and her green and purple fighting attire was that of the Celtic Elvenfae warriors. She seemed to keep to traditional attire, same as when Serena first lay eyes on her back in her room all those years ago.

"I hear you, and I will accept your help, Serena, but for now I have found my people and they are not in a good way. Come."

Serena followed, slowly lifting her sword Long Leaf from her scabbard. Shaylee was already standing firm with her sword Howling Tooth in hand, named for the sound it made when waved around and the handle being carved from a rare dragon tooth from thousands of years earlier. As they crept close to several doors, Serena, with sword in hand, lifted her Zaxis 104 for the chip extraction. They were ready for this. Serena stalled for a moment, slowly lowered the Zaxis and realized they would need serious help.

≈

Eric was concerned. He had realized that Serena was not part of the teams and as the doors were continuing to open, he couldn't help but think that maybe she had taken a wrong turn down one of the prison corridors.

"Stone, we've lost someone. Serena's not here and neither are the so-called slaves. Can we send a search party?"

Stone looked over at Eric and noticed things weren't going to plan.

Time was being wasted, and they were losing people faster than they had anticipated.

Suddenly a bright flash lit the room. Shaylee appeared in front of the whole group. Everyone was staring and Shaylee was becoming a little uncomfortable until Serena burst around the corner and shouted, "Don't shoot, please, I can explain. She is with me."

Serena was puffing and panting. She felt envious that she couldn't fly around like Shaylee could, then appear at the drop of a hat in another place.

"This is Shaylee. Her people are trapped here too and need your protection. They are unlike beings you have encountered before, they are ..."

Serena paused for a moment. Even though she knew all the history of their encounters, it felt weird saying it all out loud.

"As I said, this is Shaylee. She is princess of the Fae, from a world parallel to our own, and some of her people have been enslaved, including her mother, who is very important in her world. The other part is they ..."

Serena really was struggling with this part. She knew that Shaylee's world was a secret world. Humans had tried to find it and ruin parts of it, that's why the harsh penalties had been put in place, but Serena knew that these people would understand and would help Shaylee out without question. Well, that's what she hoped.

"The last thing is that they are very tiny and can take on full forms when they want to. The reason they cannot do it now is that they are bound by the Sasquatch and need them to survive. Transitioning into full form cannot happen while they are under control."

Serena finished explaining. After everything that Wilkes had told them previously, there wasn't much left for them to question—they were on a spaceship, in another dimension, and so on.

There was a brief pause, only for a moment, before Eric asked, "Do you know where they are?"

Serena smiled at him. She could see he understood the whole situation now.

"Yes, we must hurry, but you need to understand one more thing. Some of her people are weak and very angry, so we need to be very quick and careful, as they will attack us."

Stone looked over at Serena with the same expression on his face as he had during his earlier speech about deviating from the plan. Then he gave the command.

The soldiers ran, following Shaylee, who stayed in full form and was running fast with her sword Howling Tooth in hand. The soldiers stopped just before she did. The noise coming from the cells was now deafening. Stone had all the teams in place, ready, as Shaylee glared at Stone, seeming to indicate that if he made the wrong decision, he would get the pointy end of her blade through his skull.

"OK, carefully, and keep it steady. When the doors open, we'll need room and empathy. There may be different sizes to deal with, so I want all of you Zaxis 104 operators to zap straight away."

The soldiers backed off and Shaylee, along with Serena, took a step to the side, leaving the others to free the slaves.

Simon, Eric, and Dakota were ready. This time they were only going to open one door at a time. The others had the weapons lined up.

Just before Simon was about to open the door, Shaylee fired up again. "This blade will be for anyone who kills my family, not for rogue slaves, so be aware I do not discriminate or care who you are."

All the WOSER members along with Eric, Spencer, Eleanor, and Dakota stood still, all staring at Shaylee's blade.

Serena said, "I am with her," as she took Long Leaf and looked directly at Eric. Her face was serious, no winking this time.

Simon moved forward, pressed the door release, and waited in anticipation for what was about to exit.

≈

Charlie and Delta teams were in a fluster of pulse firing, flash grenades, and hand-to-hand combat, before attaining the advantage over the lower hybrid soldiers. A horrific mess surrounded them and sirens were going off from damage to the ceiling piping and structures.

The team moved forward after the last of the blasts. They had lost three members of the group, but that wasn't the worst of it. They were lost. Walking through halls and looking into doors provided no solution to their predicament. Even the radios were cut off for some reason and communication was now completely lost between Stone and the rest of the group.

The two teams gathered together and found the entrance to a lift. Desperate to get away, one of the soldiers just started pressing buttons randomly. This action would soon have them fighting for their lives.

The door opened on the third level of the south side of the ship, far from where Stone and the rest of the civilians were at the time. There seemed to be a lot of mist and smoke, and the environment was quite damp and humid, as if they were at a swamp in the early summer heat.

Charlie team slowly emerged out of the lift first and went to the left while Delta took the right. The air in the room was not of Earth's atmosphere and it was very dark, so they all locked down their goggles to enhance vision. The leader of both the teams, directly under Stone, was Sergeant Merring. Though he was leading Charlie team, he was still in charge of both contingents. It was now his leadership that would be put to the test.

"Everyone back in the lift now, we are not supposed to be here."

As Merring finished speaking, a scream echoed from the Delta team, then another. The team was scurrying, trying to make their way back. Their vison was unclear, but there were heat signatures everywhere, screams coming from all directions.

Merring made it to the lift with only some of his soldiers remaining. As he went to close the lift, a human-looking male, fully naked, was trying to pull back the doors. His strength was that of two men, and he almost succeeded pulling the doors open but wasn't strong enough to withstand the brunt of a pulse shot to the head. Corporal Papolous had opened fire and left nothing sitting above the shoulders. The body fell to the ground, and they saw more creeping humanoids edging closer before the doors finally shut.

"Is everyone alright?" Merring said, puffing.

"What in the world are they, Sarge? They look human, but they don't. Not like the small hybrid soldiers we just faced. And why are they naked?" They all wanted answers but Papolous had asked the same questions they were all thinking about.

"They must be the new Zeytar hybrids, extra strong, with their brains intertwined with those of their own kind. Remember what Wilkes said? This must be one of the life pod release sections," Merring explained. As the remaining soldiers gathered themselves together, he went on. "OK, boys and girls, listen up, we are in the fight of our lives now and we don't have much time. Our mission is to set the flash zeeps all along the checkpoints that Wilkes explained. They are not in the way of the Zeytars, although with the hybrids waking as we speak and readying for the war on Earth, we need this done now, and we may not be coming home, are we all clear?"

The lift was silent for a few moments, all the soldiers looking at each other, some holding on to photographs of loved ones and others clutching spiritual icons and dog tags.

Then, from all of them in unison came, "Sir, yes, sir!"

Merring looked stern and proud as he hit a button which, according to his map, directed the lift to take them to the first power core location.

"It's time to save our people and bring these mothers down."

FLAYED FACES

ALEX HAD BEEN RUNNING AT TOP SPEED for hours. He would reach the particle accelerator soon, as the signal on the first of his clocks had internally sounded, indicating a milestone of power and time. The android stopped. As the signal was sent out, the clock slowly molded into becoming part of its body, leaving no trace of the sophisticated mechanism, just a normal metal humanoid chest. The clock on the droid's left side, however, was still counting down. It would let ALEX know when there were only hours to go before Zero Time, letting the main clock count down and build the last of its power to open the door here on Earth.

ALEX had come to a town with a population of around seven hundred. It was a very small town, not shown on too many maps. Because it was so small, the android would stand out and its dark cloak and white mask would instill fear in the locals. The sun was high in the sky and there were very few places to hide so it scanned for a human to sacrifice for a better disguise.

After lurking in the shadows for a while, it became apparent that most people in the town were in groups. ALEX did not want to make a scene this close to its target, so it left the town center for the residential area where it scanned the houses looking for people who were alone.

It found a house at the end of a quiet street, old but not ruined. ALEX read a single life signature inside. It approached the veranda and walked up the stairs. As it lined its fist up to break down the door, ALEX noticed a button to the side which said "Push me." The droid stood there for a moment, then did what the sign said. With its gloved index finger, it pushed the button and a country song started playing. ALEX jumped back, its index finger now a long-edged weapon ready for attack.

Before the song ended, someone on the other side of the door said, "Who is it? I don't want anything today."

The male voice sounded elderly. ALEX didn't care, it had wasted enough time searching for a single person, this was going to be good enough for now. ALEX had to look as human as it could before reaching Waxahachie with its higher population, as it would need as much cover as possible to blend in with all the rogue spies out there. ALEX couldn't take the chance of getting stopped before the clocks ran out. If the V.I.Z.I.N.D.A.L.E.X. didn't make the Zero Time rendezvous, it would still open a rip with its electromagnetic power, but not long enough for all the ships to come through. The particle accelerator was needed to provide the rest of the power to open a rip which would remain open for the required time.

The old voice repeated, "Who is it? I don't have time for games, just go away."

ALEX pressed the doorbell again, annoying the old man so much that he opened the door quickly, thinking it was kids playing games with him. ALEX just stood there. It would let the man speak before it proceeded with its disguise. But when the old man saw ALEX with its tiny white-lipped smirk, dressed in his black cloak, black gloves, and hood covering most of its face, the old man dropped to the floor grabbing his chest and moaning in pain.

ALEX took a step inside the house and shut the door. In no more than a few minutes, it re-emerged, this time without the cloak, gloves, and mask. It was now a complete twin of the old man, using all of his skin to replicate and cover its whole body, molding every part, to the finest detail of growths and stray gray hairs. It hitched its pants up and started down the stairs, leaving the flayed old man lying in a pool of blood.

ALEX was learning at a rapid rate, and so were all the different

Geno-drones. It was getting very good at communicating with all of them and symbiotically functioning at its peak. There would be very few people who would be able to tell it was an android, however it wouldn't be long before the aged skin would start to show signs of the robotics. Any scratch or tear would reveal the truth even if only for a short time while the Geno-drones worked at fixing it. ALEX needed a younger person and it would get that in Waxahachie.

≈

ALEX had finished its business in the small town, and walked through the center openly to test its new look out. It received some strange gazes, as it had been some time since the locals had seen old man Higgins outside due to his heart condition. The droid was satisfied with its new shell.

After it reached the end of the town, ALEX looked back to see if anyone was watching, before it kicked into power-building mode and started off to the next town, Waxahachie, Texas.

ALEX hadn't realized that something was in fact keeping an eye on it and had been following it. The android hadn't done a full scan to see if there were any human witnesses that could make a report about an old man running hundreds of miles an hour. But something else was watching, and a scan would have picked it up. ALEX usually scanned continuously, but being more confident now that it was human-looking, this time it failed to register a high-tech stealth drone the size of a grapefruit. The drone had seen it and was already reporting back to the rogue base where Wilkes would confirm what he already knew and feared.

ALEX reached the outskirts of Waxahachie. There the second clock signaled, and a surge of power kicked in. ALEX was not far away now from reaching the particle accelerator and with each movement felt more power come into itself. The clocks were winding it up, and when the android finally let go, it would release a torrent of power.

The Geno-drones were working feverishly to keep repairing the damaged skin. The force of the running had peeled half of its face off, leaving the left eye, cheek, and part of its mouth revealed. ALEX had to find somewhere to stop and repair for a moment before continuing. It also had to find another poor human, much younger and stronger this time, to make it to the Super Collider.

ALEX found a large tree away from roads or houses and it sat underneath while the overworked Geno-drones finished the repairs. After a short time, the repairs were complete, and the destructive apocalyptic machine registered a slight whirring sound coming from a mile away. Its senses had been restored now with a full Geno-drone update.

ALEX stood up, turned to the deserted mountain road, and scanned. His detailed vision and sensors fixated on a light-sounding whir not from any organic bird or animal. ALEX activated a wave blast decoder and brought down the drone that was watching it. Then, satisfied it was alone for the time being, ALEX moved on and scanned for a younger victim.

The bad thing about it being found out was that it would attract all the wrong attention. It was getting desperate. The last clock was nearly at Zero Time and the X-Clock was not far from its final tick. Seeing an isolated house with empty beer bottles scattered on the ground, ALEX scanned it and found three life signatures inside. The bedroom at the end of the house was the closest to the signature it was after, so it wandered around the back and entered through the unlocked door.

ALEX followed its scan to the left into the bedroom of the male victim who lay passed out from too many beers from the previous night's entertainment. ALEX didn't even wake the young male, who had no clothes on and was spread over his covers like he landed that way. ALEX put a quick sharp implement from its fingers into the man's spine and began with the flaying and cover conversion to look like the young man. The Geno-drones including the Medi-drones were working feverishly, with the entire body skinned quickly and ALEX placing each part onto its now naked metal default form. It expanded itself to become a little taller while the flayed skin became part of its makeup.

This time it would not require any cloaks or mock clothing at all. It would be an exact replica of the human man, the same height, weight, and hair length, as the Geno-drones worked the DNA to predict exact outcomes of size after scanning the body and calculating the rest. All ALEX would need now is the right clothing.

It rummaged through the drawers of the deceased young man and found a pair of military cargo pants and a shirt, along with other army attire. It seemed this man had been on break from military duties. ALEX smiled with its new face, thinking it couldn't have worked out any better, as it would need to pass through checkpoints once inside the particle accelerator. Now it wouldn't have to kill everyone, it could just blend straight in and set up the Super Collider while waiting for the time to pass.

ALEX finished with its upgrade and snuck out the back door. It wasn't too concerned about retaliation as the signatures of the other two young men indicated they were sound asleep. ALEX took to the main road and began his final few miles to the Superconducting Super Collider.

≈

The team had arrived at the particle accelerator and had already put checkpoints and staff evacuation instructions in place. It was a secret facility in the first instance, so there was no need to worry about any leaks or backlash from civilians. The scientists were obviously a little pissed off, but these drills were becoming commonplace lately, with more interest in the area than ever before.

Staff Sergeant Felon had in place a skeleton crew of twenty-four soldiers all at different sections of the building. Some were there solely as an evacuation team and made the rounds escorting the small number of scientists and administration staff off the premises, while the remainder stopped anyone else from gaining access.

Felon knew it was a suicide mission, given the information Wilkes had passed on to them on the capacity of the V.I.Z.I.N.D.A.L.E.X. The whole team were happy to play their part. Felon gave them all a speech when they first arrived and the main part of that speech, repeated many times, was the destructive ability of the android, the human look of it so it could fit in, and the levels of persuasion it would have as now its learning cortex would know more about humans than they knew about themselves. It would be shifty, devious, and highly dangerous.

Once the staff had been escorted out and Felon had all checkpoints cleared, he informed his soldiers to take up posts and watch for anything unusual. There were several drones flying incognito around the building, sending messages and video back to him. The pilots were on standby for the next stage of the mission, so for now it was wait and report.

ALEX had made it to the Super Collider. It wanted to destroy the drones, however knew that would give away his position. So it scanned the area for the weakest entry point, which was the main doors at the front of the building. Felon's theory was that the android wasn't just going to walk into the place as it didn't want to be detected, so he put only two soldiers at the doors.

ALEX went through all types of scenarios and human psychology that it would use on the soldiers, hoping it would have minimal impact so it could get straight to the area where it needed to be to wait for the final countdown. The droid moved to the doors and could see the soldiers gearing up to fire. They were all ordered not to trust a soul. Even if their own mother walked up, they were to report back to Felon straightaway, or if they noticed anything, they were to open fire so the others could approach that area as soon as possible, before calling in the pilots to level the place.

Felon wanted to avoid decimating the whole place at this stage as it would put many lives in and around the area at risk, but whatever it took to slow or stop the android, he was willing to undertake.

ALEX had his hands in the air, and Corporal Manning and Sergeant

Farris were just about to fire when they both noticed that it was a young soldier.

Manning yelled out to the young man, "Hold it there, soldier, what is your reason for being here?"

But Farris unexpectedly chimed in as she lowered her firearm. "Ryan you are supposed to be with the second unit over in Nevada, have you been redeployed?"

Farris was certain that this was her brother's best friend, Corporal Ryan Leech, but Manning was not as sure, resulting in some to and fro between the two, all while ALEX stood there, watching.

"We don't know if this is really him, Rachael, it could be the machine. I'm sorry, but I need to tell Felon." Manning got straight on the radio, but just before he could get any kind of message out, Farris smashed the radio out of his hand, hurtling it to the ground and leaving Manning shocked and ready for a fight.

"Felon will kill or order us to kill anyone, even our own families if they turn up. What if this *is* Ryan, my brother's best friend? I'm not having his blood on my conscience," Farris said, shaking.

Manning wasn't buying it, though, and responded assertively. "You knew the risks, you have been briefed, and seen what's coming. I cannot have you risking all of us with your sentimental crap, now let me take care of this." As Manning finished saying his piece, he lifted his rifle and pointed it at ALEX, who had not budged.

Farris knocked the gun out of his hand and it went off, hitting the glass doors behind them, then pointed her own rifle at Manning before saying, "You are not doing this, I will stop you. I outrank you, soldier, and I am giving you a direct order to stand down."

Felon and the rest of the soldiers heard the blast and were all given the order not to move. "Farris, Farris, what's happening there?" Felon's voice rang out after giving the others orders to stay at post.

"Everything is fine. Manning misfired after playing around with his rifle."

Manning then yelled out in desperation. "It's here, come quick it's—

" Before he could finish, Farris turned the radio off and gave Manning a clip over the head with her rifle, knocking him to the ground.

By now ALEX had encroached into their space and was standing next to Farris. As he looked deep inside her eyes, a small blue laser light sparked out of the droid's eyes and burst some very important blood vessels in her brain, and she fell, convulsing, to the ground.

The others worked out something was not quite right, and after Felon failed to reach either Farris or Manning, he made the call to get all soldiers to the area at once.

After ALEX had broken Manning's neck, it walked inside the building where it was going to spend the last few moments before Zero Time. It had a complete database of the area, so it knew the best places to hide before taking out each soldier one by one until its signal activated. There was still a little time for some fun.

≈

Felon had all the soldiers at the front door. ALEX was nowhere to be found and without any description of his current appearance, Felon had nothing to pass on to his troops. Felon should have ordered the attack to level the buildings, but knowing that was a suicide mission he wanted to try and take it down. If he couldn't destroy the machine, he would call in the bombers at the soonest possible time. It was more ego now with the Staff Sergeant and he didn't care that he was putting other soldiers at risk.

ALEX had sent out brainwaves that were confusing the soldiers. Its ability to fully confuse and turn people on each other was its new favorite toy and it seemed to be working with Felon now. Though it hadn't wanted to make a big entrance, it was looking forward to the opportunity of a hunt before preparing the particle accelerator for the atoms to collide and open the door. To do that, ALEX needed the soldiers gone.

Felon directed the units to split into four teams, then disperse to all four levels of the building, the first three levels covered by five soldiers until the last remaining soldiers were at the bottom floor along with the Super Collider entrance.

ALEX had no problem taking them out. Dealing with the first five at the top level was like shooting fish in a barrel. None of them saw ALEX until it was right on top of them. There was a flash of gunfire and some bloodcurdling screams, and ALEX left piles of body parts and gunk on the ground, illuminated in the half-light of the flashing security lights that had activated.

Felon had the pilots on standby. He was now adamant that he wasn't going to use them until right at the end. Whatever the android did was enough to obscure the plan without actual brainwashing. Felon was on the fourth level, but he heard the gunfire and was waiting with the last seven of his team. He had some keeping watch, with others setting up some explosives along the base of the particle accelerator.

ALEX was now onto the lower second level which had been placed in darkness for security. It had perfect vision as it moved down the corridors alongside offices, and could see all five soldiers hiding behind desks and doors awaiting its entrance. ALEX wanted to toy with this lot, so it crept up and grabbed them one by one, holding its hands over each victim's mouth and whispering in their ears words that changed some neurons in their brain. They abandoned the search for ALEX, but now wanted each other's blood. It was hypnotic suggestion with a brainwave from the android and now they were hunting one another.

ALEX finished with that floor, climbed into the lift shaft and lowered itself down to the third floor, listening to the screams and gunfire from its level two fun. Once on the third floor, it forced open the lift doors. As it walked out, all five soldiers started firing together, with one soldier throwing a grenade at ALEX as well. It writhed around and felt every bullet and shockwave, but the android's Geno-drones got straight to work fixing it.

As the smoke of the blasts started to dissipate the machine was back to its full original robotic form. It let each soldier share in a huge blast of electro-energy so powerful it blew them all apart leaving nothing more than a crimson mess on the floor.

ALEX was getting close. The final ticks were coming up as it clicked around faster. The exposed clock was nearly all in sequence, matching all the intricacies of the chronometer and starting to glow blue, like it had just about reached full charge. ALEX had no more patience and when the lift opened again finally on the lower fourth floor, it expected to see the soldiers waiting. However, they were nowhere to be found. Even scanning picked up nothing.

ALEX had very little time now and went straight over to the computer system of the collider. In order for it to work, ALEX had to start the particle accelerator at full force and have the electron volts at TeV pushing the particles at a high voltage to collide just a little back from where the android would be set up. The collision, along with extra power from the droid, would cause a rip. The rip would create a larger tear and under the direction of the android would be guided and controlled to grow exponentially at the same time as the ship's portal doors opened. ALEX would then hone the sequence of the dimensional signal and release all its electromagnetic power that would burst through the roof out of the man-made covered hole designed for that moment.

ALEX would be attached to the collider, its clock open, and the energy released, pushing all power from the collider through ALEX's core and out into the atmosphere. ALEX would keep spewing out dangerous proportions of electromagnetic photons of power, keeping the portal doors open until all ships were through. The power was so strong it would create a super-shield across the area for twenty miles, so nothing could get in or out, a built-in safety measure.

ALEX turned on the machine and set it to standby as it powered up. It had forgotten the others for a moment, so it switched back to search mode and left the operations center of the accelerator. The android turned down a narrow corridor, still scanning, and eventually picked up some life signatures. It realized its effect on Felon had taken a much better turn than it had at first anticipated. ALEX entered the room and saw the eight humans cowering in the corner. Felon was standing over the seven remaining soldiers with his rifle pointing at them and repeating to them, "It will be over soon, it will be over soon, they are coming, they are coming."

ALEX planted some hypnotic residual messages in Felon's head, although was quite impressed with the lasting effects, as it didn't have mind control at all, only the ability to use human psychology and manipulate it with suggestive commands. Who knew what kinds of things the android would have been capable of if it wasn't about to complete its mission and receive its final commands from the Leader. Wilkes had failed to anticipate this outcome.

ALEX was not concerned now and walked out of the room and back to the control center. Xandar was standing in the hallway, ready to assist the android.

"Are you ready, ALEX, do you have long?"

Xandar was wanting this part over. The whole process was very stressful, for if this part failed, he would have the Leader's wrath on him and he did not want that, not one bit. They both walked into the massive room where the entrance to the main particle accelerator stood awaiting them. The whir of the machine was very loud even though it was on standby, but it was about to get a whole lot louder.

≈

Xandar left ALEX and went back into the control room. He had vast experience with the machine at hand. ALEX walked over to the entrance where it moved out with all its strength a piece of the cylindrical conduit wall that housed the exact impact of where the protons would collide. It was designed to break apart for the purpose of ALEX taking control of that section of the collider. Once the collision occurred, ALEX would proceed to unlock and adjust itself, pointing its fast spinning clock upwards, spewing all the power and redirecting the aftereffects of the collision with all its own power through the roof to the sky, thus opening the portal.

ALEX was just about in position when the last signal went out. It had five minutes to prepare before its clock turned into a conduit of power. Looking over at Xandar and nodding, it noticed all the remaining soldiers were watching from afar, not worried about furthering their coup, just in awe of what was happening, all in a trance.

The android's clock finally ticked its last tick and the large abdominal clock started spinning around so fast that it was spitting out blue light and photons. ALEX set itself in place of the open gap in the last of the collider's cylindrical walls, with its clock in position, pointing up to redirect the explosion. The Geno-drones had filled the remaining gaps, and everything was in place looking normal but for the large circling light sticking out of the collider. Xandar was in front of the control panel awaiting the final signal, which was time. He had to count down five minutes from the final signal. That would be enough time for ALEX to reach full power potential before the subatomic particles did their job.

Time was up and all the physics, building, and planning for this day had come down to now. It would either blow the whole state sky high, send the world into a black hole, or it would succeed. Many decades of planning were about to unfold.

Xandar pressed a few buttons, entered a sequence of codes, and before long began colliding two opposing particle beams of protons-protons allowing electrical connectors between the bending magnets that would hold at 10 TeV per beam, 20 TeV in total, the most powerful and dangerous ever tested or trialed in all the particle accelerators around the world. This would be enough to kick off the sequence of events for ALEX who was now at full potential. As the particle accelerator began its job, ALEX was in fine form awaiting the subatomic particles to collide just before it, and they fulfilled their function without destroying the planet. ALEX controlled all that energy and redirected it as planned through the now opened X-Clock, swirling and forcing out an immense amount of power.

As the beams shot up into the roof, opening a wide hole big enough to fit a football stadium, the soldiers watching the event were torn apart into trillions of pieces. The rip was opened and normally it would have been a tiny tear, but after the collisions, ALEX had focused all its electromagnetic energy and vibrational waves to amplify the rip's size until a massive vortex half a mile long started to appear in the sky. ALEX had also sent out a vibrational signal that matched that of the Leader's ships which would allow a doorway from the dimension they were in to open, so it would not just be a random portal to anywhere.

The noise was deafening and as the three stealth bombers came in to level the place, they too were torn apart. The military had found out, sending fifteen other bombers, and after witnessing the destruction of the stealth craft, their thinking was to go high and drop the bombs from a great height. Although fine in theory, the execution was a failure. The bombs dropped and the protective shield that ALEX held just bounced them off and obliterated them so they did nothing, not even a tiny blast.

The military pulled back and left the area which was now a monster vortex of blue, red, and purple swirls of wind, along with a high-pitched squeal that would shatter eardrums for miles. In the whirls of color and noise, a dark cloud overtook the whole area with lightning sparking from every angle.

Through the dark of the clouds, the tip of a craft started poking through. The ship was so big, it covered the whole sky. As it protruded through, another two ships, one on either side, started showing.

ALEX was vibrating and swirling so hard it started breaking apart in small doses. Tiny Geno-drones fell off at times, although the sheer force of its power enabled it to continue. ALEX held fast. This was its time to shine and the most powerful machine in the universe was succeeding.

The first three ships made it through safely with humungous conduits and cables flowing out of each of the saucer-shaped craft connecting the ships to each other. ALEX could not fail now.

FLUTTERING EXTRACTION

STONE WAS SHOCKED. There in front of him and his team were hundreds of tiny lights flickering around their faces. Then a huge beast stepped out from the rear of the cell. It wasn't like Levi. Its eyes were quite dark and red. It started lunging for the group before Simon fired his extraction gun. The faeries and sprites were making their way down the corridor thinking they were going for another victim. Serena and Shaylee, along with Eric and a soldier, followed them to the end of the corridor. The extraction gun didn't work on them. Eric fired, but they were not large enough to take the full brunt of the force.

Shaylee yelled out, "Save your firepower for the beasts, it is they who control my people. Give me time to help them."

And with that Serena fired a stun at the cluster of sprites, leaving them suspended in mid-flight although still fluttering continuously. Flapping their wings was like heartbeats or breath, something they constantly had to do as a safety measure at that tiny size to protect them from prey.

Shaylee approached the whole group. The looks of snarls and contempt on their once lovely peaceful faces were enough to bring tears to her eyes. She was once caught under the spell herself, remembering the hate, fear, and lack of self-control she had while under the spell of the sinisters' poison.

She reached into a sash on her left hip and sprinkled dust over the cluster of her folk. Then she waited. One soldier coughed as the dust found its way inside his throat.

"Don't worry, sweetness. It will only make you feel happy and kind for a few hours," Shaylee joked with him while seriously hoping that this concoction was strong enough to finally break the grip on her people once and for all.

After a moment the snarls and hisses dissipated into silence and with a massive shot of light, three of them turned to full form, breaking the control spell.

"Mother!" Shaylee yelled, as she ran over to the now free Queen and her people. Shaylee wrapped her arms around her mother tightly and whispered, "I missed you so much. I have fought hard for this day, so hard, and I knew you were alive." Tears were streaming down Shaylee's face as well as Serena's.

The Queen of the Elvenfae whispered back, "I cannot remember much, my dear, but I felt like I was in an insidious dream that I could not awaken from, knowing you would somehow wake me. But we cannot stay here." Tianna was desperate to get home. "We will not make it without the beasts and the energy of home. We have to go now." The Queen was insistent and as the others released the beasts from other cells, Stone ran over with his soldiers, awaiting Eric's orders to open the first doorway back to Earth's realm.

"We need to get this lot back along with the little folks. I am not responsible for these freed ones. It's on you, Eric."

Stone wasn't being nasty. He just had very few men left and needed to move the mission along. There was no way Wilkes would have allowed them all to do that.

Eric was already preparing. He pulled out the vocalization portal device and lined it up in a clear area, took a deep breath, and blew into it, failing miserably.

"I've got this, hang on," Eric muttered, as he took a couple of deep breaths, relaxing himself before giving it another burst and finally opening the vortex.

The beasts didn't even think about it. After they came around from the chip extraction, they saw the doorway and like it was second nature just ran through it, with the tiny sprites all following along.

Shaylee and Serena held back. Queen Tianna was holding her hand out for Shaylee to come as the door was barely holding.

Shaylee yelled out, "I will meet you soon, I have to make sure all our people are free."

Tianna smiled. She knew her daughter well and she was prouder than ever of her. As Eric pulled the VPD from his lips, nearly passing out, the Queen disappeared into the vortex and on to Earth, where her kind would escape to their own dimensional abode awaiting the return of their saving heroine.

"Why didn't you go, Shay?" Serena asked, knowing full well that there wouldn't be many, if any, of her kind left behind on the ship.

"You have helped me, now I will repay you. We have to stop them for good."

Shaylee, with sword in hand, once more ran down the corridors behind the Alpha and Beta teams, opening all the remaining cells and freeing as many of the beasts as they could.

≈

Merring had his team working hard. They had already planted two of the flash zeeps. The hardest one to plant would be in the conduits that connected all the ships together. If they could at least get that one done, they would be well on their way. The map was helping. As they approached the top section of the ship, the remaining soldiers were not as often jumping out into the firing line, as the Zeytar hybrids were fewer. Most were still connecting with their new bodies and were slowly being given uniforms, ready for the invasion.

The team was ready. Only three were being utilized for the job at hand, while the others were on watch, because the more people involved, the more chance of capturing unwanted attention. Merring hung back with the last few soldiers, letting Harris, Fleming, and Gossing do the deed. As they made their way up the ladder to the entry point of the conduits, Merring whispered to them, "You've got five minutes, guys, hurry."

The three nodded and continued into the lower roofing of the ship. One slip would be fatal, so with hasty care they raced along the beams, over to the central ladders and along to the connections to the very large metal pipes that were still attached to millions of Zeytar hybrids in stasis. The pipes met up in the middle, where they needed to place the flash zeep. Gossing took the explosive. He was the most agile, and with previous acrobatic experience, he was the best candidate to complete the task.

Moving closer over the thin ladders, Gossing reached within inches of his destination. A rumble occurred and then a major alarm. Gossing just managed to lodge the charge inside a small crevice under the connecting piers to the ship's conduit system before he slipped. He reached out and grabbed the thin ladder rung with one hand, but then came another rumble and shake.

The alarms were loud and deafening, Gossing couldn't hear the two shouting at him to hang on. He made a last ditch attempt to get a good grip, but vibrations took over the ship again and Gossing fell hundreds of yards to the inner roof of the ship, breaking his back and cracking his skull like an egg over a metal air pipe sticking up through the roof's ventilation system.

Fleming and Harris screamed for their mate. Moments later another shake-up was underway, and they scurried back down to the others who were waiting with bated breath.

Merring looked up as the two of them slowly came down the ladder. Harris glanced back at Merring, shook his head, and said, "He was brave, Sarge, very brave. The charge is in place, but the ship's movements ... poor timing, he is gone."

Merring lowered his head, then faced his remaining troops, but before he could give them comfort, his radio kicked in. Stone was trying to communicate.

"Sarge, Sarge, are you there? The comms are back, it must be due to the movement. I don't know how long we have, but if you can, meet us at the rendezvous point ASAP."

Merring lifted his head.

"Did you hear that, boys? We are back. The other flash zeeps will have to wait. Stone, can you hear me? We are heading down now."

And with that they got back on the lift and headed to the rendezvous point.

≈

Shaylee and Serena seemed to be enjoying this moment a little too much. Their faces were serious, with a glint of pleasure, hinting they had done this on many occasions. Ducking and slicing, jumping, and dodging, they were getting more hits on the board than some of the soldiers. The hybrid soldiers were no match for their speed and agility. Shaylee would transfer to her tiny form and reappear moments later behind her adversary, slicing them down with her sword Howling Tooth. She even pulled her wings back and outwards to slice through the enemies' waists while at the same time cutting their heads off with her sword. Serena had Long Leaf and she was not far behind Shaylee. Even without her shrinking abilities, she was still able to mow down hybrid soldiers easily.

Eric was now using the pulse. All the beasts had been freed and there were no more prisoners on that last level. He was watching Serena's and Shaylee's remarkable skills with the sword and was thinking to himself in between blasts, "Who is this woman I have fallen for?" Highly impressed and less anxious about having to look after her, he continued to his final mission, that of finding his daughter.

As they got closer to the rendezvous point, the final alarms rang out, and they could feel the ship moving. As the last of that group of hybrid soldiers were cut to pieces, Stone took some time to call for Merring to meet them. Serena and Shaylee cleaned their blades with the scraps of a lifeless hybrid on the ground and placed them back in their scabbards. Though the room they were looking for was around the corner, the ship's alarms were going crazy, and its movement and rumbling were starting to frighten Eric. Would he get to Stacey in time?

After Stone had given Merring the message, they burst around the corner and through to the meeting place where Stacey was told to wait. Eric bolted through first and there in front of him stood Vargzin, right next to Rovan. Eric fell back hard on his right side, and blinded by the thought that these beings were his enemy and not having recognized the Draconian from their earlier encounter, he lifted his rifle to shoot. In a split-second Stacey emerged from behind Varg and yelled, "Don't shoot, Dad, it's OK, please!"

Stacey was desperate and as Eric turned to face the voice, his whole persona changed. He could have been in a room with a million enemies, but at this time he did not care. He had found her. Finally, his little girl was back with him.

"Stacey, Stace, it's really you?" Eric said pulling himself up and racing over to embrace her.

They held each other in their arms tightly for what seemed like an eternity, too scared to let go and not saying anything but quietly crying inside each other's embrace.

Serena reached over and gently said, "Hi Stacey, I've heard so much about you."

Stacey looked up. With tears rolling down her face, she said, "Thank you, thank you all for saving us."

Stone jumped in with, "We aren't out of the woods yet, people. We have to detonate this place and get out now."

Just as he finished speaking, Merring and his troops rushed through the door, but they were jolted by the sight of the Draconian and warden Zeytar standing there, along with a Zeytar hybrid boy staring back at them with innocent eyes.

"Well, we're all on the same side. So, if there isn't any further business, Eric, get us the fuck out of here."

Stone had had enough of this nightmare and did not want to lose any more troops. He had protected these people and fulfilled his mission without Wilkes being there, just like he said he would. In his mind, it was time to go.

Rovan stepped forward. "There is one more thing to do and I need some people to help. It's a suicide mission, so I don't expect volunteers," he said noting the excitement of leaving turned to a flat look of disappointment on everyone's faces.

"What is it, Zeytar?" Stone asked Rovan in a condescending manner. Even though he was friends with Wilkes, he didn't trust any other of his kind.

"We need to kill the Leader. I need a couple of volunteers, so I can set a charge in his control room. I am a warden, and only a master has access. I will blow the door and will distract him, while someone sets the charge. I also need some lookouts as I can feel another here wanting to stop us. The Leader won't know we are coming as the ships are now in motion. The V.I.Z.I.N.D.A.L.E.X. has started opening the Zero Time portal. We only have twenty minutes before we are all sucked into Earth's realm along with these ships. Who can I ask to help and who is going to go?" Rovan sounded desperate, but a few hands rose.

Simon nodded. He was a science nerd and had never had so much fun in all his life; his hand was the first. Eric knew he would be needed to get them back, so he raised his hand as well. Stacey also raised her hand, but Eric turned to her and begged, "Stacey, I just got you back, there's no way I am going to lose you again." Eric was firm with his plea, although he knew it would be to no avail.

"I'm coming, Dad, and there's nothing you can say to change my mind. I could say I don't want to lose you again, how about that?" Stacey gave her father a smirk and looked over at Merring and Stone who had their hands raised.

"We are in if you send my troops home now," and with that Rovan had his last band of brothers and sisters to assist in the final battle.

Eric said goodbye to Serena first, and as they finished kissing, he whispered in her ear, "I won't be gone too long."

After saying goodbye, Serena said, "When we get back, I will escort

Shaylee home to her world, and I will meet you at the campsite after she is safe. There is so much to tell you, starting with I love you."

Eric smiled and gave her another kiss before reciprocating with, "I love you too," and as their fingers slowly slid from each other's touch, Eric gripped the VPD in his other hand and opened the portal. The remaining soldiers, civilians, Serena and Shaylee, along with Dakota who had the boy in his arms, vanished through the vortex. Serena had looked back shouting something out to Eric before the portal shut, but he couldn't hear her. Eric, holding the VPD, was left with Vargzin, Rovan, Stacey, Simon, Sergeant Merring, and Lieutenant Stone to finish the job.

THE DARK AND
THE LIGHT

THE LEADER'S CONTROL ROOM was easy to find, and there didn't seem to be too many guards to knock out of the way in the process. The only battle came as they reached the section where he kept his first successful Zeytar hybrids as guards. There were only two of them, as that's all he felt he needed.

The soldiers tried with pulse, then the flash grenades. The Zeytar hybrids were very fast and had great agility. Stacey got caught in between the soldiers at one point and found herself in the grip of one of them. With her quick thinking and martial arts skills, she was able to escape its hold and send it back for a moment with a spinning heel kick to its large head. This stunned the high performing humanoid who was trying to hypnotically change the humans' thinking so they would turn on each other. Eventually these hybrids would have the ability to do this, but they were still rummaging their way through their new bodies and so had to make do with intelligence and brute force for now.

Stone ran forward to try to get Stacey out of the way, as Eric had his own troubles in trying to pull Simon away from the other hybrid that had a full grip on his neck. Merring rushed past Stone when Stacey was free of danger and as he pushed her out of the way Vargzin ran in with full force and dropped the Zeytar hybrid to the ground. With the power of his scaly arms, he snapped the humanoid's neck, leaving a pulsating wreck on the floor.

As this was happening Merring ran to help Eric. The Zeytar hybrid threw Simon against the wall, then launched on them both. His strength was amazing to the point he had Eric, who wasn't a small man, and Merring both in his grip. Merring dropped the rifle and as he squirmed to get out of his vice, the humanoid snapped Merring's neck like a twig. Witnessing this and full of rage, Stone unleashed a barrage of shots at it.

"Stop it, you will hit my father!" Stacey screamed, but her plea fell on deaf ears as Stone continued to battle with the fiercely strong humanoid.

By this time Eric had been able to struggle enough to break free.

Stone yelled, "Go, all of you, go, I will deal with this one."

Without hesitation they all rushed past while Stone kept firing at it. Once away from the carnage they headed around a corner in the corridor. Simon was first around, having shaken off his wall hugging adventures. Peering up through the smoke of a flash grenade he saw a beast walking up to him. The smoke made it difficult to see its face clearly, but it was the same color and had similar markings to Levi. Simon was certain it was Levi but as he welcomed the beast to the group, he soon realized that it wasn't. It was another one that had eluded them before, still with a control chip and angrier than ever. Someone had let a heap of beasts out of the prison cells earlier on and that is why some of them had been empty.

The beast picked Simon up by his head and crushed his skull like a chocolate egg. As the lifeless body fell to the ground, Stone's screams echoed through the halls. It wasn't looking good for them; they were so close to reaching their target, yet so far.

Vargzin angrily pursued the beast and as they got into a struggle, Anders poked his head out from behind the beast's legs, shocking Rovan to the point he nearly fell over.

"I know why Wilkes got himself one of these as a pet. They are, or should I say in his case, *were*, very handy." As Anders finished his devastating remark, he let out a sickening giggle, making Rovan feel even more uncomfortable.

"Who is this? What does he mean, Zeytar?" Eric snapped, but before Rovan could answer, Anders chimed back in, all the while trying to stay clear of the fight going on in front of him.

"Well, I couldn't have asked for a better result. I've had such a bad week and in a few short hours I managed to kill your beloved Wilkes with his pet, and now the rest of his little human pets. And oh, the sweetest part is I get to pull the real Stacey apart, not a clone or copy. I will suck your blood myself, pretty one."

Eric screamed. They knew it was Anders now and even though he was in his Zeytar form, he still looked strong and crazy. Eric ran forward but halted when Anders lifted his finger up and pointed.

"Nope, stop! Tell him, Rovan, what will happen if he gets any closer."

Rovan looked at Eric, then back at Anders, before saying, "Nothing, Anders, you are finished."

Because while Anders was busy talking and threatening the group, Stacey had managed to kick a Zaxis 104 over to Vargzin who immediately sucked the chip from the beast. Anders turned to see what the so-called threat was, just as the giant reached down, lifted him up, and pulled him apart at the waist, before dropping both pieces of the gray to the floor.

Blue blood was leaking everywhere as the life of the darkest Zeytar that ever lived quickly faded away. The beast then without warning as if it had its own agenda, gave a high-pitched yell and in the blink of an eye had vanished through his own vortex of light, off the ship and free to roam wherever it wanted.

As they gathered themselves to continue to the doorway several yards in front of them, Rovan was suddenly grabbed from behind and pulled back into the darkness by the remaining Zeytar hybrid who had just killed Stone. His scream echoed across all the corridors, like a haunting cry, until there was silence.

Eric just stood there. It was on him now, he thought, but without Rovan, how could he enter the room? He was no match for the Leader.

"The arm, Eric, take the arm from Anders while it's still warm." The voice came from the darkness leading up to the doorway.

"Show yourself, now!" Eric screamed.

As the voice's owner appeared out of the shadows, a familiar face greeted them.

"Father! Father Michael, what, how?" Eric stuttered and fidgeted, not knowing how to deal with another surprise.

"Come on, now, there is no time to explain. Grab the arm and let's go."

Eric was still staring at Father Michael, stunned, so Vargzin, the only level-headed one left, besides Stacey, pulled a large knife from his scabbard and cut the arm from Anders' body. The dead Zeytar seemed to be staring at Varg as if it interested him, although he was completely gone.

Vargzin thought he would be funny and threw the arm straight at Eric, giggled, and watched for Eric's response.

"Not funny, large lizard thingy man, not funny at all."

Stacey said, "Varg, Dad, his name is Varg."

Eric nodded, like it was semi-funny, then bent down and picked up Anders' arm. Holding it with its lifeless two fingers and thumb was so weird and repulsive for Eric, but he had no choice.

They approached the door. There were just four of them now. They examined the hand indentation print reader next to the door which would give them access to the room. All they needed to do was to place Anders' hand on it and they were in. But the Leader's mind could destroy them all with just a look, so this wasn't going to work, Eric thought.

"Are we all ready?" he said. "Stacey, you stay back, Vaaag and I will go in. You remain with Father Michael."

Stacey looked pissed off at her father. "It's *Varg*, Dad, and I will not remain here with a defenseless priest, I'm sorry."

Eric had no choice, there was no time to argue. He placed the hand on the imprint reader and a large green, red, and blue light activated.

Once all three lights flickered for a few moments, they heard a click and the very large door lifted.

Hesitating, they peered inside. It was dark, as the ship's power was now in low mode to focus all the energy on getting the portal open, even though ALEX was doing all the heavy lifting at its end.

Stacey brushed past the others and as she ran into the room she saw the Leader wasn't at his post, but waiting for them like he knew they were coming. He slapped Stacey to the ground, knocking her out cold.

Eric ran in to see if she was alright, along with Vargzin, but in a split-second the Leader had them suspended in the air with a pure and simple thought, as easy for him as taking a breath. Then Michael walked in slowly after them, with his black suit and white collar looking like he was in completely the wrong place.

"Put them down, beast from another realm. Stay away from them. They do not belong to you. They are guarded and loved by another, far more powerful than you."

Michael was making no sense, thought Eric, who was able to see and hear, just not move at all.

"You have no power against me, priest. I am and will always be stronger than your kind." As the Leader finished speaking, he raised his long arm and swiped across the semi-lit room, trying to knock Michael over. The action failed, though, as if Michael had been standing behind an invisible wall.

The Leader was massive. He stood a good fifteen feet or more, and his arms seemed to extend over a large area, more gangly and wiry than the masters' arms. He still had two fingers and an opposing thumb on each hand, however his head was very large, pulsating and flashing on the inside, as if his neurons were all firing at once. He was still connected by conduits and organic cords to the control center of the hive and through to the Zeytar hybrids. His body was slender, though he seemed to have a slouch. But it was his glowing red eyes that instilled fear in everyone. They were evil-looking and piercing too, almond-shaped liked those of the others, glowing above two slits for nostrils, and a slender thin-lipped mouth. His face was gaunt, although the sheer size off the upper levels of his head took all the attention away from this feature of his face.

Michael stood there defiantly, strong and confident. He was a man who could hold his own, but against a malevolent creature like this bent on the destruction of humanity, how much could he do?

Eric just wanted to get down and get out in one piece with his daughter, but the likelihood of that happening was zero to none, he thought.

Michael faced up to the giant Leader once more.

"This is your last warning, creature. Let them go and cease all action here at once, or you will feel the sting of my resolve."

The Leader broke out into deep laughter. Now focused entirely on Michael, he released Varg and Eric, who fell from quite a height, disorienting them for a moment. The Leader, with both arms up, let loose with a barrage of psychokinetic pulses directed at Michael to break his mind with multiple blows.

Michael took the first and flicked it off, then the second. As if it was a light windy day, after the third and fourth he started moving backward a little. Eric crawled over to Stacey and wrapped his arms around her. There was a whirl of wind and power starting to come alive inside the room, still directed at Michael, but affecting the other three too. The wind whirled more and more, as the Leader built up power for an imminent strike on Michael.

The priest turned to Eric and whispered into his mind, "Go, Eric, go now, tell them what you all did and what happened here."

Just as he finished mind-blending with Eric, the Leader thrust all his power toward Michael. The priest rose up into the air, his upper clothing was ripped away, and he pulled out the largest broadsword the humans had ever seen. With gold markings and ancient text written all over the blade and hilt, the sword was taking the brunt of the powerful attack. As he rose higher, his hair turned dark and long, down to the middle of his now uncovered back, where wings appeared, holding him up in the air. Wings of white, flapping slowly, kept him high above the creature.

Michael yelled out once more, "Go, now! Destroy it all."

Vargzin took Stacey into his arms, with Eric assisting him, and they exited the room. Michael thrust down hard at the Leader with his sword, cutting the creature's arm.

As he exited the room, Eric threw a real grenade into the maelstrom and closed the door after them. All they could hear were the screams of the Leader.

Eric blew into his VPD and hit the detonator. Starting from the Leader's room, the ship began exploding as if in a wildfire of energy and destruction. The vortex opened and Vargzin and Stacey went through. But fire and earthquake-like eruptions were knocking Eric around and he slipped from his hard stance. The VPD was knocked out of his hand. There were explosions coming in his direction as the vortex began closing. Time was not his friend now. The flames climbed higher and higher, roaring around him. He had but seconds until he was fully enveloped by the destruction.

He rolled over and reached for the VPD, but as his fingers touched it, the device rolled away. Eric was out of time as he whispered under his breath, "I love yo—" Before he could finish, the ship was rocked with another explosion, launching the device into Eric's chest. He grabbed it, sprang to his feet, and blew hard, while he stared down his fiery death, watching flames engulf the entire area he was standing in The vortex closed. The ship was an inferno, exploding and burning.

≈

Most of the ships had come through by now, but it didn't matter, as Xandar couldn't beam onto any. He was outside, where he'd been watching and preparing for their arrival. Now his head lowered as he watched them explode into the vortex of lights and wind along with darkness and snow in parts.

ALEX was still at full capacity. Now all the destruction was falling over the area of the particle accelerator, the dimensional portal was cutting out and opening others, before leaving a torrent of fire over the entire area. The force field was sucking in all the remaining ships which were exploding into themselves, creating their very own buzz of fire and devastation. As the rest of the ships that made it through crumbled over ALEX, its magnetics started to malfunction. The droid's power was still at its maximum, and it began to overload as the suction of the portal continued, until it all came to a climax of chaos with an explosion that leveled Waxahachie and several towns around it.

The energy field was still there. It now reached over an entire half of the state, sucking everything in and leaving only lightning, thunder, and a continuing vortex of black swirling cloud, growling and exploding until it reached its peak. It was like a life-form made of clouds and lightning. What it was inside was unknown, but all the ships were now part of the destruction, and the area was too deadly for survival.

Nothing could survive such a powerful force and as it wasn't growing in size, everyone around it was warned to stay at least five miles from the edge of it until the military could work out whether it was safe or not. The video that Valinda uploaded had worked. The military personnel who were not under the Zeytars' control had their suspicions and as the global switch did not happen, they were able to help in the recovery of lives and the complete shutdown of areas of Texas and beyond. There would be a press conference from the President of the United States after everything had settled, but at this time right now, everything was chaos and what unfolded would take a toll on people for some time.

≈

Eric awoke not long after getting back to the Klamath woods. The force of the blast knocked him out for a moment. As he came around, he noticed a small number of medics and military personnel were assisting all the wounded. He looked for Stacey, who was being treated next to him. As he rubbed his head, she whispered, "So, Dad, where are we going for our next camping trip?"

Eric lay back and laughed as the medics started treating him. His laugh turned into quiet sobs and before long he was up and stumbled over to his daughter.

"I am so proud of you! You have the strength of ten gorillas, the perseverance of ten lions, the heart the size of a football field, and you are my hero, sweetheart, now and forever."

They embraced in a hug and let another lot of tears flow. Eric had his daughter and although this entire experience would change them all, it would only be for the better.

After a few moments, Eric let the medic work some more on Stacey as he brushed off help for himself. He wandered over toward the sealed section where Wilkes and Valinda were. He thought he felt a tug on his back, but he brushed it off, until it happened again. Feeling annoyed, Eric turned to see what the issue was, only to be staring at the chest of a huge bipedal creature. It was wearing a sling. Eric looked up and saw the patches all over it and a bandage across its neck.

He heard a little growl, before he burst out, "Levi, you're alive! Come here, big guy."

Eric wrapped his arms around the giant beast for a few moments until he couldn't take any more of the smell.

"I'm so glad you are OK, big guy, but now that there are others roaming around, you might want to have a bath first." Eric smiled as Levi tilted his head and huffed, before stomping off.

Eric entered the sealed tent area. Valinda was sitting up in her bed. She couldn't be moved just yet, until they could get a chopper in and fly her out, but she was smiling, and even more so when Eric walked in. She carefully put her arms up and gave him a hug.

"Look at you, hero, come here."

They embraced for a moment before Eric whispered into Valinda's ear, "Michael was there, Val, he saved all of us. I can't quite explain it just yet, but he is the hero here today."

Valinda didn't say anything. She just hugged Eric tighter and shed a couple of tears through her good eye. Her face was bandaged on the right side and she had a medical patch on her eye.

"Can one of Wilkes' devices fix it for y—"

But before Eric could finish, Valinda said, "No, Eric, without Wilkes to guide them, no one knows where it is. Besides, I've accepted the wounds, not just for myself but for all of us to remember what happened here today, and the violence that we were nearly overcome by."

"Whatever you say, Val, you are always beautiful to me. And what a story you will have for your grandchildren!"

They both had a chuckle and just sat with each other for a while until Valinda said, "Now go to your gorgeous Serena. She said she would be back soon."

Eric gave her another hug and headed to the end of the sealed off medical area. Just before he went out, he looked over at the lifeless wounded body of Wilkes, thinking it would be a good idea to just give his condolences. Eric found himself holding Wilkes' hand and thanking him.

"I'm sorry this happened to you, Wilkes. Without you risking yourself for hundreds of years, we would not have been successful. You taught us all, took a chance on some humans, and risked your own life for our world. There will never be enough thanks that we could ever give to show you how much we appreciate it. You will be taught about in schools and you will never be forgotten." Eric lowered his head and still holding the hand of his teacher and friend, he couldn't help but shed a tear for him. It was an emotional time and he needed that closure for Wilkes.

After a while, Eric went to move away from Wilkes, but there was a pullback. Eric tried again, and although Wilkes' eyes were closed, he pulled back and squeezed a little harder.

"Thank you, Eric, I knew you could do it. I chose right."

Eric stood up. Wilkes opened his eyes and said, "Take care of Valinda and Levi for me, Eric. Help me up, I don't have a lot of time."

Eric wasn't going to argue with Wilkes, not ever again, so he helped the frail Zeytar up and led him out of the sealed area. Wilkes had sensed something and was holding on to the last of his energy to understand it before he went.

Outside, Eric led Wilkes to a large tree on the edge of the forest and sat him down against it.

"Bring me the boy please, Eric, the Zeytar hybrid boy."

Eric raced over to where the medics were looking after the young one. Eric had to argue with them, but Stacey was now with him and said it would be OK, promising he would be back soon.

The boy held Stacey's hand as they wandered over to where Wilkes was sitting. He looked deathly white for a "gray" and they all knew he didn't have long.

Stacey sat the boy next to Wilkes. The boy had no personality at all, due to the fact he had no mind essence. He would have to grow and learn just like everyone else, although he would be the oldest baby in the world.

Wilkes reached over, put his two hands on the boy's face and whispered, "You will be OK, you are the last of us now," and as he sat there for a moment, his eyes slowly closed, his hands falling away from the boy's face. Wilkes slumped to the ground, lifeless. It seemed that he had wanted to meet the boy to see the work that the Leader had created before he slipped away.

"Dad, take Wilkes back please. I don't want the boy to have another meltdown like on the ship."

Eric picked up his friend's body and took it straight back to the sealed area, while Stacey walked back to the medics with the boy and explained that he was going to live with her after he got the all clear.

Eric was feeling the pressure now. He had searched everywhere for Serena. It had been many hours since she left with Shaylee. He wandered into the forest to get some thinking space when he heard some whimpering behind a tree.

Eric rushed over to the spot and saw a woman with very long dark hair in some kind of dark purple medieval attire. Her sword was red, she had blood on her face, and some older scarring was visible on her upper shoulder where her clothing had been torn.

Eric bent down, and as he did, he noticed a baby wrapped in blood-soaked material. It was nestled up to the woman on the ground, restless and about to cry.

Eric whispered to the woman who hadn't realized anyone was there, "Are you alright, ma'am, you look hurt, can I help?"

Eric touched the woman's shoulder, but she sprang back, holding the baby, and in a frightened state shouted, "Get away, get away from us, you will hurt us no more."

Eric's eyes widened. "Serena, is ... is that you, sweetheart?"

The woman looked up at Eric for a moment. Her demeanor changed quickly, and she began sobbing harder before responding, "Eric, am I finally home?" He grabbed her just before she passed out, screaming for Shaylee. As confused as he was, he could see Serena was in a world of trouble, along with the baby.

A short time later, Serena, still unconscious, and the baby were taken on the chopper to the hospital, with Valinda and the hybrid child. Eric was not going to get any answers this day. He felt very confused about how she was in possession of a baby, and that she had changed so much in such a short amount of time, though he was very relieved to have her back with him.

After a final debrief with the backup military team that Wilkes had had on standby, everyone involved was cleared to move along. Eric got onto another chopper to meet Serena at the hospital and as he pulled at his sleeve, he noticed the Zeytar hybrid patch on his upper arm. In a fit of anger, he grabbed the patch and tore it off, but what he saw next shocked him to the core. Wilkes had his own patch underneath it. It was showing the letters D.A.A.T., with a human holding a Zeytar hybrid's skull in the air in one hand. There was fire in the background, strange creature skulls on the ground, and the human had a pulse rifle in the other hand. At the bottom of the patch, the acronym was spelled out:

The Deception Anti Apocalypse Team.

Eric lowered his head and whispered to himself, "What have you kept from us, Wilkes, what more were you expecting of us?"

The chopper went higher into the air as Eric's face stayed lowered. He shook his head as the chopper flew out into the morning sunlight, disappearing into the glare.

EPILOGUE

ERIC WENT TO PICK UP VALINDA from the hospital. It had been two days since her surgery and she was about to be discharged with strict rules to rest. Eric volunteered to care for her, with Stacey helping, as Eric also spent lots of time keeping a bedside vigil of Serena when he could. She had not awoken, and the doctors seemed to think she was suffering from major exhaustion from a highly traumatic event. The baby was in a bed next to her, also very weak.

Eric walked into Valinda's room, gave her a kiss on the cheek and said, "It's time to get out of here, Val."

Valinda smiled. "I have a huge favor to ask, but first you need to go and see her. I have five minutes or so before the doctors will fully discharge me."

Eric smiled. He was coming back later that afternoon to visit Serena, but he wasn't going to miss an extra chance to see her.

He exited the room and walked down the corridor, turned left, and entered room number 205 where Serena was lying in the same place as the night before when Eric left her side to get some rest.

He approached the bed and pulled a chair up, seating himself next to her. The curtain was closed around the baby's cot and Eric tried to be as quiet as he could. He picked up Serena's smooth pale hand and placed it in both of his. He stared at her for a moment. He couldn't help but notice how young she looked, like she was in her twenties again

He began to whisper, loud enough for Serena to hear, yet still soft enough to not disturb the baby. "It's funny, well not funny, more ironic how you are here asleep from a trauma and I'm looking out for you. The tables definitely have turned, but I would trade places in a heartbeat, my love."

Serena didn't flinch. Eric knew that somehow she could hear him deep down, so he continued, "I have been blessed to be around such indomitable, compassionate, and independent women. I wouldn't be here if it wasn't for all of you. Valinda is so strong and for her to come out of this experience with all that has happened makes me feel so positive about her future recovery. Stacey has grown so much. She has always had great intuition and I could not be prouder of anyone in my life. Then there is you, Serena. You took a chance on a man going through major trauma. Your faith in me kept me positive about finding Stacey, and you have loved me through all my flaws, all while protecting us from harm and battling your own wars, which I will hope to understand one day."

Eric lowered his head and a few tears ran down his tired face.

"I love you, Serena, please wake up soon."

As he slowly placed her arm gently at her side, Eric quietly stood up, placed the chair back, and turned around to see Valinda standing there, smiling, with a tear in her good eye.

"Eric, that was so beautiful. She is lucky to have you too. We all are." Valinda reached out her hand and they made their way out of the hospital, not saying anything, just holding hands, comforting each other, until they made it to Eric's car.

Eric opened the door for Valinda and loaded her bags into the boot. As he got into the driver's seat, he asked, "Now what was this favor, Val, the sky's the limit today." Eric smiled as he turned on the engine.

"Can we please go to the church where my mother was shot? I would like to place some flowers before we lay her body to rest next week."

Eric nodded and after making a trip to the florist, they arrived at the church car park. Police tape still surrounded some areas. Valinda just ducked under with Eric. As they sat near the tree where Marjory fell, no words were spoken, Eric just held Valinda with his arm around her shoulder.

They sat there for a while until Valinda had cried all the tears she would cry for the day. Eric asked if she was ready, and when Valinda nodded, he helped her to her feet. As they walked to the car, they glanced once more at the empty church. They saw a man dressed in a black cassock, thinking it was obviously the new priest, but when the man looked up, it was Michael standing there. He smiled, waved, and turned to walk into the church out of their view.

Eric ran over to where he'd been, but the priest had vanished. He looked inside the windows and all the outer doors, but the sign on the front said "Closed until further notice." Eric tried the doors, but they were all locked. Had he imagined it? he thought.

Valinda was waiting for Eric at the car; his face said it all, and Valinda had to validate it for him.

"It was him, Eric, wasn't it?"

Eric looked at her for a moment then nodded. "After everything I've witnessed, I believe it was."

They both stared at the empty church for a few minutes before Eric said, "Now, time to get some rest."

At the same time Eric and Valinda were driving home, Serena woke up suddenly and, sitting up, shouted "Shaylee" at the top of her lungs, before sliding back down on her pillows and whispering, "Eric, Eric, I need you."

Tears flowed down her face as she slipped back out of consciousness.

Meanwhile in Ireland, at the exact time the ships fell, a group of children was playing in the fields of a large green paddock that overlooked some spectacular tranquil scenery. A couple of adults had set up a camping site and were having a few drinks as the children played. It had been a nice clear day with no clouds and as the sun had just set for the day, one of the children yelled out in excitement, "Look, up there, above the mountains, it's a dragon."

The adults were talking among themselves, happily drinking their wine. One of the men snapped at the child. "Finnegan, cut it out, no one wants to hear your stories today."

Finnegan was seven years old and had a very imaginative mind. He was always making up stories and his father wasn't having any of it tonight.

Angry that they didn't believe him and had laughed it off, Finnegan yelled out again, "Please, Dad, I'm telling the truth, just look over at the mountains."

Just then, they all heard a mighty roar from miles away. They turned to see what it was. They witnessed a shadow blocking much of the large bright moon, creating the silhouette of a giant creature with a long tail with spikes on the end, and huge wings reaching out wide, as it climbed higher up.

As it gathered upward momentum, a silhouette of what seemed like a man could be seen standing on top of a mountain that had not been there only minutes before. The man thrust a sword up in the air as the moon began turning a bright red before hiding behind thick dark clouds, and then he was gone. The noise of the monster's shriek continued to be heard throughout the fields as it roared above the witnesses watching it with fear. Then after a while it flew off and disappeared into the night.

Two days after the events of Waxahachie, the President was in the White House preparing to go live with his second press conference. The first had been to inform the public of a catastrophic event that happened, with many lives lost, about which he had very little information at the time. The President now had an all-important update to the recent events and wanted to soothe the public's fears.

"Sir, we are ready to go live."

President Jacob Devlin was adjusting his tie for the camera. The Democrat had been responsible for disarming all Americans to protect them from themselves, which left them vulnerable to threats from abroad. He knew this and was in crisis mode. Even though the threat had been contained for now, it could have been so much worse. The information that had been broadcast live by Valinda had sent the planet into a frenzy and it was his job to calm the nation and the world, to reassure everyone that the threat was over.

The military was working hard to keep the area contained and to sustain order as people tried to deal with the situation in different ways.

"And, we are ... on." The cameraman flicked the light to red and the President was now streaming live to all countries.

"My fellow Americans and nations across the sea, we have been blindsided by a race of malevolent beings for generations as our lack of knowledge and trust in things we don't understand almost cost us our freedom and lives. We had been infiltrated from the inside and controlled.

"I stand here today in front of you to thank all those involved in the destruction of this malevolent force. I cannot go into all the details yet, however a portion of Texas is a no-go zone. All residents in the vicinity are warned not to go near the dark zone. We have lost millions of people and I do not wish to lose any more from this evil force. There will be a complete disclosure update when all the facts are at hand.

"Ladies and gentlemen, as we sit here and contemplate what might have been and pray for those we lost, let's take some time to reflect, and change our future. By embracing each other, cultures, religions, and races, we can live together on this planet. It's the only one we have. We have been tricked for many years, so I am announcing there will be no more conspiracies and war, no more famine or untreatable sickness, and no more civil unrest between us. We don't know if this was an isolated attack, so we must be prepared. That is why I, in discussions with other world leaders, will create a unified taskforce on all outside invaders that want to subjugate. People, disclosure is upon us, and we need protection from these dangers."

The President went on about his new plan, and as he neared the end of his speech, the camera zoomed in closer. He gave what looked like a smirk and for a split-second a sharp blue glow from behind his eyes shone out across the Earth.

As the world was falling apart, it was being tricked yet again.

COMING SOON *FABLE*

About the Author

Troy M. Williams has researched and investigated all different facets of the paranormal over the last fifteen years. Heading his own team, Troy has documented and researched many cases over that time. From ghosts, UFOs, and cryptids to folklore, history, and the strange. Troy has been a guest on several radio shows in Australia discussing the field and had his own blog for many years.

In his spare time Troy pursues his other love, Taekwondo. A 3rd dan black belt, he is passionate about instructing and coaching at his local club which includes his two boys. He has won medals over the years in Sparring and Poomsae, but after a car accident he focuses more on developing those interested in competitions.

Troy also has a large comic book collection, and as an avid Batman, sci-fi, and fantasy fan, he enjoys collecting those hard to find items.

But it is writing that keeps his fires burning, ever since his younger days when he wrote short stories. His strong understanding of the paranormal field feeds his creative mind, and he delves into horror and dark poetry at times, combining fact and fiction with fantasy and history to create his own worlds.

His book *Shrill* is the first of many to come.

www.ingramcontent.com/pod-product-compliance
Lightning Source LLC
Chambersburg PA
CBHW022210010726
47493CB00002B/502